The Unfortunate Side Effects of Heartbreak and Magic

The Unfortunate Side Effects of Heartbreak and Magic

♦ *A NOVEL* ♦

BREANNE RANDALL

Published in the United States by Alcove Press, an imprint of The Quick Brown Fox & Company LLC.

Alcove Press and its logo are trademarks of The Quick Brown Fox & Company LLC.

Library of Congress Catalog-in-Publication data available upon request.

ISBN (paperback): 978-1-63910-573-1
ISBN (ebook): 978-1-63910-574-8

Cover design by Kara Klontz

Printed in the United States.

www.alcovepress.com

Alcove Press
34 West 27th St., 10th Floor
New York, NY 10001

First Edition: September 2023

10 9 8 7 6 5 4 3 2 1

For GG, who always believed in me

To mom, who still does

And for Evelyn, my little daydreamer

♦ 1 ♦

THE SUN WAS COLD, the teakettle refused to boil, and the wretched scent of old memories burned from the logs as Sadie Revelare built up the fire. Even the grandfather clock, which never paid attention to time, warbled out ten sad magpie notes.

A sign I must not miss.

Sadie threw the tedious old clock a withering look and kicked it at the base. It swung its gold pendulum as though wagging its finger in warning. Irritated, but not one to mess with the sign, she crossed herself with a cinnamon stick and then crushed it under her boot heel on the front porch.

Back inside, the house echoed its silence like a gentle reproach. Gigi had already left for the day. Seth had been gone nearly a year. Not that she was counting the days. She wouldn't give her brother that satisfaction. She glanced at the toothbrush holder as she washed her face. One lone toothbrush.

Long ago, she let herself dream of her own house, a pair of toothbrushes, maybe even water spots on the mirror from a child brushing their teeth too close.

But her curse made that impossible, and she'd given up on romance too long ago for it to make a difference now. Some people needed flowers and pretty words. Sadie needed truth and kept promises. She finished getting ready, and on her way out the door, with coffee in hand, the clock chimed again.

"I took care of it!" she shouted back.

But on the short drive to work she had to swerve twice: once to avoid a snake in the road and another time to dodge the crow that nearly swooped into her windshield. She shivered. Portents of change and death, respectively. Still. She shrugged them off. Business didn't stop for bad omens. Actually, it thrived on them.

The winding canyon road was in its full autumnal force as Sadie rolled down the window, the chilly air kissing her face. She inhaled the smell of leaves and mossy rocks and the promise of a sharp noon wind. But there was something else there too. River silt.

"No, no, no." Her foot pushed harder against the pedal as she rounded the last sharp bend faster than she should, and Two Hands Bridge came into view.

Despite the lack of rain, it was flooded. Only a little. But enough. Sure as sunshine daisies, it was the third bad omen of the morning. There was no more ignoring it.

Even townsfolk who didn't believe in magic knew what a flooding meant: someone was about to return.

She slowed down, her tires sluicing through the muddy water, her knuckles white against the steering wheel.

Cindy McGillicuddy, a neighbor from a few doors over, slowed down as she approached in her four-by-four truck, the back weighed down with a dozen bales of hay for the horses she kept. She rolled down her window and then pointed at the bridge.

"River flooded," Cindy said knowingly. She was a no-nonsense kind of woman, her six-foot frame built with solid farmwork muscle. And even she was worried about the flooding.

"I know." Sadie sighed.

"Maybe your brother is coming back, huh?" Cindy said hopefully. "Wouldn't that be nice?"

Sadie forced herself to smile, even though it felt tight against her teeth. Sure. Nice.

"Maybe. Either way, I'm sure everything'll be fine."

Sadie drove away, knowing that Cindy would spread the news far and wide. She took her duties as the town's resident busybody seriously. There wasn't a pie that Cindy's finger wasn't in, and if you needed help or information, she was always the first stop. She was a meddler, but in the way of a good fairy who secretly dropped off food for families that needed it or brought firewood to the elderly who were too weak to chop it themselves.

Everything is fine. It'll be fine, Sadie told herself again.

Sadie hated that word *fine.* It was a Band-Aid, a sugar-coated pill to mask the bitterness beneath. *Fine* was what you used when it was anything but. But fine was what she had to be because if it wasn't, everything would unravel. Sadie so often walked the line between who people expected her to be and who she really was, the lines blurred until sometimes she forgot who she actually wanted to be. But the townsfolk had expectations. And she liked to exceed those as often as possible.

Still, her fingers tingled with fear. *Someone is returning.*

Who, who, who? The question echoed through her head as she arrived at A Peach in Thyme, the café she owned with her grandmother. The day was still waking up, but her mind was already caught on the hamster wheel. The single word was like a constant drop of water as she started mixing up three batches of carrot-cake cookies with cream cheese frosting. The ginger would humble the eater while the carrots would take them back to their roots.

Maybe she had her brother in mind; maybe she didn't. At any rate, she'd timed everything perfectly, as she always did. The kitchen was warm and comforting as a hug, the smell of the oven heating up reminding her that everything would be okay. She settled into the noise. The *shick* of the whisk against the metal bowl, the slide of the baking tray against the counter, the whip of the dish towel as she settled it over her shoulder. The repetition and ritual soothed the constant stream of persistent thoughts. The unwanted, obtrusive worries that only went away when she was lost in the rhythm of movements and measurements.

But when the first batch of cookies came out so spicy that she had to spit a mouthful out in the sink, a tingling began in her toes and worked its way up her body. She tried to brush it off by throwing a dash of ginger over her shoulder and dabbing lavender oil behind her ears, but it clung firm. The rituals weren't working. The images kept slithering in. The flooding river. The snake and the crow on the road.

"Rule number six," Sadie groaned. One of the more unfortunate rules her grandmother had pressed into her since childhood. Seven bad omens in a row meant a nightmare was around the corner. And she'd just reached bad omen number four.

Sadie had learned the rules of Revelare magic while growing up at her grandmother's feet, her grubby little toddler hands searching for earthworms as Gigi explained why mustard seed helped people talk about their feelings and how star anise could bond two people together. The sweet tang of tangerine rinds scented the air as her little fingernails were perpetually stained orange.

And always, Gigi warned her how their creations would speak to them. If you were in love, things tended to turn out too sweet. If dinner was bland, you needed some adventure. And if you burned a dessert—well, something wicked this way comes.

Sadie listened to those lessons among the bitter rutabagas and wild, climbing sweet peas, drinking in every word, and letting them take root in her heart. She grew up comfortable with the knowledge that she was strange, weaving the magic around her like ribbons on a maypole.

Now, she made her living from selling that strange. A little dash of dreams in the batter and a small drop of hope in the dough. The magic had been in her veins for so long, sometimes she forgot who she was without it. Like layers of phyllo dough, they were nearly impossible to separate.

Gigi had arrived and was in the front, "pottering about" as she called it. Sadie could hear the crinkle of plastic wrap being taken off pitchers. The clink of jars bumping into each other. The common little noises that turned the café into a symphony. The cookies, perfectly spiced this time, were fresh out of the oven for the early customers, the sweet scent beckoning them in like a childhood memory. Mason jars filled with fresh lavender and wild buttercups dotted the tables, and the pot of crystalized ginger sugar was turned just so toward the pitcher of hazelnut-infused cream.

The glass case brimmed with orange-essence croissants sprinkled with candied zest, the card in front reading, "Will cause enthusiasm, encouragement, and success." Its neighbor, the fruit and basil tartlets that glistened like a long-forgotten dream read, "Use for good wishes, love, and serious intent." And the cinnamon streusel cake that some locals swore would turn your day lucky had a card that simply said, "Stability." Generations ago, the townsfolk would have rebuked or shunned such blatant displays of magic. Now, even if they didn't understand it, they welcomed it with relish and a rumbling stomach. It was part of a routine that had woven itself into the DNA of Sadie's days. And it was about to begin again.

Sadie excelled at routine. The tiny town of Poppy Meadows, much like Sadie herself, ran like clockwork. All up and down Main Street lights were clicking on, tills were being counted, and "Closed" signs were rattling against the glass as they itched to be flipped. She settled into the rhythm, her shoulders relaxing as she scanned the wooden walkway connecting the hodge-podge of brick-front buildings. Her eyes traveled to the end of the street, where a nineteenth-century, steepled white church stood. Its stained-glass windows, which local legend claimed caught prayers in the wind, were casting jewels of light on the sidewalk, when a figure caught her eye. No. It couldn't be—

"Sweetheart," Gigi hollered in her foghorn voice.

"Coming!" Sadie called quickly, stomach churning as she shook herself out of the past and pushed through the double doors into the kitchen. Absolutely not. It was impossible. And much like everything else in her life, she shut the door on the thought. The possibility of who it might be. She'd trained herself to take every thought captive, shoving them away where they were safe in darkness. Otherwise, they'd spiral out of control into full-blown anxiety. It didn't always work. Even now the tightness was squeezing her chest again.

"Sugar, if you don't move this honking bag of flour, one of us is going to trip and break our neck." With Gigi, someone was always going to break something, get a "crick," or "ruin their lovely hands."

"Maybe some necks deserve to be broken, Gigi," Sadie answered sweetly, hoisting the twenty-five-pound bag of flour and settling it against her hip.

"Stop that or I'll pop you one. I know when you're talking about Seth. You get that mean little gleam in your eye."

Before Sadie could answer, she tripped on the rubber mat that lined the floor and watched, as though in slow motion, as the flour cascaded against the ground and billowed into a cloud of white.

A mess in the kitchen was bad omen number five.

"You little pissant!" Gigi laughed with her deep smoker's rumble. Gigi—a nickname that made her grandmother sound much more French and much less feisty than she actually was—shook her head. Her short hair was a cotton-candy puff, perfectly curled as always and a peculiar shade just between rust and copper.

"I know, I know. *'Disaster follows me around like stupidity follows a drunk,'*" Sadie quoted, gritting her teeth as she secured the top of the flour.

"Says who?" Gigi demanded, rounding on Sadie with a hand on her hip and a look that threatened trouble.

Sadie shrugged.

"That brother of yours isn't too old to have his mouth washed out with soap." Gigi sighed.

"But he'd have to actually be here in order for you to do that." Her voice went flat as oat cakes as she absentmindedly smoothed her apron.

"Don't go down that road, sugar," Gigi said as Sadie's eyes slid into the past. "Whoever digs a pit'll fall right into it. It wasn't your fault."

"I'm sure he'd say differently," Sadie said with pursed lips.

"That boy has got his own demons to fight," Gigi said. "And he will. Now, I'll get this cleaned up before we open while you go wipe that mess off yourself."

At the bathroom sink, Sadie rinsed her mouth and tried to finger-comb the flour out of her long auburn hair. She hoped for the best, refusing to glance in the mirror, as that was only to be done at dawn, midday, or dusk, for fear of what else might appear in the reflection. It was one of the many oddities that were as sure as sunshine in the Revelare family, like burying found pennies in the garden at midnight, always wearing green in some form or another, and never whistling indoors. These were truths that Gigi had taught Sadie from the cradle.

The bell tinkled merrily as Sadie opened the front door and stood there a moment, letting the last of the morning chill clear her mind. She could smell waffle cones from the ice-cream parlor a few stores down on the right, and bacon wafting across the street from the diner. The half wine barrel full of marigolds on the sidewalk swayed in a sleepy morning hello. The streetlamps winked out, one in particular blinking a few times, as though sending her Morse code. Her shoulders loosened. Even without magic, this would still be the most perfect place on earth to her.

Just as she flipped the sign to "Open," Bill Johnson stood at the threshold, his kind face lined and worn with a smile that fell into place like it was meant to be there. He was a little younger than Gigi and held a special place in Sadie's heart for the simple fact that he was secretly in love with her grandmother. His flannel shirt, fresh and clean as always, hung loosely on his lanky frame. His shaggy, grayed hair gleamed smooth in the morning light but failed to hide his large ears that stuck out like jug handles.

"Morning, Sadie," he said, ducking his head.

"Good morning, Bill. What'll it be for you this morning?" Sadie asked warmly, walking behind the counter while making sure her apron was tied securely in place.

"What's Gigi Marie recommend?" he asked, staring behind the counter, as though his eyes could drill a hole through to the kitchen.

"She recommends you mind your own taste buds, you big galoot," Gigi called from the back.

"Surprise me, then," he said with an indulgent smile.

Sadie, her back straight and shoulders squared, poured his coffee: black with two sugars, because that part of his order never changed. Then she cut him a slice of peach mascarpone pie and put it in a to-go container.

"And what does this do?"

"If anything has been ailing you, you'll feel right as rain today." Sadie grinned. "And it might just give you a bit of extra energy, to boot."

"I could use it." Bill raised his eyes to the heavens.

"Old Bailer?" Sadie guessed, and Bill nodded. The restoration of the local landmark had been experiencing some unexpected setbacks.

"That place is twelve thousand square feet of trouble," he said right before his eyes swiveled to Gigi like a magnet. Her grandmother stepped out of the kitchen, wiping her hands on her apron. He cleared his throat and bid them both a good morning before leaving, but not before Sadie saw the flush that colored his cheeks.

"You just can't help yourself, can you?" Sadie demanded with a grin. "Poor Bill has been sweet on you for ages. Why can't you be nicer to him?"

"Hush," Gigi barked with harsh laughter, "Nobody's after a doddery old fool like me. And don't you pretend like half the young men in this town aren't pining away for you, Revelare name or no. Why do you think that boy proposed to you?"

Just then, they both shivered as the back of their necks grew warm. They looked up to see Ryan Wharton walking by. As he caught Sadie's eye, he gave her a sad smile and a half wave before trudging on. He was the temptation Sadie had almost given into. Not out of love—nothing like it. But comfort. Companionship. Someone to hold her hand or listen to the story of her day. In the end, though, it wasn't fair to him. He deserved more than lukewarm affection, especially since he'd been in love with Sadie since they were in grade school. Her need to do the right thing was greater than her desire for the relationship. She'd wished, more than once, that she could do something for herself, no matter the consequence of injustice. But the guilt always ate at her before she could follow through.

"Speak of the devil." Gigi laughed with indulgence. "None of the boys around here are good enough for you. Because that's what they are—boys."

"It's a good thing I'm not in the market, then," Sadie said drily, pouring herself another cup of coffee. She added a blend of cinnamon and sweetened German cocoa and swirled the spoon around thoughtfully.

"I've told you a hundred times. Love is more important than magic, sugar." And Gigi, who was never prone to displays of physical affection, laid a gentle hand on Sadie's cheek for the briefest of moments.

"Easy for you to say. You don't have a curse that'll take yours away," Sadie said, sliding an arm around her grandmother.

"Honey, I've got curses coming out my ears."

"You do?" Sadie asked, startled.

"Never you mind." Gigi pulled her in for a hug and patted her waist. "Now, get back there and finish those cookies before I sugar 'em to death."

Sadie hurried to her dough, checking the timer as she did and wondering what kind of curses Gigi was talking about and what had brought on the physical display of affection. With eight minutes left, she gave the frosting a contemplative stir.

Heartbreak for Sadie wasn't a passing folly, to be recovered from with time and chocolate and tears. Because of her curse, it could take everything from her. Which made falling in love a risk that wasn't worth taking.

Something drew her to the oven despite the six minutes left on the timer. Peering in, panic scorched down her body like chili flakes when she saw the cookies were starting to burn at the edges. The message was clear as cold ice: *"Something wicked this way comes."*

"No, no, no," she whispered, hastily grabbing the nearest dishtowel. But the pan burned her hand through the fabric.

She yelped and dropped it on the stovetop with a reverberating clang. Someone, or some*thing*, had turned the oven up to five hundred degrees. She waved the dishtowel frantically, trying to fan away any scent of the evidence, because if Gigi caught so much as a whiff, she'd banish Sadie from the kitchen for the day.

She hurriedly scraped the burned cookies into the sink and turned on the garbage disposal. A familiar fire was burning along her veins, and her fist ached to hit something. The sixth bad omen. The sachet of lavender and buckbean she kept in her apron pocket was doing little to keep her calm the way it was supposed to.

In front of her, peppered on the countertop and the long wall shelves, she eyed her canisters. Each one had a label, written by Gigi. There was no cinnamon, basil, clove, or marjoram. Instead, "Youth" sat next to "Friendship," while "Love," "Kindness," and "Forgetfulness" were relegated to their own section. "Stability," "Health," and "Fertility" kept "Good Wishes" company, while "Misfortune" was pushed to the back like a dark secret.

Sadie reached for the glass jars labeled "Traditions" and "Protection." She inhaled the scent of freshly ground cinnamon before sprinkling some into the dough. Traditions—would this do the trick?

With careful fingers, she grabbed a pinch of salt and whispered a quick blessing over it before dashing it into the bowl, hoping it would keep whatever was coming at bay.

Sadie stirred the ingredients in with her wooden spoon, carved by hand from the white oak tree in the forest behind Gigi's backyard. Her grandfather had loved wood carving in his spare time. He had passed away when the twins were six, and she didn't remember much about him other than his famous pastrami sandwiches and the little wood figurines he'd sculpt for her. He had traveled a lot for work as a technician and would always bring Gigi a small collector spoon from whatever state he'd visited. Sadie had loved those little spoons, tracing her finger over the intricate filigree or studying the resin design. She hadn't thought of those spoons in years.

"Querido amado." A high, musical voice barged into her sanctuary just as she slid the baking tray into the oven. "Did a tornado hit in here?"

Sadie turned and frowned at the raven-haired woman. Raquel, her best friend since childhood, scanned the room with wide, expressive eyes. Even when she was still, she somehow seemed to be in motion. Fingers or foot always tapping, eyes so thoughtful you could practically hear her talking even when she was silent.

"I thought I banned you from coming in here if you couldn't say anything nice," Sadie retorted, holding up her wooden spoon like a sword.

"I'm not worried until I see the fire in your eyes." Raquel laughed. "That's when I know we've really got a problem."

Sadie hugged her best friend and then pinched her on the arm.

"Ow!" Raquel cried, her face drawn into a frown.

"Pinching is my love language." Sadie shrugged, checking the timer.

"What's wrong?" Raquel demanded, leaning against the counter and eyeing her best friend, waiting.

Sadie's lips pursed. She never could hide anything from Raquel and found it rather inconvenient the way best friends could see into you even when you refused to look yourself.

"Hello!" Raquel snapped her fingers. "You in there?"

"I'm thinking."

"You're always thinking. Sometimes it's healthy to just say what's on your mind, you little control freak."

Sadie laughed.

"I'm just—you know, just wallowing in a bit of self-pity. Freaking out about being alone for the rest of my life. I had a minor panic attack over toothbrushes this morning. So, you know, the usual."

"Were the toothbrushes on fire? Did they insult you?"

"More the fact that there was only one."

"Exactly how many toothbrushes do you need?" Raquel demanded, arching a perfectly lined eyebrow.

"I'll only ever have one. You know, because I'll always be brushing alone." Sadie dragged a finger along the countertop, trying and failing to stop the ache that bloomed in her chest.

"Do you want me to brush my teeth with you? All you have to do is ask, you know."

"Shut up." Sadie laughed again. "It's just the curse," she started.

"The curse, the curse," Raquel chattered. "When are you going to let that go? Listen, you're not alone. Nobody is abandoning you. Your brother is going to come back. Gigi's not going anywhere. Neither am I. You run a successful business. You're loved. We're all here to support you." The words came out in a rush, like they'd been rehearsed. For all Sadie knew, maybe they had. She wondered when she'd become the friend who had to be talked off a ledge so often that Raquel had a speech for it.

Sadie took a deep breath and let the words wash over her. Reassure her. But for some reason, they couldn't pierce completely through her armor. Because the truth of the matter was that Seth *wasn't* back, and even if he did return, there was no guarantee he wouldn't vanish again. Gigi wouldn't be around forever. They'd both leave. Just like her mother. Just like Jake.

"And now that I've buttered you up . . ." Raquel started.

"Oh no." Sadie groaned, again folding the thoughts in half and tucking them away. "What are you roping me into this time?"

"Let me start off with the good news." Raquel was practically beaming. "They said *yes*!"

"Did you propose to someone I should I know about?"

"Hilarious. And no. You're the only one for me. But the school board said yes to *Carrie*!" she squealed. "I had to sign an agreement swearing I'd personally clean the blood off the stage, but it's totally worth it."

Sadie laughed. Raquel was the local high school music teacher and always directed the musicals. Sadie had been cornered into her fair share of sitting through hours of long auditions and backstage teenage meltdowns.

"What do you need me for?" she asked with resignation.

"You're an angel, you know that? I was wondering if you and Gigi could help with the gym costumes. You know, the toga-like ones?"

"Your parents own literally the only costume store in town! They don't have anything?"

"Um, excuse me. The Mad Hatter is a costume and *tux rental* store. We also do prom dresses. And no, they don't have what I need. I was also thinking maybe you'd want to host a bake sale or something to raise funds?" Raquel smiled obscenely.

"Okay, okay," Sadie said, laughing. "Done."

"Now I just need someone to help me with the lighting. It needs some strong design. Know of anyone who could help?"

Before Sadie could answer, the air in the kitchen suddenly pulsed with an energy that felt like endless summer nights where anything was possible, or of first frost on Christmas morning. It was anticipation, pure and clean.

Sadie nervously wiped her hands on her apron again, her stomach dropping to her feet. The "Traditions" and "Protection" hadn't had time to bake through yet.

"No, no, no," Sadie moaned with a hand over her mouth. The noise of the world faded to a hum. It buzzed in her chest like a painful memory. The kitchen went eerily quiet, even the popping and creaking of the hot oven gone silent.

Beyond the double doors, something pulled her. Something warm that smelled like sweet summer peaches.

Pushing the door open a sliver, she peered out the front window. The hum turned into a roar, and her ears burned hot as she saw him.

The omens. The flooded river. That quiet voice in her head snickering and whispering.

Jacob McNealy.

He stood on the sidewalk like a living, walking daydream. Her mouth went desert dry, and it was like she'd been thirsty for years and hadn't realized it. Looking at him was like stretching your limbs after a long nap.

The first heartbreak that had sparked her curse to life.

And seeing old sorrow before noon was the seventh bad omen. A nightmare was on its way.

Carrot Cake Cookies with Cream Cheese Frosting

These will humble the eater and remind them of their roots, where they came from—you know. Carrots help you understand that to find fulfillment, you have to seek answers from your past, no matter how gritty it is. The salt and cinnamon ensure that those traditions and memories will be protected. Focus on positivity while baking, or they'll turn out bitter. I adapted this recipe from my Uncle Sun, who brought back a bag of lunar white carrot seeds from his tour in Vietnam.

Ingredients

For the cookies

1 c. all-purpose flour
1 tsp. baking soda
½ tsp. salt
1½ tsp. ground cinnamon
⅛ tsp. ground nutmeg
½ tsp. ginger
¼ c. coconut oil melted and cooled to room temperature
½ c. dark brown sugar
¼ c. granulated sugar
1 large egg
¼ c. peach puree (can use baby food or just puree canned peaches)
2 tsp. vanilla extract
1 c. shredded carrots

1 c. old-fashioned oats
½ c. sweetened coconut flakes
½ c. raisins

For the frosting

1 oz. cream cheese at room temperature
1 c. powdered sugar
1 T. milk
¼ tsp. pure almond or vanilla extract

Directions

1. Preheat the oven to 350°F. Line a baking sheet with a Silpat baking mat or parchment paper, and set aside.

2. In a medium bowl, whisk together flour, baking soda, salt, cinnamon, and nutmeg. Set aside.

3. In the bowl of a stand mixer, combine coconut oil and sugars, mix until smooth. Add egg and vanilla extract, and beat until well combined. Next, add the shredded carrots and peach puree. Mix until combined.

4. Slowly add flour mixture until just combined. Stir in oats, coconut, and raisins.

5. Drop cookie dough by heaping tablespoonfuls, 2 inches apart, onto prepared baking sheet. Bake for 10–12 minutes or until cookies are slightly golden around the edges and set. Remove cookies from pans; cool completely on wire racks.

6. While the cookies are cooling, make the cream cheese glaze. Mix together the cream cheese, powdered sugar, milk, and extract in a medium bowl. Using a spoon, drizzle the glaze over the cooled cookies. Let cookies sit until glaze hardens up. Serve!

2

"WHAT THE HELL?" RAQUEL cried just as the smoke alarm went off.

After a moment of sheer panic, Sadie grabbed a dishtowel and jumped on a chair to fan away the sudden onslaught of smoke, the acrid scent making both their eyes water. Raquel snatched another and windmilled her arms like the force of nature she was. A second later Gigi came rushing through the door just as the shrill beeping cut off, leaving them in an echoing silence.

"You trying to give the customers a heart attack?" Gigi demanded, and then stopped short when she saw the look of horror on Sadie's face. "Okay, toot. You're done for the day."

"*Dios mío*, I saw her put those cookies in," Raquel said, making the sign of the cross. "How did they burn that fast?"

"I'll call Gail for backup," Gigi said, her voice going soft as she patted Sadie on the arm. Gail, Gigi's oldest friend and part-time employee at the café, would be there in under ten minutes with ready hands and a smile on her face. "You need to get out of here before you blow this place to bits. What's rule number twenty-one?"

"'*Don't mess with Revelare magic.*'" Sadie groaned, her heart beating hummingbird fast. It wasn't even noon, and her world was crumbling. Her chest tightened, her lower back seizing up. The kitchen, which had been stifling before, was strangely cold now. It was all smoke and ice and heavy silence, like everything had been blanketed in snow.

"That's right. Some things you can change, but those you can't are best left well respected. Take this with you," she added, pushing a small vial of salt and angelica into Sadie's hands before shooing her out of the kitchen.

Sadie washed her hands and slid all her rings back on like a soldier strapping on battle armor. Then, she silently followed Raquel out the kitchen door after making sure Jake was nowhere to be seen. Several customers called warm greetings to her as she passed, and complimented the orange essence croissants. She smiled absentmindedly while a burning heat climbed stickily up her neck.

The air was brisk as ginger snaps as the sun made its daily commute into the sky, but it only served to make her skin clammier. Though it was still early, Sadie could see Cutsie's Diner, across the way, filled with breakfasters. Standing there on the sidewalk, it felt like looking in on a dream she couldn't quite touch.

"So that went well," Raquel said, breaking into Sadie's thoughts. Her brown skin seemed to give off a glow in the early light. She linked Sadie's arm through hers and pulled her across the street. When Raquel took charge, there was really nothing to be done, so Sadie let herself be pulled. For someone who was always in control, it was a foreign feeling.

"Ten years," was all Sadie said.

"I know." Raquel sighed.

"He was my first heartbreak. He's the one who started my curse," Sadie said with such force that her face flushed with the heat of memory.

"You're so dramatic," Raquel said with pursed lips. "I told you, curses are only real if you believe in them."

"That's what you think! Do you remember what happened to my, my—you know what," she whispered, eyes scanning the sidewalk, "after he left?"

"I'm extremely terrified of what you're referring to." Raquel raised her eyebrows.

"My magic!" Sadie hissed.

"Oh yeah. Something spontaneously combusted every time you walked into the kitchen. That *was* weird," Raquel said thoughtfully.

"And the plants in the garden kept dying. And the electricity in the house kept going out. It was a disaster. The same thing happened after Seth left. My magic is only now settling back in. Both times it took almost a year for things to go back to normal."

"Your definition of normal could use a little work." Raquel laughed, her stick-straight raven hair blowing in the early autumn breeze, carrying with it the scent of strawberries and anticipation.

Sadie nervously scanned the street and down the sidewalk. But he was nowhere to be seen. They waited at the crosswalk, and Sadie shivered. There was no stop sign here, only a blinking stoplight up ahead at the four-way intersection that led further up the street, and crossways to smaller, winding neighborhoods or large pastures with even larger barns. Here there was only a friendly sign, its pole wrapped in cheery climbing ivy, that read "Look Both Ways!"

"If I were a real witch, I'd have hexed you by now," Sadie said, but her heart wasn't in it.

"Real witch." Raquel rolled her eyes. "Please. Did you or did you not brew a tea in middle school that made Annabelle Bennet tell the whole student body the truth about how she stuffed her bra?"

"She was a bully! She deserved it for teasing all of us for not 'blooming early' like her."

"Uh-huh. That's why she still hates you. And did you or did you not bake a quiche that helped poor, zit-faced Phillip Lee conquer his fear and ask that very same Annabelle to the high school winter formal?" she asked as she held the door open to the diner.

"How could I not help him? I was duty bound." Sadie laughed, the feeling starting to come back into her fingers. The smell of diner coffee and fried potatoes made her stomach growl, even though it felt too twisted up to eat.

"That's why your customers always come back. It's not just food. It's magic. It's hopes and promise and love and all that stuff. You don't call that witchcraft?"

"I plead the fifth."

"Which means I'm right." Raquel grinned as they walked into the diner.

They both laughed as they slid into their favorite booth in the corner, along the windows that overlooked the street. The cracked leather depressed with a creak as they slid in. A few moments later, Janie sidled over. Only a few years older, she'd been working there since the girls were in middle school and seemed almost as permanent a fixture as the diner itself.

"How are my two favorite customers?" she asked with a smile, pulling out her ticket pad.

"I bet you say that to everyone who walks through those doors," Raquel said, smirking.

"Only the ones who tip as good as you do." Janie winked. "What can I get you ladies?" Sadie noticed the way her hand held the pen over her notepad and made a mental note to bring her some Cat's Claw salve for her arthritis.

"Gold Rush scramble with egg whites, please," Raquel said without glancing at the menu.

"Just coffee, thanks," Sadie said.

"She'll have the Gold Rush scramble too. But the biscuit instead of toast."

"I will?"

"I know you've probably had four cups of coffee and two cups of tea already, with nothing to eat, so yes, you will."

Janie laughed and wrote their order down, flexing her fingers as she slipped the pen into her apron pocket.

"You're bossy," Sadie said as she closed her eyes and listened to the chatter of the diner. Water being poured from pitcher to glass, the clink of knives and forks against plates.

"Part of my charm." Raquel grinned. "Plus, you told me to remind you not to drink so much caffeine."

"Well, that was before I found out you-know-who was back in town!" Sadie shot back.

"What, Voldemort?" Raquel asked with an arched eyebrow.

"Funny. Hilarious," Sadie deadpanned with an evil glare and pursed lips.

"You know, that's actually what I came in to tell you. But your stupid sixth sense got the better of me. Apparently, he's a firefighter now. Wonder how he looks in that uniform . . . I hope he's gotten fat."

Sadie knew Raquel was trying to get a reaction out of her, which was exactly why she didn't answer. She had to keep the last shred of control before she lost it completely. Her heart hadn't stopped beating erratically since she'd seen Jake standing on the sidewalk. But she couldn't let it show, or her best friend would pounce like a ravenous lion. Already, Raquel's eyes kept finding themselves plastered to Sadie's face, watching for any sign of emotion.

"Stop staring at me like that." Sadie threw a dirty look across the table.

"Don't tell me what to do with my eyes." Raquel's voice was as imperious as her pointed expression. "Anyway, I guess he was at a big station in southern California but wanted something a little more relaxed, so he decided to move back home."

"How do you even know all of this?" Sadie demanded, curiosity getting the better of her.

"I ran into Nancy at the gas station this morning, who heard it from Katie Sutherland."

"Great," Sadie groaned. If Cindy McGillicuddy was the town busybody, Katie Sutherland was the town gossip. Her mantra was, "It's not gossip if it's true." No consideration given as to who she hurt in the process. She once caught Sadie kissing a boy behind the pastor's house during junior high youth group, and told anyone who would listen that Sadie was using her "devilish ways" to lure innocent boys into sin. Of course, then Gigi had shown up at her door with a cake soaked in misfortune, telling her that if she spread any more nasty rumors, Gigi would return with a shotgun.

"Apparently, he's going through the process to get hired onto the fire station here in Poppy Meadows," Raquel went on.

"He couldn't wait to get the hell out of Dodge back in the day. I mean, I knew. I *knew* he never wanted to stay. And I fell anyway."

"You always were a glutton for punishment."

"I don't know, I guess I just thought we'd—well, it doesn't matter. I was dumb. Naive."

"No, your problem, *cariño*, is that it's practically impossible for anyone to get in that heart of yours. And when they do, you love them forever. No matter what. No matter how much they shit all over you."

"Raquel, I'm seriously going to stab you with this tiny coffee straw if you don't shut up."

"Truth hurts," Raquel shrugged, dragging a finger along the tabletop and staring innocently off into space. "Seriously. Aren't you tired of living your life ruled by all your routines and lists? Don't you want to give up just a *teeny*"—she drew out the word in a high-pitched voice as she pinched her thumb and forefinger together until they almost touched—"bit of control and, you know, have some fun? Stop obsessing over Jake being back, like I know you are in your head, and let's have a girl's night. Wine. Junk food. Crappy movies."

"First of all, my life does not revolve around Jacob McNealy," Sadie hissed, her stomach pooling into a mess of nerves as she finally said his name aloud. "I'm not even thinking about him." Just then a whoosh of cold air shot into the diner as the door opened, and Sadie, whose back was to the entrance, whipped her head around so fast her neck cracked. She let out a shaky breath when she saw it was only Mayor Elias.

"I'm so convinced right now," Raquel deadpanned. "Look how convinced I am."

"I haven't seen him in ten years. I shouldn't even care that he's back in town," Sadie said, massaging her neck as the corners of her mouth pulled down into a frown. She knew full well that *shouldn't* didn't mean much when it came to Jake. "I *don't* care, even if—"

"Mayor incoming," Raquel hissed, cutting off her lies.

Sadie immediately sat up straighter. Raquel smoothed the napkin in her lap and ran a hand over her hair.

"Sadie, Raquel," he said, walking over.

"Mayor Elias."

"And how are my constituents this fine morning?" he asked, running a hand down his tie before sticking his thumbs through his suspenders. Impeccably dressed as always, Elias cut a striking figure with his dark skin and darker hair.

Sadie and Raquel mumbled their answers, always reverting to their teenage selves under Elias's gaze, which had turned stern. He had the unique ability to make you feel like you'd done something wrong, even if you hadn't, because he knew, at some point, he'd be right. He held up a hand.

"Lovely, lovely. Now, about the autumn window displays," he started just as his husband, James, called his name from the corner booth. "Well, more on that later, I suppose. Breakfast beckons." He patted his stomach and left them.

"Saved by the bell," Raquel whispered. "Now, back to Jake."

Sadie groaned.

"I mean, it's not like he 'dumped you.'" She made quotation marks with her fingers around the last two words. "You're allowed to move on a decade later, you know?"

"I—we . . . it was complicated."

"Was it?" Raquel demanded, her tone dripping with skepticism.

"The river flooding, seven bad omens in a row. He's obviously the nightmare."

"At least we finally agree on that. He's a dipshit. Always has been."

"You're only saying that because he broke my heart."

"Duh. You're my best friend. You'd hate any idiot that broke my heart too."

Just then Janie stopped by to drop off their Gold Rush scrambles and Sadie's coffee. Sadie inhaled the steam coming off the hot plate, eying the maple sausage hungrily. Her stomach rumbled, and Raquel gave her an "I told you so" look. Ignoring her, Sadie picked up a rasher of bacon and dunked it in her coffee before folding the whole piece into her mouth. Stress eating at its finest.

"That," Raquel pointed her fork at Sadie's coffee, "is disgusting. You just contaminated your drink with pig parts."

"It all goes to the same place, you weirdo." Sadie rolled her eyes.

"You're going to be okay, you know," Raquel said in a casual voice that wasn't quite convincing. "I know it sucks, but—" She shrugged.

Sadie picked up her coffee, the mug warm in her hand, but as she brought it to her lips, her temperamental magic turned the ceramic cold and the bitter taste of ice-cold coffee hit her tongue. The back of her neck prickled, and she scrunched her shoulders, forcing herself not to turn around again. The urge to throw a dash of salt over her shoulder, or at the very least squeeze the buckbean in her pocket, was almost overwhelming. Goose bumps rose on her arms. *"Something wicked this way comes."* She tried to brush it under the rug like she always did, but the rug wasn't budging. Some things refused to be swept.

"Camilla is trying to convince Mom and Dad to let her get a tattoo," Raquel said out of nowhere, changing the subject and breaking into Sadie's thoughts.

"What!" Sadie laughed. "In what world?" Raquel's parents were stricter than strict. Raquel had once been grounded because she played an April Fool's joke with a fake nose ring. When Sadie had tried the same trick, Gigi had told her how darling it looked.

"I know, right? 'What kind of example do you think you're setting for Sofía!'" She imitated her mother's voice and accent. "Mind you Camilla is nineteen and Sofía is sixteen, but God forbid they go against *Mamá y Papá* Rodriguez. Been there. Failed that. Remember when I tried to skive off my therapy session when we were in middle school? I thought Papá was going to have an aneurysm." She laughed. "He sat in the waiting room every time after that. I think he'd *still* sit in the waiting room if I let him."

"Only because you're his princess," Sadie said with a smile. "How are your meds, by the way?" She usually asked every few months, but Raquel had been so stable she'd forgotten to check in and felt a little guilty for it.

"Dr. Attenburg upped the dosage a few months ago, and it's—" She shrugged. "It's good. It numbs me a little too much sometimes, but it's better than the alternative."

The alternative, Sadie knew, could be disastrous. She'd sat with Raquel while she'd spiraled into a catatonic state, been with her when her manic episodes threatened her safety, and cried with her as her as she begged not to be broken. Raquel's bipolar disorder was a roller coaster, but it was one that made her best friend the strongest and most courageous person she knew, even if she herself didn't see it.

"And how's yoga?"

"Working on the eight-angle pose. It's a sight to behold," Raquel said. "But the more I take care of my body, the better I feel."

Just then, Annabelle Bennet walked by and threw a condescending smile in their direction. She'd never quite forgiven Sadie for outing her bra stuffing, and made it her life mission to make Sadie feel as small as possible. Still, Sadie smiled back and offered a wave as Raquel scowled.

"I can never decide if I should try to be nicer like you, or if I should try and make you more of a stone-cold bitch like me," Raquel said as Annabelle took a seat at a table across the diner.

"I'm not nice," Sadie countered.

"You would literally let someone shit on your doorstep and then apologize for not cleaning it up fast enough."

"That—that's disgusting, first of all. And second, it may *seem* like I'm nice, but really, it's scathing sarcastic subtext. It's a subtle art of insulting but doing it in such a way that the person doesn't know if you're joking or not. I mean, Annabelle tries, bless her, but the hatred shows in her eyes too much, you know?"

"Whatever you say, *cariño*. But everyone knows you're a big ol' softie."

Sadie stirred her coffee thoughtfully, opened her mouth, couldn't think of anything to say that seemed true, and closed it again.

"Stop editing whatever you're thinking about saying, and just spit it out."

"Fine," Sadie huffed, "even though that's a rhetorical question because you're my best friend, and you obviously know how I feel. My stomach is in knots at the thought of him being in the same town, let alone actually seeing him. And now I know what all those bad omens brought. But a nightmare you know is better than one you don't because then you know how to handle it. And whatever Jake's doing in town, I want nothing to do with it."

And that, as far as Sadie was concerned, was that.

After they ate, Raquel wouldn't let her go home, forcing her to walk down Main Street with her, arm in arm.

"Face your fears," she said. "Just a little stroll, and then you can go home and bury your hands in the dirt like I know you're going to."

"I'm going to bury your head in the dirt," Sadie said, her eyes roving everywhere, scanning faces as she hoped and feared a particular one she might see.

Meera Shaan waved as she swept the stoop outside of Shaan's Salon. The gold threads on her peach-toned sari winked in the sunlight like little promises. Mrs. Shaan had been trimming and setting Gigi's hair since they opened shop several years ago, after they moved from Aurelia.

"Tell your daadee that the tea she gave me for Akshay has been helping him sleep much better," she said with a grateful smile. Her ten-year-old son, Sadie knew, suffered from severe obsessive-compulsive disorder, and his anxiety kept him up at night.

"I'll tell her," she promised.

They passed Delvaux Candles & Curiosities, the sign outside swaying slightly in the wind. If you tilted your head just right, you'd swear the three candles burned into the old wood flickered like they'd just been lit.

And then Sadie felt the pull as they neared Poppy Meadows Bookstore. She heard pages fluttering, calling to her. It was a siren song, one she usually couldn't resist. The sign in the display window was painted with an open book that had bright orange California poppies sprouting out of the pages. The logo had always made her think of falling into a book the way Alice fell down the rabbit hole. Behind the glass, there were books in white enamel bird cages and hanging from the ceiling by invisible strings.

"No way," Raquel said, dragging her by the arm as Sadie's feet slowed down. "Time ceases to exist for you in bookstores, and I am not sitting by for three hours while you get hot over books you have no intention of buying."

"But they need me," Sadie argued. Her hand was on the door, although she didn't remember reaching her arm out. "Even if I don't buy them, they need to know they're loved. That someone wants to look at them. Caress their delicate pages."

"You are so weird," Raquel said, sighing and following her inside.

Sadie inhaled.

"Your anthropomorphism knows no bounds," Raquel added as Sadie waved to the books.

"Shh, you're going to offend them."

"Hello, ladies," said Mr. Abassi from behind the counter. Sadie had grown up with his rich voice welcoming her into the shop, the brightness of his white crestless pagri dimmed only by his even more brilliant smile.

"I am glad you stopped in," he said in his light accent. "Your Nanni would not take payment for the arthritis salve she gave me, so I set this aside for you." He pulled a book from underneath the counter, and Sadie gasped as she read the cover: *An Illustrated Guide to Rare Floriography and Its Uses.* She'd been drooling over the intricate watercolor designs again just last week but couldn't justify yet another addition to her ever-growing collection.

"Mr. Abassi, you really don't have to," she said, but her eager hands were already reaching for the book.

"Please," he said, "it's the least I can do. I do not know what Poppy Meadows would do without Gigi Revelare." He waved them out of the shop with a farewell in the form of *"Khuda hafiz."*

"That wasn't so bad, was it?" Sadie asked, her fingers trailing over the embossed flowers on the cover.

"Not this time."

"Am I allowed to go home now?"

"Feeling better?"

"Marginally," Sadie admitted, kissing her best friend on the cheek.

On her drive home, Sadie finally released a long breath it felt like she'd been holding ever since the grandfather clock went off that morning. She pulled into the driveway and cut the engine, the silence snaking around her.

The Revelares' three-bedroom home sat further back off the street than the others in the neighborhood. It was nearly antebellum, with its sweeping front porch and white pillars, though the lemon tree out front had wide reaching branches that made it look more suited to an African plain than California. And no matter how hot the days got in the summer, the shade underneath would cool you until you were nearly shivering. Rumor had it that sucking the juice from a lemon off the Revelare tree could show you what you wanted most in the world.

Sadie had tried it dozens of times growing up, her cheeks pinching at the sour-sweet taste, but all she ever saw was the house in front of her.

On the other side of the yard stood a tall, proud red maple tree. When Seth and Sadie were younger, they'd painstakingly carved their names in the trunk with a pilfered kitchen knife. The markings wept syrup for weeks afterward. Every time the twins would visit it, Sadie cried for the tree's pain and what they'd done, while Seth merely dragged his fingers through the sticky sweetness and licked it off. That's how it always was. When he tried to start fires with a magnifying glass, she was the one putting them out. When he forgot to empty the trash, she did it for him so he wouldn't get in trouble with Gigi. Looking back, she thought maybe he could have used a little scolding. Maybe her treatment of him was enabling. Or maybe it was easier to help others than it was to help herself. Whatever the reason, whenever she saw someone needing help, she stepped in.

But it wasn't just memories of Seth in that yard; there were memories of summer picnics, when Uncle Brian would visit and barbecue one of his freshly slaughtered pigs. Aunt Anne and Uncle Steven setting up the badminton net. All the cousins there and endless games of hide-and-seek and secrets and sprinklers. Sticky watermelon fingers and sidewalk chalk. As the years went on, the memories stuck, but the get-togethers didn't. Sometimes she missed her aunts and uncles so much it felt like pieces of her were searching for little pieces of them.

Shoving down the past, she slammed the door of her beat-up old Subaru and—first things first—unlaced her boots and kicked them off. A sigh escaped as the warmth of the pavement spread across her feet. She inhaled the smell of hot, wet concrete where water from the sprinkler had edged its path to the driveway. For once, the wind had died down, and everything was still. There was the chatter from a pair of squirrels up in a tree and the whicker of a horse in Cindy's field across the way. Something inside Sadie stilled too. Poppy Meadows wasn't a town of much commotion, but being on their little plot of land, away from the noise and café chores, the tightness in her chest began to uncoil.

Her fingers trailed the sky-blue hydrangeas that circled the house, their delicate petals filling her with courage. Finally, in the garden, she sat in the dirt below her favorite potato vine, her toes burrowing into the pebble walkway, her fingers plugged into the earth, as though to recharge her. Usually the garden brought peace, but as she looked around, it felt different. The fairy lanterns swayed, and the tomato vines rustled, but something was out of place. And that's when a movement at the edge of the forest caught her eye. It was just the smallest slip of movement before it vanished behind a tree. A film of white that could have been animal, ghost, or intruder.

After a moment, the sound of sharp little toenails on flagstones startled her. Gigi's miniature Manchester terrier, Abby, barrel chested, wheezing, and far too fat for her size, waddled excitedly over to Sadie. And by the time she looked back to the woods, the figure was nowhere to be seen. She brushed it off. The woods held all kinds of secrets, and none had bothered her yet. Abby, meanwhile, realizing it wasn't Gigi, gave a disdainful sniff and marched straight back through her doggie door.

The backyard was small, but every inch was covered in herbs, fruits, and vegetables. Foxglove and lavender bushes lined the perimeter to keep the deer away. The smell of green tomatoes and earth and pine mingled into a memory. Into comfort. Sadie could name every genus and species in that garden before most children could spell their own name. By the time she was thirteen, she could trace their origins and recite their symbolism, tell you the history of each plant and how it had been used medicinally or magically. Sometimes she wondered if her very blood was laced with the nectar of those blooms. The path from the back porch to the garden was lined with fairy lanterns hanging from twisted wrought iron poles. Among the garden itself were nestled solar lights that gave off a warm, ethereal glow, and the peach and plum trees' trunks were wrapped in a garland of tiny, muted white lights that twinkled like stars. At night, Sadie would feel the space calling to her until she snuck out and danced among the sweet peas and rainbow chard as the plants swayed in a secret welcome.

Seth, meanwhile, had been barred from the Revelare garden by the plants themselves. When he'd try to eavesdrop or sneak his way in, an errant vine would wrap itself around his ankle until he tripped.

"Only Revelare women have this kind of magic," Gigi would tell him kindly but sternly in her gravelly smoker's voice. "Revelare men have magic of a different sort."

"I don't want your stupid magic anyway," he'd shout before stomping off.

"What kind of magic do Revelare men have?" Sadie had asked.

"He'll find out when the time comes, never you mind," Gigi had told her in a tone that said, *"Case closed."*

"What about the curse?" Sadie had pressed, never knowing when to leave well enough alone. The curse was the most mysterious part of their legacy. All the Revelares had magic, but they also had a curse to accompany it. For nature demanded balance, and that was its way of keeping things in check.

"You're not supposed to know about the curse until today, sugar. But I suppose your Aunt Tava has been whispering in your ear." Gigi had sighed, leaning back on her heels, with her knees caked in mud. "I guess we better get into it. Every curse is different. Some don't take effect until you've nearly forgotten about them. Maybe you thought you'd get away scot-free, only to find it slumbering like a queen of the night," she said. "You and your brother, you'll find your magic. But your curse—well, that'll find you. For now, don't borrow trouble unless you've got the shoulders to carry it."

The promise of magic seemed worth the cost of a curse. And the first time she made the night jasmine bloom during the sultry heat of a June day with a single word, she knew that her magic lay in the earth, same as her grandmother's. It was so tangled up in her, she could never quite separate the two. The one truth she hung on to, always, was that family was more important than her magic. Because if she lost that, she was nothing. An unmoored ship, a kite without a string. And right now, with Seth gone, that meant Gigi. Her grandmother was the anchor that kept her grounded and the string that let her fly.

The property line behind their plot abutted the edge of the forest, where sweeping pines and ponderosas slumbered gently in a dream. The light filtering through made the space feel like Sadie's very own secret garden.

Except now, it seemed as though an insidious presence had infiltrated her private space. Because through the trees, less than a mile down a winding dirt deer track, stood a house. *The* house.

She hadn't thought about it in years. It was a large, two-level home, straight from a storybook, painted in robin's-egg blue with white trim. Nestled against a hill, Rock Creek ran right through the seven-acre parcel, the bubbling water a siren's call to forest animals. The attic, with its dormer window, had been turned into a reading nook.

Sadie knew this because she'd snuck into the house with Jake over ten years ago, when the property had been up for sale. They'd sat on the faded leather couch in the dying sunlight, the walls creaking in the charged winter wind as they ate rum-soaked peach muffins with streusel topping, to incite euphoria and preserve only happy memories. The air was cold and brittle and sweet as they talked about everything they'd do to renovate the house.

"I'd build a slide from the roof down to the creek," he'd exclaimed.

"That sounds like a lawsuit waiting to happen," Sadie had protested, laughing.

"And a zip line from here to your grandmother's house," he added, grabbing her hand and tracing the lines on her palm.

"She might murder you for that," Sadie answered, willing her stupid heart to get used to the way he touched her, even though it never would listen. She inhaled the musty scent of the old house and listened as the beams groaned, wanting the moment to last forever, the summer heat cocooning them like a secret.

"And this couch," he said in a low voice, "it would have to go. I'd definitely need a bed here. Look," he said, pointing to the skylight. "Perfect for stargazing." He leaned back, pulling Sadie with him until they were two sardines in a tin can, pressed against each other on the tiny couch. His body against hers, igniting a heat in her core that had nothing to do with the balmy air. She hated the way he was close, but still not close enough. She wanted to sink into him until she didn't know where she began and he ended. Her eyes caught his as they'd darted to her lips, and even a decade later she never forgot the hunger she saw there. It had pulsed through her, the air filling with static electricity around them until he broke the stare.

"Yeah, this thing is way too small. Only room for one," he'd said with a laugh, right before pushing her off.

She'd landed with a thump on the floor and let out a strangled cry of gleeful rage. She'd pounced, catlike, and landed on top of him, pummeling his shoulder. He'd laughed and grabbed her hands in a gentle iron grip.

"You know how this always ends up. You lose. Just give up before you hurt yourself," he warned her.

Sadie had yanked with all her might, but his grip held fast. He pulled her closer, moving her arms until they were pinned behind her back, and she and Jake were chest to chest, breathing hard.

Sitting in her garden with her eyes closed, Sadie could still smell the fresh soap and bonfire smoke that had clung to his skin. And just like woodsmoke, his essence had clung to her long after the fire had been put out.

She'd refused to think about that house for ten years. There was something about the promise of it that was far more painful to think about than even the night they'd first kissed. The desire that had her panting to catch her breath. To think straight. To think of anything other than how she wanted his rough hands scraping over every inch of her body. The way she'd finally found something she wanted to lose control over.

She inhaled. The smell of him was so strong that, with the memory of it, she could almost feel his smooth skin.

And then someone cleared their throat.

Sadie's eyes snapped open.

And there he stood. A delicious memory brought to life.

Her stomach dipped and knotted—and it all came rushing back.

It was the satisfying crunch of a sharp knife cutting through ripe watermelon. It was green citronella spirals burning down and sunscreen squirting hot out of the tube. It was banana pancakes on repeat and the tang of river silt clinging to tanned skin. It was summer. And freedom. And youth. And heartbreak so hot it cauterized.

"How long have you been standing there?" she demanded, her heart going staccato.

"Long enough to know you haven't changed," he said somberly.

He had sorrow in his eyes. Just a shadow of sadness, hidden behind the crinkle when he smiled. She used to make it her mission to make him happy. And she had. There was something about being the one that brought out his booming laugh. It unlocked something inside her. Made her realize who she wanted to be—the one who made his eyes smile. But she'd also never found out why he was sad in the first place.

His voice was a recollection, the siren song of the past, and damn it all if she didn't want to climb inside it and live there. Before she knew what her legs were doing, they were walking her to the gate.

He held out his arms, and she hesitated. *It's just a hug. A friendly hug,* she told herself. And then she was running.

His arms went around her and he squeezed, and for the first time in ten years she felt small again. Against his broad chest. His strong shoulders. Her body's muscle memory urged her closer, where her head nestled in the crook of his neck. This was why she could never settle for Ryan. For anything less than the way her ribs turned into a steel drum, echoing her thudding heart in a summer drumbeat of hopes long abandoned.

Home, home home—the rhythm reverberated in her chest.

But when she leaned back, still in his arms, and registered the little lines beneath his eyes, she remembered the years that had stretched into a decade since they last met, and the echo stopped short. She stepped out of his embrace, her cheeks pinker than they had any right to be.

"Before you start yelling, I brought something for you. Just let me give it to you first, and then you can attack." He took a small blue box out of his back pocket and handed it to her as her eyes narrowed. There was a clear cutout in the top and nestled there in white satin was . . .

"You brought me a tiny spoon?" she asked, vacillating between confusion and incredulity.

"I remember you saying how much you loved when your grandad would bring one to Gigi. You said that even though you never wanted to leave Poppy Meadows, you liked the thought of having little pieces of the world. And I went to a conference a few years ago in Texas and saw it, and—look, I know it's about ten years too late," he said. "I'm sure you hate me. I'd hate me too. I was an ass. But I was young. And stupid. And didn't know what I wanted. Not that that's an excuse. I've apologized to you in my head twenty times in the last ten years, but I was too much of a coward to do it in real life."

The longer he spoke, the more the initial glow at seeing him turned to ash. She hated him for remembering that. For it softening her toward him now, when all she wanted to feel was righteous anger.

"I trusted you," she said in a quiet voice. "And you ruined me." She'd been waiting to say that for ten years. But now that the words were out, they didn't make her feel better, like she'd hoped they would. "Do you know how hard it is for me to trust people? Do you know how much you screwed me up?" she demanded. As soon as the words were out, she winced. He wasn't the only one to blame. She'd held on too long. And as always, she said too much around him, revealed too much. He was the one person she'd allowed herself to lean on, to tell her truth to, show her mess to. And then he'd left. She'd sacrificed her self-control for him, and when he'd gone, she vowed that no one would hold that power over her again.

"I know." He ran a hand through his hair, his face a reflection of the anguish Sadie used to feel every single day. "I just thought, maybe, I could try to earn your forgiveness. You were my best friend, Sade. And I didn't . . . I shouldn't have left like that."

A hundred thoughts were at war in Sadie's head. The dark part of her longed to lash out and punish him. The rational side said they could be friends and leave it at that. And the emotional side that she constantly tried to keep hidden whispered that it was impossible. Control. She had to fight for control. Everything in her life belonged in neat little rows and columns. There were no surprises—only managed expectations. And here he was, obliterating them.

What she really wanted to do was to yell at him. To unleash the wild inside her that she usually channeled into dirt or dough. But she had to shut it down. She hadn't needed anyone for ten years. She wasn't going to start again now.

"What do you want, Jake? I can't just let you back in," she said finally, hating the note of brokenness that had weaseled its way in there without permission.

"I'm not asking you to. I just . . . needed to apologize."

The ground grew warm beneath her feet, the heat snaking up her legs until it wrapped around her chest and squeezed her heart. It was fall. The air should have been crisp. Instead, the stillness she'd come home to earlier had turned even warmer, and she swore she could smell honeysuckle. Like her garden was trying to make her remember the summer she'd fallen in love with him. As if her brain needed the encouragement. Jake's hand rested on the fence, his fingers curled over the top. He looked like a permanent fixture. Like he'd been wandering around in a fog and had finally found the lighthouse.

The thought of seeing Jake every day for the next decade made her blood jump. The ground was steaming now and rose in tendrils around her legs. He glanced down and jumped back.

"You should go," she told him, proud of herself for sounding firm, even though her hands were trembling by her side. "I need time to think."

"I understand," he said softly, staring sadly into her eyes.

She remembered every amber fleck hidden in there, but forced herself to ignore them.

"I want to be friends," he continued, although his voice came off pained. "Do you think we can, eventually?"

"I don't know," she whispered, refusing to look at him. "I hope so. Maybe."

She turned away before she could do something she'd regret, like forgiving him on the spot or screaming at him or giving in to the memories and the way her heart still ached for him. For the first year after he'd left, she wouldn't let herself think about a reunion. It was a Revelare fact that daydreaming about the desires of your heart was the surefire way to make certain they never came true. The second year was harder. She imagined the obscenities she'd yell at him. The third year she dreamed of the ways she'd make him pay if he came back asking forgiveness. On his knees. She'd played the scenario out in her head so many times in so many different ways, it felt like a soap opera on repeat.

Most times she imagined yelling at him until she was hoarse. Other times she thought about refusing to even acknowledge him. But her favorite scenarios, the ones she rarely let herself think about because kindness was her kryptonite, were when he showed up unannounced while she was gardening, with a bouquet of flowers in his hands and an apology on his lips. And yes, it was a spoon instead of flowers, but it seemed her daydreams had some power after all. Only in her head these imaginary encounters ended up with a lot less clothing involved.

After a few moments, she heard the crunch of gravel as he walked away. When she turned around again, he was at the sidewalk. By the time he was out of sight, some of the feeling had come back into her legs. She exhaled an unstable breath. Maybe

Raquel was right, and she was a glutton for punishment. But the little blue box felt heavy in her hand as she lifted the lid, and her fingertips grew warm as she ran them over the cool metal. Three inches in length, the handle had a background of white, red, and blue, with the outline of Texas and a horned bull laid over. She loved it. She didn't want to tuck it away. Gigi had always let her use her grandfather's spoons for fake potions and feeding her dolls because she said special things were meant to be used and treasured instead of simply stared at. She wanted to use this spoon to stir sugar into her coffee and reflect on the fact that Jake had been thinking about her while he was gone. She nestled the spoon carefully back in its home and slipped the box in her back pocket, where it felt like a sort of talisman.

She glanced in the direction of Rock Creek House just once before shaking herself. Memories wouldn't get her anywhere. She had work to do.

Her knees sunk into the earth as she pulled weeds, dirt embedding itself under her fingernails since she refused to wear gloves. She pulled a clump of Queen Anne's lace and shivered as she remembered the feel of Jake's arms around her after so long.

Damn it damn it damn it.

She knew she was screwed.

Her weeding paused when she reached the smattering of pastel gladioli that towered like a stack of bonbons dusted with sugar. Remembrance.

The stalks swayed toward her in an enticing dance. Setting down her garden shears, she plucked a bell-shaped bloom and squeezed a drop of juice from the petals, the taste sweet on her tongue.

She had to remember. The pain. She couldn't forget; there was far too much at risk. He wanted to be friends—and that's exactly the same trap she'd found herself in before.

But as the fog rose up around her vision, it wasn't Jake she saw, but a series of dark symbols at the bottom of a lukewarm, blue-patterned teacup.

As her eyes closed, a looming flutter of white appeared again from the forest.

Rum Soaked Peach Muffins with Streusel Topping

Careful with these. They incite euphoria and preserve only happy memories. Peaches are a symbol of youth and immortality. Walnuts symbolize the gathering of energy, especially in beginning new projects. Use this recipe sparingly or it'll prove the worse for you. You've been warned. People who don't listen to old folk's wisdom are too stupid to pour piss out of a boot before they put it on.

Ingredients

For the muffins

¼ cup all-purpose flour
1½ teaspoon baking powder
½ teaspoon salt
⅔ cup white sugar
¼ cup brown sugar
1 cup finely chopped peaches canned in syrup divided ¾ and ¼
½ cup milk
1 egg
¼ cup vegetable oil
1 tsp vanilla extract
2 tbsp dark rum

For the streusel topping

¼ cup all-purpose flour
3 tablespoons white sugar

½ teaspoon baking powder
½ teaspoon cinnamon
3 tablespoons cold unsalted butter

Directions

For the muffins

1. Preheat your oven to 350 degrees Fahrenheit and prepare a large muffin tin with 12 muffin cups.

2. Dump peaches into sauce pan and add brown sugar and rum, bring to a boil. Turn down to low until all liquid is reduced. Let cool.

3. Add the flour, baking powder, salt and sugar to a large bowl and whisk together to combine.

4. Add ¾ c of the peaches and stir well to coat.

5. Add the milk, egg, oil and vanilla extract, and stir together with a rubber spatula just until the flour disappears.

6. Portion the batter out into the muffin cups evenly (about ¾ full).

For the topping

1. Combine the flour, sugar and cinnamon and baking powder in a small bowl and stir.

2. Add the cold butter in chunks and break it up with your fingers in the flour mixture until it resembles coarse crumbs.

3. Top the muffins with the remaining peaches and with a spoonful of the streusel topping.

4. Bake at 350 degrees Fahrenheit for about 20 minutes until golden brown and a toothpick inserted into one of the muffins comes out clean.

♦ 3 ♦

SADIE WAS THIRTEEN YEARS old and wiping dirt-covered palms on her stained jeans. She had to do something to keep her mind busy while Seth was inside with Gigi. She had no idea what was coming, only that it was important. A ceremony of sorts—the day she'd find out her Revelare curse. Seth, having been born four minutes sooner—something he never let her forget—had gone first. Out in the garden, she straightened and looked at the back door so often she felt like a groundhog peeping its head out of the earth. Seth would tell her what to expect as soon as he came out. She knew he would. Still, she used her forearm to wipe sweat from her forehead despite the spring rainclouds hovering overhead.

Just as she kneeled down again, her knees caked in mud, the screen door banged open.

"Your turn," he called out, jumping the stairs in one go.

She scrutinized his face, looking for some hint.

"What was it? What happened? What's your curse?"

"I swore on the lemon tree." He shrugged, but there was a tightness to it.

"You *what*?" she demanded. "Why?" She tried to keep the hurt from her voice and failed.

"She made me. Go on—she's waiting for you."

"You're the worst," she spat out, shoving past him and up the stairs. Before she yanked the screen door open, she scrunched her eyes shut. Seth had never kept anything from her. But she wouldn't let it dampen this day. She'd been waiting for it since the first moment Aunt Tava had told her about it in hushed tones as she painted Sadie's fingernails in pink sparkles when she was seven years old.

Though her stomach was a raging sea of angry lightning bugs, she made sure her face was composed. This was what she'd been waiting for. She appeared to be calm, cool, and collected, even if inside she was anything but. It was an art she'd mastered at an early age. Too early. But if she'd learned not to care about the secrets and whispers and children calling her names like *witch* and *freak*, then maybe it wouldn't hurt so much. Fold the worries in half. Tuck them away.

The house was uncommonly warm. The kitchen table, set with Gigi's nicest linen and china set, made Sadie's heart thrill. The teapot had ceramic clusters of blueberries that were so cheery and full they looked half alive. There was a gentle, fragrant haze in the air from the clary sage and frankincense incense that added an air of magic and mystery to the whole ceremony. Both scents, Sadie knew, were supposed to invite clarity and focus.

"He can't keep it from me," Sadie said after she'd taken in the scene before her.

"He can and he will. Your turn now, sugar," she'd said. "Sit." She pushed a saucer and empty cup toward Sadie. "Eat," she added, holding out a plate of pomegranate tea cakes.

"What do I need to be brave for?" Sadie asked, her eyes narrowing and focusing on the fruit dotted throughout the cake.

"The future always needs bravery, toot. Eat."

The seeds burst in her mouth, the sweet, buttery taste coating her tongue as Gigi poured the vanilla jasmine tea with a hint of black pepper and cinnamon.

"It's hot," she warned.

Sadie blew on the top, watching the tiny ripples and inhaling the sweet warmth of the vanilla.

"Now, what do you want for your future?" Gigi asked conversationally.

"To do magic. To grow things. To help people," Sadie answered without thinking.

"And what does magic mean to you?" Gigi asked, and Sadie thought there was a hint of sadness to her voice.

"Everything. Or almost everything. Seth means as much."

"I know he does. Drink," she commanded.

Sadie felt the valor of the pomegranate sink into her. She let the clarity and focus seep into her from the incense. Her curse wouldn't be that bad. Whatever it was, it would be worth it so long as she could keep her magic.

She drained the last drop, set her teacup down, and rotating it, pushed it toward Gigi.

"You know the legacy. Every Revelare has magic, but they also have a curse. I told you your time would come, and it's arrived, sugar. Your choice, of course, is to forgo the curse by sacrificing your magic."

"What did Seth say when you asked him that?" Sadie challenged.

"Your brother and I had an entirely different conversation and ceremony, which you're not to know about. Focus on your own future," Gigi told her in a stern voice.

"Whatever his future is, mine is the same. We're twins. That's how it has to be. And I know Seth: he'd never give anything up until he understood it fully, and he doesn't; so I can't either, and I wouldn't even if he did!" she said.

"This will change everything," Gigi warned.

Sadie didn't answer, but nodded once and watched as Gigi finally looked down into her cup. She turned it this way, then tilted it that. She swirled the remaining tea leaves, her lips pursed thin as paper.

"There's a heart broken into four pieces and a chain. I see a clover, but it's so near the bottom that the luck may not arrive before you're old. And a snake. Bad omens, always."

"What does it all mean?" Sadie asked, her heart hammering.

"It's a curse of four heartbreaks, sugar." Gigi shook her head almost as if she were angry. "Each one will be worse than the last. They'll be so deep they'll rend your soul in two. And if you're not careful, when all four heartbreaks come to pass, the curse will consume you, and your magic will flee, leaving chaos behind, bitter as milk thistle. This curse will follow you like storm clouds, leaning toward you like wheat in the wind. Love only as you are willing to lose your magic."

From that day, the magic had wrapped itself around her heart and built a wall of thickest vines until not even a tendril of hope could get in.

Though she thought of her curse every day, she hadn't pictured the tea-reading ceremony in years. "Rule number seven," Sadie said, sighing, "'*If it's done, it can't be undone.*'" She'd forgotten what her grandmother had said about Seth's time with her and wondered, for the first time in three blood moons, just what Seth's magic was.

They used to be inseparable. They'd been every cliché, from finishing each other's sentences to knowing when the other was in pain. But Seth was never content; he was always digging and asking questions about their magic and their parents, which was a mystery thick as cold clover honey. The only thing Gigi would tell them was that their father had never been in the picture, and their mother was gone. Not dead nor that she'd left—just gone. Like a puff of dust in a summer breeze.

Sadie never understood her brother's need for answers or the way his cheeks would flush with embarrassment when neighborhood kids teased them about being the grandchildren of crazy Marie Revelare. Seth tried to hide from the strangeness, run away from it, deny it until he stopped asking questions altogether. Unlike Sadie's magic, which showed up externally in the garden she tended and the food she made, in the way she could stir her finger in a pot of cold water and it would boil seconds later, Seth's magic was internal. It was a hidden thing he never utilized as far as Sadie could tell. And no matter how many times she asked, demanded, pleaded, and pouted to know what it was, he would respond only with silence, headlocks, or vicious glares. But on full-moon nights when they were young, when the clouds whispered their secrets across the sky and the church bells chimed in the distance, Seth would sneak into Sadie's room with chocolate biscuits and a jug of milk. They'd settle a blanket across the hardwood floor, and with their knobby knees drawn up and moonlight splashing across their faces like a blessing, he would finally talk. He asked questions about her magic, their future, and—most of all—their mother. What did Sadie think she was like? Why did she leave? Where was she now?

In Sadie's mind, if her mother had wanted to leave, then good riddance. Magic was the truest thing she knew, and she was good at it. And if she focused on becoming the best, then she didn't have to think about the way Seth had left her exactly the way their mother had. Seth's disappearance had been heartbreak number two. The last year had been spent trying to find a neat little box to put the pain into. Something she could label and wrap with a bow. But the heartbreak was ugly and defied any sense. She hated that. Not having answers. Not having control. And even with the memory of those secret nights, she never found out what his magic was.

"I'm not like you. I don't think what I have, what I can do, is good," he'd confessed one night. They were older then, thirteen, and he'd brought Gigi's cooking sherry instead of cookies and milk.

Sadie's heart had hammered, wondering if this was finally the moment.

"I can't tell you because I don't know," he'd snapped. "Honestly, stop screaming your thoughts into my brain." He'd softened a moment later at the hurt look in Sadie's eyes. "One day, okay? I promise."

"You swear on the lemon tree?"

"I swear on the lemon tree."

But he'd still left.

"Every Revelare leaves at some point," Gigi had told her with a bright and distant sorrow.

The fingers that had been carefully combing through the zucchini were now clenched into fists. She forced her hands open, carefully harvesting dozens of squash and zucchini, separating them into bundles, avoiding their spiky vines and doing her best not to look toward Rock Creek House or think of Jake, and failing miserably at both.

There was a small pile of zucchini for Sunday night dinner and a larger one for the table at church. Folks always brought their surplus of fruits and vegetables for whoever wanted them. As a last-minute thought, she made another pile for Bill. She'd make some zucchini and coriander seed bread for him and his crew working on Old Bailer.

As she bent over to pluck an errant weed that had escaped her notice, the hairs on the back of her neck stood to attention, and a shiver worked its way along her shoulders. A moment later, she heard a scuffling sound beyond the lavender.

"Hey!" she shouted, picking up a zucchini and getting ready to launch it in the direction of whatever creature was trying to eat her garden. But then, squinting through the brush, she saw a small chocolate lab puppy staring back at her.

"Oh, puppy!" she called, instantly melting. "What are you doing? Come here, pup." She held out a hand, and the dog took a bounding leap over the bushy lavender, landing in a heap as his short legs went every which way.

"Hello, little Bambi," she said, scratching his velvety ears as he cascaded into her. "Who do you belong to, hm?" she asked, feeling around his collar for a tag. "Chief?" she asked, reading the engraving.

The dog quirked his ears and peered at her with what Sadie thought to be sad eyes.

"I agree. That's a silly name for a puppy. I think I'll call you Bambi." Turning the tag over, she didn't see a number. Why would someone put a collar on the dog without a number? Her chest tightened with indignation.

"Don't you worry. I'll take care of you, boy."

She'd check in with the shelter later; he did have a collar, after all. But something in her felt like Bambi was meant for her. A dog was loyal. A dog you could train with treats and table scraps and attention. Maybe if she could keep him, he wouldn't leave her.

She gathered up the baskets of vegetables and, smiling, called the dog after her. Finally, something today had gone right.

Bambi lay on the back porch off the kitchen while she whipped up three big loaves of zucchini bread. With every ounce of focus trained on the task, nothing went horribly wrong. Seth used to say that she bent over backward just to make everyone like her. She'd argue that she just liked doing nice things for people.

"There is no truly selfless act," he'd told her.

"It doesn't have to be. If it makes me feel good too, who does that hurt?"

"People should like you for *you.* Not what you do for them. You're always afraid people are going to leave, so you do anything you can to make them stay."

She hated the way he always saw into her. Revealed truths she didn't want to look at. She wanted to tell him that it wasn't true. But the lie refused to roll off her tongue.

"People can't be boiled down to black and white," she said instead. "We're made up of too many memories and prejudices."

"When you stop being so afraid of being alone, you'll realize your worth and stop letting people walk all over you."

Shaking off the echo of Seth's words, she filled her car with crates of lavender-infused honey for Wharton's Market, sachets of good luck buckbean tied with twine, a set of silver welcome bells for Poppy Meadow's Florist and Gift Shop, and a fresh assortment of ice cream for Lavender and Lace's. The bells were meant to be rung when visitors arrived, as a sign of welcome and gratitude for friendship. Sadie had dipped them in violet-infused water under a full moon, to ensure peace during the visit.

With everything loaded, she set off for Lavender and Lace's Ice Cream Parlor, always first on the route. The freezer bags only lasted so long.

"Let me help you with those," Lavender half shouted from her place at the counter when Sadie came in. Her long, shiny black hair rippled like a flag in the wind as she jumped down.

"No, let *me* help you!" Lace said even louder, scrambling to grab the bag from Sadie's shoulder first. "What is it this week?"

"Honey vanilla with toffee and then a pumpkin stracciatella," Sadie told them, glancing around the immaculate parlor. It was set up exactly like an old-fashioned soda fountain, with its long counter and vinyl stools and acres of chrome, but instead of black or red checkerboard, everything was in shades of softest lavender and cream. If you stuck out your tongue, the air tasted sweet, scented with the fresh waffle cones they made every day.

"Your flavors are always the first to go," Lavender said sweetly.

"Stop puffing her up, dummy. She knows hers are always the first to go." Lace rolled her eyes at her sister. Where her sister's hair nearly reached her waist, Lace's was cut in a sharp, angular bob that framed her face with frightening intensity.

"I was just being nice," Lavender said through pursed lips.

"Like you know how," Lace sneered.

"You heard the news I see?" the twins asked at the same time, turning to peer at Sadie.

"What do you mean?" Sadie asked cautiously.

"Your eyes are star crossed," Lavender said with a dreamy smile.

"And your aura is clouded," Lace added in that no-nonsense tone of hers.

"Jake McHotty Hot Pants, of course," Lavender said when Sadie just stared blankly at them.

Sadie let out a groan as the two started bickering about what was to become of her love life.

"I'll just—I'm going to go." She pointed her thumbs to the door and started to turn around when Lace stopped her with a hand on her shoulder.

"Have you seen anything lately?"

Sadie pursed her lips and tried to ignore the apprehension pooling in her stomach. Knowing Lace and the way she asked, the question immediately brought to mind the flash of white at the edge of the woods.

"Why?"

"There's something hanging about. I can't tell what it is yet but . . . do you want me to do a card reading for you?" Lace gestured to the back of the shop, where a velvet lavender curtain hid a small room that Sadie knew was the complete opposite of the soda shop vibe. The last time she'd been in there was right after Seth left, when she'd been seeking answers from any available source. The little room was dark, and beaded tapestries hung on the wall next to palmistry posters. There was a small wood table with black lace and white candles. It was where the sisters read cards and crystal balls, along with auras and palms and fortunes. Magic of a different sort than Sadie's, but powerful, nonetheless. Particularly when those practicing weren't charlatans.

"It's not a precise art," they'd warned her when she came knocking. "We don't always get to choose what we see."

And indeed, when they'd tried to see Seth, all they could tell her was that he didn't want to be found.

"Not today, thanks," she said to Lace. "I don't think the cards would have anything nice to say, and you know what they say about mean tarot cards."

"No." Lavender shook her head, looking interested.

"Uh, you know—that you shouldn't read them because then it just encourages them to keep telling people bad things," Sadie invented wildly.

"You're saying they need to be taught a lesson?" Lace asked with a wicked gleam in her eye. "They're like children?"

"More like men. Anyway, thanks but no thanks. Deliveries." She nodded to her car outside. "And whatever it is, I'm sure it'll be fine." That word again. She wished she could delete it from her vocabulary.

She glanced at her café across the street, longing to lock herself in the sanctity of the clean kitchen there and try to block out the rest of the world by kneading out her problems on some unassuming dough.

Everything is okay, she reminded herself. *This is a normal day. Just do what you always do.* She tamped down the rising anxiety, her chest tightening in spite of the hollow words.

Tearing her eyes from the café, she took the next crate into Wharton's. The old blue door creaked, and a bell dinged. She smelled salami from the deli counter on the right and jasmine from a candle display on the left. The store had always reminded her of a soup Gigi would make in the winter that she called "Everything but the kitchen sink." It had every odd and end you could imagine, and some you couldn't. There were baby clothes and stuffed animals along with metal art sculptures and motor oil. Lamps with hand-painted shades and lighters with marijuana plants engraved on them.

"I'm back here, Sadie!" a deep voice called from behind the small deli counter. Jimmy Wharton, the town bass in the church choir and "Christmas Shoes" soloist every winter was warm as apple cider unless he was on one of his drinking binges. His head was in the case as he organized salamis. "Money's on the counter here. And can you make any more of the blackberry wine? We sold out in days last time."

"Give me a couple weeks, and I'll have another case for you," Sadie told him, pocketing the money.

"How's that grandmother of yours?"

"Feisty as ever," Sadie said with a smile.

He cleared his throat and her heart sank.

"Not going to be breaking any hearts this week, I hope, hmm?" His bearded face smiled, but there was a hint of sharpness in his eyes. He'd never quite gotten over Sadie turning down his son, Ryan.

"No plans yet, but it's still early I suppose," she joked with a tight smile. She grabbed the money and left before he could see her eye roll. Meddling. Always meddling, her town. Jake had been back for less than twelve hours and was already wreaking havoc.

A few miles past Main Street, she passed the sign for the historic Old Bailer and pulled into the freshly paved parking lot. The three-story brick mansion sat right near the edge of the two-lane highway but was shrouded by towering silver birches planted closely together. The windows were boarded up, and the low wall of stone out front was crumbling sadly, though it did nothing to dim the grandeur of a bygone era. Whenever she passed, Sadie swore she could hear the subtle chatter of ladies wearing bell skirts and a distant, haunting waltz.

Old Bailer had been built by T. J. Bailer, a wealthy entrepreneur from out of town. He'd fallen in love with Evanora Revelare, from one of the seven founding families of Poppy Meadows, who was rumored to be a witch.

The legend, according to locals, was that with her charms, Evanora had bewitched T .J. to build the house on sacred land belonging to her family. And once the job was almost done, she turned him out and cursed him. In retribution, he set fire to the house that turned the grand staircase to ash and left a stench of misfortune for decades to come. And so it had sat unfinished for nearly two hundred years—until it was turned into a historic landmark and slated for refurbishment.

Sadie dropped off the zucchini bread with coriander seed, which would help Bill see the hidden worth in things, and jars of honey butter and boysenberry jam. She swore Old Bailer whispered to her as she drove away, but she couldn't make out the words.

And then, because her day hadn't been strange enough, she nearly had a heart attack as she approached her house not twenty minutes later. There, balanced on the top rung of a twelve-foot ladder, stood Gigi.

Sadie slammed her foot on the accelerator and screeched into the driveway. When she heard Sadie's door slam shut, Gigi looked down and wobbled, her gloved hands full of leaves and muck from the gutters.

"Gigi!" Sadie half shouted, heart pounding and heat climbing up her neck. "Get down from there. I can hire someone to do that!"

"Fiddlesticks," was all Gigi said. "I'm almost done."

Sadie, heart now firmly in her throat, held the ladder for the next ten minutes, knowing better than to try to convince Gigi to do anything. Already there were piles of trimmings and leaves scattered around the yard. Gigi was obsessive about lawn maintenance the way Sadie was about her garden.

When her grandmother was on solid ground again, Sadie hugged her hard. "Could you please *never* do that again?"

"No need to make my problem someone else's," Gigi said in a businesslike tone. "And the answer is *no*. I remember once, your grandad came home after I'd spent hours working on the yard. I'd even used a pair of kitchen shears to trim the grass in places. He took one look and suggested it needed a little more. So, I took gasoline and poured it all over the grass and lit it on fire. He never said another word about the yard again."

Sadie made a small noise, thinking of her grandmother setting fire to the grounds. Of course she would.

"Now let's go in. I've got chicken for Abby."

Homemade dog food, another of Gigi's specialties. Heaven forbid her Abby have anything as common as store-bought dog food.

"Okay, but just leave the piles. I'll put them in bags later. What's this?" she added when she spotted a can of paint and a drop cloth in the entryway.

"I'm going to touch up the baseboards. They're unfit to be seen." Seeing Sadie's look, she said, "The moment I'm useless is the day I'd rather die."

"Are we expecting company?" Sadie asked. It felt like Gigi was preparing for something.

"I've let this house fall into disrepair," Gigi said, pouring boiling water over instant coffee as she turned the burner off on the chicken.

Sadie glanced around the immaculate kitchen and spotless floors but didn't argue.

"Now, come out back and have a cigarette with me," Gigi said.

"Oh, um, I forgot to tell you," Sadie started to say, but it was too late. Gigi had opened the screen door, and Bambi started whining.

"What crock of crap do you think you're cooking up?" Gigi demanded, staring at the dog and then at Sadie.

"You're always taking in strays!" Sadie argued as she opened the gate and Bambi bounded out, gluing himself enthusiastically to her side.

Gigi laughed, lighting up one of her Virginia Slims 120's and sinking back into her rocker. Abby, claws scrabbling on the deck, jumped up onto her lap trying to get away from Bambi.

"Alright, you little pissant," Gigi said, her rumbling laugh softening the words. "Did I ever tell you about the chicken I adopted when I was a girl?"

Sadie shook her head, even though she'd heard the story a dozen times. She'd lie every time if it meant hearing Gigi's stories told in that gravelly, bullfrog voice of hers. She listened raptly as Gigi told her about the chicken that waited for her after school every day and how her father had threatened to kill it for dinner. Gigi, in turn, had threatened to cook her father for dinner.

"Café made it through unscathed?" Sadie asked absentmindedly in the quiet that followed.

"Gail's got it all under control. It's a good thing you left when you did. Now you mind telling me what in God's name happened?"

"'Seven bad omens in a row.'"

"Well, crap. Rule number six."

"I know."

"The nightmare?"

"If I had to guess, I'd say Jake McNealy."

"That little shit ass," Gigi shook her head, though a small smile played about her mouth. "What's he doing back in town?"

"I don't plan on finding out."

"You never could stay away from that boy." Gigi's deep laugh made the day that much brighter. "You and your mother. You know your momma was a rounder. Round heels. Round as a moon cake. She'd fall back for anything or anybody."

Sadie stilled. Gigi rarely, if ever, spoke about her mother. And she didn't relish the implication that she was like her in any way. Her mother had left. Sadie never would.

"One time I thought someone was stealing meat from our freezer in the garage," Gigi continued. "I went out there every day for a week, and the stock was dwindling. So finally, I stayed up one night with a shotgun to catch whoever it was. And it was your mother. There was a naval ship docked a few towns over, and she was taking all the meat to them as payment for passage onto the ship." Gigi shook her head.

"What do I do?" Sadie asked, thinking about the hundreds of times she'd asked Gigi that same question during their back-porch talks.

"One thing your heart's never been is fickle," her grandmother said with a pointed look, which was about as close to a warning as she was willing to give. "Rule number twelve."

"'*Curses are for keeps, so make sure they're worth it,*'" Sadie quoted. "And it has been. Worth it, I mean." She thought of the years she'd spent trying to find a loophole in her curse. "But sometimes I wish . . . I guess it doesn't matter. I've got two heartbreaks left, and I'm not wasting another one on Jacob McNealy."

"We'll see about that." Gigi's rumbling laugh ended in a cough. "Your problem is you try to keep everyone at arm's length. You're so afraid to lean on someone because it means there's trust there. And if you trust, it hurts worse when they leave."

"Seth used to say I'm too nice because I want people to like me," she argued.

"There's a difference between needing and wanting. You use that sharp tongue of yours as a shield, and you use those capable hands to soothe the wounds."

Sadie leaned back against the porch rail and stretched her legs out. Sitting out here with Gigi was always her favorite part of the day, but she didn't like the razor-edged words that were burrowing under her skin. They felt like a mirror she didn't want to look into.

"I don't need anybody anyway," she answered. "I have you and Raquel."

"And your brother."

"Really?" Sadie asked, looking around in mock earnestness. "Because I don't happen to see the shithead here."

"Just because he's not here doesn't mean he's gone," Gigi countered.

"Gone is gone," Sadie said quietly. She wanted to be so mad at him that she didn't care he'd left. She wanted to be rid of any last shred of hope. Because the hope was what hurt so much.

"Listen, sugar," Gigi said, clearing her throat. "There's something I want to talk to you about."

Sadie's eyes snapped open, and she leaned forward, not liking the tone in her grandmother's voice.

"I want to start by saying I've had awhile to come to terms with this, and I know in time you will too," she started, and

Sadie's whole body went numb. There was a pressure in her ears that made everything muted.

"It's stage four," Gigi continued, and Sadie's heart constricted. "I'm an old broad—I've lived a long time. I couldn't ask for anything more." Her tone was sure as summer rain as Sadie's world started falling apart.

She didn't move. Couldn't.

The dirty *C* word.

Cancer.

She stared at Gigi as a fire raged through her veins.

"Magic," she croaked out.

"Honey, magic can't cure cancer. If it could, I'd be a saint by now, and we both know I'm rotten to the core."

"You're not," Sadie said, shaking her head like a buttercup shuddering in a gale. Her eyes burned with their ache to cry. But if she started, she might not stop. And she refused to break down in front of Gigi. "Okay," she said, taking a deep breath through her nose. "It's going to be okay. We're going to get through this. Everything will be fine."

"No, toot, it won't be. Not for a while, at least. And there are things I need to tell you. Traditions you'll have to take over. Legacies you should know about. You and your brother," she started.

"No," Sadie shook her head frantically. "No, I'm not listening to this. How can you be so calm? Why have you already given up?" Her voice was frantic. This couldn't be real. She wouldn't let it be. She tried folding the thoughts in half, but they wouldn't budge. They were wedged in concrete. Gigi was her world. And her world was unraveling.

"Sugar," Gigi said, reaching out a hand to her granddaughter. "I know this is hard. I know it's turning your world upside down. I'm calm because I've been expecting something like this for a long time. I'm just surprised it didn't come sooner."

Sadie stared at Gigi's hand on hers, the age spots and wrinkles in stark contrast to her own smooth skin, and jumped to her feet.

"I took on this curse for my magic. The least it can do is be useful to fix this. I'll find a way. I will," Sadie said, her hands clenched into fists at her side.

And before Gigi could say anything else, Sadie left, the pit in her stomach growing heavier with every footstep.

She stomped through the garden and into the woods.

Gigi couldn't die. She wouldn't allow it. Seth had already left. And if Gigi—but no, she wouldn't.

Still, one thought kept reverberating around in her head. *One day, I'll be left completely and utterly alone.*

She had never hated her curse more than in that moment.

She wiped the traitorous tears from her eyes and hardened her heart against the pain. She couldn't dwell on that now. She couldn't risk heartbreak when she needed her magic now more than ever.

Vanilla Jasmine Tea with Black Pepper and Cinnamon

If you don't like spice, you won't like this. It's a spicy floral tea that will give you the clarity to see what's missing in your life while helping draw those things to you through good fortune. But remember, good fortune will only get you so far, and for the rest you'll have to rely on your own wit and wisdom.

Ingredients

jasmine tea
1 vanilla bean pod
1–2 drops cinnamon bark oil
1–2 drops black pepper oil

Directions

1. Scrape vanilla bean pod into pot of boiling water, strain, and use to brew tea.

2. Drop in cinnamon bark oil and black pepper oil. Enjoy.

(To increase clarity and focus, diffuse 4 drops clary sage and 4 drops frankincense while drinking tea.)

♦ 4 ♦

SADIE SLEPT FITFULLY THAT night. She awoke with a crick in her neck and a sour taste in her mouth, finally trudging out of bed at dawn with the phantom smell of ash trailing her like a bad decision.

In the sleepy little kitchen, she put the kettle on to boil and thoughtfully eyed her jumbled collection of tin canisters filled with various blends of teas and herbs. In a mesh bag, she mixed one teaspoon of mango black tea for focus and energy, a sprinkle of dried lavender for calm, and a few buds of clove for both dignity and the ability to withstand troubles. Tying the bag with string, she dropped it into a cup of water that measured exactly two hundred and twelve degrees. As it steeped, she added a dash of cinnamon for stability and a drizzle of honey for sweetness.

The old hardwood floors creaked as the sound of pattering paws reached her. Bambi, tail wagging, sat at her feet.

"Today will be better," she told him, scratching behind his ears. "Today will be a good day. We've got work to do. Nothing is happening to Gigi on my watch."

She sipped her tea, the bright floral earthiness dancing on her tongue, and tried not to think of Seth. Or to wish that he was here.

Their last argument had been brutal. "You use people," he'd seethed. "You're so afraid of your curse that you let people love you until you get too close, then you push them away. For your *magic*. You're a manipulator. Only using people for what they can do for you."

"I've never treated you like that," Sadie had argued.

"You didn't have to! Jesus, Sade. You couldn't not love me. I'm your twin! And I see who you could be if you weren't so goddamn afraid of who you'd be without what you can *do*. There'll come a time when people figure you out, and they'll get sick and tired of the way you take and take without ever loving in return."

"I don't just take! I give! That's why my magic is so important; I help people," she insisted.

"Helping people isn't the same as loving them, Sadie."

She shook off the memory as she drank the cold dregs of her tea and started making a list of healing herbs. She loved Gigi. And magic would save her. That, as far as she was concerned, was that.

She ran through possibilities. Adder's tongue and amaranth, of course, not to mention goat's rue and heliotrope. She would start off with something small. Maybe trying to heal a dead plant. Or if she could find an injured animal in the forest, even better. This would work. It had to.

She snapped her notebook closed, and with determination in every step, prepared for the most important task of her life.

She got to the café far earlier than she needed to gather the rarer herbs she kept in the kitchen. After work she'd round up the other herbs from her garden and prep them for the spell.

She drank in the quiet comfort of her shop. The long front counter, made from reclaimed wood, was spotless. She watered the plants and herbs in their clay pots, where they rested on hand-milled wood shelves. Next to them, old black and white framed photos of Poppy Meadows in the 1940s hung on the wall. All throughout the space, Edison bulbs dripped from the ceiling at different heights. Hand-strung crystals rained down from horizontally suspended manzanita branches, reflecting rainbows of early morning light across all of the surfaces. It smelled like the holidays from the cleaner she made herself. Clove and lemon and citrus, with a hint of eucalyptus. It was like walking into a Christmas morning memory. And it was quiet. The peaceful kind of quiet that was laced with hope and expectation.

The large glass front cases were stocked with the day's offerings, their handwritten cards placed tidily beside each dish. There were apricot and basil shortbread tarts for protection, and peach thyme crumbles in individual cups, if you weren't feeling like yourself. There was lemon and lavender pound cake that had been baked in mini Bundt tins, if sleep was eluding you. Sadie served it with decaf Duchess Grey tea with extra milk and a generous dollop of clover honey. Now she sat at the high counter along the far wall, where all the stools were mismatched but perfect neighbors.

She took a deep breath. Everything was ready. Everything felt right.

"Today is going to be a good day," she said again, speaking into the cheery silence of the shop.

Sadie's optimism lasted until exactly 10:02 AM.

She'd tried to get Gigi to go home. To relax. Conserve her energy. But her grandmother had laughed outright before making Sadie swear an oath of silence about her cancer. She made her swear on the lemon tree, an oath that couldn't be broken without severe consequences. Watching her grandmother bustle about the shop, it was hard to believe the news she'd shared last night. And that, somehow, made it easier to believe she could find a cure. To be okay with going about their day as if Sadie's routine, her heart, her thoughts, weren't coming apart at the seams.

It was Saturday, their busiest day, and Gail and Gigi were taking care of customers up front while Sadie was cooking up half a dozen chilled lemon cream and lavender pies.

Three were for the store and three to bring to church the next day. She'd stored a bowl of melted butter on the high shelf, so it wouldn't be knocked over. But as she reached up to grab it, her fingers slipped, and the butter sloshed out.

The slick mess coated the right side of her hair, face, and shoulder like a greasy rain. Her eye was clamped shut to keep the butter out, and she felt blindly around for a dishtowel. Cursing and coming up empty-handed, she banged through the door, to grab some napkins from behind the counter, only to see through her one good eye a group of men coming in.

No, no, no, this was not happening. Three were firemen that Sadie knew. And the fourth . . .

She couldn't move. The butter had somehow leaked into her brain and scrambled it.

Her eyes darted back to the kitchen, and when they swiveled forward again, she was staring straight into the startlingly dark eyes of none other than Jake McNealy.

Here she was, squinting like a buttered-up pirate, and there was the bane of her existence, doing everything in his power not to laugh and utterly failing.

Excellent. This was so, so excellent.

"Sadie makes the best desserts in town," one of the men said, clapping a hand on Jake's shoulder.

Before yesterday she never in a million years would have imagined him in her store. And seeing him there, a smile taking up half his face—well, she wasn't sure if she wanted to laugh or cry.

Last night she'd thought it would be easy to shove him out of her mind. To forget about him yet again. And now the universe was mocking her, delivering him on a silver platter while she was drowned in butter.

"Sadie," he said in greeting, trying to stifle his laughter, "you . . . um, you have a little something," he gestured to his own face where the butter was mirrored on hers.

"I . . . it was—I couldn't . . . I mean, the butter," she stuttered.

"Ah," Jake tried and failed again to contain a laugh. "I see that hasn't changed then. Your eloquence is as astounding as ever."

Sadie let out a strangled groan and rolled her eyes, grabbed a fistful of napkins, and started wiping.

"What are you doing here?" she demanded. "I thought I told you I needed time."

"Oh, I'm not here for you. I've got a bit of a sweet tooth, and Vinny told me I haven't lived until I've had the cinnamon apple tarts here."

"I did. I said that. Told him, I know just the place. Sorry Sadie . . . I didn't really think . . ."

"Yes, well. I'll, um—hang on just a second. I'll be right back." She darted back into the kitchen and grabbed onto the counter to steady herself.

"Gigi Marie," she heard his booming voice call out. "How is it possible you seem to be getting younger?"

Sadie peeked through the slit in the doors and saw Gigi hugging Jake, her hand patting his side. Her head barely reached his navel.

"You little shit ass." She laughed. "I can't believe you have the nerve to show your face around here," she teased. Gigi liked to pretend that she held a grudge against Jake for leaving town all those years ago, which she probably did. But she also happened to be susceptible to his charms whenever he decided to turn them on.

Sadie finished wiping the butter off while her heart was trying to do a triple-time waltz right out of her chest.

You are a twenty-eight-year-old adult woman, damn it. Pull yourself together, she reprimanded herself silently.

Yanking her hair back into a ponytail, she groaned in frustration when the elastic snapped. Her hair, normally wavy, had tightened into thick, spiraled curls. The strawberries she'd been simmering on the stove suddenly bubbled over, filling the air with a thick, pungent sweetness. When she reached to turn off the burner, static electricity zapped her fingertips.

Gigi strode through the door and took in the mess on the stove, Sadie's hair, and her heaving chest.

"I'm fine. Just gathering my wits," Sadie assured her.

"Rule number nine, sugar."

"'*High emotion equals unpredictable magic,*'" Sadie recited. "I know."

"You remember what happened when that boy left?"

Sadie nodded. She'd nearly burned Gigi's kitchen down.

"'*Guard your heart, for from it flows the wellspring of life,*'" she quoted. "But don't guard it so closely that you'll never get hurt. Because if you can't get hurt then you can't love, and if you're gonna live like that, I wouldn't have read your damned tea leaves. Now, go on," she commanded, pushing Sadie through the doors.

Sadie wanted to say something about the curse, about how she refused to love, about how absurd that advice was when she'd only seen Jake for less than five minutes in two days. But Gigi had an iron fist when she wanted to, and Sadie's shuffling feet carried her forward with trepidation.

"Vinny was right," Jake said around a mouthful of tart. "This is the best thing I've ever eaten in my life."

"You're just trying to get back on my good side."

His eyes pierced into hers. "Of course, I am. Have *you* ever been on your bad side? That place is hell."

"Maybe you shouldn't have waltzed in here today, then," she said without meaning to. Vinny's eyes were darting back and forth between them like he was following a table tennis match.

"I deserve that," he agreed, swallowing. "You know, when I left, you'd only just started baking. And now look at you. Owner of your own café."

"Co-owner," she corrected. "Gigi is really the brains of the operation."

"Hush," Gigi chided. "Sadie is the miracle worker. It all started with peaches, remember, toot?"

"Really?" Jake asked, his eyes catching Sadie's.

"It's, well, that's what sparked the obsession with baking, yes. I started out with traditional peach pie. Then it was peach and thyme cobbler or peach hand pies with reduced bourbon and blueberry drizzle," she rambled, not meeting Jake's eye.

"Sadie makes the best peach pie in the county!" Gail piped up from the register, her chin tilted up and a proud smile gracing her face. "She's won the county fair pie contest five years in a row."

Gail, a compact firecracker in her late forties, put the Energizer Bunny to shame. She was endlessly telling everyone about Sadie's accomplishments, like she was her own daughter. Her short black hair was streaked with gray and teased into an Afro that never seemed to stop moving.

"What was it that won this year?" she asked. "Oh!" she snapped her fingers, "Peach turnovers with sweet lemon cream drizzle and mint julep ice cream. Mmm, I can still taste it. Dee-vine."

"The mint julep ice cream is Gigi's recipe, though," Sadie said.

"Used to make it for you and that brother of yours on hot summer nights when neither of you could sleep, little pissants. But you made it better than I ever did. And it went just right with the peaches."

"I've always had a soft spot for peach pie," Jake said, his eyes swiveling to Sadie again.

"Hmm," Sadie intoned. "I don't remember that." As if. Her eyes glanced to the wooden sign hanging from the walkway out front: "A Peach in Thyme." It had sounded innocuous enough when she came up with it. *Peaches for Jake. Thyme for courage. Leaving one and embarking on the other.* She had spent hours hand-drawing the logo: a full, ripe peach in the background, with another peach in front, cut in half so the pit was showing. "A Peach In Thyme" curved over the peaches while "Café and Bakery" curved underneath. And on either side were sprigs of thyme that were so lifelike you could almost smell the fragrant herb. Now that logo seemed like a beacon that had led him directly back into her life.

"Well, lucky for you, honey, Sadie's always got some peach concoction here," Gail told Jake. "Don't matter what else she's makin' because she always makes whatever suits her fancy, but you can bet your boots that's the truth. I don't know how she gets 'em to produce year-round, but we all know Gigi Marie Revelare's garden has got some kind of magic in it."

"I hadn't heard that," Jake answered, finally tearing his gaze from Sadie and smiling at Gail.

"Everyone in town's heard that, man," Vinny piped up. "That place is legendary."

"Anyway, you'll have to get in line if you want to court our Sadie for her peach confections," Gail said, giving Jake a sharp look.

"Not necessary," Sadie said quickly, seeing Jake wince. Yeah well, he *should* be uncomfortable.

"Enough of that, you superstitious buffoons," Gigi said with pursed lips and a terse shake of her head. "Now, Jake, family dinner is tomorrow night and you're coming. No arguments. Be there at six."

"What?" Sadie spluttered. "Gigi, I'm sure he already has plans. Or—"

"I don't, actually." Jake grinned. "But thanks for trying to get rid of me, Sade."

Sadie winced again at the nickname. There were only two people who called her that. Both had broken her heart.

"As a matter of fact, I can walk right over. I've got a viewing of Rock Creek House later in the afternoon," he added with a wry smile.

Sadie froze, her eyes trained on Jake. Was he doing this on purpose? She wracked her brain for something clever and nonchalant to say, but her thoughts were focused in on a tiny couch in an old attic and Jake's fingers tracing lines on her palm.

"Why there?" she asked finally.

"Just looking for some peace and quiet," he said, not quite meeting her eye. "I'll tell you all about it at church tomorrow," he continued. "For now, I've got to head to the station to finish up some paperwork, so I'll take whatever peach desserts you have on hand."

"On the house," Gigi said, who'd already been wrapping up several to-go boxes filled with one of everything.

As Sadie watched, she couldn't help but feel a tad bit betrayed.

"You sure know how to win a man over, Gigi Marie," Jake declared. "Nice to see you, Sadie." He winked before finally, *finally* heading for the door.

"He's looking at Rock Creek!" Sadie hissed into her phone. "He'd be less than a mile from me! What's he playing at?" She was standing on the tiny back patio behind the café, where she usually escaped for her breaks to have a little peace and quiet. Now there was none of that. But the vent from the kitchen, pumping out warm air and the smell of cinnamon dolce challah bread, grounded her, and she took a deep breath.

Raquel breathed out a string of Spanish. Sadie, whose Spanish was almost nonexistent, still caught the words *idiota* and *imbécil* and couldn't help but agree.

"Maybe he just likes the house," Raquel said, though it ended up sounding like a question. "Listen, I'll see what I can find out from Gina. I think she's the one who listed it. Just, you know, chill. Take a breath. Don't burn anything down."

"If I ignore him, I'm being childish. But if I let him get too close, I'm screwed. And I need my magic now more than ever."

"Why?" Raquel asked suspiciously.

"Because the holidays are right around the corner," Sadie invented wildly, "and I need to be on top of my game if I want to make enough to reroof the house."

"Dream big," Raquel said, and Sadie could practically hear her eyes roll. "Listen, Jake McNealy has always been in your life, even when he wasn't. Just try not to freak out, okay?"

"Right. I'm about to make garlic and fennel knots," Sadie added, as if that explained everything.

"Because Jake's turned into a vampire?" Raquel asked in confusion.

"Garlic wards off the bad—the *negative*—and fennel gives you strength. I'll be fine. Everything will be fine. If Jake is going to waltz back into town, then I plan on showing him just how great I'm doing."

"Whatever you say, *cariño*," Raquel said, sighing.

"How's *Carrie* coming?"

"I conned Jenny into sitting through the auditions with me, so you're relieved of that duty. As the English teacher, she's basically required by human decency to help. She asked if she could bring vodka in her thermos since it wasn't technically school hours."

"She didn't!" Sadie laughed, grateful for the distraction. Sadie had met Jenny a handful of times. Jenny was an outsider, having moved to town only a few years ago, and constantly flouted the small-town ways, which made Raquel practically gleeful.

"She did. *'Don't ask, don't tell,'* I told her. Listen, do you want to meet at the Milestone after you're done with work? Maybe you could help me figure out the lighting thing."

"I, um, I can't." She ached to spill the beans about Gigi, but Sadie never broke her promises. "Gardening," she added evasively.

Sadie spent the next several hours making the garlic and fennel knots and then covering tiny dried-lavender buds in white chocolate, losing herself in the repetition and routine. With her mind occupied on menial tasks, she didn't have to think about anything—or anyone—else.

Pulling the cold lemon and lavender pies from the fridge, she scattered the tops with white chocolate–covered lavender until it looked like they were blanketed with a thin layer of sweet snow. By the time that was done, she still wasn't ready to let her brain think. And so, with well-practiced hands, she drew down the ingredients for croissants.

For ten minutes she kneaded with vigor until the dough was smooth and elastic. After forming it into a ball, she put it in a proofing bag. The process for croissants was long, from hammering out the cold butter and carefully folding it into the dough to turning it every hour, for the next three hours, before leaving it in the fridge overnight. It was just the kind of work she needed to keep her hands occupied. When Gigi came back in the kitchen, Sadie opened her mouth to speak, but Gigi cut her off.

"No, ma'am," she said in a tone that brooked no argument. "We're not discussing this here. And whatever hare-brained scheme you've got going in that head of yours, you should just let it go."

"If you said we're not going to talk about it, then you can't tell me what to do," Sadie countered.

"Shit ass," Gigi mumbled.

The rest of the day passed uneventfully, and by the time her work day was over, the notebook in her pocket was filled with pages of ideas to heal Gigi. Some of them were "a crock of crap" as Gigi would say, but others, Sadie thought, had promise. It had taken her three summers to perfect her blackberry and basil tart recipe. Dozens of attempts where *something* was off. And she hadn't quit until she knew it would win the tri-county dessert contest. It had. Quitting wasn't in her vocabulary. And this particular recipe, whatever it wound up being, would save Gigi's life. When life hangs in the balance, it tends to narrow your scope of focus, bring priorities into sharp relief, with pointy edges that leave nicks in your heart. And Sadie's whole world was narrowing down to the piece of paper in her pocket.

When Gail's daughter, Ayana, came to relieve Sadie of her shift, she followed Gigi home, her old Subaru whining to keep up with her grandmother's PT Cruiser. The woman drove like a bat out of hell.

Sadie changed into loose linen pants and a soft cream sweater, sweeping her hair into a messy bun. The coils had finally loosened to soft waves. By the time she got back downstairs, Gigi was already watching TV, with Bambi at her feet and Abby on her lap. Sadie poured a glass of red currant wine and took it outside, sipping the symbolism of a fresh start, listening to the chatter of the television mixing with birdsong. A breeze blew from the west, and Sadie followed it with her eyes, to the tree line, the forest, and the direction of Rock Creek house.

Kicking her shoes off with a sigh, she dug her toes in the pea gravel, just as she did every evening, and closed her eyes. The dwarf orange tree was just blossoming, and its sweet citrus scent felt more like summer than the cold weather she knew was coming. The garden rustled thickly despite the gentleness of the breeze, as though it were calling to her.

"Shh," she hissed at them, and the plants gently settled.

She played the day over in her head and slowed when she reached the part where Jake entered it. She unwrapped the memory bit by bit, savoring it like a lemon drop.

Her stomach dipped deliciously as her mind brought up every detail that she'd tried so hard to forget. His hair, still the same summer honey-wheat blonde, still completely free of gray. Fine lines crinkled around his eyes when he smiled, and told stories of his easy laughter. And his shoulders . . . obviously, he hadn't given up on the gym, which made sense since he was finally living his dream of being a firefighter. She could practically feel the smooth expanse of his stomach as she trailed her fingers across it.

But those were memories. She'd make sure they stayed that way.

It used to be a dance with Jake. Around desire and convention. The curse made her fear, but in the end, love cast it out, and she knew beyond the shadow of a doubt that she would sacrifice her magic for him if it came to that.

That's what scared her the most.

On a smoky summer night when she was eighteen, she'd made chrysanthemum biscuits and slathered them with wildflower honey. As he ate, the scales fell from his eyes, and the truth was unveiled. With his heart laid bare, he told her he loved her, and with sticky fingers and a voice made pure with honesty, he made a vow by the lemon tree that they would be together forever. That he would never leave her.

But in the morning, when the magic had worn off, he left. Breaking every promise in his wake.

For years Sadie had blamed herself for tricking him into the truth. But despite the guilt, her anger grew like chickweed. He was a coward. Knowing the truth and not accepting it. Denying it and lying to himself, but worst of all, denying Sadie the love she had been willing to sacrifice her magic for. Sadie held onto the past like a drunkard clutching his whisky. Vices like that were a comfort blanket when you feared the future. If she could hang onto her bitterness toward the past, in a way it protected her heart for the future. At least, that's what she told herself.

The garden started to rustle again, swaying restlessly, trying to get her attention.

"I'm coming, I'm coming," she muttered, finishing her wine and grabbing the clippers. But as she made her way past the climbing sweet peas and saw the patch of garden dedicated to herbs, her stomach churned.

"No," she whispered. Her fingers trembled and her throat clogged as she fell to her knees. More than half of the small space had been burned. She could coax it back to life, but the fear of who would do this—and, more importantly, *why*—had her shaking.

Did anyone truly hate the Revelares enough to risk breaking and entering? To destroy something so beautiful? Her chest ached from the sight of so much destruction. The heartbreak of wasted beauty.

She turned around to tell Gigi and stopped. She couldn't worry her grandmother with this. She'd have to figure it out by herself.

Her throat tight, she mechanically dragged a rake over the burned patch as she talked herself down. But it was getting hard to breathe. Swallowing was becoming more difficult as the urge to cry almost overpowered her.

She threw the rake down and, instead, cut the healing herbs that hadn't been burnt. Bay leaves and fennel. She even dug up a garlic bulb and picked some blackberry thorns from the bush at the edge of the garden that always threatened to overtake everything.

She crushed the thorns with an amber stone and then laid them, along with a stick of selenite and the herbs, in a copper bowl and filled it with water. They would need to charge under the moon for six days before she could use them.

The garden started to rustle again, swaying restlessly, trying to get her attention.

"What?" she demanded, picking up a pebble and throwing it toward the tomato vines. The tomatoes trembled violently and then stopped abruptly just as Sadie heard a man's voice yelling in the distance. She stilled, strained her ears, and leaned forward, trying to make out what it was saying.

"Chief!" the man yelled. "Come here, boy! Come home!"

And through the screen door, Sadie heard Bambi's mild whine in answer.

She knew that voice. Damn it. *Of course*, Bambi would be Jake's dog.

A movement near the tree line caught her eye.

There was nothing there, but a sense of something, a presence, unsettled her. The air seemed to ripple, and the smell of burned herbs grew so pungent her eyes watered. The tomato vines trembled violently beside her.

The back of her neck tingled.

That slow-moving shiver down her spine that made her think of spidery fingers inching over her shoulder or the weathered shadow of a face you always fear seeing in the corner of the mirror.

And that's when she heard it.

A low, haunting sound that slithered under her skin and wrapped around her bones. There were no words, just an eerie, sinister snarl. No words. But Sadie knew a threat when she heard one.

She wanted to run into the house, scattering salt behind her.

Instead, she forced herself to walk at a leisurely pace, her heart pounding with certain dread the whole time.

Mint Julep Ice Cream

Use this to clear out the past and start over by painting all past painful memories in a happier light. Don't eat too much, or you'll be forgetting other things too, until you're a doddery old fool like me, who can't remember what day of the week it is. Getting old really is a son of a bitch.

Ingredients

1 c. sugar
½ c. water
½ c. bourbon
1 tsp. vanilla
2 c. milk
2 c. heavy cream
6 large egg yolks
8–10 large sprigs fresh mint (plus extra for garnish)

Directions

1. Bruise the leaves of the mint leaves to release oils and flavors. Combine the sugar, water, and the 8 mint sprigs in a small saucepan over medium heat, and bring to a boil, stirring to dissolve the sugar. Cook for 2 minutes. Remove from the heat, and let cool completely. Strain through a fine-mesh strainer, then add the bourbon.

2. Combine the milk and cream in a large nonreactive saucepan, and bring to a gentle boil. In a small mixing bowl,

whisk the egg yolks together. Whisk 1 cup of the hot cream mixture into the egg mixture. In a slow, steady stream, add the egg mixture to the hot cream mixture. Continue to cook for 4 minutes, stirring occasionally, until the mixture thickens enough to coat the back of a spoon. Remove from heat and let cool completely.

3. Whisk the bourbon mixture into the cream mixture. Cover with plastic wrap, pressing the wrap down against the surface of the mixture to keep a skin from forming, and chill in the refrigerator for at least 2 hours.

4. Remove from the refrigerator, and pour the mixture into an ice-cream machine. Churn according to the manufacturer's directions. For an extra kick, add a spoonful of bourbon over ice cream before serving.

♦ 5 ♦

"QUIT YOUR FIDGETING," GIGI scowled, swatting at Sadie as they drove to church. Gigi was always crotchety on the way to church because, in her words, "If you're gonna drag my ass to God's house, He better know I'm not coming willingly."

Her grandmother's Baptist roots wouldn't let her go too long without attending, despite her feelings on the matter. And today, Sadie needed backup. Everything was going, as Gigi always put it, to hell in a handbasket. The burned garden. That sound from the forest. Gigi. Bambi belonging to Jake. There were too many thoughts to fold in half. She'd need an origami master to make any kind of sense in her brain.

The second she pulled into the Poppy Meadows Community Church parking lot at the end of Main Street, thirty minutes early, she let out a shaky breath. The church wasn't fancy, but it held fond memories of vacation bible school and potlucks, fundraisers and talent shows. The main building was bigger than normal for a church built back in the 1800s, and had been expanded on with a cluster of buildings recessed from the street and connected by charming walkways lined with cheery flowers. There was a large kitchen, Sunday school rooms, and meeting rooms, with a swath of meticulously manicured grass in the middle. Wrought iron bistro tables and hanging bougainvillea made it feel more like a

European bed-and-breakfast than a place of worship. But perhaps the beauty was its own kind of worship.

She had barely opened her car door when she saw Miss Janet speed-walking over. Her floral dress stretched across her chest and swayed like a dance as she huffed to a stop.

"Sadie Revelare, you got those pies?" Miss Janet was in charge of the kitchen, which meant she handled the roster for who brought what refreshments for the coffee stand.

"Right here," Sadie answered, reaching into the backseat and grabbing the three boxes.

"Good, good. Walk with me," Janet demanded, and started off at a steady clip. "Now, you cut those pies and put them on individual plates. We don't want everybody making a mess and getting their dirty fingers all over the place. And don't make the slices too big, mind you," she said, her mouth running faster than a motorboat. "And have you thought about your booth for the Fall Festival? You know I need the forms by the end of the week. Oh, and this is Jake—he'll be helping you in the kitchen this morning," Miss Janet finished as they entered the long galley. "I'm off to set up the coffee urns. Be quick about your work, child—we don't have much time."

Sadie blanched as she saw Jake standing in the kitchen with an apron tied around his waist. His dark jeans were ten times nicer than anything he used to wear, and his freshly pressed button-down shirt was the perfect shade of blue to set off his eyes. The slim fit of both made Sadie think of things she was pretty sure you weren't supposed to think about in church.

Damn him. How was he *everywhere*?

She cast her eyes for something to land on. Anything other than staring at his hands on the counter. The hands that had once trailed up her inner thigh, the callouses snagging at her soft skin. The fingers that . . . *No. Find something else to focus on, you dirty trollop,* she scolded herself, feeling the heat that rushed her cheeks. Her eyes traveled the kitchen, which was dated but sparkling clean, with the strong chemical smell of Lysol. As the door swung shut, it blocked out the sound of the worship pastor's acoustic guitar. The only noise was the hum from the giant, ancient refrigerator.

"That woman should consider coming up for a breath of air once in a while. Do you know she actually inspected my hands after I washed them?" he said with mock incredulousness.

"What are you doing here?" Sadie asked, regretting how stupid the words sounded as soon as they fell from her lips. It seemed to be the only thing she could find to say to him these days.

"'Do you mean in a metaphorical sense?"

"I mean in the 'what are you doing here in this kitchen, serving at church, you pain in the ass' sense."

"Watch it, dirty mouth! God might smite you down."

"If anyone's going to be doing any smiting, it'll be me," Sadie mumbled. She avoided his gaze and instead made quick work of opening the boxes and getting out the pies.

"I volunteered," Jake said, setting out paper plates. "I came by last week and talked to Pastor Jay. It was nice. We spent an hour catching up. I told him about my mom buying a vacation house in Florida and what Jessie was up to. It's nice being in a small town again. Where people care."

"How is Jessie?" Sadie asked with warmth in her voice this time. Jessie, just as much of a spitfire as her brother, and probably even more reckless, had always made Sadie laugh.

"She's a real estate agent in New York," he said with pride.

"Damn," Sadie breathed. "New York? I can't imagine. I've never even left Poppy Meadows."

"Wait, seriously?" Jake asked with a furrowed brow. "Never?" His body had stilled, his big hands laid flat on the metal counter, his whole countenance focused on Sadie. She swallowed hard.

"I mean, I've been a couple counties over." She shrugged, trying to make it look casual. "But I love it here. I've never felt the need to leave." She gave him a pointed look.

"Poppy Meadows is great, but there's a whole world out there, Sade," he said, shaking his head.

"Yeah, you would say that," she snorted.

"We're not all like the great Sadie Revelare. Some of us have to figure out what we want," he said.

She thought about telling him that knowing what you want is its own kind of curse. Because when else are you so aware that you're never going to get it? Not knowing meant possibility and dreaming and hopes. Instead, she looked away from those piercing eyes.

"Dish," she ordered, sliding the cut pie toward him. "And don't mangle it, or I'll be forced to harm you."

"Word around town is that your food has magic in it. What's the secret? Drugs?"

"It's a superpower. I'd tell you, but it comes from within and is derived from great wisdom and maturity. Obviously, you're not there yet."

"Obviously. Still a bit rough around the edges. Must be why we get along so well," he said, leaning against the counter and staring at her with eyes that held an invitation, a dare. It was always the verbal sparring with him.

She could smell a heady mixture of shaving cream and cologne, and was torn between running out of the kitchen and getting as close to that scent as possible. It was woodsy and sweet and . . .

Maybe she could give in. Just once. That's it. And then she could go back to hating him. Not love. But a meeting of needs. That would be safe enough.

Without thinking, her body took a step toward him, as though it couldn't stand not to. The space around them shrunk, pressing in on all sides. His breathing turned heavy, and when she looked up to his face, his eyes had darkened to a stormy sea.

He stood perfectly still.

Warmth spread from her cheeks down to her neck, and she caught herself leaning closer without meaning to—when suddenly all of the burners on the stove behind them ignited at once.

Jake jumped back and yelped in surprise.

"What in the world?" he cried, automatically pushing Sadie behind him and shielding her with his outstretched arms. "This place must not be up to code. That's a fire hazard!"

Sadie laughed shakily and stepped around him. Her hands trembled as she turned the knobs, and the flames went out.

"I'll just start taking these out," he said, his brows furrowed and eyes darting around as though other fires might spring up at any moment. Sadie had always thought Jake might have an inkling of her abilities, but either he hadn't seen them in action long enough, or maybe she credited him with more awareness than he deserved.

She took a deep, steadying breath after he left. Her body's memory wanted to lean into him a lot further than she had. Her lips wanted to trace his jawline with lingering kisses as they had when she was a teenager. But Jake broke promises like cinnamon sticks. It was, she realized, perhaps too dangerous of a gamble. Even if her curse wasn't in play. Even if Gigi wasn't sick. It would be too much of a risk.

She made a beeline for Raquel, who was speaking with Alice Grossman, an elderly woman who pretended she was practically deaf but actually had the hearing of a bat.

"You have to sit with me," Sadie hissed, grabbing Raquel's arm.

"Excuse me, Mrs. Grossman," Raquel said at a deafening volume, and then steered Sadie away. "My very rude friend is in need of assistance."

"God bless you," Mrs. Grossman shouted, nodding like a bobblehead on a bumpy road.

"Sit with me," Sadie said again, her eyes scanning the sanctuary.

"I'm working in the nursery today," Raquel said, frowning. "What's your problem? Why are you being so weird?"

Just then Raquel's eyes swiveled to the entryway of the foyer, where Jake was entering.

"Ugh, *there's* the problem. Yours, not mine." She threw several yards of shade in Jake's direction.

"I need a buffer!" Sadie hissed as Jake walked over.

"Jake," Raquel addressed him, nodding with a tight-lipped smile.

"Good to see you too, Raquel," Jake said in a tone that meant he expected every ounce of coldness from her. "How've you been? What are you up to these days?"

"Oh, you know, teaching music at the high school, taking care of my cat. Trying to decide what kind of blood is easiest to wash off the stage floor. Living my best life."

"Always go with water based," Jake said evenly.

"Do I even want to know how you know that?" Raquel's eyes narrowed.

"Pranks." He shrugged. "What about you and Seth? You two finally together?"

"What?" Sadie demanded in a sharp tone.

"Where is Seth, by the way?" he asked Sadie. "I haven't seen him around yet. You two are usually inseparable."

"He's not here," Raquel answered for her. "And what exactly are *you* doing back here, anyway?" Raquel asked with a warning look toward Sadie.

"Seems to be the question around town these days. Really, I just missed Gigi Marie's cooking."

"She's not even here right now. You don't have to suck up if she can't hear you," Sadie said, rolling her eyes.

"Maybe I just missed your charming eye rolls and biting tongue, then," he said, his eyes settling on her as his eyebrows quirked up, daring her to contradict him.

"If you missed her, then maybe you shouldn't have left. Now, if you'll excuse me, I need to get to the nursery."

"Where are we sitting, Sade?" Jake asked, taking Raquel's snub in stride.

"Over here." Her shoulders slumped in defeat as she led him to their row.

When they stood for worship, his shoulder kept bumping into hers. She tried to ignore the low timbre of his voice. The way it seeped into her like lavender honey.

When Pastor Jay called for the congregation to greet one another, Jake kept a hand on her shoulder as she begrudgingly introduced him to the surrounding families. She surreptitiously tried to shrug his hand off.

"Sorry," he whispered, dropping his arm to his side. "It's weird to be the new guy at a place I basically grew up in. You're my buffer."

Buffer. Exactly what she said she'd needed against him. The ember in her stomach with Jake's name on it pulsed a little bit. She looked up at him, and he was staring down at her. The pulse turned into a glow. She quickly threw dirt on it, to smother it.

When they sat for announcements, the length of his thigh was warm against hers.

Why aren't these damn chairs bigger?

Sadie tried to listen to the sermon on the meaning behind the seven bowls of God's wrath in Revelation, but Jake kept pushing his knee into hers.

"If you don't stop that, you're going to feel *my* wrath," Sadie whispered.

"Your wrath sounds nice," Jake whispered back, leaning down so his breath tickled her neck. The hairs on her arm stood on end.

She surreptitiously poked him hard in the rib cage, and his chest quaked in silent laughter.

Gigi, sitting to her left, smacked her on the leg.

After that, she kept her hands to herself. As soon as the pastor gave his parting benediction and the congregation broke out in a rumble of conversation, Sadie jumped up.

"I've got to get Gigi home," she said, turning her back on Jake.

As they were nearing the foyer Sadie heard a gingersnap laugh and turned to see that Annabelle had cornered Jake. Annabelle's grandmother, Mrs. Bennett, was standing near them with a faraway look in her eyes. Sadie had always gotten the impression that Mrs. Bennett's head was a rabbit hole she'd gotten lost down a long time ago.

Jake looked over at Sadie with pleading eyes, but Sadie only grinned wickedly back.

"I'm just so glad you're back," Annabelle said with her sugar-spun voice. "I never had enough time with you back then, did I?"

Sadie knew the smile she would be wearing, so saccharine it hurt her teeth without even seeing it.

"Oh, I don't know," he said, trying to inch slowly away from her. "I'm really not that great once you get to know me."

"Nonsense. Maybe I can convince you to join the town council," she practically purred, wrapping her red-taloned fingernails around his forearm. "We could use someone like you."

"Oh, um . . ." Jake intoned nervously.

"Sugar?" Gigi called from the door.

"Coming!" Sadie answered gleefully.

"Remind me not to do that again for another six months," Gigi said when they were back home. "Leave the wolves to their feeding."

Sadie had forced her grandmother to sit so she could make them both a glass of iced coffee. Bambi was lying splayed on the cool floor at Gigi's feet, eagerly awaiting the bits of heavily buttered sourdough toast she'd drop down for him.

Sadie hadn't yet had the nerve to tell her grandmother that they'd dognapped Jake's puppy. Abby sat on Gigi's lap, staring down at Bambi with what Sadie swore was a look of superiority.

"It's not that bad, is it?" Sadie asked halfheartedly as she swirled caramel around the inside of the glasses. The kitchen had that stuffy feeling of windows too long closed, and Sadie opened the one over the sink to let in the apple-crisp breeze.

"Pfft, a bunch of holier-than-thou, Bible-thumping, small-town hicks, the lot of them."

"Some of them might be," Sadie conceded. "But not all of them. It's community," she said offhandedly.

"I know, I know. I'm just being a grouchy old crone. But you're always doing all the work for everyone. You never stop. If it's not the café, it's something for me or the neighbors or that church."

"Now I wonder where I got that work ethic from?" Sadie asked with a pointed look.

"Somebody stupid, probably," Gigi said, laughing outright.

"Anyway, you know my philosophy. It's safer to do things *for* people than it is to love them."

"Sweetheart, you're so worried about somebody breaking your heart that you're gonna end up breaking your own. Now,

I'm going out for a cigarette, and then I'm going to sit my butt down and watch the idiot box until it's time to start dinner."

"Do you really think you should be smoking?"

"Because quitting will make the cancer go away? It's in my stomach, sugar, not my lungs. And on that note, I know you're still not ready to hear it, but there are things you need to know."

"The only thing I need to know is that I have a bowl of herbs charging under the moon to use for a spell that's going to cure you."

Gigi only shook her head.

"I recorded *True Grit* for you last night," Sadie added, knowing how much Gigi loved John Wayne.

"That piece of trash? He should be ashamed of himself for filming that movie," Gigi said in disgust. "I'll just find an old episode of *NCIS*. And remind me to mop these floors before Jake gets here—they're disgusting," Gigi called from the living room.

Sadie looked down but couldn't see so much as a smudge or speck of dust. The cherrywood floors were nicked and scratched with deep gouges in places, but polished to a high shine on the monthly. Gigi revered those floors, sweeping, vacuuming, and mopping them so often that Sadie thought they were probably cleaner than she was. In Gigi's eyes, clean floors reflected a clean life.

"Now, sit," Gigi said when they were both on the back porch with coffee in hand. She patted the chair next to her and Sadie sat. "And tell me what you want out of this life."

"What?" Sadie laughed.

"I'm serious. I was never going to live forever. Now, I know the suddenness of it is a real son of a bitch, but you can't tell me you've never thought about what comes next when I'm gone."

"I haven't, really," Sadie said truthfully.

"Sugar, you have to want more than to live in this little old house with nothing but an old woman and a dopey dog for company. You do nothing but read and run the café."

Sadie didn't argue because it was the truth.

"Now, this town is in our blood. I'm not saying you need to leave it to make your mark. But I'm afraid your curse is stopping you from dreaming. So, what do you want out of life?"

"I"—Sadie started, searching for words—"I'm happy with my life."

"Didn't say you weren't. But there's a difference between being happy and being fulfilled. Happiness you feel in your skin. Fulfillment you feel in your bones."

"I feel like you're going somewhere with this," Sadie said tightly.

"You don't need a partner to complete you. But it sure as hell is nice to have someone to lean on. And what about that cookbook you wanted to make? Why'd you give that up? Or those online cooking classes you wanted to teach?"

Sadie hadn't thought about the cookbook or classes in years. She'd gotten so lost in the mire of running the café and taking care of the townsfolk that her dream of sharing recipes and teaching others how to make them had gotten put on hold.

"Now you listen up, toot," Gigi continued, covering Sadie's hand with hers and giving it a pat. "I'm not going anywhere yet, but someday soon you're going to need to ask yourself if you're content with just being happy or if you want to be fulfilled."

The moment she was alone, the knot in Sadie's chest tightened ever so slightly. Between Gigi's questions and cancer, and Jake's return, her predictable life had gone haywire. Knowing she shouldn't care about his presence and actually following through with that notion were two completely different obstacles in her mind.

She put a drop of white angelica oil in her palms and inhaled the Earl Grey scent of bergamot, the bright floral of ylang ylang, and the rich earthiness of sacred sandalwood, for protection and positivity. She needed every last tattered shred she could get.

Glancing at the clock, she saw she had a few hours until he'd arrive. The thing was, Jake didn't owe her anything. Not really. Sure, he'd promised her forever, but those were the whimsical vows of youth, tainted with berry-stained fingers and the truth-telling properties of chrysanthemum.

At least, Sadie assumed that's what they had been for him. For her, of course, it was the catalyst that set her life on its course. But maybe, perhaps, they *could* be cordial.

It would make life easier, anyway. Clearly, she was going to be seeing him all over town. And she didn't have to let him in. She could fortify her walls.

Her head heavy with that thought, she started on the orange balsamic marinade for the chicken she'd be grilling later, the bright citrus scent making her think of summer. The sound of the "idiot box" filtered in from the living room and just as she started to grate the zest of the orange, a knock sounded on the front door.

"I'll get it," she hollered to Gigi, wiping her hands on her apron. She hadn't changed out of the short-sleeved red wrap dress she'd worn to church, and noticed that a few specks of olive oil had managed to splatter themselves on the skirt. Par for the course. Her brain usually worked faster than her hands and often resulted in toothpaste on her shirt, coffee grinds all over the counter, and things falling off the shelf from where she'd stuffed them away too hastily.

"Jake!" Sadie cried in surprise when she opened the door. "You're, um, you're early," she said, not opening the door all the way and glancing to the living room where Bambi had made himself comfortable on the couch.

"I thought maybe I could help with dinner since you said I didn't need to bring anything. Even though I brought these, anyway," he said, holding up two bottles of wine. "Pinot gris, because I know you don't like reds, and a zinfandel, in case you're feeling brave and want to try something new."

Sadie just stood there staring at him, trying to figure out what to say, when she heard the tiniest whimper come from the living room.

"Are you gonna let me in?" he called out.

"I—oh yes! Just, um—hang on one second." And she shut the door in his face. "Bambi!" she hissed. "Come here, boy."

"What are you doing with that dog?" Gigi demanded at full volume.

"Shh!" Sadie waved her hands in a wild attempt to shush Gigi. "I'm putting him in my room. Jake's here, and I, um—I don't know how he'll react around strangers."

"Jake or the dog?" Gigi asked with narrowed eyes.

Sadie didn't answer as she bounded up the stairs, Bambi following after her.

"Good boy," she said, giving him a quick scratch behind the ears. "I'll sort this out, I promise," she told him. She told her heart to stop pounding, but as usual it didn't listen. *It's just about the dog,* she told herself, refusing the urge to look in a mirror and make sure her eyeliner wasn't smudged.

A second later she opened the front door again. Jake turned around and she smiled, forgetting for a moment about trying to figure out how she should treat him. After all, he was still Jake. Surely it couldn't be that difficult for them to be normal around each other? If she could just shove the past under a Texas–sized Band-Aid.

"Okay, come in," she said, stepping aside.

"Hiding all the magic books and candlesticks?" he asked with raised brows.

"And the animal innards we use for divining. You know, you really don't need to help with anything."

"Well, what else was I going to do? Sit in my Elmwood Motel room by myself?"

"Can't stand your own company? I totally sympathize."

"Be nice to our guest!" Gigi hollered from the living room.

"Listen to your elders," Jake said with a solemn tone and a teasing glint in his eyes.

Sadie reached out to smack him on the arm, but he darted out of the way. She wanted to point out that he was *not* there by *her* invitation. Damn Gigi and her meddling ways. What was she playing at, anyway?

"Give me those," she said, grabbing the wine from his hands and turning on her heel.

Jake followed her into the kitchen and watched as she uncorked the bottle of pinot gris he'd brought. Of course, he remembered that she didn't favor the reds.

"What can I do?" he asked, always helpful to a fault.

Go back where you came from?

Never have left?

Kiss me, maybe?

Shut up, Sadie.

Silently, she handed him a glass of wine and ignored the gentle tug on her heart.

"Thanks, by the way, for abandoning me with Annabelle."

"Sometimes the best kind of torture is the one where I leave you to your own devices. I mean, you should expect it. You're the talk of the town."

"Well, good to know some things never change, at least." He smiled.

"Hubris. Lovely."

"You've never cared what people think. It's one of the things I admire about you."

On the spot, she decided that she better start carrying a small posy of white and lavender heather to keep her on the safe side of sunset. Because it was statements like those, the ones that led back to dusty memories, that reminded her just how well he knew her. Better than anyone aside from Seth.

Instead of answering, she gave him a knife and pointed to a pile of onions for him to chop.

"Yes, ma'am," he said with a smile.

They worked in soft silence, moving around each other like water, practiced and smooth. When his arm brushed against hers as they worked, her skin reacted by breaking out in goose bumps. And when she went to get the butter from the fridge, it was already melted in its container.

A scratching noise came from upstairs.

"Gigi still taking in strays?" Jake guessed.

"Um, yeah." Her laugh sounded manic even to her own ears as her eyes refused to meet his.

"You know, one of the things I was really happy about moving here was that I could finally get a dog. Got the dopiest chocolate lab puppy, but the dumb guy ran off while I was looking at the house."

"Oh, really? That—well, how unfortunate," she said with wide, innocent eyes, even though her chest filled with something that felt terribly like guilt. "Maybe you should have put your number on his collar. Like a responsible adult."

"The machine at the pet store was broken. I ordered one and had it shipped to the motel, Miss Bossy Pants."

"Oh," Sadie said, and her face fell. Damn him.

Bambi whimpered and barked, and Jake narrowed his eyes at the sound, recognition coloring his features.

"I'm letting Bambi out!" Gigi called before Jake could say anything.

"No!" Sadie shouted, but a few seconds later the lab in question came bounding into the kitchen.

"Chief!" Jake shouted, dropping to the floor as the dog covered him in wet kisses. From the ground Jake looked up at Sadie with pursed lips.

"Did you steal my dog?"

"What! I mean, no! I mean . . . he just wandered into our garden. He begged me to take him. I tried to get him to leave. I said, 'Shoo, dog. Be gone!' But he wouldn't listen, and . . . and . . . yes, I did. I stole him. But I didn't know!" she blathered, her skin going clammy.

"Sadie, we're in the country!" Jake huffed in exasperation. "Sound carries. Didn't you hear me calling him last night?" He stood up, crossing his arms, and Sadie could swear he was trying not to smile.

"It was muffled," she mumbled, staring at her shoes.

"Sadie Kathryn Revelare. Did you know this was his dog?" Gigi demanded, standing in the doorway of the kitchen.

"I may have considered the possibility, yes."

Just then the dog in question started barking when there was another knock at the door. Raquel walked in, arms full of fabric, just as the puppy chose that moment to relieve himself, and the timer went off, and the water on the stove boiled over.

This was not part of the routine, and it made her chest tight and a headache pound at her temples.

"Jake, go turn on the barbecue, please," Gigi said, commandeering the situation at once. "Sadie, take the puppy out back to finish his business, and then grab some basil from the garden for me, sugar. And Raquel, honey, get me some towels so I can clean this mess up."

Everyone scattered to their respective duties. Sadie, head bowed, followed Jake and Bambi outside.

"I can't believe you stole my dog," Jake said, his voice hinting at suppressed laughter. "I mean, seriously? Dognapping? Go on, boy," he added to the puppy, ushering him past the lavender.

"It was an accident," Sadie said, kneeling in the dirt and carefully plucking basil leaves.

"Sure, it was," he said, laughing full out this time. Sadie let the sound fill her. She didn't have to let him in, but she could appreciate the way that sound made her stomach dip.

"I would've given him back. I just wanted to make sure you were worthy first. Caring for a dog is a lot of work." Sadie heard the click and light of the barbecue from the back patio and jumped.

"Well, aren't you Miss High and Mighty," he said, leaning against a post. "I may not be great at commitment, but at least I don't freak out at the tiniest bit of disorder in my perfectly fabricated life."

"If my life were perfectly fabricated, you wouldn't be here for dinner, now would you?" she asked, though there was no real bite to the words.

Gigi hollered from the kitchen. They looked at each other for a second before Jake followed her inside. When Gigi called, troops rallied. She issued more marching orders, and there was no more time for idle chitchat as the chicken and zucchini were put on the grill, the salad tossed, and the honey-glazed cornbread put in the oven.

Sadie reveled in the heat as she turned the zucchini, carefully ensuring each side was seared to perfection. Tasks were easier to contemplate than feelings.

The light breeze tasted sweet, with a dash of promise, and mixed with the char from the grill. Bambi was yapping playfully, and the sound of plates clanking together sang out from the kitchen. If she closed her eyes, nothing had changed. It was just another evening. Just another family dinner. *I can do this,* she told herself, not quite believing it but wanting to, and wasn't that the whole point?

"Dinner's ready!" Gigi called out as Sadie brought in the platter of chicken and vegetables.

"Where's Seth?" Jake asked, looking around as they all took their places.

Sadie looked mutinous. Gigi frowned. And Raquel was the one who answered.

"He's out of town," she said simply. And it was true enough. "I got the rights to *Carrie*," she added, glancing at Sadie, whose eyes were thanking her for changing the subject. "It was a total flop when it came out, so buying the rights was pretty cheap, comparatively. And it's not terribly heavy on choreography, thank God. I really don't want to inflict my dance moves on those poor kids."

"I could help," Jake said. "I'm known for my dance skills." He moved his arms like a robot.

"Thanks, but no thanks."

Sadie was surprised to hear her best friend laugh.

"What I really need is someone to control the lights. Mr. Mason, the math teacher, is helping me with lighting design, because he's a masochist apparently, but he'll be out of town for the actual production."

"I can do it," Jake volunteered, sounding serious this time.

"Why?" Raquel narrowed her eyes.

"I went to that high school too, remember? You'd just have to tell me what to do."

Sadie saw the war playing on Raquel's face. She didn't want to accept his help, but she wasn't going to look a gift horse in the mouth either. Or a gift fireman, for that matter.

"Okay," she said slowly. "When I finish the design, I'll teach you how to do it. But if you back out on me, I'll sic the kids on you."

"Deal." His deep rumble of a laugh echoed in Sadie's heart.

"'Better to screw than get screwed,'" Raquel said, looking expectantly at Sadie.

"'You'd probably think it's bizarre,'" Sadie continued, providing the next line of the song "The World According to Chris" from *Carrie*.

"'But that's the way things are!'" they both sang out at the same time.

"You two scare me," Jake said, looking between them.

"Raquel's made me memorize practically every musical since the dawn of time. *Carrie* has always been one of her favorites."

"Small town, crazy mom, awkward teenage girl, buckets of blood—it's basically my biography. What's not to love?"

Sadie sat on her hands throughout the rest of the dinner. And when she wasn't squeezing the life out of her fingers, she was passing the basket of bread or refilling water glasses and urging Raquel and Jake to take second helpings.

Everyone was silent as they ate Sadie's pumpkin and ginger pie. She'd actually baked it for herself, humming Don McLean's "American Pie" as she did. The ginger was meant to add stability to traditions while making the eater more civil, and the pumpkin was supposed to give encouragement to try new things.

In the quiet of the table, Sadie absentmindedly ate a few forkfuls. Jake had two slices and wiped the plate clean with the tines of his fork. As soon as he finished, Sadie hopped up and started gathering dishes.

"You put those down this instant, or I'll pop you one, young lady," Gigi ordered. "I have all the time in the world for washing up later."

"Gigi, Sadie, that was the best meal I've had in months," Jake declared, scooting his chair back. "You sure I can't help with dishes?" he asked Gigi. And when she raised a threatening eyebrow, he laughed. "Now you," he added to Sadie. "Let's go."

"Go where?"

"For a walk."

"No" was tipped on her tongue, ready to roll off. But the pumpkin and ginger were hard at work in her body, absorbing into her, pulsing through her blood. She thought of half a dozen rude things to say, but none of them would come out.

His eyes softened. "Please, Sade. I . . . I have something I need to say." She raised her eyebrows and crossed her arms, but as if anticipating her barked *"So say it,"* he added, "Privately."

There was something in his eyes when he looked at her. Just what else could he have to say? "I should help Gigi—"

"Don't you dare use me as an excuse, you pissant! I have everything well under control here. Raquel and I will work on the costumes. *Go.*"

Sadie's eyes locked with her grandmother's, and a silent war ensued between them. Sadie lost. As usual. She sighed, and Jake grinned in triumph.

"We'll be back, Bambi," he said, rubbing Bambi's tummy as the puppy stretched out on the floor. When Sadie looked at him with raised eyebrows, he shrugged. "It's more fitting than Chief. He's always tripping over himself like Bambi on the ice."

She looked back at Raquel, who was clearing dishes and singing "Unsuspecting Hearts" with a little too much meaning.

Her own heart was swimming in her chest as they followed a trail around the edge of the woods. The crickets were chirping noisily, and Sadie wished she'd brought a glass of wine with her. Their silence stretched taut. If he had something to say, she wasn't going to drag it out of him.

When everything turned golden as the sun began to set, she tried to stay afloat amid the crashing waves of uncertainty and nerves.

"So, what's the deal with Seth? Why's everyone being so mysterious about him? Did he land himself in jail or something?" Jake asked, finally breaking the silence. She winced.

"He's gone," she said, and it wasn't really a lie. That was one of their rules they'd established a decade ago, and Sadie knew it still stood. With a guy like Jake, those kinds of promises didn't change. No matter what, they always told each other the truth.

"Gone where? The afterlife? Mexico?"

"I honestly have no clue, Jake. Okay? He left. That's it. That's all I know." The words came out hard. Harder than she'd intended. Even though it had been a year, she still hated talking about it. Hated not having answers. It made her feel out of control, and if there was one thing Sadie liked, it was having things sorted out.

"Damn," he said softly. "I'm sorry, Sade."

"It's fine—can't you tell I'm over it?" She laughed with a bitter edge. "Anyway, Rock Creek, huh?" she changed the subject. "You going to buy it? I've always loved that house."

"That's because you love broken things," he said in a pointed tone.

"They have a certain charm that everyone else overlooks. Or something like that." Sadie laughed, but it came out a little strangled. The path narrowed, and Jake's arm brushed against hers. She tried to ignore the way it sent sparks skittering across her skin.

They walked for another twenty minutes in silence until they came to a large pond and Sadie stopped, kicking off her shoes to let the earth seep into her.

The air was damp, and the crickets were louder here. She wished they were loud enough to drown out the sound of her beating heart. Her eyes trained on the lily pads, swaying sleepily on top of the water. Drifted to the brush along the shore and the blackberry bushes farther up. Remembered her and Seth spending hours picking berries and going home with purple tongues and pricked fingers and baskets nearly empty. If only she could let go of the past the way other people seemed able to. Maybe the future wouldn't be quite so terrifying. But memories lived forever in Sadie. Indelible. The good and the bad.

"What's going on in that head of yours?" Jake asked in wary voice, coming up behind her.

"What am I doing here?" she asked, avoiding his question. "What are *we* doing here?"

Jake sighed and placed his hands on her shoulders. Sadie stood still as starlight, letting herself revel in that small point of contact for a quiet, shining moment. It sent warmth all the way down her and pooled low in her stomach where it was on the verge of turning into longing.

"If you didn't want to come, why'd you say yes?" he asked.

"When have I ever been able to say no to you?"

"Frequently, if I recall correctly." His laugh was quiet and filled with memories. "Listen. I asked you to go on a walk with me because I need to tell you something."

Her heart dipped.

"Someone just said that to me a few days ago, and I got some news I really didn't want to hear. So, no thanks. Whatever it is, I'll pass."

"You can't control everything, Sadie." He sighed. "I learned that the hard way."

"You don't think I know that?" Sadie demanded, turning around to face him. Which, in retrospect, was a mistake she realized the moment she looked up into his eyes. She backed up a step, the silt chilling her feet.

Don't be an idiot, Sadie, she reprimanded herself. *You don't want this.* But the lie tasted bitter and sharp as white peppercorns. *Just leave.* She couldn't seem to move her feet.

"What happened to the wild girl I used to know, huh?" he asked, taking a step forward as she took one back.

"My heart got broken two too many times," she answered.

The water lapped at her heels and she closed her eyes, her breathing ragged. Sadie never minded having dirty feet, always going barefoot as often as possible, but only on dry land. There was something about murky water that terrified her. It was not seeing what lay underneath, not being able to control what her foot landed on. Not knowing what was brushing up against her.

"Maybe you just need a friend to help remind you how to live a little." He took another step toward her and Sadie found her feet fully submerged in the water.

"Why are you doing this to me?" she demanded.

"Because I still love watching you unravel," he answered in a low voice.

"You're an ass," she said, pushing him hard in the chest. He barely moved.

"You're a control freak," he said, gently pushing her back. Sadie stumbled and found herself calf deep in the water. A shudder tore through her body. There was probably all manner of horrifying things in that water. Fish that would love to feast on her toes and slimy, algae covered rocks.

"Come on," he taunted. "I dare you to jump in." He pulled his sweatshirt off, wadded it in a ball, and threw it back to dry land. His shirt went next. Sadie refused to look below his chin and her eyes strained with the effort.

"You're out of your mind," she breathed.

But she didn't stop as he kept walking toward her, pushing her out further into the water. Out of her comfort zone. The way he always had. The hem of her dress skimmed the surface before submerging and clinging to her skin.

"Just breathe," he told her, his voice calm and reassuring.

But it was a feat more easily commanded than accomplished. This new version of him, the slow, gentle, kind Jake, he would be her undoing.

"What was that?" Sadie squeaked as the surface of the water rippled not teen feet in front of her.

Jake laughed, turning around to inspect the spot she was pointing at. At that exact moment something brushed against Sadie's calf. She screamed and jumped onto Jake's back, scrambling for a hold on his neck as she wrapped her legs around his torso. Anything to get out of that water.

"What the . . .?" Jake choked out, still laughing.

"Something touched me!" she yelped, her hands tightening around his neck. His body was warm, and she thought maybe she should lay her cheek on his shoulder, just for a moment. How easy it would be to pretend to be her age. With normal worries. It was the first time in years she wondered just how much her magic had taken from her.

Jake felt around in the water and brought up a clump of weeds.

"You were lucky, it could've torn your leg off," he said, his tone serious.

"Funny," Sadie groaned. "Okay, I'm a big fat baby. You have permission to mock me forever. As long as you please take me back to shore." The longer she was wrapped around him the more aware she was becoming of his body. Their closeness. Muscle memory was threatening to surface again, and she wasn't sure how much longer she could fight it. Or if she even wanted to.

"Oh, I could," he said, and she could hear the smile in his voice. "But I think this will be much more entertaining."

"Don't you dare," she hissed as he walked further out into the water. "Jacob Theodore McNealy," she yelled, pounding on his chest. "Stop right this second!" He was waist deep and Sadie tried to shimmy higher up his body.

"Okay," he said. And then, without warning, he jumped, falling back like a tree until they both dropped in the chilly water. The cold took her breath away and pricked at her skin.

"You," Sadie spluttered, wiping water from her eyes, "are the absolute *worst.*" But she couldn't stop the laugh that bubbled up.

"That wasn't so bad, was it?" he asked, wading back to the sand with Sadie still clinging to his back. His body was slick and glistening in the dying light. Her tongue felt thick in her mouth. Like there was something she was supposed to be doing with it. Something that had to do with the space of skin just below Jake's ear.

She hopped down the second they were on the shore, her red wrap dress clinging to her body and dripping water. She shivered in the autumnal chill as Jake gently moved a strand of hair that was stuck to her cheek.

"Fun?" he asked.

"Fun," she agreed, nodding with reluctance.

Her hands twitched by her side. If she'd been wearing her apron, she would have wiped them on it, twirled the string around her finger. As it was, her fingers itched to trail up his arms, along his shoulders, and thread themselves through his hair.

She took a step closer to him without meaning to. She wanted to reach out and touch him. Wanted to close the inches between them. Just to make sure he was real. That he'd actually come back.

"Sadie," he said in a low voice.

His body leaned toward her like a magnet.

The frogs and crickets and lapping water were their own kind of symphony.

They were both completely still.

She waited. For something. Anything. For him to tell her that he came back for her. That he wanted to start over or try again. That a piece of him had been missing for the last ten years.

His silence was deafening.

"I can't believe you're here," she whispered, her body aching to lean into him, to feel him against her, to steal his warmth as wisps of steam curled off her body. And suddenly, something shifted in him. He stiffened and pulled away, taking his warmth with him.

"That's what I wanted to talk to you about." He sighed and cleared his throat uncomfortably.

Before she could answer, her phone rang. And the ringtone made her heart beat triple time.

She tore her gaze from his, frantically searching for the jacket she'd discarded when they'd arrived at the pond. The lapping waves of the water turned distant. Her hand gripped the phone so hard her knuckles hurt, and her eyes went blurry as she stared at the name and picture flashing across the screen.

She should ignore it. It would serve him right. But the thought wasn't even fully formed before the phone was at her ear.

"What?" she spat.

"It's Gigi," was all he said. There was a beat of silence. She wanted to hug his voice and strangle him at the same time. "She fell. We're on the way to the hospital. You need to get there."

Orange Balsamic Marinade

Orange represents attraction, determination, and success. When they're combined they help the eater to entice and catch whoever it is they're interested in. If the intended party is already interested, which they probably are if I'm any kind of smart, then all the better.

Ingredients

¼ c. extra virgin olive oil
3–5 T. balsamic vinegar (depending on your taste)
2 T. Dijon mustard
½ tsp. salt
½ tsp. pepper
zest and juice of one orange (or ¼ c. orange juice)
¼ c. honey

Directions

1. *Combine oil, vinegar, mustard, salt, pepper, orange juice, and zest, and whisk together. Marinade chicken in mixture for a minimum of 1 hour.*

2. *Pour the marinade into a saucepan with the honey, and simmer until the volume is reduced by half.*

3. Use this mixture to glaze the chicken every *5–10* minutes as it cooks.

♦ 6 ♦

SADIE'S INSIDES WERE IN upheaval. Every time she moved, the contents of her stomach threatened to come up. She'd sprinted back to the house with Jake at her heels, and he'd insisted on driving her straight to the hospital, twenty minutes outside of town in the slightly larger city of Aurelia. With blood thrumming in her ears, her eyes manic, she let him.

Jake parked the car, and Gigi was getting X-rays when Sadie arrived. Her heart stuttered when she saw Seth leaning against the wall in the hallway. He was only a few inches taller, but stockier, broader. The freckles across his nose washed out in the hospital lighting. It was the face of her childhood. The male version of the one she saw in the mirror every day. There were dark circles under his eyes and a secret lurking in his expression.

"When did you get back?" she asked, hugging him on autopilot.

"About forty-five minutes ago."

Jake walked up and pressed a coffee in her hands. She looked down at the cup and was surprised to see her arms clad in his sweatshirt over her still damp dress. When had that happened? She briefly remembered him turning the heater on full blast and angling the vents toward her as they drove.

"Thanks," she croaked, the light of her anger toward Seth dying out just as fast as it came. "But you don't have to be here.

You can go." Her voice felt scratchy, as if the words had to claw themselves out of her throat. The smell of bitter coffee reached her and mixed with the stale hospital air.

"I've got nowhere else to be," he said before bumping his shoulder into hers.

A doctor rounded the corner, his glasses slipping down his nose and his white coat bulging over his stomach.

"Revelare?" he asked. They nodded, and he motioned for them to follow him as he walked. "Looks like nothing is broken, just some bruising." His words were short and colored with exhaustion. "Honestly, a fall like this isn't unexpected in someone her age. Especially with her diagnosis. I've prescribed some eight-hundred-milligram ibuprofen, and that's about all we can do for her. Have you considered a fall alert bracelet or button for her house? Or maybe putting her in assisted living?"

"I live with her," Sadie said mutinously.

"Oh, well." He shrugged. "Good then. I'll have the nurse start her discharge paperwork. Here's her room."

And with that, he left.

"Fucking doctors," Seth hissed. "And what did he mean about her diagnosis? What diagnosis?"

Before she could answer, they heard a small, familiar cough. Sadie threw open the door and rushed inside.

"I'm fine, sugar," were the first words out of Gigi's mouth as she held a hand out to her granddaughter. "But if those idiot nurses don't let me out of here for a cigarette soon, I'm going to have to clock them one."

Sadie choked out a laugh as she hurried to take Gigi's hand, enclosing it in both of hers and sitting on the edge of the bed.

"What happened?" she asked with a quiet hiccup. "You needed a break from me so badly you decided to send yourself to the hospital for a little holiday?" she joked, trying not cry.

"It's my damned back is all, honey. But I wish everyone would stop making such a fuss. I'm fine. I . . ." She started and then stopped. "I can't remember what I was going to say. This getting old business is a real son of a bitch, let me tell you."

"I don't think that has anything to do with getting old," Sadie argued with a small laugh. "I forget what I'm going to say half the time. Maybe it's a Revelare trait."

"Or maybe it's the painkillers," Seth countered from the doorway.

"Seth," Sadie said through gritted teeth, "why don't you do something useful and see if you can go find the nurse and charm her into getting Gigi out of here faster."

"Jesus, Sade. Lighten up. Gigi's a fucking pioneer, okay? A little fall is nothing."

"I know what Gigi is," Sadie said, rising up from the bed and rounding on him. "I know *who* she is. You? What do you know? You fucking left. And now you're here like it fixes everything, and it doesn't."

Damn him. *Damn him*. For always making her say more than she meant to. For being the one who loosened her control.

"Sadie Kathryn," Gigi warned.

"No, Gigi. He's here now because it was an emergency. That's all. I'm sure he'll be gone again by morning. I mean, what more could we possibly expect from you, right?" she demanded, turning back to him.

"You're being a child," he said flatly, his eyes mirroring Sadie's own in their anger.

"That's enough out of both of you," Gigi cut in. "Sadie, you look like a bedraggled cat. Go home and get some rest. Seth will stay here with me. I'll be home before you know it. Stop worrying, honey. Everything's gonna be fine."

"You're kidding me," Sadie spat. Her throat started to close up, but she flat out refused to cry in front of her brother.

"Come here, toot," Gigi said, holding out her hand again. Sadie automatically walked forward, reaching for her. "Look at me. I'm fine. I promise. I've got some time left."

Sadie looked at her, really looked. The color had come back into her cheeks, her voice was steady and strong as it ever was, her grip as she held Sadie's hand was sturdy. The overwhelming need to be in her garden, working with the herbs and spell that was going to heal Gigi almost choked her.

"Okay, fine, I'll go. But only because it's what you want," she said to Gigi.

"I'll drive you home," Jake called from the doorway. He looked like he wanted to come in but wasn't sure if he should.

"Get in here, you little shit ass," Gigi said. "Take care of my baby, you hear me?"

Jake nodded with a solemn smile and leaned down to kiss Gigi's hand.

"Now go on. This old broad needs to get some rest. Seth is the only one who won't hover over me like a mother hen. You two get out of here, you hear me? And don't forget about Bambi and Abby. There's grilled chicken and rice for them in the fridge."

"Of course there is," Seth said, amused.

Sadie sighed and kissed her grandmother on the forehead before leaving.

Jake was silent on the way to the car, his demeanor calm. Sadie, meanwhile, had collected herself, had her emotions back under control. Only Seth could get her riled up in that way. And though she wanted to punch through the metal door of Jake's truck, outwardly, judging by the serenity on her face, she could have just left a yoga class.

"Do you want to talk about it?" he asked as he started the engine.

"No."

"Where has Seth been?"

"Hell if I know," she answered.

"And you have no idea why he left?"

"Jake, I said I don't want to talk about it."

"Right, right, sorry. It's just weird seeing you two like that. But, you know, Gigi will be okay."

The moment he spoke the words, a lump formed in Sadie's throat. She nodded.

"Of course, she will," she said tightly.

They were silent the rest of the way, Sadie's shoulder blades aching as she tried to keep hold of her emotions. She couldn't break down. Not in front of Jake.

When he pulled into her driveway, her chest lightened when she saw Raquel's car was still there. She opened the door before the truck was fully in park.

"Thank you, really," she said. "I'll be fine. Talk to you later."

"Sadie, wait," Jake called, rolling the passenger-side window down.

She turned to look at him, not sure how much longer she could hold it all in. He looked on the verge of saying something comforting or life altering or heartbreaking, Sadie wasn't sure which. But then his eyes cleared as he seemed to change his mind.

"Can I have my dog back now?"

A wild laugh burbled out of her.

"No," she said, and left him there, but not before she caught sight of the smile that took over his face. It was soft, but sharply dangerous in the way it threatened to pierce through her armor, and she tried to kick the memory of it away before it reached her heart.

Raquel was waiting with open arms, and Sadie sighed as she sank into her best friend and told her everything the doctor had said.

"I knew she was going to be okay," Raquel said, relief coloring her voice.

"My stupid brother," Sadie groaned miserably into Raquel's shoulder.

"I know," she murmured, guiding Sadie in and closing the door while simultaneously using her foot to maneuver Abby away from where she was searching for Gigi.

"When did you know?" she demanded sharply.

"When he showed up here thirty seconds before Gigi fell. Like he knew the exact time it was going to happen."

"Asshole."

"Can't disagree." Raquel smiled, and there was something behind it. "But you've kind of got to admire his style."

"Of course, he has to be the hero."

"Sadie . . ." Raquel's voice was gentle but held reproving. "I don't think it was like that."

"Who knows what it's like. It doesn't matter. I'm sure he'll be leaving again as soon as she's home."

"I don't think so," Raquel said. "I saw suitcases when I helped him get Gigi in the car."

"Maybe I don't want him here."

"He's your family, Sade. He's *supposed* to be here. Give him a chance."

"I'll give him a chance. A fat chance. In hell."

They both laughed, and then Sadie fell quiet, wrapping her palms around the warm mug of tea Raquel had just handed her.

Her best friend gave her almost a full minute before she couldn't take it anymore.

"So?" she asked, drawing out the vowel with raised eyebrows. "Are you freaking out on the inside right now? Because you know I can never tell since you're like a weird statue whenever you're experiencing emotion."

"I'm . . ." Sadie took a deep breath. "I don't know. How should I be? I mean, Gigi's in the hospital. Gigi. The woman who once pulled a massive tree stump out of the ground using a shovel and her bare hands. The woman who climbs the tallest-ass ladder there is and cleans out the gutters because she won't ask anyone else to help her. How am I supposed to feel?"

"I don't think you're supposed to feel any way. I think you're allowed to feel however you want."

Sadie's throat was almost too tight to speak. She forced the lump down and squeezed her eyes shut until it was painful.

"She's all I have."

"Hey," Raquel said, reaching over and grabbing Sadie's hand. "I'm here. We'll get through this together. It's okay to be upset, you know."

"I know," Sadie said, wiping her nose on the sleeve of Jake's sweatshirt. "Ugh, I'm sorry," she choked out as she tried to wipe away the tears without Raquel seeing them.

"For what? Having emotions?" Raquel huffed. "You apologize too much."

"You're the only one I can cry in front of, you know." Sadie laughed through her tears and got caught on a hiccup.

Raquel sighed. "I know. Look, I get that Gigi is all you have. And I know you're pissed at Seth for leaving *and* for coming back.

And you're trying to keep Jake at arm's length and still run the café and be a good person and blah blah blah. But I just think maybe you should try and let go of the past a little bit. Maybe you could try and forgive Seth, at the very least."

Sadie snorted and stretched her neck from side to side, trying to alleviate some of the tightness that had settled there in the last few hours.

"What're you, his new spokesperson?"

"Your problem," Raquel went on, "is that you pretend to be a hard ass. You pretend you don't care. But you never let go of hope. Because if there's even the tiniest chance that someone can be redeemed, you'll never let go."

"Because I'm stupid," Sadie groaned. "I mean, if anyone should have learned from the past, it's me. But my skull is thicker than a ten-foot fence."

"That makes absolutely no sense," Raquel said, laughing.

"You know what I mean! I'm dumb. Slap my ass and call me Sally. Put a fork in me. Whatever. God, I can't even get my 'isms' right. It's just—yeah, you're right, I guess. Shut up. Do not respond to that. But I do have a hard time letting go. Despite all the heartbreak. And damn, the hope is what kills you, you know? That's why I have to smother it. No smoke. No embers. Stamp it out."

"My dad says that the thing about the past is that when there's pain, that's all you remember. But when there's joy, even if it's a little bit, you forget all the shitty things that went along with it. I mean I added the 'shitty' part because you know he'd never say that. But that's why people make terrible decisions over and over again."

"Do you think I make terrible decisions over and over again?"

"I think you don't give yourself enough credit."

"Gigi asked me what I wanted out of life."

"A loaded question if ever there was one," Raquel observed.

"She asked me why I never pursued my dream of publishing a cookbook. Or teaching those cooking classes."

"Oh my gosh! Remember how you outlined an entire series? It was all color coded and everything, you little freak. Why *did* you give up on that? You know what? Don't answer that. Look, I know you're happy here. Nobody loves this town more than you do. But it's okay to have dreams too, you know?"

The crunch of tires on gravel heralded Seth's arrival. She was out the door before he'd even turned the car off.

He carried Gigi to the couch despite her protestations, and Sadie could tell by the look on his face that Gigi had told him about her cancer. There was a hollowness to his eyes she hadn't seen there before. Raquel kissed Gigi, hugged Seth, and then cupped Sadie's cheeks in her hands.

"You've got this," she whispered before she left.

"Stop hovering," Seth hissed as Sadie rearranged the blanket around Gigi for the third time.

"Mind your own business," she answered back.

"God, I forgot how annoying you were."

"Too bad I didn't forget what an ass you were," she answered.

"You two," Gigi croaked, and though her voice was tired it still held all the command it had when they'd fought during their childhood.

"Sorry," they chorused.

"I told you there were things you needed to know," Gigi said as soon as the door closed behind Sadie's best friend. "And now's the time. I've got a story to tell, and you're not going to like it and you're not going to like how it ends. But this is the way of things, and I've kept it in order for as long as I can, but it's time to know the truth. Matters need settling."

"Well, how's that for fucking ominous," Seth said, blowing out a sharp breath.

"Shut up and let her tell the story," Sadie said.

"It starts with your mother. Of all my kids, I know I've never talked much about her. Raising five children, it's—well, you do the best you can. But there are some things you need to know. Just remember, I did the best I could. And I didn't know—but then again, I'm getting ahead of myself. Your mother—boy, she was wild as a March hare from the moment she could walk and talk. The older she got, the worse it got. I swear that girl didn't have a brain in her head sometimes. Florence—your mother—she was the middle child, the wild one. And then your Aunt Tava, she was . . ."

"The unhinged one?" Seth chimed in.

"Quirky," Sadie corrected him. "I miss her."

"She was the oldest," Gigi continued. "So, she got to figure out who she was without anyone telling her who she should be. And then Kay—hoo boy—my second born. It's been years and years since you kids have seen her."

"I remember covering my ears a lot when she would visit," Seth said.

"She never did know how to talk quietly," Gigi said with amusement. "She's the dramatic one. Her magic was always unstable, too volatile. Your Aunt Anne, the second youngest, she was always a little nervous Nellie. She was sick when she was young. I think I coddled her too much, and it stuck with her. And then the baby, your Uncle Brian. The genius Mr. Know-It-All.

"For each of them, their magic was different. They all took to it in different ways. But Florence, she was a firecracker, all right. It wasn't until she turned eight that I realized she was an amplifier, a conduit."

"A what?" Seth asked at the same time Sadie breathed, "Oh."

"An amplifier. You remember, sugar?" Gigi asked Sadie, who nodded numbly.

"I forgot my witch dictionary, so what the hell does that mean?" Seth demanded.

"Every hundred years or so in every magical family there's a sort of prodigy born. Their magic is stronger, amplified, more unpredictable, and it swells until it spills over."

"Okay? So? Our mom was what, like a super witch?"

"Stop saying 'witch,'" Sadie said. "We're not witches. We use symbolism and the power of the earth, that's all. Magic doesn't mean witches."

"Potato, potahto." Seth rolled his eyes. "What does it mean, then?"

"It means they act as a conduit to amplify another person's magic. And it sends out a kind of signal."

"Bat signal?" Seth asked.

"Can you be serious for five seconds?" Sadie demanded, annoyed.

"A signal," Gigi interrupted them, "that those who would want to use someone like that for their own, usually dark ends can take advantage of. Instead of living in fear, your mother was fearless, and anybody who came for her be damned. She tried to use her magic out. By the time she was a teenager, she trailed sparks behind her wherever she went. Started fires without meaning to. Anyway," Gigi went on, "she moved out as soon as she turned eighteen, tried to leave all that magic behind her. Much like somebody else we know." She gave Seth a sharp look. "It didn't work. It never works." She sighed, shaking her head and pulling a blanket over her lap as if to keep out the chill of old memories. "People loved your mother. Even if she was hard and cruel, and especially when she was convincing you to do something you shouldn't. Men fell in love with her after a single glance, and she couldn't shake them. Well, I knew the second she brought Julian home that he was bad news. See, he had the magic in him, but it was bad magic. Dark, let me tell you. He was a seeker, alright. The bastard. He wanted to use your mother as a conduit."

"I don't get it. What could he do? Wave a magic wand and steal her, like, essence or magic, or what?" Seth asked.

"It doesn't work like that." Sadie's sigh was exasperated.

"Hush now," Gigi told them both. "He lured her in. Your momma, she was enchanted. At first by his charm and promises. He told her he could get rid of her magic. They performed a dark ritual together, but it wasn't to rid her of her magic. It was to make her fertile."

"What?" the twins demanded at once.

"That took an unexpected turn," Seth added drily.

"Most times, the amplifier's curse, it's to never be able to bear children. That's one of the reasons they're so incredibly rare."

"So, wait—we weren't even supposed to be born?" Seth's voice was incredulous, and Sadie couldn't blame him this time. This was news to her.

"How?" was all Sadie said.

"I don't know the details. But I knew it was dark magic. And I knew that nature would try to stop you both from coming into this world. Too much power. Too unpredictable. Now, to save a life takes a life, and I took Julian's. Only, I didn't know there were two of you. And by the time we found out, it was too late. No sacrifice would have been enough."

There was a beat of silence. It seemed to press in on them. Like the walls were leaning, aching to hear the secrets that hadn't been spoken about in decades. Time seemed to trickle through the hourglass. The grandfather clock ticked louder. Sadie wanted to scream. Or laugh. Or both. She wasn't quite sure.

"Slow down," Seth said, extending his hand. "Let's back up here a second and focus on the 'taking a life' thing. Are you saying you *killed* this Julian guy? Our father?"

Gigi nodded. Just like that.

"She came home." Gigi sighed. "Tried to leave him. Told him he was never going to see her again. And even though I threatened him, he stuck around. And then, when I was gone one day, he forced himself on your mother, the jackass. I didn't know until later, of course, when she started showing. Not that that's an excuse. I should've known. I should've . . ." She cleared her throat, her hand frantically picking at an invisible thread in her sweater. "I was about to get the shotgun and shoot his fucking balls off. I wanted to shoot his heart right out of his chest. But even though I may be dumb, I wasn't *that* stupid.

"She was a mess. He'd beaten her everywhere the babies weren't. You were too precious. Too important to his plan. The only ritual I knew to save life, required life. Balance. And . . .'" Gigi paused and cleared her throat. "Well. He ended up being the sacrifice."

Sadie was too shocked to say anything at all. Gigi just sat there like nothing at all had happened. Like she hadn't just admitted to *murdering* a man. Their *father.*

"For one of you, at least. For the other, I cast magic to ensure you lived, tied the darkness to me to make sure you could have your light. But it's never been enough. Life demands life. Where do you think this cancer came from?"

Both of them sat there a moment. Silent. The bile rose in Sadie's throat until the acid threatened to come up.

"It's our fault." Sadie's words came out fast, before she'd fully formed them in her head. She wasn't sure if it was a question or a statement.

"Sugar, it's nobody's fault but Julian's—may he rot in hell."

Sadie was too stunned to believe her. It was like a puzzle piece had fallen into place. But the picture still didn't make sense. Some of the pieces were turned over, just blobs of brown in a sea of color. Other pieces were mangled or missing, but the image, blurry though it may be, spoke to Sadie of a truth long harbored in the dark recesses of her heart. Maybe she really wasn't supposed to be here after all. Maybe that's why everyone left. Maybe that's why her curse was one of four heartbreaks. She was swimming against a tide of fate.

"What did you do with the body?" Seth demanded, always practical.

"Called your Aunt Anne," Gigi said, as though it was the most obvious answer in the world. "She helped me pack him into the trunk, and we buried his sorry ass at Old Bailer, where Evanora could keep an eye on him. Now, certain magic always comes with a price. I helped save you two. But in exchange, your mother had to leave. That magic, it created its own kind of curse, and she couldn't be near you two without endangering you both. It was the price of the magic. Part of the sacrifice." She drew a deep, shuddering breath and arched her back with a groan.

Sadie's eyes automatically tracked to Seth, who was breathing heavily.

"She didn't want to leave," he said.

"She wasn't ready to be a mother," Gigi said, her voice tight and scratchy as though it was hard to get the words out. "She still had wildness left in her. She was so young. Every Revelare leaves—you know that."

"But they always come back, right? Isn't that part of the stupid prophecy?" Seth demanded.

"When it comes to you two, things are different," Gigi said, not exactly answering his question. Like her. She'd never left. And she never would.

"Well, we can figure it out, though. Right? We'll find a way around it. It'll be fine," Sadie babbled.

"You don't understand," Gigi shook her head. "My magic, my sacrifice . . . I should have died to save you. I've lived too long—it's unbalanced; and now it's going to rebound on one of you to collect back what is owed. I've been fighting it all this time, sustaining the bond, but even my death, it won't be enough. When I'm gone, you'll need a sacrifice."

There was silence for a beat as they both took in her words. Seth, in particular, looked like he was working through an essay question he couldn't quite wrap his head around. And then . . .

"Wait. *What?*" he burst out.

"You mean we'll have to *kill* someone?" Sadie laughed this time, and it came out hysterical. "There's a workaround here somewhere. A loophole. Right? Isn't that one of the laws of nature? Of magic? There's always a loophole of some kind?" It all seemed utterly impossible. From the pages of a book titled *How* Not *to Use Magic.*

"Well, sugar," Gigi said, sighing, "if there is one, you'd be the one to find it. But this is all uncharted territory." She grimaced and put a hand to her back as she stood. "Would you mind making me one of those coffees of yours while I go have a cigarette?"

"Of course," Sadie answered, on autopilot.

"Don't burn the kitchen down while you're in there," Seth sniped, but his heart wasn't really in it.

Sadie tried to busy herself with hazelnut-infused coffee, but her movements were sluggish, and she finally sat on the stool and buried her head in her hands. It was all too much. Her stomach churned, and she was grateful she hadn't eaten much dinner; otherwise, she was sure it would be making its way up.

She tried not to think about Seth being back.

She tried not to think about the secrets sticking to Gigi like freshly tapped syrup.

She tried not to think about Jake's sweatshirt, still wrapped around her, or his laugh as he'd dunked her in the lake.

And she failed miserably at it all.

The room was spinning, and her eyes, as she stared at the counter, were blurry. It was all too much. Everything was piling up. Her curse. Jake. Seth. Gigi's cancer and the conduit magic. She'd never believed in coincidences; another Revelare rule. Everything had a purpose, a reason. Which meant that something bad, very bad, was coming. And she didn't think she could handle anything else. She needed time. To process. To grieve. But magic, she realized, was useless when it came to that.

A cold hand settled on her shoulder for the briefest second, and then Seth started making the coffee.

"The doctor came in again after you left," he said into the silence. "He guesses she only has a few weeks left." His voice was hollow as a bird's bone.

"I'm working on it," Sadie croaked, surprised to find her voice worked.

"What's that supposed to mean?"

"It means I'm working on something to cure her." *Duh. Double duh,* she thought.

"Don't you think if magic could cure cancer, someone in our extremely strange family would have figured it out by now?"

"You sound like Gigi. But I don't care. It's going to work. It has to."

"You always were bad at accepting reality."

"Maybe I just refuse to give in without a fight," she argued.

"Or maybe you're running away from the truth, like you always do."

"Excuse me? Pardon me? Are you not the one who left? Oh wait, that's right. You *are*." Her voice broke then, and she swiped angrily at the tears that began to fall. Seth looked at her and opened his mouth for a retort, but then he put the coffee down and shocked Sadie by pulling her into a hug.

"You can be such an ass, you know that?" he said into her hair as he held her close.

She was stiff against him at first. Thought about pushing him away. But this was what she'd missed. His ability to be strong for her when she couldn't be for herself. And so finally, she sagged against him, her head on his shoulder as her arms wrapped around him and returned the embrace.

"Ditto," she said, though the word was muffled against his shirt.

"Cheer up, ugly duckling," he said, pulling away with a grin. "We've got this." She shoved him in the chest, and he laughed, and for a moment they were kids again.

"Hand me the cinnamon oil," she said, pointing to the cupboard.

"So, am I the only one who's fucking terrified about this sacrifice thing?" he asked, handing her the bottle. And Sadie could see it then, the cloud of fear in his eyes and the tension in his shoulders.

"No, I think on that point we're fully united."

"But you'll find a loophole, right? Neither one of us is going to die."

"Gigi isn't going to die either," she said, her voice hard, adamant.

Seth said nothing, but doubt was etched in his face like it didn't want to be there.

The kitchen filled with the soothing sounds of the electric teakettle bubbling, the slide of mason jars across the counter, and the tea tin lid being popped off. She poured cold brew, steeped Earl Grey tea, and added a drop of cinnamon oil to the salted cold foam, watching as it frothed.

"Earl Grey helps ease anxiety," she said, turning the hot tea cool with a gentle touch before pouring it in on top of the cold brew. "And the salt keeps you from bewitchment." She added a dollop of foam to each glass.

"Little late for that, I think," he said with a raised eyebrow.

"Never say never."

Finished with the coffees, she handed him one of the mason jars, and taking a deep breath, together they went out to Gigi, the creaking screen door echoing in her bones. She looked at

Seth and somehow, she knew he'd been waiting for her to ask the question.

"Which one of us is it?" Sadie's voice was quiet. She stood unconsciously close to Seth, their arms almost touching. Like if she was close enough to him, he would absorb the answer. She wondered if he was right. If she spent too much of her life living in the shadow of truth.

Gigi sighed and took a drag off her cigarette. Took a drink of her coffee and closed her eyes as she savored the taste.

"I wish I knew," she said. "But what it boils down to is that one of you is safe, and one isn't. The magic of Julian's sacrifice went into one of you, and the other I've been keeping safe by tethering a ritual of protection through me. The magic, it knows where to go. But it sure as hell doesn't tell me."

"It's probably you," Seth said, lighting one of Gigi's cigarettes for himself and closing his eyes as he inhaled. He looked like a modern-day James Dean as he leaned his head back against the porch pillar. "You're the one that loves this shit. Maybe that's why. You've got all this extra power that's been repressed for so long. You're the one just waiting to be set free."

"I love this 'shit' because it's our family legacy. Because Gigi taught me. Because I'm *good* at it."

"Exactly my point." He shrugged, tapping the ash off. "You're good at it. I'm not. I've always—" he started to say, but stopped himself with a look at Gigi. Sadie knew he was going to say he'd always hated it. She could just never understand why. "I've never exactly excelled at it," he amended.

"It probably is me." Her voice grew tighter as her hair burst from the rubber band that held it and coiled into curls.

"Sugar," Gigi warned.

"No, I mean, why not, right? It would explain so much. Why my magic is so damn tetchy all the time." She gestured at herself, and the tenuous peace they'd formed in the kitchen cracked like crème brulée. "I'm the one that's been bleeding her dry ever since. Blame me. You always do. Maybe I'm bad at coming to terms with reality but at least I always take responsibility for my actions, my life, instead of blaming someone else."

Seth looked at her. Controlling his temper as always. Curbing his words, as always. His eyes were cool as they studied her. Almost disappointed. He blew out a perfect ring of smoke before stubbing the cigarette out and announcing,

"I'm going for a walk."

The moment he was gone Sadie collapsed next to Gigi in frustration.

"I'm sorry I never told you," Gigi said without looking at her.

It took a moment for Sadie's brain to track. To understand what her grandmother was apologizing for.

"You saved our lives. There was a price to pay for it, but I'd never, ever begrudge you for it. You know that," she said in a softly remonstrative tone.

"You'll forgive me for killing a man and sending your mother away for almost thirty years." Gigi's gravelly laugh made Sadie smile. "But you won't forgive your brother for trying to find his place in the world for a year because he had the audacity not to tell you about it. You're a Revelare through and through. Now help me to the couch, sugar. And stop borrowing trouble. Everything will work out, I promise."

Wrapping a blanket around her shoulders, Sadie waited until Gigi had fallen asleep, one hand on Abby, who slept on her lap, and the other on Bambi, who rested beside her. The chocolate lab looked at Sadie with a question in his eyes, his head quirking up. Sadie shook her head, and the dog lay back down but kept his eyes on her. Sadie memorized every line of her grandmother lying there on the couch, wanting to imprint every moment on the lining of her heart until it was incorporated into the fabric of her skin. She was shocked how the threat death could make you miss someone before they were even gone.

She wanted to go back to the way things were. She wanted her brother before he'd abandoned her. Gigi before she'd shared her secrets. Jake before he'd broken her heart. Life before the threat of death.

And that's the thought that kept snagging in her brain.

One or more of them was going to have to die.

Unless she could figure out a way to stop it.

Salted Cream Cold Foam Cold Brew with Earl Grey

The bergamot in Earl Grey helps to alleviate anxiety, and the caffeine gives a boost of energy. The salt helps to keep from being bewitched. See, even a simple cup of coffee can serve its purpose.

Ingredients

cold brew coffee
Earl Grey tea, brewed and cooled
skim milk
salt
maple syrup
cinnamon oil (optional)
mason jar

Directions

1. Combine your preferred amount of skim milk with a dash or two of salt, a quick pour of maple syrup (or more if you like it extra sweet), and 1 drop of cinnamon oil, if you're using it, into a mason jar. Shake vigorously for a minute or two.

2. Fill a glass with ice, and then fill halfway with Earl Grey and the rest of the way with cold brew. Top with salted cold cream.

• 7 •

SADIE WOKE LATE THE next morning, having finally fallen asleep around five o'clock, the time she was usually waking up. Seth was nowhere to be seen, and Gigi's PT Cruiser was already gone. She'd left a note telling Sadie to take the day off. There was no stopping that woman, even with cancer. Sadie knew she'd be kicked out of the café if she dared step foot in there, so instead she brewed a cup of tea, rolling her neck from side to side, trying to work out some of the kinks that had taken up residence there.

The quiet of the kitchen worked its magic, settling into her bones. The hum of the refrigerator and the creak of the window over the sink as she opened it to let in fresh air. She cut a few stalks of lavender and lilacs and arranged them in an old milk bottle on the counter. Normalcy, that's what she decided she needed. Some good old-fashioned deep cleaning. Because Gigi was going to be fine. She had to be. Sadie could *make* everything okay. Seth was wrong. It wasn't that she was running away from the truth. She was going to bend the truth to her will. Only a few more days until the herbs would be ready. Her notebook was nearly filled with scribblings. Ideas for spells and stones and talismans in case the first one didn't work. After all, Gigi had done the impossible and saved two lives; why couldn't Sadie save Gigi's?

Sadie's cleaning was interrupted with a visit by a group of ladies from church who were stopping by to check on Gigi, which devolved into a kindhearted interrogation about Seth, which morphed into a cascade of questions about Sadie's love life.

"You've got to get back on that horse, honey," said Maggie, the most outspoken of the group. Her long, curly brown hair was threaded through with gray and bounced as she spoke, her gold-toned eyes sparkling shrewdly. Everything always came back to dogs and horses with Maggie, who had used both to help her through her own bout of cancer a few years back.

"I don't know, Mags. It's been awhile since I've been in the saddle."

"I think they'd be chomping at the bit," Maggie said, grinning now.

"Is that your unbridled opinion?"

"Hay, what do I know?"

"This is all so spur of the moment. Hang on, hang on, I'm just reaching my stride."

Maggie laughed and shook her head.

"Oh, come on, I could do this all day," Sadie said with a smile. "Look, I appreciate everyone's very misplaced concern over my love life, but I better get back to cleaning. Why don't you ladies head to the café to check on Gigi? Tell her I sent you and to give you a coffee on the house." Sadie bustled them out and leaned back against the closed door with a sigh. The grandfather clock let out a series of short chimes that sounded like a laugh.

"Keep it up, buddy, and I'll turn you into firewood," she said, and it immediately stopped its chuffing.

With the well-meaning women gone and her hands chafed from cleaning, she decided to bake. No sooner had she pulled down the ingredients than there was a knock on the back screen door. Jake stood there, gray through the old screen, and her heart, though she told it not to, still flipped inside her chest. He smiled timidly, like he didn't know quite what kind of reaction to expect from her.

"Don't you have a job?" she demanded with a frown. "Seriously, shouldn't you be putting out fires? Rescuing babies and careless women from burning buildings?"

"What do you think I've been doing all morning? A hero's work is never done," he joked. "But actually, I'm burning through sick leave from my station in southern California while I'm trying to get hired on here." He hesitated. "Can I come in?"

"I'm not stopping you," she answered, cutting cold butter into cubes and trying to ignore the fluttering in her chest.

"It's locked," he said, rattling the handle on the screen.

"Oh, draw a line in the salt on the ground," she told him.

He mumbled to himself but did as he was told, and when he tried the door again, it opened with ease.

"What kind of black magic do you cook up in this house, woman?"

"Wouldn't you like to know." She angled her body away from him as she measured pecans into a food processer.

"How's Gigi?" he asked.

"She ordered me to stay home while she went to work, so . . ." Sadie shrugged.

"Of course, she did," he said, laughing. "I don't think a hurricane could stop that woman. What are you making?"

"Did you know the pecan tree can survive for more than a thousand years? Chocolate pecan pie is one of Gigi's classic desserts. So, I thought it would be nice symbolism for her."

"Why, because she's going to live for a thousand years?" he asked with a laugh, popping several whole pecans in his mouth and leaning against the counter—too close for comfort, Sadie thought.

"Don't be ridiculous," she said, shooing him away.

"I've never had pecan pie," he said thoughtfully.

Sadie stilled and settled her glare on him.

"That's blasphemy," she said seriously.

"Listen . . ." He cleared his throat. "I need to—" But he paused, rubbing a hand along the back of his neck.

He had the eyes of someone who had a secret he didn't want to share, and Sadie's skin tightened. She wasn't sure she could handle any more bad news.

The silence thickened until he shook his head.

"Can I help?" he asked.

"Don't you have anything better to do?" she said, breathing a small sigh of relief.

"Yes," he answered candidly. "The sale is going forward with Rock Creek House, but the place is a total disaster. There are a ton of supplies I need to get because as soon as it's mine, there are a dozen projects I need to start. But I'm not in the mood, and I think you could use some good distracting." Sadie rolled her eyes.

"Fine. You can keep me company," she said, squinting as she dashed some cinnamon into the bowl. His steady presence soothed her nerves; she wasn't sure that was such a good thing.

"Need a hand?" Jake asked.

"I don't exactly trust your cooking," she said, forcing lightness into her voice.

"I had to learn how to cook at the station," he told her, sitting down at the breakfast bar and watching her work. "When you're on probation at first, you're basically everyone's servant. You have to cook, clean, be on your best behavior."

"Must've been hard for you."

"Practically impossible," he said, his eyes following her around the kitchen. "This is like watching a cooking show. Aren't you going to narrate for me?"

"No," she said, and surprised herself by laughing. Shaking her momentary mirth off like powdered sugar, she scraped cream cheese into the bowl and began to rub the mixture between her fingers to make a coarse meal. Seemingly unable to sit still, Jake came up behind her, hovering so close it was worse than if he was actually touching her. The back of her neck tingled, and her ears burned hot.

"What's your secret?" he asked.

"Always stir clockwise," she told him, adding the cold butter before spooning the whole mixture into a gallon plastic bag. Her apron strings tightened around her waist the closer he got to her.

"Why?" he asked.

"I don't know. It's just one of the rules. One of the things Revelare women know."

"And what else does a Revelare woman know?" he asked.

"That crescent moons are for making wishes and curses, but a waning moon is for breaking them," she said, trying to scare him off with talk of magic. It didn't work.

"What else?" he asked, leaning over her shoulder to watch as she used a rolling pin to flatten the cold butter into thin flakes.

"River water is for moving on and seawater is for healing. Storm water is for strengthening or, if you're feeling ambitious, curses. Water that falls as lightning strikes will cause disaster sure as a cracked mirror or walking under a ladder."

She didn't know why the words were coming out. She'd never talked to anyone about this, other than Gigi. Seth had never wanted to hear it. Raquel was never in the kitchen long enough. It was like her words needed a home, and Jake was the front door. She blinked rapidly, shaking her head and trying to find her way out of the fog that he produced in her brain anytime he was near her. She reached for the bottle of vinegar.

"I like watching you in the kitchen," he told her.

"Why? I'm a disaster." She frowned, her eyebrows inching together suspiciously, and she eyed the countertop, which was already in disarray.

"True," he said, and laughed, a low rumble resounding in his chest. "But you're so focused. Everything you do has passion in it. I used to tease you about being dramatic, but . . . it suits you."

His words echoed through Sadie, and she leaned into them. Looking straight ahead, her eyes were on level with his chest. They trailed up and caught on the column of his neck. Further up, the strong line of his jaw. She didn't have to look at his eyes to know he was staring at her lips. She felt it. Felt the burning glance seared there until she finally connected their gazes. He took a ragged breath. They weren't even touching, and she could still feel him. The ghost of him pressed against her. Every line matching up. Fitting perfectly. And she knew he remembered it too. Could tell by the way his eyes darkened, the pulse in his throat hammering erratically.

He was going to kiss her. Every warning sign that had been blaring in her head like sirens went quiet. He smelled the same, woodsy and bright, and she wanted to bury her nose in his neck, but he didn't move. His hands curled into fists at his sides, and every line in his body went taut. He wanted it—she knew he did. But he was holding back.

"Jake," she whispered.

"I'm sorry," he said suddenly, taking a step back. "There's something about this kitchen. It . . ." he shook his head as though trying to clear it. His eyes were dreamy as he looked at Sadie. Like she was a promise. Water in the desert he longed to quench his thirst with. But he didn't come closer. "I know you wanted time. And space. I'll go." But he waited a moment before turning. His eyes begged her to tell him not to.

The words formed themselves in her mouth, but her lips wouldn't open. With the space between them, her brain started working again. She had gotten comfortable. And being comfortable with Jake meant her guard would be down. She knew where that would get her. Straight into heartbreak number three. Gigi was worth more than her temporary happiness. Family over everything. That's what it came down to.

She finished the chocolate pecan pies, making sure that none of her tears fell in with the Karo syrup.

The pie was barely in the oven when a lancing pain burned through her chest, as though an invisible hand were squeezing her heart. She gasped for breath and coughed a moment later when the pain vanished. When she could breathe again, the smell of smoke had her running out to the garden.

She shuddered as, before her eyes, all of the plants along the edge of the fence shriveled and died.

They were nearly charred in their blackness, with a sticky, tar-like substance clinging to some of the remnants. A pungent aroma painted itself across her skin, her eyes watering. The ruin stopped just past the fence line, at the thin, towering stalks of dill, planted for the express purpose of keeping out malevolent magic. But they'd sacrificed themselves in the process.

Years ago, Sadie had laughed when Gigi instructed her to plant the herb in abundance. After all, what kind of garden needed that much protection? But as they had planted under the soft, deep light of a Flower Moon, Gigi's eyes had continually flitted over her shoulder, past the gate, to the stars. She'd crushed a moon blossom under her left heel before picking all the herbs for a protection talisman.

"What is it?" Sadie had asked.

"This work," Gigi said in a low rumble, "it's not without its blood, its wounds, its ghosts. Even though it's meant to help, magic makes enemies. Remember that when someone knocks on the back door asking for you to fix some damned thing of theirs. Your decisions will leave you with a past to make you proud or a future that has too much risk to measure. Make sure you know which one you want."

Sadie had scoffed at the time, but the more she tried to help fix the broken things, the more she wondered if she was meddling in places she oughtn't. There always seemed to be an unseen consequence: the heather refused to grow back for weeks; certain animals wouldn't come near her without hissing or growling; fires refused to light for her until she bathed her hands in goat's milk and lavender to purify herself; and sometimes, a viscous scent trailed after her that smelled gray as ashen sorrow.

What kind of blood was on her hands? What sort of ghosts were following her into her future?

She got to her knees and with heavy arms began to rake the detritus into a pile with her hands, her nails instantly turning a sickly black. As she moved across the ground, the first tingling of fear started to trickle through her, her body growing dense with dread.

She could feel a pair of eyes watching her, slippery as eel skin and just as slimy.

With slow movements, she looked up as something caught her eye beyond the fence line. In the dense thicket of trees, she saw a figure looming.

Sadie had seen ghosts before, and this wasn't one. A spirit, maybe. Someone with unfinished business or a grudge to settle.

The longer it stood there without moving, the more her chest tightened, until she could barely breathe. Was this the thing that had tried to wreck her garden?

At the thought, her blood turned hot, fire chasing away the ice, until her fingertips were vibrating with the chaos swirling in her breast. With steel mettle, she picked up a handful of dirt and watched as her anger lit the edges, flames licking across her palm until it burned in her hand and the ash took to the wind like the vengeful light of dying stars. But before the ashes could reach the figure, it vanished without a trace.

Something, or someone, was trying to get in. Without the dill, the garden needed a new defense. Sadie spent the next hour raking the burned foliage, removing every last vestige. She couldn't let Gigi see this. Couldn't add another worry to her plate. Sprinkling the dirt with ground asafetida root and soil from the four corners of the garden, she then burned the whole lot. The smoke was as pungent as bad dreams and bitterness.

When the ashes were cool, she sprinkled them around the perimeter, a protection that would last for a few nights, at least. As she sprinkled asafetida, she saved a little for herself. For if it could protect a garden from unwanted spirits, surely it could keep her from heartbreak.

It was time to take matters into her own hands.

At six o'clock she dragged herself upstairs to shower off the stench of ashes and soot and dirt. By the time she was finished, the scent of fried chicken was snaking its way under the doorjamb. She dressed in loose-fitting jeans, worn thin at the knees, and a cream cable-knit sweater. It was evening, so she allowed herself a look in the mirror. There were half-moons under her eyes, and her olive skin, though still tan from summer, was washed out. She rubbed some blush in. Not for herself, but so Gigi wouldn't worry about her lack of color.

Slipping her feet into her well-worn leather sandals, she walked into the kitchen with heavy footfalls that thundered up to her heart and echoed bad omens. Gigi was there at the stove, watching over an enormous pan filled with fried chicken. The cornflakes were crisping golden as a summer sun, the hot oil filling the air like a promise. There was a pot of peas and corn simmering too. Sadie could still see the large pats of butter slowly melting.

"Hey, toot," Gigi said.

"What's all this?" Sadie asked.

"I just felt like cooking," Gigi told her. "Baked beans are in the oven. And I've got a fruit salad here, but I don't think it's any good. Try it," she demanded, handing Sadie a fork with a strawberry speared on it.

"Exactly how much sugar did you add to the fruit salad?" Sadie asked as she chewed.

"Now don't you pitch a fit. It wasn't edible without it." Gigi leaned against the counter, her hand on her back as a grimace of pain flitted across her face. "I'm fine," she said before Sadie could ask her.

"Mm-hm. And brown sugar in the baked beans?" Sadie asked, trying to keep her tone light but not liking the way Gigi's body was bent over like a shepherd's crook.

"And bacon. It's the only way to make them," her grandmother said resolutely, checking the chicken with a fork. "You know the Revelares were one of the founding families of Poppy Meadows, but my mother, she was a wanderer. Always chasing a man. I grew up here, but we settled in Oklahoma for a time. It was there she dropped me off at the bus station when I was twelve She told me she'd be back, but that if she wasn't, to get on the bus to Chickasha and stay with my granddad."

"By yourself?" Sadie asked horrified. "At twelve?"

"Things were different back then. Well, she didn't come back. She was too busy to care. And I spent the summer with my granddad and hated every damn second. So, he told me that if I could save the money, I could take the bus to Newport Harbor, where my daddy worked in the shipyard. So, I sold my bike for thirty-five dollars, and that was a lot of money in 1942, mind you. Then I went door-to-door selling Cuticure, a miracle salve. If you had an ailment, Cuticure could fix it. When I finally got enough money, I took the first bus to Oakland."

"And? Was it better than Chickasha?"

"Pfft, please. Daddy was seeing some dumb bimbo." She stirred the corn thoughtfully. "I got to his apartment and she answered the door. Made me wait in the hallway until he got home from work. They didn't want me. Nobody ever did. But I stayed anyway. And she'd lock me out while her and daddy had their 'private time,' so I spent every afternoon at the pictures until I had every newsreel and film memorized."

"That sounds horrible." Sadie frowned, absentmindedly eating the fruit salad with her fingertips and licking the sugar from her thumbs.

"Every Revelare leaves, but they always come back. That's the saying. But my mother didn't. I did. I always knew this was where I was supposed to be. But listen to me, blabbering on like an old fool. I just wanted you to know. Nobody ever wanted me except for your grandad. At least that's what it felt like to a short, painfully shy kid like me with my huge nose and bullfrog voice. But I always wanted you and your brother. From the second I laid eyes on you, I knew you were meant to be mine. I hope you know that. I know it's not good enough. I know I'm not your mother," she said in a businesslike tone, taking the fried chicken from the pan and transferring it to the paper towels, waiting on the counter, to siphon off the excess grease.

"Gigi," Sadie said in a voice soft as challah dough. But Gigi clucked her tongue. She never was one to get emotional. "Just so you know, your love has always been more than enough."

"For you, maybe. But not for that brother of yours. And that's okay. I just wanted you to know."

Sadie didn't like the way Gigi was telling stories like she needed someone to hear them. It sent a shiver down her spine much the same way sucking a lemon or getting a paper cut did.

Seth came in just as Gigi put the last piece of chicken on a paper towel.

"It's time you two start being civil to each other before I knock your heads together in the hope of knocking sense into you both. I'm going out to have a cigarette. You two eat. And talk."

"Gigi," Sadie started but was cut off.

"Do this for me. We'll talk more later, I promise." And Sadie thought how amazing it was that Gigi could smile while holding such command in her voice.

She and Seth stared at each other. Her fingers twitched at her side. How could you want to hug and throttle someone at the same time? Sibling love was no joke.

"I feel weirdly like we've been set up on some kind of twisted blind date," Seth said, looking at the platters of food. A laugh bubbled out of Sadie. She felt like she was going insane. Like nothing fit together. Like all the pieces of who she thought she was were unraveling at the seam, and she couldn't quite figure out how to keep them together.

"What are we going to do?" she asked her brother.

Seth looked at her like she really had gone mad.

"We're going to eat," he said, as if it was the most obvious thing in the world. "Because if we don't, Gigi will lock us in here like it's the end of fucking days, and I swear to God but that woman actually terrifies me."

Gigi had already put a basket of garlic and parsley biscuits on the table. Seth grabbed one and tore into it as he tossed another to Sadie. She took a bite and as she chewed, she rolled her eyes. Her grandmother had put a dash of white mustard powder in the dough, which was meant to help the eater get things off their chest and deal with challenges.

"Sit down—I'll make your plate." She sighed, wiping her tears and washing her hands with lemon verbena soap. "We better get this over with."

When she had two heaping piles of food, they sat down, and both looked at their plates as if they held some kind of answer. Before taking a bite, Seth cleared his throat.

"She gave me a very specific set of rules and instructions while we were in the hospital." He opened the notes on his phone.

"We're not allowed to mope about, and we're not allowed to treat her like she's dying."

"Even though she is," Sadie said, her voice granite hard.

"Even though she is," Seth echoed. "We're absolutely not allowed to tell anyone. That was her first rule. And we can't try to convince her to take treatment, and we have to be nice to each other. Hey, it's in the notes," he said when Sadie rolled her eyes again. "And when she gets bad, if she starts to get dementia or whatever, we're supposed to drop her off at the hospital and leave her there."

"Like that's going to happen," Sadie snorted.

"I know, I'm just telling you what she said. Oh, and you're supposed to re-salt the perimeter every night, whatever the hell that means."

Sadie nodded, even though her world was fracturing. She could do this. She would do whatever Gigi wanted, even if it was insane. Her greatest fear was coming to pass, and she thought she would shrivel up, curl into a ball, and weep until she submerged herself in a river of her own tears. But to her surprise, a resolute calm was slowly working its way through her system, burning down her throat like elderflower cordial. She would take care of everything.

"Okay, thanks," Sadie said, nodding slowly. "I'll take it from here. You don't have to worry about anything."

"What do you mean?" Seth asked, genuinely confused.

"I mean"—Sadie waved an airy hand—"you do what you do, and I'll do what I do. You're busy, you have a life, you were—"

"Would you quit pushing me away?" he cut in.

"I thought that's what you'd want," she said, her brows pulling down in the middle. "I figured I'd be doing you a favor."

"God, for being my twin, you really don't get it." And just like that, the tenuous peace they'd been forming snapped like peanut brittle. "Do you even know why I left? Because I couldn't take living in your goddamn shadow anymore. I was drowning in magic that I had nothing to do with."

"You never wanted it anyway!" she argued. "All you cared about was being normal, separating yourself from us, living your own life."

"Yeah, and that's worked out really well for me, hasn't it?" He shook his head like she had no idea about anything.

"Oh, I'm sorry Gigi's dying and that you have to actually involve yourself in our lives. But please, don't do us any favors." She wanted to cross her arms but knew it would look petulant.

"Listen, we can't do this. It's one of Gigi's rules. Can you please just believe me when I say I'm doing the best I can? I was a dick, okay? I shouldn't have left like that. I should've told you. I should've answered your calls. But I couldn't. I was in a black hole. It's like I have this demon living inside me that dictates when the darkness comes, and I can't stop it. Some days it's quiet, and I wake up and think I can do it, I can make it through the day. But other days I'm just suffocating, and I hate not being in control like that. So yeah, I was a dick. And I'm sorry."

Sadie stared at her brother. He'd never spoken like that before. Tendrils of guilt started to hook into her heart. What kind of twin was she? What kind of sister that she didn't even know, couldn't even guess that he was going through any of that?

"Why haven't you gotten help?" she asked quietly.

"Like a therapist?" He laughed without humor. "How do you think that would go? 'Hey, shrink. My magic is giving me depression and anxiety.' Yeah, I don't think so."

"But look at Raquel. Her bipolar disorder has gotten so much better. It's manageable now because she's on the right meds. She sees a psychiatrist and a therapist."

"Yeah, and I'm really fucking proud of her for that. It's not that I don't believe in therapy, I just don't believe in it for me. Our magic, it messes everything up. We're not normal."

"All I ever wanted was for you to be proud of being a Revelare," she said. "I never understood why you tried to run away from it. I've never known myself apart from you. And I didn't—I don't like it. I missed you," she confessed. "I blamed myself for your leaving. I thought if I'd tried to help you with your magic more, or if I'd tried to be more normal, maybe you'd have stayed."

"Sadie." He was shaking his head. "Listen, I was a selfish dick. I can't take it back. You've always known who you were, and even while I was gone, you found more of yourself apart from me. I was just trying to live up to that in some small way."

"But you were trying to do it on your own. And that's what family is for. You'd just never let us help you. You've always wanted to blame the magic, the family name, instead of just accepting that it's what makes us different. Instead of understanding that *that's* why it's so important for us to stay together."

"Maybe I wanted to see who I could be apart from all that." He shrugged coldly.

"As always, you're missing the point," she said, frustration making her hair curl. "You never told me about your magic or your curse. But I'm incapable of keeping anything from you, so I told you the minute after the ceremony was over. Remember? A curse of four heartbreaks? Jake was the first. You were the second."

Sadie couldn't tell if that was a revelation to him. They were both so good at the game of keeping emotion from their face that sometimes it was hard to remember it was just a defense mechanism. She knew how easy it was to shut out the people you loved the most, needed the most. Because maybe, if you didn't need them so much, it wouldn't hurt as much when they weren't there for you. She loved him the most, and so he had the most power over her.

"I *needed* to leave. Don't you get it? I was drowning here. You think it's healthy that I'm the only one you had?"

"No, I think that's the way family is supposed to work, you idiot. Now I'm two heartbreaks away from completely losing my magic altogether. And I need it now more than ever."

"God forbid you lose the thing that's actually the most important to you." He laughed derisively. "That's what this is really all about, isn't it? You're pissed I left, but you're even more pissed that you're one step closer to losing the most precious thing you have because you're so afraid of your goddamn curse coming true, and you love your magic more than you let yourself love people."

"Fuck you," Sadie spat, her fingertips growing warm, itching to release some of the anger flooding through her. The dishes rattled in the cupboard and the teakettle on the stove blew a jet of steam.

"There it is." He folded his arms and leaned back in his chair. Like he'd just been waiting for her to snap. A small smile played around his mouth, tugging at the corners. "Say whatever you want to me now. Get it all out. Feel however you want. But Gigi doesn't want us arguing. So I'll be as civil as possible until this is all over. And you will be too."

"Did you happen to forget about our new little family secret we just learned? One of our lives is in the free and clear, and the other is doomed to God knows what. And how are we supposed to fix that? Huh? If we can't even have a civil dinner together when Gigi is dying."

"We'll—" he started, but Sadie cut him off.

"I swear on all that's holy, if you say, 'cross that bridge when we come to it,' I will lose my ever-loving mind."

Seth actually laughed, and it stopped Sadie in her tracks.

"What," she demanded.

"I almost forgot how annoying it was to have a twin."

"Lucky you," she said.

"Are you done yelling at me? Can we eat now?" he asked, not waiting for an answer, but pulling his plate toward him.

Something happened in those few moments of silence that followed. A sliver of peace returned to Sadie. Maybe it was finally telling him how she felt. Maybe it was Gigi's biscuits at work. Either way, she hated the push and pull of the emotions eating at her. Each moment was different from the next. One second, she was calm and in control, and the next she wanted to scream.

"Nothing can ever go back the way it was," she said.

"Would you honestly want it to?"

And she didn't have an answer. So instead she asked, "Did you at least find what you were looking for? When you left?"

Seth looked at her thoughtfully but was silent as he began to clean his plate. Sadie followed suit, taking a bite of chicken. And every bite seemed to say that it was all going to be okay.

"I found something," he said finally. "I'm just not sure exactly what it is."

"Was it worth it?" she asked quietly, wondering if she really wanted to know the answer.

"As mad as you are, you know I would never do anything to hurt you on purpose," he said pointedly, almost as a challenge, a reminder. "I do actually love you."

"I know, but sometimes it's nice to hear it."

"Don't get used to it." And after a pause he added, "You always knew I was going to come back, right?"

"If I knew you were going to come back, I don't think it would have broken my heart. When you're as close as we are, and something comes that far out of left field, everything you thought you knew up until that point goes up in smoke. You start questioning everything. Thinking maybe you built it all up in your head." She wondered if she was talking about her brother or Jake, or both.

"Shit, Sadie." He sighed and ran a hand through his hair. "I guess I just thought you knew. Or that you'd understand, at least."

"I'm starting to," she admitted.

"Look, you've always been the strong one. I admit that, but . . ."

"I'm not," Sadie countered. "I feel like everything is going to crumble any second."

"But you keep going. That's what I mean. No matter what, you never give up. I respect the hell out of that."

"Maybe it's just stupidity," she said, staring at the biscuit in her hand.

"It's not."

"If I'm strong at all, you know why I am. We're only as strong as the people we love. And the ones that love us. Nothing else matters."

"Even magic?" he asked archly, raising an eyebrow.

"Magic comes from family."

"I know I said you don't accept reality, and I meant it. But it's also kind of a compliment, you know? Like the way you see the world is so forceful that reality has to fall in line or get the shit kicked out of it. I wish I had some of that."

"You have more than you think."

"This is the part where you apologize for saying I blame my problems on everyone else."

Sadie narrowed her eyes at him, wondering if he'd apologized just to get one in return, but he laughed.

"Jesus, Sade, it was a joke. Lighten up." But there was an undercurrent to the way he said it, and she realized what it was in an instant.

"Sometimes it's hard to own our shit," she said slowly. "And I didn't mean to generalize." She chose her words carefully. "You don't do it all the time. Just with certain things. But we all have our issues we're working through, and more than anything else, I'm sorry that saying it that way hurt your feelings."

Seth looked down at the table and then idly twirled the butter knife between his fingers, like he was doing a magic trick. He cleared his throat.

"Thanks."

"Of course. We may fight like idiots, but I'd never, ever want to hurt you intentionally either. Irritate the crap out of you? Yeah."

"Push my buttons?"

"Duh!" She laughed. "You were the one who taught it to me as an art form."

"Look at us, apologizing and shit, like adults. Hey, maybe we're gonna make it after all."

"Of course, we are," Sadie responded without hesitation. "And I really do think you should, you know, maybe try therapy. You obviously don't have to talk about magic. But Seth, if you're battling this—these demons and depression and anxiety—you need the tools to deal with it."

"I'll think about it," he promised.

Seth left for a walk after they ate, stopping to say goodbye to Gigi while Sadie did the dishes. At least some things would never change.

"Are you two done acting like fools?" Gigi asked as Sadie sat on the couch next to her, where she was watching an ancient rerun of *Bonanza*.

"Probably not." Sadie sighed. "But we're going to try and be civil to each other only because we both love you so much." She smiled tiredly.

"I know you're not going to like what's coming. You've never been one for change, sugar. But I believe in you. We'll all get through this together. And I mean *all* of us," she added sternly. "I know you've already forgiven that brother of yours, you're just making him work for it now. And I don't blame you for it. But don't be too stubborn, like me. All it gets you is regret," she said.

If she could have her way, Sadie would have woven a garland of four-leaf clovers and worn them around her neck. She would have swallowed essence of nightshade if only she could close off the world around her and sleep in a silence where bad news would knock but never get in. Part of her still wanted to wake up tomorrow and believe that this was all a lie. That she could go on with her routine as she had done for years. But life had gotten its roots into her and she was growing, one way or another. So instead of covering her ears with a pillow the way she wanted to, she nodded.

"I promise I'll do my best." She swallowed hard and pinched her eyes shut.

"That's my girl," Gigi smiled, taking Sadie's hand in her own and squeezing it. "Now, there's a mixing bowl in the cupboard above the microwave. Get it and sprinkle what's in it around the perimeter of the house and garden," Gigi said.

"Salt and pennyroyal oil," Sadie said, and Gigi nodded.

"Something wicked is on the wing. It's trying to get in, and I aim to stop it. At least for a little while longer."

Sadie wanted to swat the omen off the way you'd smack a flea, but it stuck to her skin like flypaper. She looked out the window, and as she watched, right at the tree line, a mist creeped along the ground, spreading like snow and sending an icy chill through Sadie's heart.

Fog on a clear night meant someone was waiting for death.

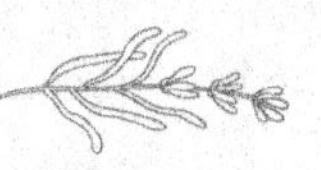

The next morning, Sadie quietly opened Gigi's door, peering in and staring at her sleeping form, tiny under the covers. One more day and the herbs would be ready. With a soft click that echoed through her heart, she closed the door and went for a run.

Sadie hated running. Her own form of punishment. But it was one of the only ways to get the anxiety out. Every strike of her foot against the pavement brought another worried thought.

Jake.

Gigi.

Seth.

She was sprinting without meaning to now.

My damn *curse. All I want. Is a simple. Relationship.*

All I want. Is. Love.

She let the thoughts flow through her, burn their way to the soles of her feet, where her shoes left black imprints on the sidewalk. Fold, fold, fold. Tuck them all away. She felt like Elsa. *Control it. Conceal. Don't feel.*

The stitch in her side forced her to stop. Her calves cramping, she doubled over with her hands on her knees. Slowing to a jog, she reached the café where Gail was already serving customers. When Sadie walked in, she silently pointed to a tall glass of lemon and cucumber water.

"Saw you comin' from down the street," Gail said. "I never seen someone runnin' with a scowl on their face." She laughed, and despite everything, the sound made Sadie smile as she tied an apron around her waist.

"I'm just going to slip in the back and pull some things out to thaw."

Now that she'd caught her breath, she let the comfort of the café close in around her. Bill was sitting by the window, with a cup of coffee and a pomegranate éclair.

"How's your grandmother?" he asked the second he saw her.

"She's well, Bill. Thank you." She hated the dark circles under his eyes and the way his concern sat on his skin like a layer of dust.

"I was going to send flowers." He cleared his throat. "But I thought she'd hate that. I know she doesn't like people fussing."

"She would absolutely hate it." Sadie smiled. "And you should absolutely send them. Better yet, drop them off yourself. She likes sunflowers."

His smile lit up his eyes.

The old ladies in their neon joggers were gossiping at a table in the middle. Lavender waved from a corner table, and Lace beckoned her over. As Sadie got closer, she saw that Lavender only had one earring in, and mismatched socks with her tan leather ankle boots. She was all soft curves and dreamy colors. Lace, meanwhile, was military precision. Her black bangs were ruler straight, and her Doc Martens polished to a high shine.

"Have you seen anything?" Lace asked her as Sadie got closer.

"You don't have to answer that," Lavender said to Sadie before frowning at her sister.

"Something is off, and I'm trying to figure out if it has to do with the Grand Revel or with"—she paused, eyes squinting at Sadie like she was trying to pierce through the veil—"whatever is going on with the Revelare family," she finished.

"The Grand Revel isn't for five months" Sadie said with surprise. And honestly, she had completely forgotten about the party that was set to take place at Cavendish Inn. Every seven years, the seven founding families of Poppy Meadows got together for a weeklong celebration, complete with a masquerade, tasks, riddles, and games.

"Now look what you've done." Lavender frowned. "You've upset her. Leave her alone. She's got enough going on."

"We're—I'm—I've got everything under control," Sadie said. The sisters didn't look convinced.

The tinkling chime over the door rang, and Sadie knew, instantly and without turning around, who had just walked in.

"Stars," Lavender whispered with a knowing smile. "They're in your eyes."

Sadie narrowed said eyes just as Jake called her name. She turned toward him like a moth to a flame.

"I'm just grabbing some stuff for the guys at the station," he said with a wary smile as his gaze darted between the three women.

"I recommend the honey lemon pound cake," Sadie said, turning on her heel and heading toward the kitchen.

"Sade, wait," he said, following her through the metal double doors.

"You can't be in here!" She tried pushing him back through, but it was like shoving a boulder, and his skin, even through the fabric of his uniform shirt, burned her fingers. She felt her hair begin to curl and the apron strings pull tighter around her waist like it wanted to show off her figure. Traitors, all.

"I just wanted to see how you're doing."

"Never been better," she answered, giving up on getting him out of the kitchen and instead pulling the container of basil-lime sugar cookie dough out of the fridge and setting it on the counter in a blur of motion.

"Okay, well . . ." he said as she silently washed her hands and studiously ignored him.

She was back at the fridge, pulling out apricot lavender shortbread dough. Turning the ovens on, pulling down baking trays and cookie cutters and a rolling pin that looked like it could be used as a weapon. And all the while, his eyes tracked her. She felt them leaving trails of stardust all over her skin.

"Right." He cleared his throat. "I'll just go."

"Jake," she said just as he reached for the doors, "thank you. I just—I need to do this. It clears my head."

He nodded.

"I'll be at the station if you need anything, okay?"

"Take the guys a box of the pomegranate éclairs too. On the house."

Sadie spent the next few hours getting lost in the rhythm of rolling, cutting, and stirring. The slide of baking trays going into the oven and the clatter of mixing bowls echoed around the kitchen like children playing tag. Every so often she'd go out and refill coffees or ring someone up while Gail restocked the pastry case. Juliana Daunton came in, and despite herself, Sadie felt her mouth pull into a smile.

"Sadie, honey," she said, striding toward the counter like a woman on a mission, "this is my second time in here today. Those mini lime–poppy seed Bundt cakes are better than sex," she said, lowering her tenor voice to a whisper. "And trust me, I've had some good sex." She winked, and Sadie couldn't help the blush that stained her cheeks like cherry juice.

"Oh well, that's . . ." *Probably more info than I needed,* Sadie thought. ". . . good," she finished lamely.

"I mean it. The card said they'd give you a kick of energy, but my God, I feel like I could dance a dozen rumbas." Juliana moved her feet in a little dance. "I've got more oomph than the kids today." Ms. Daunton ran the town's gymnastic program, and Sadie immediately felt responsible for whatever chaos went on in her classes today. "Now, you're going to share the recipe with us, aren't you, honey? It's simply not fair to deprive us of this goodness."

Sadie thought of the cookbook. Of Gigi telling her to find her fulfillment.

"I might," Sadie said, "but you know—"

"Sadie," a stern voice cut her off as the bell chimed over the front door, and Sara Watanabe steamrolled into the shop.

"I am out of bells. I have called and called, and you do not answer. I need bells, and I also need more jars of the infused honey."

"I'm sorry, Mrs. Watanabe," Sadie said, sighing internally. "Things have been a little crazy."

"That is no excuse, young lady. You run a business? This is part of business. Now, tell me how your grandmother is doing." Mrs. Watanabe's voice was stern but Sadie took no offense, it was just the woman's nature.

"Yes, how is that darling woman?" Ms. Daunton added.

Mrs. Watanabe glared at Ms. Daunton like she'd stolen her question at gunpoint.

"She's doing well," Sadie said, and even though it tasted like a lie, it sounded like the truth.

"Fine, fine," Ms. Watanabe said. "I will take a pomegranate éclair to go."

"Oh honey, you should try the lime–poppy seed Bundt cake. It's like an orgasm in your mouth."

Mrs. Watanabe's mouth gaped like a fish's, and Sadie had to stifle a laugh.

"I'm telling you," Ms. Daunton went on. "It's a shame Sadie won't share the recipe."

"Yes, I—I have often thought Sadie should offer a baking class," Mrs. Watanabe said, trying to gather herself after the orgasm comment.

"You have?" Sadie asked in astonishment.

"It would be good for business."

"What would be good for business?" Jimmy Wharton asked, coming up to the counter for a refill on his coffee. Sadie took it on autopilot and poured the specialty coffee she ordered for the shop. It had notes of blueberry and honey that gave it a clean, creamy flavor profile, and it also happened to be highly addictive.

"It is not good to butt in on other people's conversations," Mrs. Watanabe said with a frown.

"Oh, honey," Ms. Daunton said, "nobody can have a private conversation in this town. We were saying how Sadie should offer cooking classes. Or at the very least, share her recipes," she added to Jimmy.

"Sherry would love that," Jimmy said, speaking of his wife. "You could do couples classes. Like for date night."

"I'll think about it," Sadie said. The excitement bubbling in her chest felt like champagne bubbles, light and airy and making her float just a little.

"Don't forget. Bells and honey."

"Yes, Mrs. Watanabe," Sadie said, handing her a container with a pomegranate éclair and a Bundt cake for good measure. Not that the woman needed any extra energy. She was a force to be reckoned with.

Sadie went back to the kitchen, humming to herself and working on projects until she felt something calling her home. It wasn't an urgent pull, but there was a pleasant sort of siren song that resonated in her bones. She checked in with Gail, who shooed her out with a kiss on the cheek, and then started a slow walk back home.

The sky darkened, and the wind whipped through her jacket, but the warmth of the pull kept her from shivering. She was back near the house when the soles of her feet grew warm, and she laughed, the anxious thoughts finally ebbing away. There, in the middle of the empty street, with her arms outstretched and mouth open, stood her Aunt Tava, barely over five feet tall, with wide hips and short arms. With a squeal of delight, Sadie rushed over to her.

"I was waiting for you!" Aunt Tava said in a high, girlish voice. "Darling, beautiful girl, you." She enveloped Sadie in a brown-sugar-and-vanilla-scented hug before resuming her position. Her blue hair glinted nearly neon in the wild weather. There were stars painted on her cheeks, and her tiered skirt shone with glitter like technicolor stars.

"What are you doing!" Sadie demanded, eyes wide, shaking her head in disbelief.

"About to rain."

"But what are you doing *here*? In Poppy Meadows?"

"I had to travel the farthest, so I got here first. The others are coming."

"What others?" Sadie exclaimed.

"Everybody leaves, but we always come back."

"Auntie Tava," Sadie said, equally frustrated and endeared by her aunt's ability to speak only in riddles when it suited her, "I haven't seen you in years. Does Gigi know you're here?"

"Here it comes," Aunt Tava whispered.

"Here what—"

"Shh," her aunt interrupted. "The first drops of September are sacred. Catch them on your tongue, and you'll be granted your truest heart's desire. Even if you don't know what it is yet."

Sadie smiled and when, a few moments later, Aunt Tava snapped her fingers, she obediently assumed the same position. Arms out, mouth open. And sure enough. She felt a drop of rain on her arm. And then her shoulder.

It started slow. But when the first drop hit her tongue, it was sweet and earthy, like the sky was waking up. Sadie smiled.

A car drove around them and honked. Aunt Tava completely ignored it.

"Love is always the answer," Aunt Tava whispered as the smell of warm, wet pavement worked its own kind of magic. "But it'll never come the way you are. Rigid, silly girl. Dream a little. Didn't you see the flood over the bridge the other day?"

"How did you know about that? Are you who the flood brought back?"

"The flood brings everyone back, my sweet, darling niece. And speaking of my sweet, darling niece, where's my sweet, darling nephew?" she asked as their clothes started to soak through.

"Can't we get out of the rain now?" Sadie asked, ignoring her aunt's question.

"Almost."

Before the word was fully out of her mouth, a bolt of lightning so bright it was nearly purple flashed across the sky. It forked out, seeming to cover the entire neighborhood. And by the time it died down, the rain had stopped.

"There we are!" Aunt Tava clapped her hands together. "You know, baby, family is everything. Sometimes they're awful. And you want nothing more than to cut them out of your life like cancer, but you can't. Because that kind of loyalty, that kind of dedication, it won't wash out in the water. It's in the blood."

"Screw the blood." Sadie sighed, wringing water out of her sweater.

"What's good is never easy. Now, let's go get ourselves a cup of honeysuckle tea." She patted her pocket secretively, and Sadie's spirits lifted. Aunt Tava's honeysuckle tea was legendary and could make even the darkest day like noon in summer.

"Gigi know you're here?" Sadie asked again as they walked the rest of the way to the house.

"Doesn't she always?"

"But did you tell her?" Sadie laughed. "You know, pick up the phone like a normal person?"

"Don't need to. Like telling a bird it's going to rain. They just know. See?" She gestured to the house.

Sadie saw Gigi's sparkling maroon PT Cruiser back in the driveway, but that wasn't what caught her eye. Though it would appear white to any passerby, Revelare eyes knew that the smoke billowing out of the chimney was a soft lavender color, a sign that Gigi had sprinkled the wood with dried mayflower. A welcome for unexpected guests. Abby and Bambi were both at the window, barking, tails wagging, and Sadie shook her head.

"Told you." Aunt Tava smiled. "Mothers always know."

Fried Chicken

Just because it's damn good. Your hands will get messy, your clothes will smell like grease, and it'll all be worth it. The only magic here is good food.

Ingredients

5 lb. bag of boneless, skinless chicken breasts (thawed)
1 large egg
¼ c. buttermilk (half and half or milk will also work)
2 c. cornflakes (crushed)
2 c. flour
⅔ teaspoon salt
1 tsp. pepper
½ tsp. basil
⅓ teaspoon oregano
4 tsp. paprika
2 tsp. garlic salt
½ tsp. thyme
peanut oil (vegetable oil will also work, but peanut is better)

Directions

1. Whisk together egg and milk, and set aside. Put cornflakes in a plastic bag and crush lightly with your fist. Add flour salt, pepper, and herbs. Shake up, then dump into a bowl.

2. Heat a generous helping of oil in a large skillet. While it heats, sprinkle the chicken breast with more salt and pepper.

3. Dredge a piece of chicken in the egg mixture, then transfer to cornflake bowl, press down to help coating adhere, then flip and do the same to the other side. Repeat for the rest of the pieces, and then place in the hot oil.

4. Fry chicken until golden, turning it only once so you don't make it tough, about five to six minutes, depending on the thickness of the breast. Drain on paper towels.

♦ 8 ♦

"You little shit ass," Gigi's voice called as soon as they were through the front door. Abby and Bambi were going wild, jumping all over Aunt Tava until she picked up the one and pet the other. The grandfather clock was chiming its hello, and the flames in the fireplace jumped dangerously high. Wherever Sadie's aunt Tava went, a joyful pandemonium followed.

"Mother!" Aunt Tava feigned shock. "Such language!"

"Get over here." Gigi laughed reluctantly as she hugged her oldest daughter. "You didn't need to come."

"That's just utter nonsense now, isn't it, you precious little pup?" she asked in her high, girlish voice, speaking to Abby instead of her mother. "And speaking of nonsense!" She walked over to the fire, reached into her pocket, and threw something into the flames that turned them bright turquoise for a brief moment. A second later the scent of cedarwood curled in the air, and Sadie's clothes were dry before she even realized she wasn't shivering anymore.

"Ready for the chaos, my darling niece?" she asked with a grin. "And by the way, while I was on Main Street, window shopping at the antiques shop, I ran into the *most* delightful firefighter. Can you say yummy! I started chatting him up, and when he found out I was a Revelare, he said he knew you both, so I invited him to dinner."

"You didn't," Sadie groaned.

Of course, she had. And there was no such thing as coincidences when it came to her family.

"Who on earth wouldn't want to stare at that god of a man across the dinner table?" Aunt Tava demanded, as man crazy as ever. "And speaking of handsome men, you haven't told me where that brother of yours is."

"Probably off shaking hands and kissing babies," Sadie muttered. But even as she said the words, she realized how different he was since he'd been back. Less charm, more solemnity. She wouldn't go so far as to call it brooding, but he'd lost that happy-go-lucky edge he'd always carried around with him like a talisman.

"Oh pshaw, you still haven't forgiven him for leaving yet? Dear God, if I'd done something like that, Florence would have celebrated my absence, and here you are whining that he's back. But don't you worry, your head and heart will be too full soon enough."

"What does that mean?" Sadie demanded.

"Tava," Gigi said warningly.

"Where's that little firecracker Raquel?" Tava asked, ignoring them both. "Ah!" She held up a finger, and a moment later there was a knock at the door. "There she is."

Raquel barged in just as she spoke.

"Tava!"

"There she is!" Tava's tiered skirt rustled like whispered secrets as she hugged Raquel.

"I assume you're the one responsible for the glitter-dusted note demanding my presence?" Raquel laughed. "It's the last day before break, so I let the kids out after lunch. Now, what's going on in this madhouse?"

"Oh, family reunion." Tava shrugged nonchalantly, but there was a glimmer of mischief in her eyes, and a second later she burst out laughing. The air turned sweet like sparkle-dusted rainbow cotton candy, to match Tava's tiered skirt. If Sadie stuck out her tongue, she swore she'd be able to taste the sugar granules.

"What!" Sadie demanded.

At the same time Gigi said, "I knew it. You little shit ass."

"Don't blame me!" Tava squealed.

"Who should I blame then?" Gigi insisted.

"I hate to state the obvious here," came Seth's voice from the doorway, making Sadie jump. "But I'd probably blame magic. I mean, isn't that usually the explanation for things around here?" He smiled, and Sadie remembered one of the reasons she loved her stupid brother so much. No matter what was happening, no matter the nonsense or heartache or confusion, he always made everything better. Just by being there.

"My darling, handsome nephew!" Tava cried, practically cooing in delight.

"Aunt Tava. I'm never quite sure if you're actually human or part fairy." Seth hugged his aunt and kissed the top of her head. "Honestly, who knows with this family." He hugged Gigi and kissed her next. As though he'd been gone weeks instead of hours. "Sister," he said. She made a noise halfway between disgust and annoyance as he kissed the side of her forehead, though in reality she loved it. "Quel," he added, slipping an arm around Raquel's shoulders in a half hug but then leaving it there.

A knock on the front door interrupted Sadie's thoughts, and her heart stuttered, wondering if it was already *him*. It was too early. Tava had said dinner. Her hands flew to smooth her hair, but then she heard the bright, shrill voice of her Aunt Kay. Instantly, she and Seth locked eyes in unspoken trepidation and amusement. The house's lights dimmed, and even the fire died down, as though it was trying to hide.

"Um, hellooooo!" Aunt Kay called in annoyance. "Is there a reason this damn door is locked?" She rattled the handle violently until Sadie opened it. It hadn't been locked—just the house's way of playing its own prank. "Baby girl!" Aunt Kay cried. Her hands were full of gift bags and a potted ivy plant. She towered above Sadie, her long legs made longer by the over-the-knee boots she wore, with six-inch-high heels. Her hair was piled in a messy bun on top of her head, and her wrists jangled with what seemed like a whole jewelry store as she pulled Sadie into a bone-crushing hug, her cheek resting on top of Sadie's head. When she finally pulled back, tears were streaming down her cheeks, and the ivy she was holding had grown by a foot. “My baby,” she whispered quietly, cupping Sadie’s cheek with the palm of her hand. Her acrylic nails were long and Ferrari red, and the kimono she wore swayed about her slender frame like a kite in the wind. She smelled like new shoes fresh out of the box, and the scent took over Tava’s sweet cotton candy scent.

“Mommy!” she called next. As she pushed through the front door, all the lights in the house flickered as though wincing at the high-pitched voice. “Mommy,” she said again as they entered the kitchen. She started crying in earnest when she saw Gigi. The grandfather clock went off again, but this time it sounded like a cry for help. If Tava was joyful pandemonium, Kay was pure chaos in the kind of way that left you breathless.

“Now, now,” Gigi said, trying and failing to hide her irritation. “No need to make such a big fuss.” She hugged her second-oldest daughter and patted her cheek before going back to food prepping. Because family meant food, there was simply no way around it. “You all scoot on out of here. You’re like a bunch of chickens with your heads cut off, and I know the yapping will never stop now.”

“What can I do?” Aunt Kay asked, hovering around the kitchen, trying to look helpful but really just attempting to steal the tomatoes that Gigi was cutting up.

“Stop that!” Gigi slapped her hand away.

“What beautiful sunflowers,” Sadie noted, nodding to the bouquet in the windowsill over the sink.

“Humph,” Gigi said, but there was a slight pink to her cheeks that made Sadie smile.

Though the house liked to tease her, Aunt Kay’s presence brightened the room. Her magic lay in making everyone around her feel loved. A back scratch from her nails felt better than a ninety-minute massage because it was infused with focused intention and love. A compliment from Kay made you believe it instead of brushing it off or awkwardly accepting it, as women were wont to do.

Tava’s magic was more mischievous. Sadie could see it floating around her in streams of rainbow glitter. It was the kind of magic that made you do things you normally wouldn't, that made you feel like anything was possible. Very simply, it was magic of the imagination, the type that turned the ordinary into the extraordinary. A tent of blankets turned into a fairy den; a typical outfit suddenly gave you red-carpet confidence; and teas turned into curious elixirs that you would remember long after the cup was empty.

Sadie laughed, her heart bubbling in her chest like sweet soda water. The rain had stopped, and the afternoon sun was sliding through the windows, the golden light refracting against the water droplets left on the panes and casting little rainbows across the counter. Seth bumped her shoulder in a friendly way as he walked to the living room.

The day wore on, and they made up the guest room and blew up air mattresses.

"We're going to need more coffee," Gigi said as Tava poured the last cup.

The hubbub in the house continued to grow as Sadie navigated around Aunt Kay and Tava. When she went to help Gigi with folding the freshly washed blankets, Tava was already there. When she went to sit on her stool at the counter, Kay was there, drinking an iced coffee. She felt a little lost in her own home.

As evening approached, Sadie gave a sigh of relief. The kitchen, at least, would be safe.

"What are we making?" Sadie asked Gigi when finally it was just the two of them in there. Gigi took a deep breath, stopped chopping the tomatoes, and leaned against the counter.

"Lasagna and garlic bread with salad," she said in a matter-of-fact tone, as if there was anything else to possibly serve at an impromptu family reunion. "And I wish you all would stop making such a damn fuss." She used the back of her hand to wipe her brow.

"Not likely," Sadie answered, pulling down the pomegranate-infused balsamic vinegar and locally made olive oil, to mix a dressing for the salad. She added a sprinkling of herbs de Provence, a dash of mustard, and a dollop of orange honey.

"Hand me the butter, would you?" Gigi asked, setting out slices of sourdough on a baking tray.

As Sadie pulled it out of the fridge, it softened in her hands.

"Sorry," she said, sighing.

"What is it, sugar?"

"I don't—I mean—just getting used to everyone being here I guess. It's a lot of noise. Change. You know." She shrugged.

"You're more set in your ways than I am," Gigi observed. "It's not good for someone as young as you. Now go pick some lettuce for the salad, missy. And take these damn dogs with you before they get stepped on." Bambi and Abby, both sitting at Gigi's feet, waiting for scraps, whined.

Sadie's toes curled as her bare feet hit the cold, still wet gravel in the garden. She had a basket under one arm for the butter lettuce, and the dogs were dancing around her heels. She could hear her aunts chatter humming from inside, and the smell of garlic wafted through the screen door. She closed her eyes, the basket half full of lettuce, and tilted her head back to the sky. Fresh, wet earth; cold hands; and the promise of a hot dinner . . .

"I can't tell if you're praying or falling asleep standing up." His voice came from the fence line, and Sadie snapped her eyes open. His hair was damp, and she could smell him from there. Cedarwood soap and a hint of pepper. He had a bottle of wine in each hand and wore a smile that wedged between Sadie's rib cage like a tickle. "We need to talk about something," he added.

"About the fact that you're spying on me?"

"You know, in the city, I lived in an apartment with paper-thin walls. I could hear the families on both sides. All the drama. When the kid would come home past curfew. When the husband would stay out too late drinking. It was like my own personal soap opera I couldn't turn off. Made me think of you."

"Are you calling me dramatic?" she demanded, her eyebrows shooting up.

"Not if I value my life," he said with mock seriousness. "But I remember you always eavesdropping on people and whispering their secrets to me."

"I forgot about that." She smiled. "I never was good with boundaries. I wanted to know too much. What was it like? Living in the city?"

"You'd hate it," he said, grinning, and then proceeded to regale her with stories before asking questions about what had changed since he left. As they talked, Sadie felt her guard slipping. He was so much more than the boy she'd fallen in love with so long ago. He was a constellation of memories and fresh revelations. A man who held her gaze when she spoke, and didn't just hear her, but actually listened. And she found herself wanting to talk more because of it. He was laughing at her story of the old ladies in neon joggers who always tried to set Sadie up with their grandsons, when there was a shriek from inside the house.

"What the hell?" he asked, alarmed.

"I think another one of my aunts is here," Sadie said. "We're definitely going to need those," she said, her eyes tracking to the wine in his hands. "And maybe a few more."

Jake followed her back inside, and she could feel the centimeters between them, the tension rising as he got closer. And it was only once they were inside that she remembered he'd said they needed to talk about something. But the thought was interrupted by another scream.

"Annie, Annie, Anne!" Kay shrieked.

And there she was, Aunt Anne, being smothered by Kay. Sadie could feel the house welcoming her. The doors seemed to glow, as though begging her to walk through them. And over the smell of garlic from the kitchen, Sadie could detect a light undertone of gardenia that seemed to follow Anne wherever she went. The cupboards in the kitchen rattled, asking Anne to make use of them, knowing she was the only one of them, besides Gigi and Sadie, that would do them justice.

"You know what those heels make you look like?" were the first words out of Anne's mouth.

"Shut up!" Kay cried as Tava laughed and the sisters all hugged each other.

Anne was exactly halfway in height between Tava and Kay, with stick-straight hair that refused to curl, no matter what, and a series of expressions on her narrow face that all meant business. She was short and slight to Kay's tall and slender, and both were beautiful in the way of their sharp cheekbones and thin noses, like paintings of old.

"Well, really! Who let the milkman's daughter in here, anyway?" Anne teased Kay, hugging Seth next. "We all know it's true. Mother just won't admit it. But she doesn't look like the rest of us, and she's a freaking Amazon. I mean, look how tall she is!"

"Anne!" Kay screeched in outrage while they all knew she secretly loved it.

"I'll order you a DNA kit for Christmas, and we'll just see, won't we?" Anne said, barely able to keep a straight face as she pulled Sadie into a strong hug.

"Mommy!" Kay screamed this time, stomping into the kitchen. "Anne is making fun of me again!"

"It's just too easy." Anne smiled at Sadie, holding her at arm's length. "You look beautiful, as always."

"Where's Uncle Steven?" Sadie asked.

"In South Africa, opening another branch. He should be back in a few weeks. And the kids wanted to be here, but Emily has her new baby and John's kids are in school. She hugged Seth and Raquel, was reintroduced to Jake, and proceeded to talk his ear off for the next ten minutes about his parents and Rock Creek House, asking him eight thousand questions but only letting him answer half. Anne's magic was as straightforward as she was. If something needed to get done, Anne was the general who not only issued orders that people were compelled to follow, but she was also on the front line, getting her hands dirty and making sure the campaign was executed flawlessly. However, that meant her brain was always going a hundred miles an hour, jumping to the next thing she needed to know or get done.

"Well," Anne said abruptly, cutting Jake off right as he'd been about to answer another question, "I better go help Mom. God only knows what's going on in there."

Jake looked to Sadie with his eyebrows raised, and she laughed.

"Aunt Anne's known for administering verbal whiplash," Seth told him.

"I don't mind it. So, where you been, man?" he asked Seth.

"Oh, you know—out sowing my wild oats," Seth answered.

"I'm getting wine," Sadie announced. "All around, I assume?" Everyone nodded, and Raquel followed her into the kitchen.

"I love your family so much," she said, sighing.

"Want to trade?" Sadie joked.

"Yeah, right. You think you could survive Rodriguez rules? No way. Why do you think I always wanted to come over here when we were younger?"

"If you were like every other girl in school who feigned interest in me, I'd say because of my brother," Sadie said, laughing.

"Well, him too," Raquel said lightly, and Sadie, for once, couldn't quite tell if she was joking or not.

Kay and Tava sat at the counter while Gigi and Anne moved around each other in a practiced way. Gigi handed her the cheese grater right before she reached for it, and Anne turned the pan handle away from the flame as Gigi lit the burner. It reminded Sadie of when she and Gigi used to cook together, and she realized with a sudden jolt that they hadn't done that in some time. They'd gotten so used to it being just the two of them that they didn't make a big fuss over dinner. It was usually something Sadie would throw together after a long day at the café.

As Sadie filled the wineglasses, there were two thumps against the back-garden window. It was the peach tree, wanting to join in the fun. Sadie looked at Raquel and nodded to the last two wineglasses, her own hands already full. Raquel picked them up, and they walked back out to the living room.

"To family," Raquel toasted, and the sound of clinking followed.

"Only Uncle Brian and Aunt Suzy are missing now," Sadie noted after a long swallow.

"I'm so glad Brian married that woman. The best addition to this family anyone could have asked for," Anne said.

"And our mother," Seth said lightly, though there was a coldness to it. "But I guess once you've been gone that long, it doesn't really count as 'missing' anymore."

"Seth," Sadie said in a warning tone.

"Sadie," he answered, mocking her in the same pitch.

"Don't even start," Raquel said, interrupting the twins' staring contest.

"Alright, alright." Seth laughed. "See? This one's so good for me. Keeps me in my place. Truce, sister?"

Normally she would have bickered right back. But then she felt Jake's hand against her lower back, the heat of his palm making her skin tingle through her shirt. And she nodded.

"Truce," she answered, her voice hoarse. She watched as Raquel and Seth made their way to the kitchen, thinking how strange it was the way they moved in sync. She sighed. She could let go of her grudge for a night. And that's when she remembered Jake's hand was still on her back. The house seemed to sigh in a contented sort of way, and the record player in the corner began to play Nat King Cole all by itself.

"Listen," he said. "I really need to talk to you."

She took another drink of wine. Turned around. She'd been meaning to say something, but now she couldn't remember what.

They stared at each other, the inches between them growing warm.

His eyes burrowed into hers, and he opened his mouth to say something. Closed it again.

Just then, a knock on the front door had Sadie springing away from him and nearly spilling her wine. She cleared her throat. Blushed. The lights flickered, and the grandfather clock chimed loudly even though it was only 5:42 PM.

"I'll just get that," she said hoarsely. Uncle Brian stood on the doorstep, with a smile that Sadie always felt he reserved just for her. He was short, stocky, bald headed, and handsome in a Bruce

Willis look-alike way. His hands were always dirty, calloused, covered in grease from the mechanic shop he owned with his wife, Suzy, who'd been so much a part of the family for so long that Sadie didn't remember a time without her. He held up a grocery bag.

"Margaritas?" he asked.

"God bless you!" Sadie laughed, squeezing him tight and then beaming at Aunt Suzy, who was carrying a covered bowl that Sadie knew was full of her favorite pesto pasta. No matter how many times Sadie tried to replicate it, she could never get it quite right. She'd had Aunt Suzy write out the recipe, but even that didn't help. Her obsessive-compulsive nature compelled her to spend half a summer trying different variations before finally giving up.

When Uncle Brian came in the house, various parts of it hummed like they were calling out to him. Burnt-out light bulbs Sadie always forgot to change and screws that needed to be tightened, and if she strained, she swore she could hear her old Subaru whining for attention. Brian's magic had always been fascinating to Sadie because it felt like a superpower: he knew how to fix anything he touched.

"We would've been here sooner," Aunt Suzy said.

"But the string of lights along the driveway had a short, so I fixed them," Uncle Brian finished.

"I've been meaning to look at that—thank you," Sadie said, not even bothering to ask how Brian had managed it, since she knew he always carried a toolbox in his car.

The smell of lasagna brought them all into the kitchen, where another round of cries and hugs went around. Uncle Brian headed straight for the blender while Suzy unloaded a basket with zucchini squash and purple tomatoes from their garden. There were three conversations going on at once, accompanied by the sounds of Gigi clanging the pot lid as she checked on the broccoli steaming on the stovetop and the hiss of cheese melting in the oven. Tava hummed while Anne continuously teased Kay. Gigi smacked hands and scolded and laughed and bossed "the kids" around. The air was warm with talk and company. It had gone from dinner for two in front of the television to having to add chairs for the ten people crowded around the kitchen table. They all grinned at each other and drank deeply.

Seth helped Uncle Brian get a leaf from the shed to expand the table while Jake brought in a bench and extra chairs. Sadie and Raquel set the table, and Suzy was already at work on cleaning dishes. A blast of heat hit the room as the lasagna came out of the oven and the garlic bread finished broiling. And finally, Gigi's bullfrog voice silenced them all.

"You didn't need to come back," she said. "But I'm glad you did. Now let's eat before this damned food gets cold. I don't even know if this lasagna is any good. And that broccoli isn't fit to eat, but it'll have to do."

For the next twenty minutes the conversation died away, to be replaced with the clinking of silverware and the setting down of plates, the scraping of chairs and the refilling of drinks. You could cook all the magic in the world into the most delicate of dishes, but, Sadie thought, nothing compared to the magic of sharing an ordinary meal with people you loved.

Sadie was sitting next to Jake, and even over the melee of delicious dinner aromas she could smell him. The cedarwood and hint of campfire smoke. When he reached for a second helping, his thigh brushed against hers, and neither of them moved away. She knew she should. Knew she was supposed to keep her distance. That her magic was the only thing that mattered right now. And still, she relished that small point of contact. Let it spread through her until it pooled at her center.

"I can't eat another bite." Jake sighed, leaning back in his chair, his hands on his stomach. "Gigi Marie, as always, that was the best meal I've had in forever."

"Well, I hope you saved room for dessert in a little bit. But before we get there, I suppose we should talk about why you're all here." The table all hushed at once, and the bubble of joy that had been growing in Sadie's stomach suddenly burst. Acid began to burn in her chest. Kay was already crying.

"You don't have to do this, Mom," Anne said quietly, all teasing gone from her voice.

"Hush, toot. I do have to. You all already know it. Or at least most of you do. I'm dying." Gigi was never one to mince words, but these came out sharp and sliced through the silence until Sadie could feel the incisions across her heart.

Kay let out a wail, and Tava shushed her. Raquel had silent tears streaming down her face. Seth's jaw was clenched so hard the vein in his forehead was visible. Brian pushed back his chair as though he were going to leave—like if he refused to hear it, it wouldn't be true. But when he saw Gigi's look of warning, he sat back down.

"Chemo," Anne started but faltered when Gigi's eyes cut to her.

"This goes beyond modern medicine. It was always going to be this way. And I wouldn't change a damn thing." Gigi cleared her throat.

The house groaned and shuddered, and the record player stopped on a dime. The grandfather clock sent out one long, mournful chime.

"So, what we're going to do now is enjoy our time together. I'll have no fussing and no hysterics." She looked pointedly to Aunt Kay. "Everybody hear me?"

They all nodded. Uncle Brian cleared his throat.

"Is there a time frame?" he asked, his voice gritty as muscovado sugar.

"Whenever the good Lord calls me home. But I'd say sooner rather than later."

Everyone was crying. Jake was squeezing her thigh under the table so hard Sadie was sure it would leave a bruise, but she couldn't bear to push him away. Instead, she grabbed onto his hand like an anchor and squeezed back. Tava's tears came out turquoise. Anne was trying to be stoic, but her shoulders were shaking. Raquel's face was buried in Seth's shoulder, and he ran a soothing hand over her back, his own tears refusing to fall.

And then, in the silence, the television turned on of its own accord and John Wayne's voice filtered through to the kitchen.

"Courage is being scared to death but saddling up anyway," he said in that trademark twang.

"I've always hated that damn picture," Gigi said with a scowl.

There was silence around the table as *True Grit* played on in the living room, and then Tava laughed. Anne joined in a moment later, and then they were all laughing through their tears. The air was still heavy as they ate Gigi's cherry cheese pie, and their hearts were still breaking, but they were breaking together, and that was its own kind of beauty.

As the people around the table dispersed to do dishes or head for the living room, Jake grabbed Sadie's hand and gave it a gentle pull, nodding to the back-patio door.

She swallowed hard but followed.

"So, Gigi, huh?" he asked once they were in the garden.

"Yeah," Sadie croaked, reminding herself that it was Gigi she should be concerned with. Not the small space between them that begged her to close it. Gigi. Not the way Jake's skin looked in the moonlight or the way he ran a distracted hand through his hair.

Her chest tightened. All the change, the family, the looming threat of death, the life debt, gave her heart palpitations. She was losing control. And fast. Constantly feeling like she was about to choke. But being near Jake—somehow he diffused it. She wondered if that was what love was. The subtle easing in her chest. The lending of strength when you needed it most.

"I know this is a bad time," he said, his hand on the back of his neck now, "but there really is something I need to talk to you about. It can't wait any longer."

The palpitations started again.

The ground grew warm beneath her feet. Seeped into her soles and wound through her body until it became so hot that Jake took a confused step back.

One more day, she reminded herself. *I have almost everything I need now. The herbs. The knot of Isis. I can do this. Just keep him at bay awhile longer.*

The nearby foxgloves, a flower symbolizing healing, began to droop in unison. Jake was talking, but she wasn't listening. The pale pink of the foxgloves reminded her of the Mount Diablo buckwheat that grew on Wild Rose Hill outside of town. It was the one flower she could never get to grow in her garden. Blooming only once a year and thought to be extinct by most botanists, it was a powerful symbol of love. More than that, it was said to be the flower that had given Evanora Revelare, her ancestor, her magic. Why hadn't she thought of it until now?

"Sadie," Jake said.

She had to get that flower.

"Are you listening to me?"

It would be the thing that put her spell for Gigi over the top. She had to find Raquel. Make her go with her. Because there was no way she was going alone to Wild Rose Hill at night.

"Sorry." She threw the word over her shoulder as she headed back to the house. "We'll talk later!"

Cherry Cheese Pie

The easiest, foolproof, no-bake dessert around. Seth would beg me for this dumb ol' pie for every special occasion he could think of, but Sadie never could stand it. That girl just has something against being peaceful, I think. A slice or two of this pie will help to ensure peace when an argument is sure to happen. Perfect for family gatherings.

Ingredients

1 (8-oz.) package cream cheese
1 (14-oz.) can sweetened condensed milk
⅓ c. lemon juice
1 tsp. vanilla extract
1 (9-inch) prepared graham cracker crust
1 (21-oz.) can cherry pie filling

Directions

1. In a large bowl, beat cream cheese until fluffy. Beat in milk until smooth. Stir in lemon juice and vanilla, then pour mixture into graham cracker crust.

2. Cover and refrigerate for three hours or until set. Top with cherry pie filling.

♦ 9 ♦

SADIE RUSHED THROUGH THE house and found Raquel on the front-porch swing, Seth leaning against the railing as they talked.

"I have a favor," Sadie said in rush.

"No," Seth said.

"I wasn't talking to you," Sadie said shortly. "Raquel, my beautiful, wonderful best friend. How would you like to go for a little drive?"

"Where to?" she asked, eyes narrowed in suspicion.

"Wild Rose Hill," Sadie answered innocently.

"You must be out of your mind," Raquel barked. "You, of all people, know that place is haunted."

"She does know. Which would beg the question: Why, sister?"

"Mount Diablo buckwheat." Her voice was a little breathless.

"Oh, come on," Seth said, rolling his eyes. "Seriously?"

"Should I know what this is? I mean I'm not exactly filled with comfort with the word *devil* being in the name."

"It's for Gigi. I'm working on a spell for her. For the cancer."

"And this flower is supposed to be crazy powerful. Where our magic originally came from," Seth added.

"Not only that," said Sadie, "but remember that fire a few years ago? Wild Rose Hill was blackened. And now it's lush again. The most powerful Revelare flower, life growing from death. It's the perfect symbolism. Please," she pleaded to Raquel. "I don't want to go alone, but I will if I have to."

"Alright, alright, keep your shirt on. I'll come," Raquel said. "But Seth is coming too."

"I am?"

"No, he's not," Sadie said with a short laugh. "He doesn't believe in what I'm doing."

"Seth?" Raquel demanded with an arched brow.

"Fine, fine. I'll go," he said after only a moment of pause.

Sadie refused to acknowledge that she was grateful for his presence. Because the second she admitted that, it would mean she was giving credence to the haunting. And everyone knows that the moment you look the dark things in the eye, they become far too real.

Wild Rose Hill was twenty minutes outside of town, and the trio was silent as they drove. They all knew the stories. And knew, too, that Gigi would have banned them from going, which is why they didn't tell anyone. Sadie idly thought about Jake. About what he was going to tell her. And knew that she didn't want to hear whatever he was having trouble getting out. She couldn't hold him off forever, but a little while longer wouldn't hurt. It was just another dark thing she didn't want to look in the eye.

The hill loomed eerily in the distance, like the arched back of a slumbering giant. Around the base was a forest of trees that stopped abruptly as the incline grew steeper. Then, at the top, was a single, towering oak.

"I already have goose bumps." Raquel shivered.

"They're just stories," Sadie told her.

"Nothing is ever just a story," Seth said from the backseat, sounding like a Revelare.

"We're here." Sadie cut the engine and let the silence fill her. None of them moved.

A rock hit the side of the car, and all three of them jumped.

"Fuck it," Seth said taking a deep breath. "Let's go. This better be worth it," he added to Sadie.

She swallowed hard and they set off—with flashlights and a resolution that didn't quite feel steely enough.

"You really believe the story?" Seth asked quietly as they reached the tree line. "That this is where Evanora got her magic?" His voice was strangely serious.

"Why wouldn't I?"

She could practically hear his shrug.

"What exactly was the price of that magic?" Raquel asked in a whisper.

"Probably whatever's left haunting this place," Seth answered.

An owl hooted nearby, and Raquel let out a small noise. Seth positioned himself between them, a knife in his hand.

"What the hell, Seth. A knife isn't going to work on what's here."

"Better safe than sorry" was all he said.

By the time they were through the thicket of trees, Sadie was sweating despite the cool air.

"Put these in your pocket," she said, handing them each a few stems of vervain.

"We come in peace." Seth let out a quiet laugh, reciting the symbolism of the flower. "It's a ghost, Sadie, not an alien."

"You remembered," Sadie said in surprise.

"More than you might think, sister."

There was something about the stillness of Rose Hill that made them draw closer together. No crickets chirped, the frogs were silent, and even the wind seemed to tiptoe. The smell of pine and wet earth grounded her, even when it felt like they were entering another dimension.

"Of course, the flowers had to grow at the *top* of this damn hill," Seth huffed halfway up.

Normally Sadie would have sniped something back. But for the first time since he'd been back, it felt like nothing had changed. It felt like a dare they'd have done when they were younger. Like the time he'd dared her to draw on the neighbor's garage. In red lipstick of all things. Never wanting to disappoint him, she'd scrambled across the lawn, heart beating at a wicked pace, and drew a dime-size heart in the far corner before sprinting back. The idea of getting in trouble was less terrifying than owning up to a failed dare. Seth, of course, had sauntered over and signed his name in large, looping letters.

Finally, they reached the plateau.

"Do the stars seem brighter from up here, or is it just me?" Raquel asked.

"I, for one, have never seen that constellation in my life," said Seth, who'd spent his senior year obsessed with astronomy, dragging Sadie out every night to look though the telescope he'd spent so long saving for.

Sadie followed his finger to where he pointed to a particularly bright quadrant of stars.

And that's when they heard it.

A low growling.

The same Sadie had heard from her garden only days ago.

No words, just that deep rumbling.

"Sadie, I think it's time to get those flowers and get the fuck out of Dodge," Seth said.

Without wasting a moment, her heart beating so hard it hurt, Sadie shone her light on the ground near the oak tree. There, growing at the base, was the buckwheat, their purple petals glinting otherworldly.

The closer she got to the tree, the stronger the presence grew, until her chest seemed to cave in with it. She hurriedly plucked several stems and stashed them in their bag.

"Do you think if I pull some up with the root, I'll be able to grow them at home?" she whispered.

"Let's debate that another day, shall we?" Seth's back was to the tree, his eyes scanning the plateau. His tone was tight and clipped to mask his fear.

An icy chill spread across the ground, burrowing into their bones. The grass frosted over, turning crunchy beneath their feet.

And then the voice spoke. The words were drawn out, long and sharp as a blade.

"Get out," it groaned.

Sadie's stomach plummeted as her eyes went wide with terror. She wanted to run, but fear rooted her feet to the icy ground as that voice made her shiver. She turned her head a fraction of an inch and saw her own fear reflected in Raquel's face, in her wide eyes and her mouth open in a perfect "o." Seth's skin had gone white as death as he clutched the useless knife in his hands.

The three looked at each other for a half second before running down the hillside. They stumbled over rocks and loose dirt and clumps of wet grass as the chill chased them with a fury that slid under their skin and threatened to stay there. Sadie slipped and Raquel grabbed her arm in a vicelike grip, pulling her back up and down the hill as their feet tripped over themselves.

They didn't stop until the car doors slammed shut, locking them safely inside the car. The only sound was their labored breathing as the chill finally began to dissipate.

"All in all, I think that went well," Seth panted out after a minute.

And Sadie couldn't help it—she burst into laughter.

Raquel followed suit, and the two of them were laughing until tears ran down their cheeks while Seth shook his head in the backseat.

"Lunatics," was all he said.

Sadie's leg began to sting as the adrenaline wore off, and she realized her jeans were sticky with blood.

She dropped Raquel off, and by the time she walked up the front porch she was trying not to wince.

"What's wrong?" Seth demanded.

"Scraped my leg on a branch when we were running, I think."

"Come on," he said, sighing.

He made her sit at the kitchen table while he pulled down supplies.

Sadie watched in surprise as he reached for the lavender, frankincense, and helichrysum and mixed them with a dollop of coconut oil.

"I'm not entirely useless," he said when he saw her face.

"I'm just surprised you remember." She pulled up her pant leg and winced as he smeared it on.

"Don't be a baby."

"Don't be an ass," she answered. But it was the friendly bickering they'd always shared, not the angry quarreling they'd done since he'd come home.

"So, what happens now?"

"Tomorrow I'm going to do the spell. The herbs will be ready, and I've got the flowers now."

"Do you want help?"

"What?" she asked, even though she'd heard him perfectly.

"If it works, I don't want you getting all the credit." He shrugged.

"Sure," she said, confused but grateful. "Come on—bed. We'll do it first thing in the morning."

It was strange following him upstairs the way she used to when they were younger. Her feet left a light trail of gray dust on every step, a fine powder from the walls around her heart that were slowly beginning to crumble.

The house was silent the next morning when Sadie rose with the sun.

"I changed my mind," Seth groaned when she tried to wake him. "I don't want to help you."

"Too bad," she said, yanking the covers off him. "Meet me in the garden."

The brisk air brushed against her skin, waking her up fully. It was the coldest morning of the season so far, and she exhaled hot air into her cupped hands before rubbing them together. Excitement brushed along her skin like confectioners' sugar. This was it.

She settled an old quilt on the cold ground and lined up the herbs: bay, fennel, and a clove from the bulb of garlic. The crushed blackberry thorns were in a small glass vial, and the Mount Diablo buckwheat next to it. The small piece of amber and stick of selenite glinted in the dawn light. And there, in a butter-soft leather pouch was the knot of Isis. Shaped like an ankh but with its arms curving down, it symbolized life and would be the talisman she bound the spell to.

The crunch of gravel heralded Seth's arrival.

"Look at this," he complained, breathing out a puff of air and pointing to the icy mist that formed there. "It's too cold."

"You volunteered as tribute, remember?"

"Yeah, well, I'm a dumbass."

"You said it, not me. And there's one more thing we need," she told him.

"Let me guess, dragon tears? Maybe a phoenix feather?"

"An egg."

"Chimera egg? Do we need to go to Siberia to get it? I hear their ghosts there are a little friendlier."

"Shut up," she said, but she laughed. "We need a fertilized crow egg. Life from death, remember? The egg represents life and crows symbolize death. And"—she took a breath—"lucky for us, there happens to be a crow's nest in that tree." She pointed to a live oak just at the edge of the wood.

"Nope" was all he said.

"Come on," she wheedled. "You used to climb those trees all the time!"

"When I was younger. Which I'm not anymore. And my fingers have actually turned into popsicles, which I hear aren't great for gripping onto things."

"You have the skills. I don't! You'd never let me climb them when we were younger."

"Have you seen yourself walk? Try to ride a bike? Of course, I wouldn't let you climb them. You're a fucking menace to gravity. And out of curiosity, if I hadn't offered to help, exactly how were you going to get that egg down?"

"Necessity is the mother of invention, and all that." She shrugged, not wanting to admit that she hadn't thought of a way. The tallest ladder they had wouldn't even reach a third of the way up.

Seth sighed.

"I guess the good news is that if I fall to my death, the sacrifice will be paid."

"Stop being dramatic. You're not going to fall. Now go on—we need to do the spell before the sun reaches its apex."

He gave her a look.

"And also because I need to get to the café," she admitted.

"There it is." He sighed. "Good to know my life is weighed against the measure of your business."

"Stop stalling, you big baby."

Sadie watched as Seth shimmied up the tree to the lowest branch and swung himself up. From there it was a ladder of footwork and small jumps to the top third of the oak. She sighed in relief when she squinted and saw him triumphantly hold up a small green egg. She'd never tell him, but she hadn't been entirely sure there were eggs in that nest.

Finally, he jumped from the lowest branch and grinned at Sadie.

"Okay, that was pretty fun," he said, wiping his hands on his pants in an effort to get some of the sap off. There were leaves in his hair, a few scratches on his arms and palms, and a light in his eyes. "Let's do this."

Sadie knelt on the blanket, trying to hold back a shiver as the wind picked up.

"So, we're going to take turns putting the items in the bowl. That way it'll have power from both of us." She picked the amber and put it in.

"This feels weird," he whispered, placing the selenite next to the amber.

When everything was in, she pulled a white candle and a book of matches out of her bag and wrapped the knot of Isis around it. Her hands trembled. This had to work.

"Now what?"

"Now we light everything in there on fire." She lit the candle and handed it to Seth, and then struck another match. She dropped it in the bowl, but it went out on the way down. The second one she cupped her hand around, but the flame snapped out. Finally, she held it directly next to the fennel, but it still wouldn't light.

"That won't work," Seth said.

And with his eyes concentrated on the candle, he held it over the bowl. The flame separated from the wick and leaped down into the bowl, curling around the herbs, and blazed bright green before dying out completely.

"How'd you know how to do that?" Sadie whispered.

"I don't know. It just felt right," said Seth, equally surprised.

"I wish you'd tell me what your magic is."

"I wish you'd stop nagging me about it," he said, but his grin took the sting out of his words.

"Shut up and repeat after me," she said, her voice still quiet and soft.

Earth below, sky above,
Fill this knot with purest love.
The morning sun will take her pain,
And she will wake renewed again.

They stared at each other.

"Is that it?"

"That's it." She nodded, unwrapping the knot of Isis from the candle. "Now we just have to get her to wear it. It should help even if she doesn't, but the closer in proximity it is to her, the better."

"Twenty bucks says she won't wear it," Seth said as they walked back inside.

"Either way, thanks," she said, bumping her shoulder into his.

By the time they walked through the screen door, the knot of Isis warm in Sadie's pocket, Aunt Anne and Aunt Tava were already in the kitchen. Anne poured them both a cup of coffee.

Sadie had dreamed of having family around for so long that she'd forgotten what it was like when they were actually there. It was nice, but so was the solitude of her kitchen in the mornings. Tava sat at her stool so Sadie took a seat at the kitchen table but jumped up again a moment later when Gigi came in, the dogs trailing behind her.

"What did you do, you little shit ass?" Gigi demanded.

Sadie held out the knot of Isis. It thrummed in her palm.

"Just prolonging the inevitable." Gigi shook her head. "But it's nice to feel better, at least."

"You do? Feel better?" Sadie asked, hope and pride blooming in her chest.

"You don't understand," Gigi said, shaking her head again. "My time is up. Nothing can stop it now. And I don't want it to. I've been tying that darkness to me for years, and it's finally catching up. I've lived my whole life for you kids; I plan to die on my terms. Now, I'm going out for a cigarette."

"Oh, baby doll." Tava sighed when Gigi was gone. "My babies." She put a hand to Seth's cheek. "Mom is right. I hate to say it, but it won't work."

"That's enough, Tava," Aunt Anne snapped. "Don't be a Debbie Downer."

"It's going to work," Sadie said quietly. "It has to. I know she thinks it's her time, but it's not. She'll see."

"Sade," Seth said, but she didn't let him continue.

"No. I'm going to get ready for work."

She scrubbed her face and pulled on a pair of black leggings, a burgundy tunic that reached her mid-thigh, and a saffron cardigan with big, loose pockets. She swiped some rose ointment on so her lips wouldn't chap, and shoved it in her pocket for later. Her hair was surprisingly tame, and she positioned it to keep her ears warm instead of wearing a hat she'd just end up taking off.

She sat at her vanity, the oval mirror tilted up toward the ceiling, as she pulled on her scuffed black work boots and laced them up. Her room, which faced the garden and subsequently Rock Creek House, was always cold in the morning and warm as the sun traveled toward night. It was the same room she'd had her whole life, and not much had changed in it. There were still colorful tapestries hung from the wall and an old green rocking chair in the corner that had belonged to the grandfather she didn't quite remember.

The large bay window had a built-in reading nook with books stacked haphazardly in piles ready to topple over. She was happy in here. But looking around, she thought again about the toothbrushes. About sharing space with someone. She had everything she needed. But was it selfish to want more? To long for something she wanted but couldn't have?

"Don't borrow trouble," she reminded herself, repeating Gigi's words. And shaking off the doom and gloom of the future, she snuck out the front door before any aunts could accost her.

At the café, Gail had already opened the shop. Sadie got to work in the kitchen, throwing herself into the routine, stemming all thoughts of Gigi and Jake and the spell and the curse and her family. Spoonful by spoonful she added butter to the babka dough, one of the only recipes she'd use a hand mixer for. Enriched dough wasn't for the faint of heart. The dough hook caught the soft dough, stretching it around and around, and she couldn't help thinking it looked like how she felt. Like a big, soft, tangled goop of a mess.

When Gigi came in, there was color in her cheeks, and she bustled busily about until Sadie couldn't help feeling the hope that was planting itself in heart. She didn't have to worry about Seth. About the life debt or who would become the conduit. Not yet, anyway. Gigi would be fine.

Sadie helped customers and lost herself in the movements, keeping her friendly smile in place at all times until it almost felt real. The air was perfumed with the rich, buttery smell of caramel, and the bell over the door continued to chime as the afternoon crowd flowed in.

When the last of the rush was gone, she allowed herself to think of Jake. She felt a little guilty for running off when he'd needed to talk the night before, even if she didn't want to hear what he had to say. So she wrapped a large slice of the babka for him, her stomach braiding itself into knots just like the bread as she thought about driving to Rock Creek House for the first time in over ten years. It was a testament to her desire to do the right thing that she would go so far out of her comfort zone. But right was right, and Gigi had taught her long ago that when you knew what you had to do, it was best to just get on with it. Maybe the walnuts with their symbol of clarity and gathering energy for new beginnings would be just the thing he needed.

Or maybe it's something you need, a little voice in her head whispered. She ignored it.

Jake was sitting on a ratty, old rocking chair on the well-worn and sadly unkempt front porch, with a beer in his hand. He jumped up when he saw Sadie's car pull up.

"Everything okay?" he asked before she was fully out of the car. "Gigi Marie?"

"She's good." Her smile widened. "Really good, actually."

She looked up at the house. Its peeling paint. The roof that needed repairing. If the outside looked this bad, she could only imagine what the inside looked like. She thought about projects. About walking the aisles of the hardware store with Jake, picking out paint samples and drawer pulls.

"It's a piece," he said, watching her watch the house.

"Why'd you buy it?"

"What are you doing here, Sade?"

"That's supposed to be my question," she shot back, noting the way he dodged her question, but not interested in pursuing it yet. "I brought babka," she added, holding up the slice that was basically half the loaf, before walking up and setting it on the railing.

"My hero," he said, looking down at her.

Focus, she reprimanded herself.

Instead, she took a step closer.

Gigi was getting better. She and Seth were healing. She was beating death itself; curses could be broken. Maybe, just maybe . . . there was room for Jake in her heart.

He didn't move, but there was a war playing on his face.

"Sadie," he said, his voice tight.

"I have questions," she whispered. "But I don't want to ask them yet. Just stand here with me."

And then, because it seemed he couldn't help himself, his hands found themselves on her waist, pulling her closer until she could feel his heart beating against her chest. He held her tight, and she remembered a hot summer day. The ground had burned her bare feet, but she didn't care as he hugged her and didn't let go. Though she hadn't known it at the time, it was the day before he'd left for good. And this moment, with his arms around her again, felt like another kind of goodbye.

His breath tickled her ear when he spoke and sent a shiver down her arms. She leaned into him, every curve pressing against him and lighting her on fire.

"You terrify me," he whispered. "You're always the one who's challenged me." One hand tightened on her waist while the other slid to her back. His stubble bristled deliciously against her jawline. She wanted to turn her head. Make his lips meet hers.

"You have no idea how bad I want this," he murmured, his fingers curling into her skin, drawing her closer.

Her stomach dipped, and warmth spread from her center up to her chest.

"I have some idea," she whispered back, her own hands trailing down his arms and then back up. She tilted her head to look at him, and he cradled her face in his hands, like she was something precious. His thumb brushed across her lower lip. Without thinking, she captured it with her teeth, biting gently and running her tongue across it.

A small, tortured groan escaped him.

"I want to live up to your expectations," he breathed heavily, "and that means I have to be honorable." He started to pull away.

"Screw honorable," she said, her heart beating rapidly as her hands pushed under his shirt, his velvet skin warm against hers—and she wanted him *now*. Needed him. To move against him. To feel his calloused palms scraping against the sensitive skin of her stomach, her inner thighs. She arched against him, closing her eyes.

"Damn it, Sadie," he ground out, his voice low and rough. "You're making this impossible. I need to tell you something," he murmured against her hair before pulling back and looking into her eyes. His hands were warm on her shoulders. Like he was steadying himself.

"What?" Her breath was ragged, and she couldn't look away from his lips.

"I'm engaged."

Her eyes snapped to his, all threads of desire doused in disbelief.

Impossible.

The heat in her stomach hardened into ice.

Whatever she'd been expecting, it hadn't been *this*.

"To be married?"

"What other kind of engaged is there?"

This wasn't happening. Not again. She pushed him, hard, his hands falling from her shoulders.

"I tried to tell you," he said, his voice a shade of agony.

"Tried? You *tried*? It's pretty simple, Jake," she spat. "Two words. Two words that could have been said at any time!" But even as she said it, she remembered all the times he'd said he'd needed to tell her something. And every time she'd pushed it away. Because she'd known it was something she didn't want to hear. And like a child covering their ears, she'd refused to listen.

"I—I know. But every time I was about to, we got interrupted. And then Gigi. And I just wanted a little bit longer. A little bit more time with you before, well, before this."

Her pulse was jumpy, and a cold sweat was breaking out on her forehead.

"How long?" she demanded.

"A few months."

"Why the *hell* did you move back here?"

He ran a hand through his hair.

"Have you ever been at a point in your life where you felt like everything was finally going the way it was supposed to?"

"Yeah, and then you left. And here we are again. With me stupidly thinking we might have a chance in hell. But of course it can never be that simple with you," she said.

"But life *isn't* simple. It's not black and white like that, Sade. It's messy and hard and heartbreaking. And those are the things that knock the rough edges off. That make life worth living."

"That's rich, coming from you. I like my rough edges just fine," she seethed, but she wasn't sure she believed herself. Not anymore.

"They don't protect you as much as you think."

She wanted to tell him that she kept things black and white because it was easier when you couldn't have it all. It made things fall neatly into one category or another: can have, can't have. It wasn't a byproduct of magic, but of her personality. Of the way she'd come to see things, growing up. It made her fight harder for the things she did have. Because she would do anything to keep them. And now, here he was again, slipping through her hands. Or no—he hadn't even been there to begin with.

"Bethany is—" he started.

"Bethany," she said flatly, hating the way the name tasted on her tongue,

"Yes, Bethany. I was happy with her. Or happy enough, anyway."

"And what? You started to get cold feet and thought you'd come back here and screw with my heart again? You're the reason I have trust issues! You're the reason I'm terrified that everyone is going to leave me. You broke my heart. You broke *me.*"

"You don't think I was broken too? I wanted to come back. To you. But I knew I'd messed up too badly. And still, you were the only one I could imagine spending the rest of my life with. When I finally decided to come back, I'd heard Randy or someone had proposed to you."

"Ryan," Sadie said shortly.

"And what was I supposed to do? Come back and screw that up for you like I screwed up everything else? I owed it to you to let you be happy, even if I was miserable. And that's when I met Bethany. So, I stayed. And by the time I found out that you weren't with Randy—"

"Ryan," she corrected him again.

"By that time, I . . . um . . . we—well, we found out she was pregnant."

He was looking anywhere but at her face.

"Pregnant," she echoed. The shards of ice in her stomach splintered apart.

"Whatever doubts I was having, I have to do right by her. I grew up in a broken home, and I won't do that to my kid. But it's more than that," he said, and she saw the light bloom in his eyes.

"You're excited to be a dad," she whispered, and her breath was so cold it came out in a fog.

"Terrified, actually, but yeah, excited too." And he sounded guilty for feeling it. "I built part of my life with this woman, Sade. And I don't want to abandon her."

"I understand," she said, and she did, even though it made her stomach turn until she felt sick. Jake, at Bethany's side, welcoming new life into the world. He was too noble to ever walk away.

"I should have told you sooner. But I was trying to forget. And being with you again, being near you, it made me realize what I'll never have. Sleepy mornings shuffling around in the kitchen. Summer barbecues and touching my feet to yours in bed at night just to feel you near me. The right to worry about you. *You.* And I wanted to live in that a little longer before Bethany got here. Can you blame me?"

"Yes," she said without hesitation. "I hate you." The way she said it sounded like anything but. "You being here—it screws everything up. I can't *breathe* when you're near. You're exactly the same. You string me along, make me love you."

"I can't make you do anything, Sade. Trust me, I've learned that by now. You and me, we're like fire and gasoline. I wish I could take it all back—trust me, I do." He ran a hand distractedly through his hair. "Just tell me what you want from me. You never want to hear from me again? Okay. You want me not to move here? Done. I won't buy the damn house."

They were both silent.

"Do you love her?" she asked quietly. She didn't want to know the answer. But she *needed* to know. Not that it would change anything.

He was silent for a moment. Hesitating. "I think I could learn to love her."

And her heart hurt for him, just a little.

"Why not just stay in the city?" she demanded.

He sat back down, grabbing his now warm beer and staring hard at the label.

"I was working at a station in the city. We deal with—or dealt with—a lot of drug calls. People overdosing, beat up from some fight or other. Our paramedics try to patch them up, or we take them to the hospital. What I didn't know was that there was a turf war going on between two gangs." He took a deep breath. Leaned back in his chair. Took a long drink. "Kids were involved. Kids, Sadie. Strung out on drugs or peddling coke or weed or meth. One night we got a call and it was—well, his name was Adam. His mother had called because he'd overdosed on cocaine. He was ten."

A noise rose involuntarily from the back of Sadie's throat. Her hand came over her mouth.

"This boy, I don't know, I felt drawn to him. I went back to their house on my days off and would help his mom. I got her sixteen-year-old son, Alex, a job, trying to keep him out of the gang, out of trouble. They started going to church with me. But when Mary's husband got out of jail and found out, he beat her. I thought I was doing something good. I thought I was helping them," he said, clearing his throat and staring at the deck floor, setting his empty bottle on the table between them.

"What happened next?" Sadie asked in a soft whisper. She wanted to reach out and put a hand on his arm, hold his hand, anything to reassure him. But she knew Jake. He needed to finish his story first, or he might not get all the way through it.

"When I showed up at their house, her husband, Tony, told me if I came back, he'd kill Mary and then me. To be honest, not a lot scares me. But Tony, I believed every word he said, and it scared the shit out of me. So, I stayed away. I went to see Alex at his job, but he'd quit. His father had forced him into the gang. I thought I would get over it, you know? But I kind of spiraled.

"Anyway, we got a call one night. There'd been gunshots in one of the worst parts of the city. When we got there"—he paused and cleared his throat again—"it was Alex. He was bleeding out on the street. Before he died, he asked me to get his mom out." Jake spoke quickly, as though expelling the memory might somehow absolve him of it.

"From that second I vowed I would do whatever it took. I couldn't fix it all, but I could do that. So, I bought an old car, and when I knew Tony would be gone, I gave her the keys and a few thousand bucks cash to get her and Adam as far away as possible."

"Did they?" Sadie asked with a quick intake of breath.

"I don't know." He shrugged. "I hope so. I think so. It was a rough area. There were drugs and violence and prostitution, and then the people who were just stuck there among it all because they didn't have an opportunity to get out. There were good people there, you know? Some of the house fires turned out to be drug dens or meth labs. A lot of the calls were incredibly depressing. Every time we went out, I was looking over my shoulder, waiting for Tony, wondering if he knew I'd helped his wife escape.

"And bringing a kid into that? My kid? I would never let them be collateral. I knew I had to leave the city, and being with Bethany is the only way I'll be able to be in the baby's life. She's—I think if I broke it off with her, she'd move back to the city in a heartbeat, and I'm terrified she'd try to cut me out."

"You think she'd deprive her child of knowing their father?" She didn't know why she was asking. It was too late for that.

"Bethany—she's great. But when she loves someone, it's like they're not allowed to love anyone else. And if I hurt her like that . . . I can't risk it. So, I cashed in on my sick time, and here I am. I couldn't handle being in that city anymore. I couldn't take the stress, the heartbreak, the paranoia of always looking out for Tony or someone from his gang."

He looked at her. "When Bethany asked me if there was a place I could go where I felt safe . . . I didn't think of Poppy Meadows. I thought of you. You'd always been my safe place. The person I could tell anything to, go through anything with. Once I started thinking about you, I couldn't stop. I figured we could start over, be friends at least. That I'd be happy if I could just be near you. But I knew the moment I saw you again that it would never be enough. I know that's not fair to you. And I'm sorry, Sadie. I'm sorry I'm so screwed up."

They were words she'd been longing to hear. The words her heart had been yearning to hear for a decade. He'd given her the vulnerability she'd been longing for. Forged a new bond between them. And it was all pointless.

She wondered if he loved her. But did it matter? When Jake decided on something, there was no one and nothing that could change his mind.

"I have to go," she told him. She needed out. Away from him.

"Sadie," he said, and his voice was broken. But when she walked away, he didn't stop her.

On the short drive home, the steering wheel was colder than a glacier. She thought she'd be crying, but the tears seemed to have frozen inside her. Her shoulders were tense, hunched, from her trying to hold herself together.

As she stepped out of her beat-up old Subaru in the driveway, the overpowering scent of crushed rosemary reached her, sending a shiver down her spine. She followed the smell to the side gate and nearly collapsed against the post. The line of salt and pennyroyal oil, meant to keep unwanted guests out, had been scattered like ashes.

"No, no, no, this can't be happening," she breathed. Everywhere she looked, devastation reigned. The garden had been destroyed. Tomato vines were uprooted, and the lavender bushes looked as though they'd been steamrolled. Herbs and vegetables were scattered everywhere. Bruised peaches lay all over the garden, as though the tree had tried to defend its family by pelting the infiltrator with its fruit.

Sadie walked to the once neat rows on weak legs. It was as though the lifeblood of the garden, having been broken, was leeching the energy from Sadie herself.

"It's okay," she said, sagging to her knees. "I can make this right. I'll fix it. You'll be fine." She sunk her hands into the earth, filling her palms with dirt as her chest tightened. It was all too much.

She couldn't draw a deep breath. Her blood vessels were closing off in revolt. Her vision narrowed until her skin went numb. With a cry she dragged her fingernails through the dirt, filling her palms and then beating them against the ground.

She felt a prickling of unease and looked up. The same figure, a green mist surrounding it, like something rotten, was hovering at the edge of the forest, seeming more solid than it had last time.

All the magic in the world couldn't prepare her for the fear that seized hold of her, as though she were drowning inside her heart.

Healing Salve

Apply this to minor cuts, scrapes, and bruises. Helps with inflammation and healing and works as an anti-infection and anti-microbial. Had to perfect this when the kids were little because they were like bulls in a china shop. Then, of course, Seth and Sadie turned out just the same.

Ingredients

2 T. coconut oil
2 drops each of:
- tea tree oil
- helichrysum
- lavender
- frankincense

1–2 tsp. beeswax pellets (optional, just makes the balm firmer)
1 oz. tin

Directions

1. In a small double boiler, melt the coconut oil and beeswax until just melted.
2. Take off heat and let cool for just a minute or two before adding the oils.
3. Pour into your container, and then refrigerate to solidify. Apply as needed. Helps speed up the healing time and fights infection.

♦ 10 ♦

SADIE ESCAPED TO THE back porch, and three glasses of wine later she still wasn't numb enough.

She didn't have the heart to tell her grandmother about the garden. Gigi, who'd refused to wear the knot of Isis. Sadie had hidden it in her room, so at least it would be near her while she slept. But doubt had already crept in. Gigi was moving slower again, always with a hand to her back and a grimace on her face when she thought no one was looking.

Kay was louder than usual, and Anne was talking faster than a speeding train, filling every silence to say all the things before time ran out, even if those things didn't matter. Uncle Brian had taken to fixing odds and ends around the house, muttering under his breath about Tava taking over the table with her sewing project. And Suzy had decided to clean and organize the hall closet. Seth, meanwhile, sat quietly next to Gigi on the couch; as always Abby was on her lap and Bambi at her feet.

There was a charged feeling to the air, everyone scattering to their respective posts, believing that if they could hang on to normalcy for a little bit longer, maybe their denial would waylay the inevitable. And Sadie couldn't stand the taste it left in her mouth.

The screen door creaked open, and Sadie recognized Seth's footfalls without turning around. He took the wineglass from Sadie's hand as he sat.

"Fucking madhouse in there," he said.

Sadie only nodded.

"What's up?"

"For starters," she said, pointing in the direction of the garden.

He squinted his eyes in the dying light and let out a sharp breath.

"Shit."

"Yeah. And I don't know," she said, answering his question before he could ask who had done it.

"Okay, what else?"

"What do you mean 'what else?' That's not enough?"

"You said, 'for starters.'"

She looked sidelong at him. He was her twin; she couldn't keep him out of her heart any more than she could keep her reflection out of a mirror. So she took a deep breath and spoke the words that had been weighing on her chest, like an anvil, ever since Jake had said them.

"Jake is engaged."

"To be married?"

"Apparently so," she said bleakly.

"Damn, sister, you can't catch a break."

"Oh, but wait—there's more. She's also pregnant."

"I feel like this qualifies as asshole fodder. Or am I wrong? Is there something I'm missing here? This just doesn't seem like Jake."

"He tried to tell me. A few times, actually, but I kept—I don't know—I pushed him away because I didn't want to hear it. It doesn't matter anyway." She shrugged, taking the glass back and pouring another serving before drinking half of it in a single gulp. "The world I've been so carefully cultivating for the past twenty years is crumbling. Nothing is recognizable anymore. I've spent so long protecting my heart from the curse that there's nothing in my life except for Gigi."

"What am I—chopped liver?" he demanded.

She gave him a sharp, challenging look.

"You realize you have to forgive me at some point, right?"

"Don't be stupid. I've already forgiven you."

"We're going to be okay, sister," he said, putting his arm around her shoulders and stealing the wineglass back. "I promise."

There was a sticky silence in the air, and Sadie was overcome with a sudden urge to dip her hands in lemon water to brush away bad luck. And that's when they heard it. Like the universe had heard his promise and laughed in his face. A thump and a cry that had them both running into the house.

Kay was hysterical. Aunt Suzy had her head buried in Uncle Brian's shoulder. The room had grown uncomfortably warm with the weight of so much worry. Anne was on the ground, trying to rouse Gigi, whose small, limp form shoved a spear straight through Sadie's heart.

Finally, after a heartbeat that seemed to last for eternity, her eyes opened.

"Fell," she croaked.

"Let's get you to the hospital," Seth said, and Sadie wondered how he kept his voice so calm.

"Pishposh," Gigi said, her tone as disgruntled as the look on her face. "Absolutely not. What are they gonna tell me, sugar?" she asked, trying to sit up. "That I've got cancer? Just help me to the couch, would you?"

Despite her best efforts, Gigi's face twisted in pain as Seth half carried her to the living room.

"Mommy," Kay cried, sinking to the ground and clutching Gigi's hand.

"Now that's enough," Gigi said in a not unkind voice. "I need to speak with Seth and Sadie. Alone," she added to the room at large.

"I'm not leaving your side," Kay argued.

"Like hell you aren't." Gigi's voice was turning crochety now.

"Everybody out," Anne said, taking charge as always, and they dutifully scattered.

Sadie was still by the door, unable to propel her legs forward until Seth gently pushed her.

"My time is coming. Soon, I think." Gigi said.

"The knot of Isis," Sadie choked out.

"I told you that damn thing wasn't gonna work." She turned to her granddaughter. "Sadie, there are spells I've done, rituals that you two will have to take over after I'm gone. You know Julian is buried on the grounds of Old Bailer. Now, that property isn't in our name anymore. It got passed to the state after it was marked as a historic landmark. But our blood is still in the land, and that's why we buried him there. Evanora has kept his spirit at bay, but every year on the day of his death, you've got to salt the perimeter of his grave to keep him where he belongs. Write his name on a piece of paper, and burn it with the flame of a black candle, saying the words I taught you long ago. You know the ones. Make sure the rope on the bell by the front door is changed on the same day."

She nodded numbly.

"Now you, you little pissant," she said, turning to look at Seth, "my lost boy. I knew you'd come back. You're wrong about not using your magic. The more you try to snuff it out, the more it will consume you. You can't run from who you are. You're meant to be a light on a hill, but you have to let your sister help you. Don't be so damn prideful, you understand?"

Seth nodded as well, but the look on his face showed Sadie it was taking everything in his power not to break down.

"As for the life debt, you have until the first full moon after I'm gone to satisfy the balance, or the forces of magic will claim what's owed once and for all, you hear me?"

"But *how*," Sadie started, unable to even find the right words to ask a question she probably already knew the answer to.

"There's got to be a spell or something, right?" Seth demanded.

"Only the one I already used." Gigi smiled sadly.

"We could—" Seth started, but Sadie cut him off.

"And create a death sentence for somebody else? Absolutely not. This is our problem. We'll fix it."

"Now, the last thing. About your mother." Gigi's cheeks were red as she held the back of her hand to her mouth. "I don't know when she'll come back, but she will. When I die, she'll be free to return. Her magic"—Gigi paused, her eyes traveling to distant memories—"her magic's not like ours. Be careful with it, but give her a chance," she said to Sadie. "For my sake, give her a chance. It's my fault she left. Try not to blame her. And Seth, she'll pull you in. Don't get too lost in her. Remember you're the only one that can define who you are. And you, Sadie, you take care of your brother. Promise me," she said again in an urgent voice.

"I promise by the lemon tree, and by the lemon tree I keep my promises," Sadie recited, the words falling heavy from her lips.

Gigi sighed and nodded, wincing as she leaned back again.

"I'm not saying goodbye—not yet. But I need to make sure everything is in order. I have to make things right. My curse . . ." She shook her head, unable to finish, her eyes pained.

Sadie couldn't look at Seth. She couldn't look at Gigi. The house was closing in around her, Gigi's fate hanging in the air like a thick, acrid smoke that choked Sadie until drawing a breath was impossible.

"I'm going to carry her up to bed," Seth said.

"Nonsense," Gigi muttered, but she didn't argue any further.

Sadie stood, lost in her own living room. Her eyes caught on the besom hanging on the front wall of the house. The twigs tied around the stick needed to be trimmed, the twine rewrapped. Gigi had taught the twins about the besom when they were little older than toddlers. The ginger moon shone through the lace curtains as Sadie got up and took the broom off the wall.

"Always start by the front door and sweep the dust inward," she heard her brother say from the bottom of the stairs, where he leaned against the wall with his arms crossed and a small smile playing about his lips.

"If you sweep outward, you'll sweep your luck away," she finished with her own sad smile. "I remember. I'd be in the kitchen doing homework sometimes, and she'd be sweeping. It always smelled like cinnamon. Like that dish soap she always made. She put cinnamon in everything. She said it brought even more luck into the house and that she knew it worked because that's how she'd always done it, and she'd gotten to be our Gigi, which made her the luckiest grandma in the land."

"It's crazy, now, knowing how she got stuck with us."

"I don't think she sees it that way."

"I know, but you know what I mean. I mean"—he shook his head—"I can't even wrap my head around it. I don't want to. I can't think about it because it feels so disloyal to her. Gigi, I mean. Not . . . not our mother."

"I can't think of her being gone. I don't know how. I just—" She blinked rapidly, trying to keep the sting of tears from her eyes.

"I know. But you can't spend your last days with her like this. I know it's hard, right? But let's try to be happy, celebrating her and her life. I see the way she's been looking at you. She'll never say anything, but I have to. Don't let your sorrow be her burden. Wait until she's gone to mourn her. You know what she's always told us: 'Don't borrow trouble.'"

It was the gentlest Seth had spoken to her in years. And that's how she knew he meant it. And annoyingly, she knew he was right, as he so often was. She would be useful, cheerful, happy, even if it killed her. Even if it felt like little pieces of her were dying right along with Gigi.

The next day, Anne was the only other one awake when Sadie ambled blearily downstairs, following the scent of fresh coffee. She'd spent half the night choking back tears and the other half letting them flow. Her eyes were puffy, and her hair settled in a wild halo, making her look like a Botticelli painting come to life.

Anne wordlessly poured a second cup of coffee.

They sat at the bar, and her aunt was still uncharacteristically quiet. Normally, her words came at the speed of thought, her internal monologue flowing out like a constant conversation with herself.

"Did you sleep?" Sadie asked her.

"Of course not," Anne answered. "I never sleep anyway."

"I'm going to the farmer's market. Do you want to go with me?" Sadie surprised herself by asking. It was usually one of the things she reveled in doing alone. Perusing the vegetables like she was picking out a dinner date; chatting with the stall proprietors; letting Jim, the potato seller, badger her about opening up her own stall.

"Absolutely," Anne answered without hesitating. "I need to get out of this house."

The sun was still cold, the morning breeze rustling through the ponderosas like whispers and secrets as they caught themselves on the sharp points of the pine needles. Anne turned the heater on and rolled down her window. Warmth and chill played across Sadie's skin, and Joni Mitchell's "Circle" blared on the radio. Her hand was out the window, the wind gliding smooth over her fingers, buffeting them like a wave, and she smiled, her head tilted back against the headrest. In that moment, she was happy. And the realization made her guilty, snatching away the slice of joy as sure as the wind whipped it from her fingers, carried away by the undertow until she drew her hand back in, and the lyrics of the song washed over her.

We're captive on the carousel of time
We can't return we can only look
Behind from where we came
And go round and round and round
In the circle game.

Sadie was caught on the carousel of life, her knuckles white against the shining, braided brass pole, but her ribboned horse seemed only to go down. And even then, the guilt bubbled like burnt sugar. Others had it worse than her. Destitute or in slavery, without food or home or love, who'd lost children. And here she was, bemoaning Jake and her brother and her grandmother. Gigi, who'd lived a long life and had given every ounce of love she'd possessed.

"What are you thinking about over there?" Anne asked.

"Do you think we have a right to our pain when so many others have it worse?"

"I don't think pain is a competition," her aunt answered without hesitation. "Somebody else's ten might be your six. You can't compare heartbreak. No matter what, it's valid. And that's all that matters. You're allowed to feel," she added, as though aware of Sadie's internal struggle.

"Sometimes I think if I let myself feel, really feel, I'll never be able to climb my way back out. I can't stuff it all back in."

"You're not supposed to, sweetheart. You're like a volcano. One of these days, you're going to erupt. Do they have jewelry at this market? I'd love to find something for Emily. You know your cousin and her jewelry."

Sadie chuckled. Just like that, Anne could never stay on one thing too long. It went against her nature.

They ambled around the market, Sadie introducing her aunt wherever they went, and Anne pouring out tidbits of her life before jumping to another subject so fast it gave the listener whiplash. The air was filled with the smell of ripe tomatoes and fresh flowers.

By the time they were halfway through the stalls, their arms were laden with cloth bags full of vegetables and fruits that Sadie didn't grow in the garden. But there were also the things she never would have bought that Anne pounced on. Lavender-scented soaps and mason jars full of local amber honey so fresh it still had bits of hive in it. She bought a hand-painted ashtray for Gigi and a bottle of pomegranate balsamic vinegar for Brian. And even though Sadie tried to convince her not to, she bought a bonsai for Seth. For Sadie she picked out a hand-carved wood birdhouse to put in the garden. And she found a moonstone pendant for Emily.

"We're going to need a wagon if you buy anything else," Sadie said with mock sternness.

"Do they sell wagons here?" Anne asked, completely without irony.

And that's when she saw him.

Jake.

Standing at Jim's stall, perusing potatoes. And there, beside him, was a woman whose intense, striking beauty seemed to sing out from her. Bethany.

Sadie had expected her to be showing, but her thin, runner's frame was lithe, with no visible bump. Of course, she had to be perfect. Her hair was a thick, lustrous curtain the black of a midnight, moonless sky. It swayed as she turned her dark eyes up to Jake. And when he looked down at her, his eyes darted back up, as though sensing her presence.

She wanted to turn around and bolt. The dread pooling in her stomach turned sour, and the bile at the back of throat tasted alarmingly of jealousy.

And then, something Gigi used to say echoed through her head, words she'd whisper to Sadie as a little girl when they'd walk down the sidewalk and mothers would pull their children hurriedly to the other side of the street. Words that would unfurl around Sadie as a gossamer protection when Seth would beg her to use her magic to make them normal, clutching her hand in his in the darkness of a fingernail moon.

"You know who you are. Never let anyone or anything mold you into something different. Don't let those idiots tell you what to do or how to live your life." And so she plastered a smile on her face as Bethany followed his line of sight. She could have turned tail and run. Instead, she puffed up her tail feathers and did the right thing.

"Jake!" Sadie called with a smile so bright she thought it might shatter her face. "And you must be Bethany. This is Anne, my aunt. She's visiting from out of town." If she let a moment of silence hang, she might crack. Thank goodness Anne could talk the ear off an auctioneer and seemed to sense Sadie's distress. The next few minutes were peppered with Anne's questions and Bethany's answers, and Sadie did everything in her power not to look at Jake, even though she could feel him watching her.

"How are you liking small-town life so far?" Anne asked.

"I'm just visiting while we decide on some things. But it's much . . . smaller than I was expecting," Bethany said carefully.

"Truer words have never been spoken," Sadie said with a light laugh. "Congratulations, by the way. You look radiant." And she did.

"I'm not showing yet," she said with a smile that didn't quite reach her eyes.

"How's Gigi?" Jake asked, his wary eyes traveling from his affianced to Sadie and then back to Bethany. "Her grandmother is sick," he explained.

"Yeah, cancer." Sadie nodded, her lips automatically pursing into a frown. "She's . . . okay, I guess. It's hard to tell with her sometimes. She never complains."

"Oh." Bethany reached out her hands to Sadie, who did the same on instinct. "I'm so sorry. My grandmother was my best friend, and she passed away from cancer two years ago." She squeezed Sadie's hands with honest concern in her eyes that made Sadie itch with discomfort.

"Thank you," she said, trying and failing not to like her. Stunning *and* nice. *Damn it all,* she thought.

"I hate to be rude, but speaking of Gigi, we better get back," Anne interrupted before Sadie was forced to think of another response.

"I hope I see you again," Bethany said with a smile, her hair wafting cardamom like a spicy wave of welcome.

"Hard not to in a town like this," Sadie told her, and they smiled at each other.

Jake looked back over his shoulder at Sadie as they walked away. This would be the new normal. Stolen glances and hidden memories, secret desire and guilt bitter as bile.

Anne was suspiciously quiet as they loaded everything into the car. The ominous sky reflected Sadie's mood. The wind tasted bitter and whispered of the changes on the horizon. Sadie shivered.

Things were picking up. And she didn't like it one bit. Her emotions were in a swirl, and her brain couldn't decide which problem to worry about. Just as she shut the trunk, a clap of thunder resounded through the sky. Storms like this always messed with her magic.

"Should I ask?" Anne asked, interrupting her thoughts.

"No point." Sadie sighed.

And surprisingly, Anne didn't say anything else—just reached over and squeezed Sadie's hand.

"What was she like?" Sadie asked, feeling it was safe to ask in the quiet space of the car, the hum of the old engine cutting through her words. She knew Anne would know whom she meant without clarifying.

"As Mom would say, 'wild as a march hare.'" Anne laughed. "She was a pain in my ass, I'll say that. We had some good times, but she had her own friends. There was drugs and drinking, and I was too straightlaced for that. Always afraid of getting in trouble. But not Florence. Trouble followed her wherever she went."

They were quiet the rest of the way home, Sadie turning the words over in her mind. Her mother. The one she knew almost nothing about. Who would, according to Gigi, someday make her way back. Soon.

They ate dinner in the living room that night since Gigi was in too much pain to sit at the table. She tried to balk, but none of them would hear it.

The next week passed in a blur.

On Sunday, Sadie refused to go to church, but Gigi put her foot down.

"I won't have you hanging around here wasting your life with some doddery old fool. I know they're having a potluck today after service, and you're supposed to bring something. You always do. So, go. And take the rest of this gaggle with you. Give me some peace. Gail has the café today, but tomorrow your butt is going back to work, you hear me?"

In between preparations for getting ready, Sadie made thyme and sesame crackers to go with her garlic dill dip. Anyone eating them would find themselves a little more honest and open than they usually were. Normally, she'd bring sweet instead of savory. But time was short, and tempers were high.

All seven of them piled in Uncle Brian's van and arrived just as worship was starting. There was only one row with enough seats together, and of course it had to be directly in front of Bethany and Jake. She tried to ignore his baritone voice and the way it burrowed into her bones, warming her.

During the greeting, Mr. and Mrs. Rodriguez came over, Sofía and Camilla trailing behind.

"Oh, mi querida!" Mrs. Rodriguez held out her hands to Sadie and squeezed them before pulling her into a hug. It was warm, and she smelled faintly of cinnamon, and Sadie wanted to sink into her forever. For all Raquel's mock complaints about her

family, Sadie had grown up envying her. Mrs. Rodriguez drew back, and Mr. Rodriguez pulled her in next.

"We're always here for you—whatever you need," Mrs. Rodriguez told Sadie. "And Raquel, don't forget you have to take your sisters to soccer practice after church," she added sternly.

"Yes, Mamá," she answered, but as soon as her mother left, added, "If she'd let Camilla get her license like a normal teenager, she could drive herself." And then she wedged between Seth and Sadie. She held Sadie's hand during the prayer, giving it a gentle squeeze.

Sadie didn't hear a word of the sermon. Her heart was brittle. There would only be one heartbreak left after Gigi. For she knew, without a doubt, Gigi's passing would be the worst heartbreak of her life. And everything would hang in the balance.

She thought how, in many ways, she'd been preparing for this heartbreak her whole life. The worst one of all. The one that claimed the person you owed your life to.

Before she realized what was happening, Pastor Jay had said his final benediction, and the stampede of feet toward food thundered in her ears.

The long tables were laden with Crock-Pots and platters and plastic bowls. Sadie didn't have it in her to eat. But she tried to be civil because that's what was expected of her.

She stood watching as Aunt Anne talked to everyone, and Uncle Brian stood quietly off to the side. Aunt Tava was drawing a heart on the cheek of Ms. Janet's granddaughter, with the sparkly eyeliner she always kept in her purse. She liked having them there. Even though they were all broken in some way, their love filled in the cracks until it felt almost whole.

Monday looked the same as Tuesday. Sadie was at the café before the rest of the house had even woken up. She made cinnamon challah bread and pinwheel pastries with elderflower jam, rosewater and cardamom panna cotta, and lavender and honey macarons. But nothing was as potent as it should have been. The macarons didn't bring peace, and the panna cotta didn't banish the negative energy the way it was supposed to. Her magic felt thin, and she thought briefly about the Grand Revel in April, when her magic was always at its strongest. If only Gigi would make it that long.

Both days, she came home with sore shoulders from kneading dough, and flour in her hair and under her fingernails. Her soul yearned toward the garden, and no matter how much she tried to wash the desire away with a hot shower and rosemary mint shampoo, it clung firm.

On Wednesday, Sadie barely made it through half her shift, when Gail forced her to go home.

"I know you're tryin' to distract yourself," Gail said, patting her cheek, "but it won't work. Ayana is on her way. So go."

Thursday and Friday looked much the same, and even though she was trying to distract herself, every hour that passed at the bakery she thought of Gigi, counting down the hours until she went home to her. Until Gail or Ayana would shuffle her out the door, demanding she go home. And still, she refused to go into the garden. She couldn't stand seeing the destruction or the way it echoed in her heart.

Anne was always finding something to do, even if it didn't need to be done. She could never sit still. Kay, on the other hand, never left Gigi's side. The two sisters were always at odds, with Tava trying and failing to broker peace.

"Why don't you rest?" Sadie asked Anne in the evening.

"I will," she answered, her hands deep in the sink, scrubbing stovetop grates.

"You won't." Sadie smiled.

"Sometimes it's easier to serve than it is to sit." Anne shrugged. "You know the story of Mary and Martha in the bible?"

"You're Martha?" Sadie guessed.

"Martha was distracted. Or she was distracting herself. Maybe both. But Mary was just sitting there at Jesus's feet. Martha asked Jesus if he cared that Mary had left her to do the work by herself, and told him to tell her sister to help her. He said that Mary had chosen the right path. But they both served a purpose, didn't they?"

"I know what you mean," Sadie said quietly. "It's like love. Sometimes it's harder to let yourself be loved than it is to love. There's more vulnerability in it. It's stepping back and saying, 'I trust you enough to love me.' Like Mary sitting there and just listening."

"Thinking of Jake?"

"When am I not?" She was too tired to guard her tongue, and the honesty slipped out like a will-o'-the-wisp.

"They say that in a relationship there's always the lover and the loved. But I don't think that's right. I think it changes. Sometimes you're the one who loves more, and other times you're the one who needs to be loved. That's what a relationship is. Bracing the other person when they need it. Love is knowing you have open arms to fall back into."

"It doesn't matter. That's all over for me. And I shouldn't even be thinking about that right now. Not with Gigi . . ." she trailed off.

"Death doesn't stop you from loving. It makes the love more important. If it's right, it'll happen. Now get over here and dry these dishes."

By Friday, Gigi was so weak she had to be carried to the bathroom.

Sadie wanted to take the knot of Isis and throw it over Two Hands Bridge. Instead, she called Gail and asked if she and Ayana could take over the café until further notice. Sadie had spent two days a week for the last year teaching Gail's daughter, Ayana, how to make all the staples for the café. Ayana didn't have the Revelare touch, so nothing turned out magic, but it was delicious, which was a magic in and of itself. And Sadie felt confident that they would take care of the café as if it was their own.

On Saturday, Gigi's lucidity started to go. They all took turns sitting with her.

Bambi whined constantly, his wet nose nuzzling Gigi's arm gently.

When Sadie took her hand, her eyes opened, and Sadie tried not to notice their glazed, milky film. But when they rested on her, they cleared.

"Hi, sugar." Her smile turned warm and soft as freshly spun sugar itself. "I think it's almost time."

Sadie forced the tears to remain unshed and sat on the floor beside the couch, gently holding Gigi's hand. Uncle Brian brought chairs in from the kitchen, and they crowded around the couch, Aunt Kay with continual, unusually silent tears streaming down her face. Aunt Tava wore surprisingly muted colors, and the series of stars that had been painted along her cheekbones had been cried off. Aunt Suzy, who had sat through her own mother's death years before, looked gravest of all, knowing, in a way the others didn't, what was coming. She made tea, quietly tidied, and whispered encouraging words in every ear she passed by. Every so often she'd run a tender hand over Gigi's forehead.

They stayed there until the light in the room softened into an evening glow, which was when Gigi started getting restless.

"I need to cut my hair," she said abruptly, trying to sit up.

"What?" Sadie asked, startled by her change.

"My hair. It's a mess. It needs a trim," she said again.

"Okay," Sadie said, confused, but willing to do anything her grandmother asked. She ran upstairs to fetch the shears she used on her own hair. Seth was waiting for her in the hallway when she came back down.

"She's getting ready," Aunt Suzy murmured quietly.

"For what? Her haircut? What do you mean?" Sadie demanded, not liking where Suzy's words were leading.

"I read it in one of the pamphlets at the hospital when my mom was . . . going through this. Toward the end, when they're not completely lucid, they think they need to get ready for something, but they don't know what. They're subconsciously trying to prepare themselves to move on."

Sadie nodded, her face going blank. She would save her emotions for later. Right now, she was on autopilot. Seth squeezed her shoulder as she walked away, and then he and Aunt Anne helped Gigi into a sitting position.

Anne trimmed her mother's fine hair. Sadie's hands were surprisingly steady as she held the mirror for Gigi, who nodded in a distracted sort of way.

"I need a cigarette," she said, her eyes growing clearer.

"You'll freeze to death out there," Sadie said, and then stopped in horror.

"Might be." Gigi smiled. "I'll risk it." Her voice was scratchy, and Sadie had an instant urge to record everything she said so she could have it forever. Why hadn't she ever been better about taking photos and videos? Why hadn't she journaled all of Gigi's stories, recorded all her funny sayings and typed out recipes so she'd never forget them?

Seth scooped Gigi up and placed her gently in her chair outside. Sadie draped a wool blanket around her shoulders and put Seth's slouchy beanie on her head. Abby tried to jump up on her lap, but her barrel chest and fat tummy wouldn't let her get that high.

"You look like a fashion plate," Sadie told her, and Gigi laughed weakly before grimacing in pain. Sadie lit her cigarette for her. Gigi's eyes closed as she inhaled. Anne joined them and lit her own.

"I've been smoking since I was thirteen," she said, her voice thin and weak. "Your grandfather was older than me, and all his friends smoked. The first time I had one I had to rush outside so I could throw up in the bushes. Did that every time I smoked for the first six months. But eventually it went away. Should have known they'd kill me one day."

"Your cancer is in your back and stomach, Gigi," Sadie said, trying to be consoling.

"Potato potahto," Gigi coughed. "That's all I can take." She stubbed the cigarette out having only taken three puffs. By the time she was back on the couch, she was shivering. Bambi stood sentinel beside her. Uncle Brian built up the fire, and Sadie layered blankets over her, but ten minutes later she was sweltering and babbling. She tried to push herself up off the couch, but Seth rushed over.

"What is it? What do you need?"

"Vegas. Have to go to Vegas. Have to pack," she babbled.

"Mom, you're not going to Vegas," Uncle Brian said in a stern voice. "Do you know where you are?"

"I have to get to Vegas." Her voice was getting more agitated as she tried to push herself off the couch.

"Listen, Gigi, you stay here. I'll go get your suitcase. Don't worry—we'll get you all packed," Seth assured her. But of course, he didn't move.

"Okay." Gigi nodded and settled back into the couch. She closed her eyes, and her breathing slowed, her chest falling flat. Seconds passed before it rose again. Seconds that lasted an eternity. She slept fitfully for an hour. At times Seth and Uncle Brian would have to restrain her arms while she tried to fight them off, until finally her breathing grew more rapid, and she opened her eyes. When they landed on Sadie, they cleared fully.

"Hi, sweetheart," she breathed.

Sadie forced a smile, unable to speak even if she could find words.

"Now you listen to me, all of you," she croaked. "There's to be no funeral. If you do, I'll come back and haunt you from beyond, you hear me? I've detailed what I want done," she wheezed. "Already paid for cremation service. Sadie, under my bed there's a green metal file box. You'll find everything you need to know in there. There's a notebook with all the ailments of folks around town, and what they need. The recipes and spells too. You'll need to take that over."

"We'll do whatever you want," Sadie told her.

"Take my hands," Gigi demanded. "I'm too damn weak to reach out for you." The twins took her hands. "My curse," she started, but her eyes filmed over, turning distant again. Her next words floated softly in the air between them, clinging to their skin like confectioners' sugar. "Part of my curse was that I would drive my own daughter away. It was my punishment for what I'd done, taking justice into my own hands. The rules of magic are clear on that, and it nearly destroyed me. But then it turned out to be my biggest blessing. Because I got to raise the two of you. You were both born with magic in your veins and a knowing in your souls. When the fire of ancient wisdom burns in you, you will know that it's me there with you, urging you on."

When her eyes closed, they didn't open again, but her labored breathing continued for hours. Sadie took Gigi's pulse religiously, her own heart beating wildly when she could barely feel her grandmother's. Her body temperature dropped, and the skin on her hands turned a mottled purple.

"It's almost time," Seth whispered.

But Gigi kept hanging on, her breathing interrupted by gasping until there was a rattle in her chest that tore Sadie's heart out. Her grandmother's spirit had already gone on, she knew, but her body remained, unwilling to relinquish its hold, as stubborn in death as in life. Her heart kept pumping, though slower and slower still. And so finally, moved by some calling within her, Sadie smoothed her grandmother's hair and folded her hands on her chest. Getting on her knees, she placed her hands on Gigi's shoulders.

"It's okay," she whispered to her grandmother. "You can let go." She murmured the twenty-third psalm, and by the time she'd spoken the last verse, *"And I will dwell in the house of the Lord forever,"* Gigi took her last, shuddering breath.

At the same moment, two hummingbirds flew in through the open window and performed an intricate dance over Gigi's body before flying away.

And now, there were thirty days until they had to satisfy the balance of magic, or one of them would pay with their lives.

Harvest Soap for Luck

Ingredients

unscented castile soap
vitamin E oil
clear cold-pressed Mexican vanilla
Essential oils
clove
cinnamon
orange
lemon

Directions

1. *In a 16-oz. glass pump bottle, combine 2 T. castile soap, a squirt of vitamin E oil, and a splash of the Mexican vanilla.*

2. *Next, add 5 drops of clove, 10 drops of cinnamon, and 15 drops each of lemon and orange. Fill the rest slowly with water.*

♦ 11 ♦

Sadie's hands slipped from her grandmother's shoulders, her brain incapable of processing. Death had a way of sneaking up on you, even when you were expecting it. It was absolutely impossible until it wasn't. Only one thought took over as she stared at Gigi's lifeless body. This was heartbreak number three. And if she'd known—God, if she'd known—she would have taken that tea Gigi had given her when she was thirteen, and thrown it down the drain with a healthy dose of sage to boot.

But she knew, as much as she wanted to, that wouldn't have stopped Gigi from dying. Even if her grandmother hadn't killed Julian, even if she hadn't had the darkness tied to her, death would have eventually exacted its toll.

Sadie had expected to cry. But none of it seemed real. Grief was sticky, and it clung to her bones, weighing her down until she could barely take another step or formulate a coherent thought.

Seth, his face also dry, stepped away to call the coroner. He called Raquel next. Sadie heard her best friend's voice on the other end of the phone. But when Seth tried to speak, he couldn't. He stood silent, his mouth opening and closing but unable to find the words. Sadie took the phone from him and whispered a few words to Raquel.

On numb feet, Sadie walked to the back patio, the creaking door echoing in her bones. The scent of Gigi's last cigarette clung in the air as she sat on the top step, hunched over her knees and trying to draw a breath through her chest, even though it was encased in iron.

It was then that everything crashed into her. Every small gesture, each word, story, gift, birthday card, phone call, and memory that she would never have again.

Her shoulders began to tremble until they quaked, and sobs wracked her body, so violent she had to grit her teeth to keep from biting her tongue. And then there were arms wrapping around her from behind, holding her together. She smelled Seth's clean soap scent and cried harder. He held onto her until the tears stopped. It was short and violent and left her feeling no better than she had before.

"What do we do now?" she asked him.

"I don't know," he answered, sitting beside her, his shoulder leaning into hers.

As they sat in silence, a hummingbird darted in their line of sight, hovering a foot from their faces. Sadie knew it was the same one that had appeared when Gigi had taken her last breath. Its wings beat so fast they were a whir of iridescence, its bottle-green plumage shining with an ethereal light. It vanished after a few seconds.

Seth demanded that Sadie stay outside when the coroner came to take Gigi's body. He didn't want Sadie's last image of her to be her lifeless body covered under a white sheet. He and Aunt Anne took care of everything.

The light was turning amber, the golden hour, and the air was filled with the scent of lavender and sorrow.

She wanted to get under her covers and sleep through winter and wake with the fresh shoots of spring, when breathing didn't feel like dying. Gigi had sacrificed her whole life for her family. She'd lost a daughter in the process. And the darkness she'd tied to herself to ensure the twins' safety—that protection was gone. One of them would soon have the power of a conduit running through them. They needed a sacrifice. And yet, there was less than a month left until the first full moon.

The smell of coffee and breakfast drew her into the kitchen. It was after midnight, but Uncle Brian was flipping bacon at the stove.

"She'd want us to eat," he shrugged, his eyes red rimmed.

Aunt Suzy was pouring coffee.

Tava was making scrambled eggs.

Seth sat at the table, silent, his gaze faraway.

Anne, inexplicably, was making maple butterscotch walnut fudge.

"Mom always used to make it for us when we needed"—she stopped, cleared her throat, and swiped at her eyes—"when we were scared. She said it would make us strong."

Sadie didn't know what to do.

What were you supposed to do after the matriarch died?

"Here," Seth pushed a cup of coffee in her hands and shoved a bear claw in her face, forcing her to take a bite. "I know you haven't eaten. And Gigi stockpiled enough of these for the zombie apocalypse."

Sadie wanted to laugh but couldn't find her voice. Bear claws were one of the staples their grandmother always had on hand—along with cheese crackers, cheese Danishes, sourdough bread, and a drawer filled with whatever candy the discount store had on hand.

"When we were kids, she wouldn't let us leave the breakfast table until we'd eaten everything on our plates," Anne said. "Even if we said we weren't hungry."

"*Especially* if we said we weren't hungry." Kay was half laughing and half crying.

When the sun finally filtered in through the windows, Sadie and Seth were the only two still awake.

Sadie, her voice soft but brittle as she hunkered under Gigi's blanket on the couch, told Seth, "I had to memorize a poem in high school. Pablo Neruda. It was a death poem. All I can remember is the line *'Falling out of the skin and into the soul.'* That's what I feel like."

"*'Death is the enemy. The first and the last. And the enemy always wins. But we still have to fight him.'* Or something like that. Pretty sure that was Beric Dondarrion from *Game of Thrones*."

And despite herself, she smiled, even though it broke her heart.

The first few days after Gigi passed were a fugue best left forgotten.

They all mourned differently.

Kay with wails and tears. Anne with action. Uncle Brian with a soft kind of sorrow that threatened to overcome him anytime he tried to speak. Tava with words and stories. Seth and Sadie with silence.

Sadie had never been depressed. Sad and worried? Yes. But this, this grief felt different. Thicker. Like a shroud she was suffocating under. She wondered if this was what Seth felt all the time. The weight of failure made her empty. Everything lacked purpose. Her words, when she spoke, came out slow, and her whole body ached. Life seemed vacant. *She* was vacant. Not a normal person. She wasn't a patient lying in a hospital bed, but she was sick, nonetheless. Just an empty human.

And every hour, more people stopped by with flowers and food and words that were meant to bring comfort but usually didn't, because comfort is an impossible task in the face of fresh grief. The real consolation was seeing their own grief reflected in the eyes and tears of friends and neighbors and café patrons because it meant they were unified in their sorrow and love for a woman who had touched so many lives.

Cindy McGillicuddy organized casseroles in the fridge.

Bill brought more sunflowers.

Gail came with stories of misspent youth and long-forgotten memories until they were all laughing through their tears.

Lavender and Lace dropped off salted chocolate truffle ice cream that tasted like sorrow.

Mayor Elias and Mr. and Mrs. Rodriguez were there. There were people Sadie knew by name, and others she only knew by sight. All of them with hugs and tears and words that left Sadie's mouth dry.

Mr. and Mrs. Abassi brought a basket of sweets and nuts.

"What will we do without her?" Mr. Abassi asked in a choked voice.

"She left me the recipe for your arthritis. I promise you'll never be without it," Sadie said around the tightness in her throat.

Meera Shaan and Akshay came with a biryani layered with fragrant rice, chicken, and vegetables in a riot of color. Before they left, Akshay slipped a piece of paper into Sadie's hand. After they left, she unfolded the smudged paper, and her tears fell onto a drawing of the little boy asleep in his bed with a red-haired angel watching over him.

There were moments where Sadie was sure she would break. For so many years she'd tamped down her feelings that now it seemed there was no outlet for them. It was too hard to sort through the jagged pain. It threaded through her body, made her limbs weak, her heart heavy as quartz. Dull. Everything was dull and muted and on autopilot. She smiled mechanically at the sympathetic neighbors and friends who came to call.

Cindy mowed their front lawn and brought over fresh coffee.

Pastor Jay stopped by and said a prayer for the family.

The Cavendish, Madizza, Tova, and Delvaux families all arrived together to pay their respects. They wore black and set up a small altar with white candles for peace, a palm stone of banded agate for courage, and sprigs of rosemary to signify a new beginning. They said a prayer and offered condolences, and their tears fell black as night.

Jake came. She knew it was him before she opened the door because the grandfather clock warned her with a long, deep note that sounded, somehow, like it belonged to him. She hadn't cried in hours, but seeing him there on the threshold, she remembered the way Gigi would pat his side when he hugged her, and laugh at his compliments, and the grief felt like a fresh wound. But when he opened his arms, she stepped into to his embrace, and it felt a little easier to breathe. They sat on the front-porch swing, and he pulled a small red box out of his jacket pocket before shrugging out of it and draping it over Sadie's shivering shoulders.

"I went to Hawaii," he said quietly. "To Kona."

Sadie opened the box, and nestled inside was another small silver spoon with a filigree pineapple at the top and "Aloha Hawaii" stamped in tiny letters along the handle.

"I love it," she whispered. "Thank you."

"It's just a spoon," he said, even though they both knew that was a lie.

He sat with her until her tears slowed to a trickle, rubbing soothing circles on her back and holding her hand like it was his anchor to this world. Ten years ago, she had loved his acerbic wit and sarcasm. She had reveled in their physical sparring matches, loved to be the object of his incessant teasing. But this softening had her falling for a different side of him, one she hadn't even known she needed.

"Hey, Sade?"

"Hmm?"

"Did you know that pet theft can get you charged with a misdemeanor and has penalties of fines and possibly jail time?"

A strangled laugh bubbled out of her.

"I'll risk it," she said.

When he left, she was still clutching the spoon in her hand.

And every day her magic caused some kind of minor catastrophe.

The upstairs bathroom flooding when she tried to wash her face.

The coffee urn shattering when she filled the filter with ground coffee.

She would wake to find dirt in her bed with no idea as to how it got there.

And always there was an internal clock counting down the days until the full moon.

On the one-week anniversary of Gigi's passing, Sadie woke on the verge of retching. Her breath came in hitches as the panic made her vision go blurry in the early dawn light. She had dreamed of the full moon, of Seth dead and cold on the ground after they'd been unable to find a way to satisfy the curse. He'd sacrificed himself, and it broke Sadie's heart. She wept and where her tears fell in the frosted grass, black obsidian sprouted up. She tried to bring him back, but his death was the fourth heartbreak, and her magic was gone. Her stomach churned as she tried to rid herself of the images.

Twenty-three days, Sadie thought. *Twenty-three days, and I might never hear that voice again.*

They took turns being strong. But it was hard, in that first week, to become accustomed to the truth of death, the reality of it.

Tava, Brian, and Suzy went home, promising to return when Seth had collected Gigi's ashes.

"Where are you going," Sadie had demanded wildly. She needed them there. Needed the anchor.

"We'll be back," Suzy said again. "We don't want to spoil the surprise. But it's a good thing, I promise."

Kay and Anne stayed.

"I'm sure you're tired of people asking," Raquel said one afternoon, "but how are you doing? Really? Slow descent into madness?"

"I don't know," Sadie answered honestly. "It's like I don't know how to feel. Or maybe I forgot how to feel. But I know that can't be true because it hurts. All the time, it hurts."

"It was always going to hurt, *cariño.* All you can hope for is that the love is worth the pain. And I know it was."

Raquel was talking about Gigi, but Sadie involuntarily thought of Jake.

"Have you tried gardening?" Raquel asked tentatively.

"No," Sadie answered automatically. "I can't go out there." Every time she'd tried, the closer she got to the back porch, the more she felt rooted to the spot, until her feet tingled and her soul seemed to stretch in the opposite direction. The magic of the garden seemed, in her mind, tied to Gigi. And Gigi was dead.

"You'll get there," Raquel told her, holding Sadie's cold hand in her own warm one.

"And speaking of getting there," Seth said, walking into the living room on the tail end of their conversation, "we need to talk about the sacrifice. The conduit."

"I'm not losing you too," Sadie said with vehemence.

"Sade, it was just a dream," he said softly. All she had to do was look at him and know he'd somehow seen her terrible vision.

"You're my priority now," Sadie said. "The thought of losing you—" She broke off.

"I know," he said. "It makes you furious and bitter and terrified. I can feel it rolling off you. But that's not how we tackle this. You're the one with systems and solutions, okay? I'm the ideas guy. We'll fix this together."

"I'm the moral support," Raquel chimed in. She tried to make her voice light, but Sadie could see the fear buried in her eyes.

Seth gave her a grateful smile and then stood, pulling Sadie to her feet. He put his hands on her shoulders and leaned his forehead against hers.

"I'm here," he said. The words echoed in the chaos of her brain. *"Neither one of us is going anywhere."*

She nodded and tried to believe him.

"Now get your ass into the garden," he said. "Get your hands in the earth. You know it always makes you feel better.

"Why is everyone trying to get me to the garden? It was destroyed, remember?"

"Because sometimes we know what's better for you," Raquel said with a smile that formed itself like a secret.

"Sometimes?" Seth asked.

She didn't go into the garden that day. She spent each hour obsessively working through all aspects of the curse, every morsel of information they knew, and making plans. And constantly she fought the urge to heed her brother's and best friend's advice until, finally, the evening light called to her too strongly to ignore. The smell of fresh earth and green stalks had been following her around too long.

She cautiously opened the back screen door, her chest tight and lips pursed, bracing herself. Maybe if she could just feel the dirt against her skin, it would make her feel closer to Gigi. Give her some kind of inspiration about the sacrifice. She braced herself for the devastation, the uprooted plants, the scattered bushes, the work she'd need to do to get it back in order. Maybe that was what she needed. Something to do with her hands, to keep her thoughts at bay.

But some kind of miracle had been wrought. Nearly everything was replanted or fixed. She walked down the tight rows, brushing her hands along velveteen leaves, soaking in the comfort of the wild sweet peas that had been reattached to the arbor. The scent of sage and rosemary mingled with mint and thyme, soaking into her skin like a homecoming. She marveled at the squash and zucchini plants, all the trampled leaves and crushed vegetables cleared away. Already there were new blossoms peeking through the foliage. Who had done it?

Certainly not Seth—the garden still wouldn't let him in—and Raquel could kill a plant just by looking at it. It had to be Revelare magic, Sadie concluded in wonder.

Sitting down right in the center of the garden, the early September sunshine warming her skin, she sank her hands into the earth. A peach plopped off the tree and rolled toward her, stopping just within arm's length, like an offering. She wanted so badly for it to be a good omen, but it was hard for her to believe in goodness just then. Even so, the garden welcomed her back. Emerald-green leaves reached toward her, and tight flower buds opened into blooms in a wave of hello. Some of the brokenness inside her began to knit back together as the very dirt seemed to call to her. She had almost forgotten what pleasure felt like, but as she picked up the peach and inhaled its fuzzy skin, the scent of summer memories and childhood mixed with the earthy soil, and it smelled like a promise.

She heard a low, grumbling meow, and a fluffy black cat slunk out from behind the sweet peas. He came straight toward Sadie, rubbing against her legs, calling out in a gravelly meow. His fur was so downy and wild, particularly around his neck, that he looked like a lion in cat form. And Sadie was instantly drawn to him. He peered into her eyes and seemed to see her sorrow and reflect it, absorbing it as he crawled into her lap, turned in a circle, and lay down. She knew without understanding that this cat was now hers. Maybe she'd have to give Jake his dog back. But probably not. *Maybe we could have shared custody of him,* she thought with a wry smile that felt foreign on her face.

"I think I'll call you Simon," she whispered, stroking his ears and head as he purred louder than a motor. And from that moment, there was nowhere Sadie went in the garden that Simon wasn't. Every time he meowed in his gravelly voice, it reminded her of Gigi's bullfrog laugh.

"Hey!" A voice from the fence line startled her. Jake.

"Hey," she answered.

"Can I come in?"

She nodded, and he pushed the old gate open. Sadie made a mental note that she needed to repaint it.

"Stupid question, but how are you doing?" he asked, and it reminded her of the way Raquel had asked it. Like they both knew there was no good answer, but they needed to know she was still in there.

She shrugged again, her throat growing tight, the ground growing warm beneath her knees. She'd been asked that question so many times, it had started to lose meaning.

He came over and sat down near her, wrapping his arms around his pulled-up knees.

"How'd I do?" he asked.

"What do you mean?" Her voice was brittle.

He gestured to the plants with his head.

Her brain was foggy. He couldn't possibly mean . . .

"You did this?" she demanded, incredulous.

"What are friends for?"

"But, *how*? When?"

"I had a small garden in the city. On the roof. It helped me, I don't know, block things out. And I had some help with this one. Cindy delivered fresh dirt, and Bill fixed the fence. Gail helped with the configuration. I know it's not exactly how it was. But when I told them what I was going to do, everyone wanted to help. This town rallies when something needs to get done."

Sadie was speechless. Warmth spread through her chest, and she wanted to cry, but in the kind of way where you were so overwhelmed that the tears are a beautiful release instead of a painful one.

"I thought it was magic," she whispered.

"Thanks," he said with a little laugh. "Sade . . ." He paused. "Can I do anything for you?"

She wanted to tell him about her curse, about the life debt, about her confusion. She wanted to tell him she couldn't do it. Any of it. That life was breaking her into a hundred jagged pieces. That she knew what she wanted but couldn't voice it because it made her a terrible person, and that thought scared her more than anything else. All she'd ever wanted was to be good. And wanting Jake was the opposite of that. So why did it feel like the only right thing in her life? It was always going to be him. She would have loved him no matter what, but this version of him? He was a new person, and that meant he had the opportunity to break her heart all over again in a new way.

"Just sit with me," she said instead.

He did.

And even though he belonged to someone else, there was a part of him he reserved just for her. A space with her name on it. She could feel it in him. And she thought that no matter how many decades went by, no matter whom they loved or lost, or where they ended up, that small piece of real estate in his heart would belong to her forever. And it would have to be enough.

"Thank you," she mumbled finally, leaning on his shoulder, just for a moment, and stealing some of his warmth.

The next morning, she woke with her chest feeling not quite as heavy as the day before. She'd sat in the garden with Jake, the silence shrouding them until the frogs and cicadas started their evening song. Until he said he needed to get back. To Bethany. And there wasn't even any room in her heart to feel anything about that.

She paused on her way downstairs, Gigi's door illuminated with a soft light. She felt the pull. The green lockbox she knew was under her bed. The one that held all the details about what she wanted for her less than traditional memorial service. But she couldn't bring herself to go in. Not yet.

Anne was already in the kitchen, the coffeepot full, the counters sparkling, and the smell of butterscotch hanging in the air.

"Here," said Anne, pushing a plate toward Sadie. "Have some with your coffee." She poured her a cup and added just the right amount of cream.

"Fudge for breakfast?" Sadie arched a brow.

"This family runs on sweets. You should know that by now."

Sadie took a small bite, and her chest went tight. It was Gigi's recipe, and Aunt Anne had done it perfect justice. The maple played with the butterscotch, and the velvety smooth texture was cut with the crunch of toasted walnuts. She chased it with a sip of coffee, the heat and bitterness cutting the butter and sugar.

"Wisdom and strength," Anne said.

"She made this when we opened the café. I remember it like it was yesterday."

"You always will."

The day passed in a slow kind of blur where time played its old tricks until the sun began to set. They were drinking coffee around the kitchen table when Anne asked about the café.

"I should check in with Gail," Sadie said, feeling guilty she hadn't already.

She took her mug and walked out front, barefoot, the cold grass anchoring her to the earth. There was something about misty fall mornings in Poppy Meadows that came straight from a storybook. All was peaceful and cozy. Smoke curling from chimneys. It was cold, but the kind you could warm up from fast and didn't need heavy clothing for. The coffee hot in her hands, she circled the lemon tree first and the Japanese maple second. The hedges were looking unkempt, and she realized with a jolt that the front yard would have to be her responsibility too now, along with the back.

With heavy fingers, she pulled her cell out and called Gail to ask how she was doing.

"You know there's nowhere I'd rather be, honey. I've got nothin' but time on my hands," Gail told her. "My two oldest goin' off to college, bless 'em. And another getting' married. And Ayana's doin' great. But how are you? That's the more important question." Her voice was thick, and Sadie knew she was holding back tears.

"I'm hanging in there." It was the barest sliver of truth. "I'm going to come into the café tomorrow. I need to—I don't know—I think Gigi would want me to go back. Not sit here and wallow. And I need something to do. Some normalcy."

"We'll be here waitin' for you, honey."

Sadie hung up and as she stood on the path, a hummingbird zoomed up, hovering not two feet from her, its wings a blur. It stayed for twenty seconds, staring at Sadie before flying up to hover outside Gigi's bedroom window. The bird seemed to say two things at once. *"Good job for getting back on the horse and do what you know needs to be done."*

"I'm going, I'm going," she told the bird. And it bobbed in the air before flying off.

Her footsteps up the stairs were soft and even softer as they padded to Gigi's bedroom. Abby followed her up, her toenails click-clacking against the wood. The poor creature was barely eating, and Sadie had never seen so much sorrow in an animal's eyes. Together, they stood at the doorway, the sight threatening to bring down the wall she had so carefully been resurrecting around her heart. Everything was exactly the same as it always was. Framed photos on Gigi's wooden chest of drawers. Scarves hanging on hooks on the wall. A pair of small, hand-painted, porcelain elephants on her bedside table next to a half-empty glass of water and a pair of reading glasses. The curtains billowed despite the closed windows, like they were happy to have someone in the room again.

Abby whined at the foot of the bed, and Sadie picked her little barrel-chested body up and deposited her on the comforter. The dog then proceeded to sniff her way up to Gigi's pillow, where she took a shuddering breath, turned in a circle, and lay down.

Sadie, focusing her eyes forward, got on her hands and knees to feel under the bed. Her hand hit something metal, and she pulled out the dull moss-green lockbox. Gigi, organized as ever, even in death, had left a page of instructions lying on top.

Sadie smiled wanly, as though her lips had forgotten how to. As she'd said, the cremation service was already paid for. Seth was to pick up the ashes, and then they were to have a family dinner in place of a memorial. Gigi had even detailed what food was to be made.

"No mourning," she'd written. *"Set the table for twenty-nine."*

Twenty-nine, Sadie thought, her eyebrows shooting up. She did a quick calculation. That meant all her cousins were coming. Even second cousins. This was everyone.

In the box were tax information and the deed to the house, which had been transferred to Sadie and Seth. There was a journal, worn and weathered, that Sadie couldn't quite bring herself to open yet. And there, held together with an old blue rubber band that came from a bunch of asparagus, was a stack of letters. Hers was on top, and she flipped quickly through the rest. One for each of the aunts and uncle Brian, Seth, and Florence.

With trembling fingers, Sadie opened hers. At times, she could barely read the words through her tears.

Hi Peapod,

Unfortunately, the task of delivering these letters falls to you. But you've always been my good girl, so I know you'll do it. Now, I'm sorry for dying. A silly thing to apologize for, isn't it? But I know how mad you can get sometimes, and I don't want to leave you with any anger. God knows Revelares are too good at holding grudges, and if there's one thing I regret, it's not letting go of them sooner. If I hadn't been so stubborn, I could have said goodbye to Dickie. But it was too late. It's not for you. It's always been so easy for you to forgive, except when it comes to the people you love the most. But you remember those manners I taught you, young lady. Your job is to forgive that brother of yours. And your mother too, whenever she decides to show up.

Now as for the life debt, I'm sorry I kept it from you for so long. But some truths are best kept like dough; they need time to proof. I shouldn't be telling you this, but there's a way for you to nullify the curse. This is a last resort, and I'm only sharing it because I'm afraid of what else you'll try. But if you sacrifice yourself, Seth will be safe. When you give up who you are, you become someone new. And that means all the old debts are forgiven, the dark magic nullified. You're a new creation. It's a baptism of sorts, that kind of sacrifice. Just make sure you're prepared for it.

Lastly, I know you've always closed yourself off because of your curse. It's easier not to lose anyone when you don't let them in all the way. But that's no way to live, sugar. You'll figure things out. And it'll get easier with time. Know that you and Seth were my pride and joy. I will love you every moment of forever. Now, go live your life, you hear me? I believe in you. I always have.

Love,

Gigi

The looped, old-fashioned handwriting, Gigi's "chicken scratch," clung to Sadie's heart. The tears burned hot on her cheeks as the lights flickered overhead.

Twenty-one days.

That was all she had left.

Twenty-one days until the full moon. Until the life debt had to be paid.

And Gigi had written about sacrificing herself as casually as she would have discussed the proper way to flip fried chicken. And what was with the ending telling her to go live her life? How could she live her life if she sacrificed herself to save her brother? It was madness. All of it. She wanted to laugh but knew if she did, she'd end up sobbing and unable to stop.

Instead, she clutched the lockbox to her chest and curled in a ball on the floor.

Through the high window she could see the waxing gibbous moon, soft and eerie, the symbol for changing seasons, life and death. Gigi's knit blanket slid off the bed and laid itself over her, tucking in at her shoulders.

Everything seemed utterly lost. Gigi was dead. Her aunts and uncles would soon return to their lives and jobs and homes. Seth had never promised to stay. And Jake—well, it was too late for that. Gigi had been the glue that held them all together. With her gone, everything unraveled. Everything she'd ever been, all that she'd known, it died with Gigi. And she couldn't do it. Even with her life, or maybe Seth's, hanging in the balance, she couldn't think of a single way to nullify the conduit magic.

And in that moment anger dominoed through her heart. Anger at Gigi for killing Julian and incurring the life debt; at her mother for putting Gigi in a position to have to; at Julian for being the world's biggest dick; and all the way back to Evanora Revelare for picking that goddamn diablo buckwheat up on Rose Hill.

The quiet murmur of voices floated up to her on the cold floor as she let the anger burn hot through her. It felt good. Even if it was only a numbing sort of Band-Aid.

And then a gentle knock on the front door reverberated through the floor, after which the grandfather clock blasted a dozen notes, like a call to arms.

Maple Butterscotch Walnut Fudge

It won't heal sorrow, but it will spark wisdom and strength, traditionally for new beginnings, ventures, or the new year. I also made it the day before Sadie and I opened the café. Running that place with my favorite girl have been some of the best years of my life.

Ingredients

1 c. white chocolate chips
1 c. butterscotch chips
1 c. chocolate chips
1 can (14-oz.) sweetened condensed milk
¼ lb. butter (1 stick)
1 tsp. maple extract (maybe a dash more)
1½ c. chopped walnuts

Directions

1. *Grease and line an 8 × 8-inch dish with parchment paper. Combine chips, sweetened condensed milk, and butter in a microwavable bowl.*

2. *Heat the bowl for 30 seconds at a time, giving it a stir after each time, until everything is just melted. Don't overdo it, or the chips will get grainy.*

3. *Stir in maple extract and walnuts.*

4. *Pour fudge mixture into tin. Refrigerate until set, and then cut into squares.*

♦ 12 ♦

BEFORE THE CLOCK HAD finished its echo, Kay screamed. Anne's laugh set Sadie's teeth on edge. The house seemed to snap to attention. Picture frames straightened themselves. Knickknacks scuttled back to their corners. Piles of dust swept themselves under dressers.

There was the sound of footsteps thundering up the stairs, and seconds later Seth burst through Gigi's door.

"You need to come downstairs," he said breathlessly.

And before she could demand why, he was gone again.

She sat up, wiped her nose on her sweater, and set the lockbox down, her heart thudding. She didn't want to go downstairs. Didn't want to see whoever was at the door. But the lights flickered, and a warm breeze shuffled through the room despite the lack of open windows, and Sadie knew it was Gigi reminding her of her manners again.

With trepidation in every step, she took to the stairs and swore they looked like they'd just been polished. Halfway down, as the entryway came into view, she stopped, her bare feet against the wood floor heavy as cinderblocks.

She looked impossibly young. Dressed in all black except for a calf-length velvet duster in a jewel-toned floral pattern. The air pulsed around her, and her inky black hair, cut in a shoulder-length bob with thick bangs, shone iridescent blue black in the porch light. Her face wore a smile that made Sadie shudder. It was Seth's smile. It was hers. Even though she'd only seen a few photos of her mother, she'd recognize her anywhere.

Kay and Anne were hugging her with abandon, but Florence's eyes rested on Seth, dark and glistening like liquid diamonds. Full of hope.

No. Not yet, Sadie thought.

She hadn't given much thought to meeting her mother, so consumed had she been with Gigi's health and the family secrets. When Gigi had said that only her death would let her daughter come back, Sadie had tucked the information away. *In years,* she thought, *maybe she'll come back. After we've had time to grieve.* Yet there she stood.

She was tired of accepting things as they came. Each calamity had stacked up until the weight made it almost impossible to breathe. She'd grown up hearing that God never gave you more than you could handle, but He'd obviously mistaken her for someone else. And this was the last straw.

Manners. Manners, Sadie. Gigi would have your hide. Instead, she said, "You've got to be shitting me."

Everyone's eyes snapped up to her.

And then Sadie saw her. She'd been partially obscured by her aunts. A girl, maybe seven. She wore a rainbow tutu over striped leggings and a shirt that read "Unicorns are real." Her Converse sneakers were scuffed, and she held a raggedy stuffed lamb in one hand. Sadie saw a slight movement to the girl's right, a shape that rippled in the air, but when she looked closer, it vanished.

"I'm sorry," her mother finally spoke. "I know this must be a terrible shock."

"Nonsense," said Kay, pulling Florence's arm and dragging her over the threshold. "Come in out of the cold. I can't believe you're here. I can't believe you're real!"

"And who's this?" Anne asked.

"I'm Sage," said the little girl. "And this is Cocoa." She held up the stuffed lamb.

"Your sister," said Florence, her eyes were guarded as she put a protective arm around the child's shoulders. Just then, Bambi ambled out from the living room and went to Sage like he'd been waiting for her. He nuzzled his nose into her little hand before plopping down beside her like a sentinel.

"Impossible," Sadie breathed, finally finding her voice. "The conduit magic—" she started, but Anne cut her off sharply.

"I've heard that lambs love hot chocolate. Is that true?" her aunt asked.

Sage nodded, her eyes wide.

"Come on then. I happen to have a *very* special recipe I think you'll like." Anne held out her hand, and Sage looked to her mother, who nodded briefly, before the girl took Anne's hand. "Come on, Kay."

"But—" Kay started to whine until Anne gave her a wicked glare. "Fine, fine, I'm coming. You're so bossy."

Bambi traipsed after them, and then they were alone, Sadie still halfway up the stairs, Seth still mute, the door still ajar.

What do I do? The thought traced itself over and over in her brain.

And then Florence held out an arm to Seth. Without a blink he walked forward into her embrace.

Sadie felt the tug of jealousy. It was what Seth had always wanted. But when Florence held out her other arm, a question in her eyes as she looked at Sadie, her feet moved of their own accord. And then, after twenty-eight years, she was hugging her mother. And they were both crying.

"I miss her so much." Florence sobbed quietly. "I never got to say goodbye. I missed so much."

Seth made a strangled noise as a sob escaped.

Sadie pulled back awkwardly, staring at the ground.

Their mother was back. But even knowing she'd left because of the magic, the curse, didn't take away the sting of abandonment she'd felt her whole life. Florence may have given birth to her, but how was she supposed to behave toward the woman when she'd never set eyes on her? What were the rules of civility when it came to long-lost mothers? Sadie, who hated trying new things for fear of being bad at them; who refused to do things in front of people because she didn't want to mess up; who liked to seem like she knew what she was doing, even if she didn't. And right now, she was a sailor without the stars.

Seth pulled out of their mother's embrace too, and the three of them stood there, not knowing what to say or do, until finally Anne called from the kitchen that hot chocolate was ready.

"I know we have a lot of things to talk about," Florence said. "Can we stay? I'll tell you everything so long as you do the same."

Sadie was surprised when Seth looked to her.

"Yes, of course," Sadie croaked out. "You're family, after all."

Sadie winced inwardly. Blood? Yes. They shared that. But family was more than blood. It was memories and love and late-night phone calls and being there when no one else was; none of which they had with this beautiful woman who stood before them, her hair so shiny it looked reflective, her eyes so eager it made Sadie's chest ache.

By the time Sage had fallen asleep at the kitchen table, her head pillowed on her stuffed lamb and Bambi at her feet, Sadie still couldn't decide how she felt. So instead, she told Florence they could take Gigi's room for the time being. Florence carried the sleeping child, her *sister*, Sadie reminded herself, upstairs.

"I'll be right back," Florence said over her shoulder. And like a dutiful bodyguard, the dog trailed after them both, his head held high, as though he'd been waiting for the assignment his whole short life.

"I can't believe she's back," Kay said again the moment she was out of earshot.

"About damn time too," Anne said, sounding exactly like Gigi.

"Did you know?" Sadie asked the aunts. "About Sage?"

"I didn't," Kay said at the same time Anne nodded. "You're such a bitch," Kay said, though there was no venom to it.

"We've barely kept in touch." Anne rolled her eyes, and their bickering continued until it stopped abruptly when Florence walked back in.

"I'm sure you have a million questions," she said, taking a seat at the table. Her voice was weary.

"What's your magic?" Seth asked, like he just couldn't help himself.

Sadie's eyebrows shot up at the question. It certainly wasn't the first one she'd wanted to ask.

"Magic . . ." Florence was frowning now, twirling a spoon idly in the air. "Magic is only as powerful as the curse that accompanies it, you know. My curse was Julian. And from that, being parted from you two"—she pointed the spoon at Sadie and Seth in turn—"and the rest of my family."

Sadie pursed her lips at the answer in the form of a riddle. It reminded her of Tava.

"I ran for years," Florence continued. "Like I said, my curse wasn't just to leave, but to be a wanderer. Always chased by sins of the past. The ghosts, spirits—whatever you want to call them—would never let me rest. Anyway, I guess it's time you heard my side of the story. I think we should start from the beginning."

And while a dark, cinnamon-scented wind picked up and made the oak tree tap, tap, tap on the window, Florence began her story.

"I fell for Julian as a teenager. I was wild, I'm sure mother told you." She laughed but there was an edge of sorrow to it. "I only wanted trouble and freedom and, most of all, to rid myself of my damned magic. I wanted to see who I was apart from this, this *legacy* that had been heaped on my shoulders."

Sadie watched Seth's face as he drank in every word, knowing he found in their mother a kindred spirit.

"Looking back, I realize I wanted to separate myself from the family to find myself. But back then, I told myself I was in love. And Julian was my ticket out.

"By the time I realized I was lying to myself, I tried to leave him, but something always compelled me back. That's when he told me about the ritual to rid me of my magic." Sadie's skin crawled as though rubbed all over with wood nettle. "Of course, it was really to make me fertile. I was stupid to believe him," Florence said simply. "I blame myself. I should have never tried to run away from who I was. *What* I was. I was too scared and stubborn to ask for help. And then I was pregnant.

"I didn't want to leave you. But you have to understand: I was physically unable to stay. The spell Gigi cast . . . I was forced away. Fate pushed me until I was outside the city limits. Even then, I stayed as long as I could. I hovered in the next town over, but catastrophe started to strike. Natural disasters appeared out of nowhere, following no scientific pattern. And then people started dying. It was my fault—I knew it was. And so I left. I didn't want any more blood on my hands. After that I could never stay long in one place."

Florence shared how she'd traveled with a carnival for a while, setting up a booth as a tarot and palm reader, dispensing fortunes and warnings like soup to the starving. She told them how she wept every night, and when she'd tried to send letters or postcards or gifts, the very envelopes and packages had burst into flame, leaving an ash that smelled of self-hatred and regret.

"I was so angry, I thought I'd use my magic to become what nature demanded I must never be: an amplifier. I learned everything I could about who we are, what we can do. I delved into the deepest, darkest parts of myself, hoping that by some miracle I could find my way back to you. But miracles are for fools who don't believe in fate."

Florence told them how she'd been at rock bottom, wondering what her damnation would be if she were to take her own life, when in reality she knew she never could. Never would. Not without seeing Sadie and Seth again. And that's when she decided maybe she could have a second chance.

She performed a ritual, fully believing it wouldn't work. She found a man with no name, and two months later was shocked to find out she was pregnant with Sage.

"It was my chance to start over. To try again. To do it right this time. Because even though the curse isn't my fault, even though I'm not the one who killed Julian, it was my fault. It was all my fault." She broke down then, covering her face with her hands, trying to keep her sobs quiet so as not to wake her second-chance daughter upstairs.

"And now Mom is dead. She sacrificed everything for me. For my kids. And I couldn't even hold her hand at the end."

"She knew," Anne reassured her. "I promise. She always knew."

"I'm more grateful to her for raising you than you'll ever know," Florence added, turning to the twins. "I know she did a better job than I ever could have. I'm sorry I wasn't there. I'm sorry I fell in love with the wrong man."

Her apologies piled up, a burning mess scattered on the floor between them, charring the wood until the smell of cherries burned Sadie's nose. Seth, by his own measure, drank in every word of her story. In his eyes, there was nothing to forgive, there was only time lost that he could finally attempt to regain. Sadie's heart, on the other hand, was like the pile of apologies glowing amber on the floor.

The longer Florence spoke, the more Sadie's teeth set on edge. Every word clawed its way in, establishing roots. Her mother wanted to be a family: that much was clear, though Sadie doubted she'd ever say it. But what was family other than blood? It was time and love and memories. It was arguments and forgiveness and compromise. Her thoughts drifted unwillingly toward Jake.

"I know mom tied one of your lives to her own," she added, grabbing Seth's hand across the table. "I know her death unleashed all kinds of things. I promise, I swear, I'll help you figure it out. If that's what you want," she added, looking to Sadie this time.

As Sadie watched her brother, the way he looked at their mother, the hunger in his eyes, she wondered if she was going to lose him all over again. She'd had him to herself their whole lives. And then he'd left. And now that he was back, their mother threatened to capture his heart.

"It doesn't have to be like that, sugar," she heard Gigi's voice whisper in her ear. *"There's always enough love to go around. You've learned to be stingy with it because of your curse. But it's time to let that go."*

"Do you know which one of us is the conduit?" Sadie asked.

"I don't. But Sage can help us with that tomorrow. We'll figure something out. I promise." Florence smiled reassuringly. "Now, there's nothing more we can do tonight. So, it's time for everyone to tell me what I've missed."

Kay started, of course, and told Florence about every detail of her job and the misery of it and the string of younger men she'd had brief flings with, until Anne finally cut her off. She chimed in about Steven, their kids, and the new grandbaby. Then it was Seth's turn.

"I guess I'm kind of like you. I never wanted my magic. Jesus"—he ran a hand through his hair—"I never even knew what it was, really. Or how to explain it, I guess. And then about a year and a half ago or so, it started getting worse. I didn't want it. I'd never wanted it. I always wanted to just—I don't know—be normal, I guess."

"Hard thing to be in this family," Florence said with a small smile. "What exactly is your magic, if you don't mind my asking?"

Sadie held her breath. She'd been wondering about that since time beyond memory.

"I guess I'm pretty good at knowing what people want. Or what they need. Even if they don't know it themselves. I know their deepest secrets," he said, his face etched in misery. "Everything from their greatest desire to their most inane wish—I know fucking all of it."

"Oh, honey," Florence said, her voice soft with sympathy, "that's got to be so tough."

"But Seth," Sadie broke in, shaking her head with brow furrowed in confusion, "that's amazing."

"Amazing," he scoffed, turning to his sister. "It's my curse. That's the legacy, right? Every Revelare has magic, but they also have a curse. Mine just happen to be one and the same."

"How can you say that?" Sadie argued. "You can use it to help people!"

"Most people don't want to hear what they need. Most people—normal people—have secrets for a reason. I don't want to know that shit, trust me. And you wouldn't either."

Florence looked back and forth between the twins, unsure of her place.

"When did you know?" Sadie asked. And when Seth didn't answer, she asked again, demanded in a voice that brooked no argument.

"Before I left, I started, I don't know . . . feeling things. Hearing them. Seeing people's wants, needs, desires. It was driving me insane. I couldn't control it at all."

"That's why you really left," Sadie whispered.

"Yeah," he intoned, his lips pursed as he nodded.

"You left?" Florence asked.

"I guess it's in his blood," Sadie said, regretting the words the moment they were out.

Seth looked mutinous.

At that moment the fireplace in the living room sprang to life, the wood suddenly popping and snapping as though it had been roaring for hours.

"I'm sorry," Sadie said, shaking herself and turning to Florence. "I didn't mean that."

Didn't you?

"Sugar, you have every right to how you feel," her mother said, and it was so similar to something Gigi would say that Sadie's throat tightened. "And you have every right to hate your legacy," Florence added to Seth. "Trust me, I did for a while too. But your grandmother, she believed in what we had. She used it to keep our family together, to help people, and God knows I'm far from that, but I try."

"I'm not saying it doesn't have its perks," Seth said. "I know what people want to hear. I can get any job I want, anything or anyone I want. I can basically manipulate anybody to do what I need them to. When I left, I did that for a while. But none of it was real."

"We're more alike than I thought, then." Florence's smile was sad and full of shadowed memories better left to midnight. "It's an empty life, isn't it?"

"I never wanted to leave. But I couldn't, I don't know, I couldn't separate myself. I thought leaving would help me figure out who I was apart from Sadie, apart from the stupid family legacy. But I was miserable. When I came back, I told Raquel everything. I don't know why, but when I tried to use my magic on her, it didn't work. So it felt safe, I guess."

"Wait a second—Raquel knows about this?" Sadie demanded, her brows furrowing.

"She tried to help me turn it off." He shrugged.

"I don't know who Raquel is, but you can't get rid of who you are," Florence said in a voice that spoke from experience.

"I'm with her on this one," Sadie echoed.

"Trust us, honey," Tava said. "We've all tried to escape at one point or another. But every time we leave, we realize there's no place better than with the people who love us the most."

"You can't imagine what it's like, okay? I go to pay for my gas, and the checkout guy, his girlfriend is pregnant by another guy, and he's so miserable all he wants is to kill himself. And I feel it so strongly that suddenly I feel like I want to kill myself too."

"You haven't felt this your whole life?" Florence asked.

"Some part of me has, I guess. But it just kept getting worse."

"And now?"

"I've basically become a hermit. If I'm not here, then I'm somewhere nobody else is. I can't go out in public."

"Seth"—Sadie reached out to him, grabbing his hand—"why didn't you tell me any of this? I'm so sorry."

"Because I knew you'd try to help, and I love you Sade, but you just don't get it. You'd want me to use it to help people. But I have to help myself first or risk losing my goddamn mind."

"You know if you actually let someone in once in a while, maybe you'd realize that you don't actually know everything," she said.

"Well then," Florence interrupted, "I guess we don't need Sage to tell us whose life is at risk."

"What?" Seth and Sadie asked at once as all eyes in the living room swiveled to Florence.

"Oh, come on," she said. "Isn't it obvious? Mom had cancer. Guaranteed she knew before she even started showing symptoms. And she hid it. It was probably around the same time Seth's magic started acting up. Because as her health got worse, the bonds of magic would have deteriorated, and the conduit magic would have spiked. *Your* conduit magic," she clarified, pointing to Seth.

"What?" Sadie started. "But I—then how come my magic has been going haywire?"

"Grief will do that to you," Florence answered with a frown. "So will any kind of strong emotions you can't control. You've always had your magic, known what it was and how to use it. For Seth, it makes sense that it was muted because of Mom's—I mean your grandmother's—enchantments."

Nothing could have stunned Sadie more, but the moment her mother spoke the words, she knew they were true. And that's when she felt it. The dread. The very reason she'd never wanted her mother to come back, even when they were little.

Florence was already pulling Seth away.

She'd lost her brother once, and now she felt him slipping away again. Seth had always had a hard exterior. If you didn't know him, you'd think he didn't care about anything. But Sadie knew how sensitive he really was. And now their mother was here to show him what Sadie could never make him believe. His worth. His legacy.

"Let me ask you something," Florence said, interrupting Sadie's dark thoughts. "It doesn't work on blood, right, Seth?"

"No, thank God. Then again, I can't get it to work on myself either," he replied. "Sometimes I wish it would."

"That would be far too easy, wouldn't it?" Florence asked with kindness. "Magic doesn't work like that, unfortunately."

"So, you can't tell what I want? What I need?" Sadie asked her brother.

"Other than a swift kick to the ass every now and then? No. But then again, that's not magic—that's just common sense."

"Hilarious," Sadie murmured, rolling her eyes.

Part of this felt normal. And how that could possibly be, Sadie had no idea. Maybe it was because Florence had a hard surety to her the same way Gigi had. She wanted to learn to love her. To forgive her. But that felt like a betrayal to Gigi as the woman who'd raised her. And how could she possibly welcome with open arms the woman who had left them, had another daughter, and now threatened her relationship with her brother? So many conflicting emotions left her exhausted. But she'd said she'd plumbed the depths of their magic, and if she could help save Seth without Sadie having to sacrifice herself, well, she could make nice for the next two weeks, at least. At the thought, she remembered the letters. The lockbox.

She left and a moment later returned, setting everything on the table.

Seth stared at the letter like it was a ticking time bomb before tucking it away in his back pocket.

Kay snatched hers up hungrily, already crying, and went to the living room.

Anne and Florence opened theirs on the spot.

Sadie excused herself to the back patio. She needed space. But Bambi had other ideas. He followed her out the screen door and nudged into her leg until she sat down to pet him. Then Simon slinked his way out of the garden and up the steps, rubbing against her other side, his tail flicking back and forth until he settled against her hip with one of his gravelly mews. Bambi watched her and then plopped down too. It was the silent support she needed in a way only animals could sometimes offer.

Now that everything had been stripped from her, she knew there was nothing worse than losing the thing you loved most. Her curse had dictated more than half her life. It had made her dread love instead of cherishing it. Push people away for fear of heartbreak instead of drawing them close for strength and healing.

She sat there until the lyreleaf opened and the screech owls sat silent in their towering trees. She pulled her sweater tight against her to keep out the cold, wrapped her arms around her middle, and hunched over her knees. All she wanted was to hear Gigi's voice, to feel the warmth of her rough hands as they patted her cheek. But mostly, she wanted to know what Gigi would have had to say about Florence, her prodigal daughter finally returned home.

"I used to sit out here and watch her garden," a soft voice said from beside her.

Sadie startled, for the door hadn't creaked as it always did.

Florence leaned her elbows on the railing. "I was never very good at it," she continued. "Tava was the worst. She had a black thumb. Could kill a plant just by looking at it. Anne, well, she was and still is a nerve ending." She laughed. Sadie could tell by the tone of her voice the way she'd missed her siblings over the years, the longing inside her for everything that had gone on without her. "She'd start a garden and harvest a few tomatoes, and then move onto the next thing, the next idea, the next project. And Kay never had any patience for it. She'd just as soon use her magic to burn your hair as to coax a bloom to life."

"Our family is royally screwed up." Sadie sighed.

"That may be," Florence agreed with a nod, "but honey, that's what family is. Every family is messed up in its own way. The drama, the politics of it all, navigating the hurt feelings and the expectations and your place in it all. There are grudges and anger and bitterness, and you say things to your family you'd never say to anyone else because you love them the most, and at the end of the day, you know they're the ones who will forgive you. You do things for family, things you never thought you'd do." Her words were spoken from experience, and though she smiled at Sadie, there were twenty-eight years of sorrow buried in her eyes. "And that's all without magic, by the way. We've just got a little more to contend with."

"How do you look so young?" Sadie asked without thinking, unable to keep the question in.

Florence laughed then, a soft, tinkling sound. It was the kind of laugh that could draw you in, make you want to share in the mirth, even if you didn't know what it was for.

"Magic is good for some things, at least," she said with a sly smile. "I stopped by your café earlier, you know. It's incredible. I'm so proud of you."

Sadie's throat tightened, and she didn't even know why. This woman meant nothing to her. She'd spent her whole life telling herself she didn't need a mother, thinking Seth foolish for his obsession. She had spent nearly thirty years painting a picture of herself she wanted others to see. Strong. Independent. But when it was all stripped away, with her mother here before her, telling her she was proud, who was she?

In that moment, Sadie hated magic for what it had taken from her. She'd always believed the curse was worth the magic. But with each heartbreak, she was less certain. All she wanted was to hold on to her beliefs, but everything she ever saw as true was slipping through her fingers like starlight.

"Listen," Florence said when Sadie didn't speak, "I screwed everything up. That wasn't part of my curse—that's just me. Even if I could have stayed, I probably would have screwed you and your brother up too. But I want to try, okay? I want Sage to have a place she can call home. I want to do right by all three of you."

As she spoke, the strange, burnt scent of asafetida drifted from the forest line. Sadie glanced that way, looking for the figure, but there was nothing to be seen.

Dream Catcher Hot Chocolate

It's more work than the instant packets, but that stuff is crap anyway. This will cure bad dreams and send the drinker off to a sweet slumber. It can also cure headaches and heartaches and make you feel like all is right in the world.

Ingredients

3 c. whole milk
3 T. good-quality cocoa powder
6 oz. semisweet chocolate (sub milk chocolate for creamier taste, or bittersweet for extra punch)
3 T. sugar
splash of vanilla extract
dash of cinnamon

Optional: Fine sea salt sprinkled on top or mixed in gives it that delicious salty-sweet flavor.

Directions

1. Bring ¾ c. water to simmer. Whisk in cocoa powder until smooth, add milk, and return to simmer.

2. Whisk in chocolate, sugar, cinnamon, vanilla, and salt, and stir until mixture is smooth and chocolate is melted—about 5 minutes.

3. Split among mugs, and top with whipped cream *and marshmallows*.

♦ 13 ♦

SADIE SLEPT FITFULLY THAT night, dreaming of lost things and garden gates that wouldn't open, no matter how hard she tried. She woke smelling the lingering scent of cigarette smoke and Gigi's perfume. And for a few blissful moments, she forgot the events of the previous night, her mother a hazy dream. She forgot until she walked past Gigi's bedroom door, and the memory of last night crashed over her, cold and salty and wild.

Her mother.

Florence was back.

Anne and Seth and Florence were moving around the kitchen in a practiced dance. Sadie looked in from the doorway, trying and failing to find her place. Even though there was room for her, she couldn't quite figure out how to maneuver herself between them.

She had thought her brother might look more worried. Had been prepared to promise him the moon. Tell him she would take care of it all, the way she always did. After all, there were only twenty days left. But she'd never seen him look so content. No hint of concern lined his face, only a quiet kind of wonder.

"Sadie!" Florence said when she spotted her. "Sweetheart, how do you take your coffee?"

"I'll make it." Her tone was shorter than she'd intended it to be. "I'm just—I'm going to take this upstairs. I'm going into the café." She pretended not to see Anne's understanding look or the flash of hurt on Florence's.

She heard Florence's soft laughter from the staircase. Her mother was already taking up too much space. Sadie could let her in, she knew. It would be an easy fall, soft as babka dough. But she only had one heartbreak left. And that would break her, and she would lose not just her magic but also more of herself in the process. She couldn't trust herself. She couldn't trust what else her magic, or her curse, might take from her.

She pushed up her sleeves and pulled her phone out of her pocket. There was a text from Raquel.

Holy shit. Is it true?

Yep.

She's back. I can't even believe it.
How are you holding up?

Exactly as you'd imagine.

I'm meeting Jake at the school, to
teach him the lighting, but want
me to come over after?

Sadie's fingers hovered over the keyboard. She wanted her best friend. But that felt like cheating. She had to be an adult, didn't she?

Yes, but no. I need to work.
Need some normalcy. See you
for Gigi's memorial dinner on
Thursday though?

Of course. Love you.

Sadie finished her coffee, thinking she should probably take a shower and shave her legs, but it seemed too monumental a task. Instead, she got dressed in fleece-lined leggings and a slouchy sweater that slid off one shoulder. She focused on the movements that felt natural but foreign. Sliding rings on her fingers and fastening a crescent moon choker around her neck that Seth had given her on her eighteenth birthday. Swiping kohl eyeliner around her eyes and trying not to linger too long on the dark circles that shadowed them. It was the first time she'd truly gotten dressed since Gigi's death, and something about it felt like a small kind of betrayal. She brushed it aside, knowing Gigi would have told her to "knock it off," and instead, her eyes slid out the window to the garden below, thinking about Jake on his knees, planting, weeding, fixing her haven, until she had to swallow around the lump in her throat. She glanced toward the spoons that held a place of honor on her messy nightstand.

You shouldn't want what's not yours, she told herself. She'd always been so set on doing the right thing. Being a good person. On justice. But her head and heart weren't matching up.

Draining the last sip of her now cold coffee, she slipped Gigi's journal into her purse and then tried to sneak out the front door, doing her best to ignore the chatter filtering out from the kitchen. But the door wouldn't budge.

"Stop it," she hissed.

The doorknob rattled in defiance.

"Let me out."

She could feel the grandfather clock watching.

"Don't even think about it," she warned it. But it let out a gong that sounded like an alarm.

"If you don't let me out right now, I'll paint you a hideous orange and never grease your hinges again," she whispered furiously.

It swung outward immediately just as the last gong of the grandfather clock died away. Sadie saw her mother from the kitchen entryway, the second before the door slammed shut. Her mouth had been open like she was going to call out to her, and Sadie tried to quash the guilt that stuck to her fingers like honey.

"You sure you wanna be here?" Gail asked from the front counter.

"I need to bake out some of this stress." Sadie smiled and took a deep breath as she entered the kitchen and turned the oven on.

While it preheated, she took out Gigi's journal, hoping that something inside would lead her to an answer. About what to do concerning the curse. About her mother. She'd even take guidance on what she should bake today. Anything, really.

She opened it gingerly with shaking fingers. She flipped through pages filled with recipes for food and spells, teas and poultices. Dried flowers were pressed between the pages, with their meaning and uses written in the margin. There were jotted memories and a few faded photos, and a newspaper clipping from the *Poppy Meadows Crier* announcing the grand opening of A Peach in Thyme. There was a random grocery list on a faded piece of notepaper.

vanilla yogurt
sourdough bread
salted butter
cherry cheese pies
jelly beans
bear claws
tomatoes
Diet Coke
bell peppers and onions

And there, on the last page, were two photos. One was black and white, of Gigi and her kids out in the front yard, the border faded to yellow and a crease in one corner. The other was of Seth, Sadie, and Gigi at the Country Christmas Festival the previous year. Sadie remembered it with a bloodred vividness because it had been the last photo they'd taken together before Seth had left.

Sadie reached the end of the journal, and a strange peace settled in her bones. It felt light and bright as starlight. She had nineteen days to save her brother. And in a flash, she was up and pulling down ingredients. Twice-blessed salt and fresh rosemary from the garden, finely chopped. She zested and squeezed the juice of lemons from Gigi's magic lemon tree. It dribbled down her arm, and as she whirled to grab a dish towel, she ran smack dab into a solid chest.

Jake reached out his arms to steady her. His hands on her shoulders sent a series of light sparks dancing in her vision.

"Where's the fire?" he asked.

"What? What fire?" she demanded, turning about the kitchen.

"Sade," he said, choking back laughter as he turned her back toward him, "it's a joke. An expression. I meant what are you baking in such a hurry?"

"Oh. Lemon rosemary cake," she said in a rush. "It's for clarity. Pure clarity. What are you doing here?"

"Checking on you."

She flitted out of his reach, grabbing a dish towel and the crystalized sugar in quick succession.

"Hand me the baking soda. And flour. And grab the vanilla yogurt from the fridge."

He laid everything on the counter as she took out measuring cups.

"You're sure you're okay? What do you need clarity for?"

"Everything," she said breathlessly.

"Okay," he said, laughing. "I love it when you go into intense mode. I'm headed back to the station. I've got another twenty-four hours, then I'm off for forty-eight."

She nodded without seeing him and thought he'd gone. But a moment later she heard his voice from the door.

"Hey, Sade?"

"Hmm?" she asked, running a finger down the recipe on the page.

"Can I have my dog back now?"

"No." She smiled without looking up, and when she turned around again, he was gone. The scent of rosemary wafted up as she ground it with mortar and pestle, and something tugged at the edge of her thoughts. Something about Jake that was trying to make itself known as the pungent herb took over her senses. But she pushed it away, focusing only on Seth and how to save his life. Nineteen days felt like forever and no time at all.

She made five loaves of lemon rosemary cake, leaving four for the café and bringing one home. She found Seth with Florence and Anne, and pulled him aside, dragging him into the kitchen, where she pushed him into a chair.

"We're going for a walk," Anne called from the front door.

"Eat," Sadie said once the door had closed, pushing a slice of cake toward him and taking a bite of her own.

He stared at the plate and then back at her.

"Listen, dumbass," she said around a mouthful. "I need your help. We need clarity. This will give us that. I'm not letting you die, got it? Now, eat." She pointed to the cake again.

Wordlessly, Seth took a heaping bite. She watched as he chewed, and her stomach flipped as his eyes went wide.

"What? What is it? Did you think of something? An idea?"

"It's all so clear," he whispered. "But no, it doesn't make sense." He shook his head, his brow furrowed in confusion.

"What! What doesn't make sense? Just tell me, and we can figure it out together." Her voice was breathless. She didn't think her food had ever worked so fast before, which had to mean something good.

"You need . . ." He paused.

"What?"

"To go on a vacation because you are way too uptight," he finished, laughing.

She screamed in frustration and threw her piece of cake at him as he kept laughing.

"I'm sorry," he said, wiping frosting from his cheek with his finger and then licking it off. "I mean, great cake, first of all. And second, you had to know that was coming."

"Seth, you're not taking this seriously!"

"Oh, I'm taking this quite seriously, sister. I just refuse to let it ruin what time I have left in case we fuck everything up, and I don't make it."

"Stay there," she said, her voice stern. It was time for something drastic.

She grabbed a piece of paper and a pencil, sketching an intricate diagram that reached the edges and then snaked right off.

"Why do I feel like this is a bad idea?" Seth said. He may not have liked the legacy growing up, but he knew enough to know a summoning spell when he saw one.

"Shut up and grab the Thieves and clary sage while I get something of Gigi's."

She almost lost her nerve as she reached Gigi's door. But she needed a charm. A totem. Something to represent her grandmother. Stealing in with silent footfalls, she quickly grabbed the knot of Isis without looking around. Next, she pulled twice-blessed salt and a pure white candle from the cupboards before forcing Seth up and outside. They trekked out past the tree line. Simon followed them to the edge, but refused to go further.

Her heart was a syncopated rhythm. This could work. It had to work. They needed answers.

Lighting the candle, she waited until there was a small pool of melted wax, and then scattered salt in to bind Gigi's spirit. She held out her hand and Seth wordlessly handed her the Thieves essential oil and clary sage, the first for fortification, and the other for clarity. She put a few drops of each on a small bundle of dried pine needles before lighting them on fire.

"I really don't think—" Seth started, but Sadie cut him off with a glare as she placed the knot of Isis on top of the diagram.

"Show yourself," she whispered under the canopy of trees. Light filtered in from above, the wind less fierce in the thick copse. The flame flickered. She closed her eyes. She smelled sap and pine and that particular bite of cold that promised rain. Sticks and rocks poked at her legs as she knelt on the ground, but she ignored them.

"I need to know what to do. Please, Gigi."

She picked up the knot of Isis and squeezed it in her hands, focusing on the memory of Gigi with every ounce of willpower she possessed.

Simon's gravelly mew from the tree line startled her eyes open. The flame was still lit, swaying gently.

"Please, please, please," she whispered over and over until the silence threatened to undo her. She grabbed Seth's hands in hers, and her eyes pleaded with him to at least try. He sighed but closed his eyes, focusing.

And that's when she felt it. A bone-seeping cold that stole her breath like a bad dream. It was back. She shivered, and her breath came out in a puff. The flame blew out, and with shaking hands she tried to relight it.

"No, no, no," her teeth chattered with cold and anger. "Not right now!" She took a handful of salt and scattered it in a circle around her and Seth.

"Sadie," Seth said, gripping her hands tighter as his palms frosted over. "What. The. Fuck," he gasped as the cold stole his breath.

She looked around but couldn't see the form. Could only feel its presence. It didn't want them here. Didn't want them doing this. It tried to linger—she could feel it pressing against the circle of salt. But it held. And after a few shaky breaths, the cold receded.

When she tried to light the candle again, her fingers shook so hard she dropped the lighter. Seth swiped it up before she could.

"Have you lost it? We're leaving. Up," he commanded, tugging at her arm.

"No, I just need to try again." Her voice sounded desperate, even to her own ears, but she still pushed him away and tried to grab the lighter out of his hand.

"Jesus, Sade." He reached down and picked her up, throwing her over his shoulder like she was a sack of flour, and stamped the pine needles out with his foot before marching out of the forest.

"Put me down!" She pummeled his back until he finally stopped at the edge of the garden.

"Is that supposed to happen?" he asked.

"I don't know. I can't see what you're talking about, you caveman!"

He lowered her to the ground with more care than she expected, and she was about to thank him when she smelled the ash and her heart sank. A patch of sweet peas that Jake had so painstakingly tied back up and coaxed back to life had shriveled up. She ran trembling fingers along the curled leaves and shuddered as they crumbled to the ground as dust.

"There's a reason you're not supposed to do that kind of magic," he said. "Where did you get that damn spell? Gigi never would have used something like that."

"Calliope," Sadie coughed as the scent of ash stuck in her throat.

"Fucking Calliope Madizza. I should have known. That girl has got a death wish."

"I needed to talk to Gigi," she said, her voice breaking.

"You have *me*," he said tightly. "I know it's not the same. But we're in this together." And when he hugged her, she sank into it. "Now, you mind telling me what the hell that was in the forest?"

"I don't know," she confessed. "A spirit?"

"No shit, Sherlock. You've seen it before? Felt it?"

She nodded.

"Great. Well, I'll tell you what. You try and stop summoning malevolent spirits, and I'll try and stay alive long enough to stop you from making stupid decisions."

"Seth?" she said as they walked back to the house with his arm around her shoulders. "I'm glad you're back."

"I'm glad you're letting me back in."

On Thursday morning, the day of Gigi's memorial dawned bright and cold. There were sixteen days left until the full moon, and they were no closer to an answer. Sadie had consulted Lavender and Lace, who had no advice but offered to help in any way they could. Seth had reached out to the Tovah family, who had their own unique brand of magic when it came to elixirs, and the Delvauxs, who were partial to spells. He refused to speak with Calliope, but at any rate, none of them had ever seen a curse quite like theirs.

"Just set it aside for today, okay?" Seth had said before he left to pick up Gigi's ashes. "Look at me, Sadie." She did. "I'm trying to be cool, calm, and collected here, but this is scaring the shit out of me too, okay? But I need you here for this." He gestured around them. "Today is for Gigi. Her memorial. Family dinner.

Whatever the hell you want to call it. We're going to do this, and we're going to do it together. When you feel like breaking, just look at me."

"And then what?"

"You'll just know. The way we always do, okay? Twin shit. You'll look at me, and you'll know I'm breaking too, and that you're not in this alone."

Sadie nodded through her tears and, absurd as it was, agreed to ignore the countdown on his life just for the night.

After that, Seth left with Florence to pick up the ashes while Anne and Sage cleaned. Anne tried to tell the girl she didn't have to help, but there was an eagerness in the child's eyes that was hard to deny. As though cleaning a home was so foreign it became fun.

Ever since the river had flooded—no, ever since the grandfather clock had chimed its warning—things had gone wrong. And it felt like nothing would ever be right again. But then the doorbell rang, and little pieces of Sadie's heart began to stitch back together.

"Uncle Steven," Sadie half shouted, throwing her arms around his six-foot-tall frame.

"Hi, sweetie," he said, a smile in his voice, but there were tears in his eyes. Behind him, the porch was a sea of cousins. Anne and Steven's three kids were there, and they had their own children with them: Liam and Lina who were almost teenagers, and Marie who was just a little strawberry-haired thing. There was Kay's daughter, tall and ethereally beautiful, with soulless jet-black hair and vegan-leather platform boots, holding the hand of her son, who had to be around Sage's age.

Hugs were passed around and the doorframe seemed to expand, wanting to let everyone in at once. The grandfather clock gonged, wanting in on the commotion, and the door had barely closed when someone honked a horn. More cousins filed in as everyone shared tears, and "I can't believe how much you've grown" was a constant refrain.

Happier than she thought she'd ever be capable of being again, Sadie couldn't help but laugh when Aunt Anne had Uncle Steven whistle through his teeth to get everyone's attention.

"Time for dinner prep," she said loudly. "All kids, outside. And that includes the menfolk! Sadie, get Gigi's instructions. John, when Gail gets here, help her carry the groceries in."

There was silence for a moment before everyone scrambled, and then the women marched to the kitchen like they were going to battle.

Aunt Anne soaked tomatoes and mozzarella in basil-infused olive oil and added a squeeze of lemon juice. Ayana baked three loaves of rosemary bread, and Sadie turned one of them into croutons and crostinis, a safe enough task with Sage's help. The message was clear in every dish. Love, remembrance without bitterness or sorrow, a celebration of life and coming together. Welcome. Acceptance. Sadie settled into the rhythm. The clatter and clanking of dishes and spoons scraping pots, all the smells dancing into a marriage of sweet and spice. Fingers dipped into sauces, and ingredients were passed wordlessly when they were needed.

Kay and Tava came knocking not long after, with flowers and hugs and more tears. The kitchen grew noisier, and Sadie opened the windows to carry away some of the racket, the breeze blowing through feeling more like spring than fall. Uncle Brian and Aunt Suzy arrived, and so did Raquel.

"Where is she?" her best friend whispered as she squeezed her tight.

"With Seth. Getting the ashes."

What a strange sentence, she thought.

"What's she like?" Raquel demanded.

Sadie thought how to answer and couldn't come up with one. "You'll have to wait and see, I guess."

"You trollop."

"Takes one to know one."

"Wow. Truly. How do you come up with such clever comebacks?"

Sadie stuck her tongue out at Raquel.

"How's Seth?"

"Stronger than me."

"You know, I spent my whole life trying to break my parents' rules. I was so different than they were. I wanted to know it was okay to be *me*. Even if I turned out different from how they wanted or expected me to be. One day I came over after a huge fight with them. You weren't home yet. Out harvesting wild yams or something, probably. But Seth was here, and he could tell I was upset. I'd been crying. He was about to go postal on someone, thinking they'd hurt me. So I told him what was really wrong. And you know what he told me?"

"To stop complaining?"

"No." Raquel laughed. "He said he knew exactly how I felt. That ever since you two were little, you'd been *you*. You knew who you were. And he still had no idea who he was."

Sadie swallowed hard.

"I don't think he's stronger than you," Raquel added. "I think he tries to be strong *for you*."

When Seth and Florence came back, both of their eyes were rimmed in red, and Sadie could barely stand to look at the box her brother carried. It was deep brown with a gold plaque and a metal clasp. Gigi returned to dust. But the sorrow was offset by laughter and togetherness and a soft remembrance. A strange and delicate sort of dance that both filled and emptied her.

When Florence entered, Raquel went stock-still where she sat at the kitchen bar, her eyes ping-ponging back and forth between the twins and their mother.

"Mom, this is Raquel," Seth said. "This is Florence," he added.

"Well, goodness, nice to meet you," Raquel said, wrapping her arms around Sage's shoulders as the girl went up to hug her mother. "How darling," she added, looking between them.

"What do you mean?" Sadie asked, brows furrowed.

"How long have you and my son been in love?" Florence asked Raquel, whose face instantly paled.

"What?" Sadie choked out a laugh.

"I—we . . . uh," Seth started, but Raquel waved her hand to shut him up.

"Oh boy. Oh, I see." Florence frowned. "Whoopsie." She laughed uncomfortably. "I'm so sorry."

"What the hell is she talking about?" Sadie demanded, turning to Raquel.

"We were going to tell you," Raquel said. "It just didn't seem like the right time. We didn't want to upset you," she said.

"Correction," Seth countered. "*She* didn't want to upset you. I said you'd be pissed no matter what."

"I don't get it," Sadie said stupidly. "You, the two of you, are *together*?" The thought didn't compute. "And you kept it from me? How long?" she demanded. Her ears were hot, her throat tight, and her chest was breaking out in hives. How many rugs did she have under her that could still be pulled out?

"Not long," Raquel squeaked out.

"Since before I left." Seth rolled his eyes.

"Shut up, Seth," Raquel snapped. "We'd talked before he left, but nothing was certain until he returned. Please don't be mad," she added to Sadie. "Are you mad?"

"I'm not. I'm not mad that you're together," she said, and realized she meant it.

"I'm sorry," Florence said again. "Me and my stupid mouth. I just thought, the way you two are"—she gestured to the twins—"I didn't think you'd have secrets."

"Neither did I," said Sadie. "It's fine," she added in a reassuring tone, seeing the worry in Raquel's eyes. *"Fold it in half. Tuck it away. Everything will be fine."* It wasn't the fact they were together, but that she'd been so entrenched in her own problems that she didn't even think to look or ask. But now all the little moments she'd seen between them made sense.

"On the plus side, if I die, you won't have to worry about it," Seth whispered between them. Sadie and Raquel both hit him. They had decided not to tell the extended family, so they could focus on Gigi's memorial.

"Stop joking about that," Raquel hissed.

At that moment, Ayana's girls, Ali and Maggie, aged five and seven, respectively, broke the silence with their giggling as they darted into the kitchen and then out the screen door to run through the garden. Sage followed them out. It had taken her barely a minute to make friends when they'd first arrived.

Sadie shoved her feelings down into a quiet, dark place in her heart. A space that was getting far too full for her liking. But Gigi's memorial dinner was not the time to let it all out.

"Hello?" Jake called from the front door. "I didn't even knock," he said as he came in the kitchen. "The door swung open on its own." His face was adorably puzzled, and Sadie inwardly decided she'd go six months without greasing that dastardly door's hinges.

He came bearing flowers and six bottles of wine and two of whisky. Once he'd set everything on the counter, he pulled Sadie into a hug that had her cheeks burning before she shooed him out of the kitchen and into the backyard with the kids.

Raquel hummed as she set the table, stopping every so often to squeeze Seth's arm or give Sadie an apologetic look. She'd been banned from anything to do with fire and was relegated to stirring or pulling down ingredients. Seth and Uncle Steven set up extra tables, end to end, until they stretched into the living room, and the whole house was full to bursting with life and food and raucous laughter punctuated with fits of tears.

The kitchen grew warmer with people and heat from the oven and all burners going at once with steamed broccoli and creamed corn and a pot of noodles boiling away for marjoram and white pepper macaroni and cheese.

The fried chicken they saved for last, so it would be fresh and piping hot. The cornflakes crisping up in the grease was a sound that heralded empty stomachs to prepare for the feast. Sadie placed the last dish on the table and called everyone to eat.

A warm, heavy silence fell around the table, cocooning them in their memories and sorrow and gratitude for the woman who had brought them all together. She'd been their strength. And now they had to be hers. Her legacy etched into their souls. Sadie thought of how her dinners always fixed a bad day. The way she'd hang a new shirt in Sadie's bedroom just because she thought she'd like it. And now, life was moving on in a strange new cadence.

It would take days and months and years yet for Gigi's absence to feel normal. But as she looked around the dinner table, she realized that without Gigi's love, none of them would be here. Her whole life had been about building a legacy. Not of magic. But of family. Because magic without family was nothing, but family with love was everything.

Without wanting to, Sadie tapped her glass with a knife, and everyone fell silent. She thought about standing but wasn't sure her legs would support her.

"I won't make a whole speech, because Gigi would have hated it." Everyone laughed. "But I will say this. Gigi had a lot of rules about life." She had to stop as her throat clogged up. She found Seth's eyes amid the sea of people. He nodded slightly and somehow it filled her with courage. She cleared her throat. "But here's to my favorite. Rule number five." She raised her glass. "*'A legacy without love ain't worth a damn, sugar.'*"

All around the table, glasses of wine and pomegranate juice and lemon water went up as everyone echoed, "To rule number five."

That was the kind of legacy she wanted to pass down. And as her curse pressed in on her, it seemed further away than the sun from the moon.

As the evening wore on, Gail and her children all left, trailing curiosity and the scent of cherry cheese pie.

Suzy tried to help with dishes, but Sadie shooed her off, demanding she relax for once. Brian, Jake, and John were playing freeze tag with kids, chasing them from the garden to the front yard and back again. And when Florence silently started loading the dishwasher, Sadie didn't stop her. They worked in a comfortable silence, listening to the children shriek and giggle through the open window over the sink.

"They're all crazy about you, you know," Florence said as she wiped down the counters. "I see the way everyone looks at you. You've got that something special the way mom did. The ability to pull everyone together and keep them there."

"Thanks." Sadie smiled, feeling for the first time in a long while that maybe her future wouldn't be filled with an empty house and occasional holiday gatherings. Sure, there'd be a neighbor through the woods that held her heart, even though she could never hold his, but she had the town, her café, her family.

"Listen, I know you don't really want me here. I know it feels like I abandoned you. It was my own dumbass choices that got us here. I hope one day you'll understand how hard it was for me to leave you." Her voice grew thicker as she spoke, until she stopped altogether.

"I think part of the reason it was so hard was seeing the way it affected Seth growing up. I care more about him than I do myself, and he always wanted answers. He needed more than Gigi and I could give him."

"Well, you know what, honey? I've seen a lot in my life, and there's some things I can tell just by looking, and that's that you will always be exactly what Seth needs. If you weren't, he wouldn't have come back to you. Sometimes, we just need a little perspective and a dose of courage to get the help we need."

Florence's tone meant she was speaking from experience, and despite herself, Sadie felt a crack in the wall around her heart.

Before it could get any wider, she reminded herself that tomorrow meant there were only fifteen days left. There was no time for sentiment if she wanted to save her brother's life.

Marjoram and White Pepper Macaroni and Cheese

I always bake this before someone leaves for a trip. It works for happiness and good tidings on a new adventure.

Ingredients

½ lb. elbow macaroni
3 T. butter
3 T. flour
1 T. powdered mustard
1 tsp. onion powder
3 c. milk
1 egg
12 oz. cheddar (however sharp you like it)
1 tsp salt
1 tsp white pepper
¼ tsp. finely chopped fresh marjoram

For the topping

3 T. butter
1 c. breadcrumbs

(I recommend doubling or tripling this if you like extra topping.)

Directions

1. Preheat oven to 350°F. Cook pasta to al dente (make sure the water is salted).

2. While the pasta cooks, melt the butter in a separate pot. Whisk in the flour, mustard, and onion powder, and keep stirring for about 5 minutes (if you don't, there will be lumps). Stir in the milk, and simmer for 10 minutes, adding the marjoram at the last minute.

3. Whisk in the egg, stir in ¾ of the cheese, add salt and pepper. Fold the macaroni into the mix, and pour into a 2-quart casserole dish. Top with remaining cheese and maybe a little Parmesan if you have some.

4. Melt the butter in a sauté pan, and toss the breadcrumbs to coat. Spread evenly over top of macaroni dish. Bake for 30 minutes.

♦ 14 ♦

THE NEXT DAY WAS a maelstrom of goodbyes with the extended family as hugs were passed around like a tray of chocolate truffles, sweet and decadent until too much made you sad for no reason. But there were promises of the holidays and talk of "next year" like it was the most natural thing in the world. It filled Sadie with hope and fear, knowing none of it would be the same if she couldn't save Seth's life. She spent the rest of the day in her room, trying and failing a myriad of spells and potions and incantations that would satisfy the balance, but nothing worked, and it left her feeling more lost than before.

"Let me help you," Seth argued the next day. She was sitting on the back porch, Gigi's ashtray still unemptied, with the journal on her lap and a blanket around her shoulders. She watched the towering pines sway in the slight wind, the chimes hanging from the eaves clinking merrily.

Sadie had been avoiding him all afternoon because every time she looked at him, all she could see was a countdown. Fourteen days. Three hundred and thirty-six hours. And she'd only responded to one of Raquel's texts asking if she was okay.

I'm fine, she'd answered. Promise.

"I'm fine," she now repeated to her brother.

"Has anyone ever told you you're a terrible liar? At least tell me what you're doing."

"Looking for a needle in a haystack?" she said, tapping the pile of papers on her knees. It was a mark of how far they'd come since he'd come back that instead of pushing him away, she handed him Gigi's journal, letter, and her own notebooks she'd kept through the years, filled with notes and recipes and spells and ideas for the garden. The dark clouds threatened rain, mirroring her mood. Seth's eyes narrowed as he read Gigi's letter.

"But if you sacrifice yourself, Seth will be safe. When you give up who you are, you become someone new. And that means all the old debts are forgiven, the dark magic nullified. You're a new creation. It's a baptism of sorts, that kind of sacrifice. Just make sure you're prepared for it," he read aloud. "What the hell does that mean?"

"If I had to guess, it means I need to remove myself from the equation," she said, her throat tight as she finally voiced the words aloud. Seth looked mutinous. "I know it can't be that obvious, though, right? There's something we're missing, and it's more elusive than a freaking well-made Gateau St. Honoré."

He looked at her blankly.

"The hardest dessert to make in the world?" she said, eyebrows raised, waiting for recognition to dawn. "Never mind," she said, sighing.

"You're weird," he said knocking his shoulder gently into hers. "But look, this can't mean what you think it means. Gigi would never to tell you to off yourself, okay? I'd rather die than let that happen, so don't do anything stupid. Got it?"

She nodded numbly.

"I'm going to make some tea while you read through everything else," she said, heading to the kitchen on legs that felt too heavy to walk. Sage was there, eating a bowl of sugary cereal at the table, with Bambi asleep at the floor by her feet. As Sadie tried to boil water, the bubbles wouldn't come, and she set the mug down, running a hand across her forehead, pressing her palm hard into her skin. She wanted to scream but wouldn't scare Sage like that. The child was tender and caught every look and sidelong glance, calculating them, weighing the words that weren't said. No matter what she felt for her mother, Sage had walked right into Sadie's heart and settled there.

"I can help you," Sage said, her voice soft as merengue clouds, her spoon poised halfway to her mouth.

"Please do," Sadie groaned. Out of the mouth of any other child she'd doubt such a claim, but something about Sage invited trust and calming. The girl walked over to Sadie and laid her hand on her sister's arm.

"What—" Sadie started to ask, but then she felt it. The coil inside of her started to unwind. Peace threaded through her veins like liquid silver. Anger and frustration melted away. Even her sorrow felt diminished. "How . . .?" she asked, but before she could finish, the water boiled.

"I can make people feel certain things," Sage explained, her clear, sweet voice a balm to Sadie's bruised spirits. "I got it from my mom. But I'm better at it than her." Her smile was sly as she said it. "Don't tell her I said that, though."

"Clary Sage," Sadie smiled.

"What does that mean?" the little girl asked, her eyebrows furrowing, unsure whether it was a compliment or insult.

"Clary sage is used for clarity, for emotional stability. And it can spark creativity and imagination. It calms the mind and spirit," Sadie said, pulling Sage in to hug her. "I've never known a name more fitting for someone. Thank you."

"You're welcome," Sage smiled again, the furrow disappearing. "It'll only last for a little while. But I can do it again when you need me to. Mom says I shouldn't, usually, because people need to work through things on their own. But . . ." She shrugged.

As Sadie got down a cannister for tea, the black cherry tin caught her eye and reminded her of the poisonous Jerusalem cherry. When she was younger she'd been obsessed with Hamlet and gotten the idea in her head to become a great playwright. In one of her many failed attempts, her heroine had used Jerusalem cherry tea to poison her lover's disapproving father, so they could finally be together.

But if you sacrifice yourself, Seth will be safe.

Sacrifice myself, she thought. *Could it be that easy? That hard?* Her death would nullify the curse. But it didn't make sense. Seth was right: Gigi would never tell her to kill herself, would she?

"What are you making?" Sage asked around a mouthful of cereal.

"It's called Athena's tea," she said, shaking herself from the morbid thoughts. "She was the goddess of wisdom, and that's what apples symbolize," she said, measuring out two spoonsful of dried apples and a measure of white tea in a mug. "This is Rooibos," she added as Sage's eyes tracked her movements. "And then you add a cinnamon stick and vanilla pod. It's used to connect your head and heart."

"Sounds yummy," Sage said.

"Let's just hope it works."

Thirteen days.

The thought of her sacrifice was a scratched record grating on every thought. She wasn't sure which was scarier, the idea of actually doing it or the fact that if she knew it would work and there was no other solution, she'd sacrifice herself in a heartbeat. No matter that he'd left or that he'd hidden his relationship with Raquel. Because for every hundred annoyances and fights and tears there were a thousand more reasons to love him.

He had everything. His magic to learn, their mother returned, Raquel's love and their future together. And what did she have? A handful of nothing. Broken dreams and empty promises and one more heartbreak.

She didn't realize she was crying until the tears fell her into her tea, causing the steam to rise in spirals.

"What's wrong, honey?"

Her mother's voice startled her, and as she wiped her eyes, she realized Sage was nowhere to be seen.

"Or should I ask?"

"Everything," Sadie heard herself answer.

"I spent so many years hating myself. Hating life. Or I should say, hating *my* life. I recognize the look on someone else."

"I have nothing left. Literally, nothing," Sadie was surprised to find herself telling her mother. She knew it was an exaggeration. She knew she had the town, her café, her family, but the thought of losing Seth made it all meaningless, and she was too heartbroken to care about being dramatic.

"You have everything," Florence said, her finely arched brows furrowing in a way that made her even more beautiful.

"How?" Sadie laughed, and it turned her tea bitter.

"Listen sweetheart, I spent almost twenty-five years alone. A thirty-second phone call here, a one-line text message there. A few times—and I have no idea how she did it—but a few times Anne got a postcard to me. Once mom tried to send me a picture of you and your brother, but it had turned to ash inside the envelope. You two weren't supposed to be born, and my curse made sure I knew it."

For the first time Sadie thought of what it must have been like for her mother. She'd always been afraid of being abandoned, of her curse bringing about her worst fear, but Florence had been truly alone.

"How did you do it? How did you not go insane?"

"Who says I didn't?" Florence laughed. "I spent a decade punishing myself. Living in that misery as my own form of penance. And it didn't do a damn bit of good. It took me another decade to start forgiving myself. To accept that the stupid indiscretions of youth, despite their consequences, didn't have to define me anymore. My misery served no purpose. It didn't make me feel better. It didn't bring me closer to you. And I knew that if I met you as I was, I'd be ashamed. So, I went on a quest to become someone you'd be proud to call your mother."

Her words were buoyant and calm, and Sadie turned them over in her mind like a sand dollar you find on the beach. She'd given a lot of thought to her mother over the years, but whether she'd be proud of her hadn't been one of them. She wondered what it would be like to be a mother. To carry the weight of your children in your heart, etched into your skin, worrying always, the way Gigi had. The way her mother had too, apparently.

"Do you have any ideas about how we can fulfill the life debt?" Sadie asked, turning the subject to what she felt was safer waters. The threat of death seemed safer than motherly love.

"I'm still working on it. But I know he needs to learn how to control his magic before it consumes him. Because for him, it'll pull him down to the depths. The darkness. And climbing your way out of that is—well, sometimes it can be too hard to do. He'll lose himself."

"But if the sacrifice is complete, it'll be easier for him to get control, won't it?"

Florence nodded.

Twelve days.

And still no answer in sight. Anxiety was a poison that made her frantic. It was cold and cushioned as fresh snow, welcoming her with its icy arms until her teeth chattered and her heart felt frosted over. It was time to pull out all the stops. The seven founding families all had elements of magic, and though they'd never heard of a curse like theirs, she was willing to try anything. And she'd start with Sorin Tovah. Only two years older than her, Sorin was an expert with alchemical elixirs.

"Maybe you could try purifying him," Sorin said, pushing her glasses up her nose. "You know, burn the curse out."

Sadie left Sorin's house with a recipe and a spark of hope.

"You want me to drink what?" Seth demanded when she showed him the paper. "You realize that mercury and sulfur are poisonous, right?"

"Only in big doses," she said. "Would you rather have a little bit of poison or be dead?"

"Touché, sister. Where do we start?"

They took an ounce each of gold flakes, silver flakes, sulfur, mercury, and hemlock and watched as it slowly melted in the glass beaker, the flames burning blue and then silver.

Once it had boiled, they poured it into small glasses and went out to the garden, where Sadie poured a circle of salt around them.

"Bottoms up?" Seth asked. His tone was light, but Sadie could see the hope in his eyes that this could work, and the fear that it might not.

"Three, two, one," Sadie said, and they both drank the elixir.

A few moments passed.

"Do you feel any different?" Sadie asked.

"Yeah, like my insides are trying to claw their way out." His skin went white, and before Sadie could ask another question, he leaned over the circle of salt and vomited into the tomatoes.

"Okay," she said, trying to hide the disappoint in her voice as she rubbed a hand up and down his back. "One down, onto the next.

Seth was still too ill, so she left him on the couch to recover and made her way to the Delvaux family's house on her own. They lived on the opposite side of town, in an all-white manor house with marble columns and a sweeping front porch. Adina answered the door in a long, flowing dress, her green eyes soft with concern as she pulled Sadie into a hug.

"I have a spell," she said, cutting right to the chase. Adina was a few years younger than Sadie and though she didn't know the girl well, Sadie liked her no-nonsense manner.

After explicit instructions and a detailed lesson in how to pronounce the French portion of the spell, Sadie left. The spark of hope was small, but it was there, and she let it fuel her as she went to the café. Seth wouldn't be ready to try the spell for another few hours, and she needed to be somewhere familiar, keeping her hands and heart busy.

It was the lunchtime rush, and Ayana was refreshing the pastry case while Gail rang up customers. Sadie slipped behind the counter, tied an apron around her waist, and slid into the swing of things. She cleared tables and refreshed coffees, delivered orders and stopped to chat with both familiar and unfamiliar faces. There was a tall, blond woman sitting by the window and a cherubic little girl in a high chair next to her.

"And who's this?" Sadie asked, smiling at the girl. She thought of Jake and Bethany, and her smile froze in place.

"This is Grey," the mom said, her eyes brightening as she said her daughter's name. Grey's blonde curls looked like golden wheat swaying in the summer sun, and her caramel-colored eyes were flecked with green. "She's only fifteen months old, but she's so tall people always think she's older. This is our first time here. We're from Aurelia and my girlfriend kept raving about this place, and I just had to get out of the house, you know? So, here we are," she said, and laughed self-consciously. "Sorry, I haven't been talking to a lot of adults lately."

"I'm so glad you came," Sadie said warmly. They continued to chat while Grey pulled things out of her mother's purse, until the bell over the front door rang and Sadie's neck grew warm. "Can I get you two anything else?" Sadie asked the woman, whose name she'd just forgotten. The woman smiled and shook her head.

"I'd do just about anything for a cup of coffee," Jake said as he followed Sadie to the counter. She felt lighter in his presence, like the spark of hope she had when she'd left Adina had grown to a small blaze in her chest. It felt like a betrayal, knowing he belonged to Bethany, but flames were tricky things that eluded whatever might put them out.

"It's your lucky day," she said, busying herself with his order. She didn't ask what he wanted. She already knew. A vanilla cappuccino with nutmeg and cinnamon on top.

"I just got off," he said. "And wanted to see—"

"How I was doing?" she finished for him. "I'm fine," she added with a smile, pushing the cappuccino toward him and then turning to package up a piece of honeyed peach and lavender tart with a dollop of fresh whipped cream. She pushed the tart toward him.

"Hey, Sade?" He paused at the door.

"No, you may not have your dog back, Jake. But if you're on your best behavior, I might let him have a sleepover."

His laugh trailed after him down the street, leaving little starbursts of light in the air.

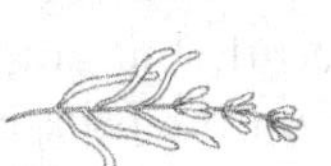

"Can't we wait until tomorrow?" Seth complained.

"Absolutely not," Sadie said, scandalized. "Excuse me but I hardly think this is the time to lollygag."

"Who even uses the word *lollygag* anymore?"

"I have another choice few words I could use instead."

"Alright, alright, I'm coming."

"Outside," she said. The aunts and Florence were in the kitchen, pouring over Gigi's journal and old recipe books, still looking for any clues they'd missed, anything that might set them on the right path for saving Seth. And she preferred to do this in nature, anyway.

Sadie made a circle out of oak branches in the clearing between the garden and the forest edge before pouring moon-blessed oil over them.

"Adina said this calls on our ancestral magic," Sadie said as they both stepped inside the circle. She held out her hands to Seth, who grasped them with a deep breath.

"Sadie," he said quietly. "What if this doesn't work either?"

"Then the next one will."

"But what if it doesn't? We need to talk about what's going to happen after."

"No." She shook her head vehemently. "Not yet. Manifestation is powerful. You have to believe. Please, Seth, just believe." Simon slunk out from behind the peach tree and slowly circled the twins, with wary green eyes.

He stared at her for a long moment but nodded his head. She closed her eyes and began.

"Par la force de l'équilibre, je convoque les esprits de la magie ancienne," she began, and Simon mewled loudly in what felt like a warning. "I implore you, blood of our ancestors, to remove this curse and restore harmony to our bloodline. Let not one twin perish, but let the magic of light and blood flow through us both, uniting us in strength and power. So mote it be."

The scent of peach drifted from the garden and mixed with pine from the forest. Sadie could feel the magic brewing in her veins, ancient and powerful, but something felt off. Her eyes snapped open as the hair on the back of her neck stood to attention. Her gaze was drawn to the forest line. Right at the spot she'd entered when she'd tried to call Gigi's spirit. The figure was back.

It was a man-shaped figure, and the more she stared, the clearer he became. He wore white pants and a matching white suit jacket with a white hat. Well, she'd certainly never seen a better-dressed spirit. She squinted and saw a brown cigarette in his fingers. And as though he didn't like her staring, he vanished. Just as he did, the circle of oak that surrounded them burst into flames and caught the hem of her pants on fire.

"Shit, shit, shit." Seth pushed her out of the circle, and faster than Sadie thought possible, had his jacket off and was hitting the flames until they died out.

They were both on the ground, panting, her terror reflected in his eyes.

"You okay?"

"Yeah, it didn't burn my skin." At that moment, Bambi shoved through the screen door and yipped wildly as he ran toward them.

"You saw that? In the forest?" Seth asked, catching the dog in his arms and giving him a reassuring pat.

She nodded, swallowing hard, unable to form words.

"Safe to say that one didn't work, I guess."

Eleven days.

Another failed attempt. This time from Calliope again. Seth had adamantly refused, and so Sadie tried the summoning on her own and suffered three long gashes in her forearm that wept angry red pus and smelled like rotten bones.

Seth rubbed ointment in and wrapped the wounds with a disapproving look that said *I told you so.*

They all sat in the living room. Florence, Anne, Kay, Tava, Brian, Suzy, Raquel, Seth, and Sadie. Sage was asleep upstairs. The grandfather clock kept sending out sad, quiet chimes. The curtains shuddered like they were trying to hold in their tears.

They'd been over every notebook and letter, Gigi's journal, and exhausted every resource they could think of.

And so they were silent, but together. And that made them feel like they still had a chance. Even if part of that chance felt like a lie.

Ten days.

The Wilde family didn't live in town anymore and weren't answering her calls.

The Blacks were on their yearly pilgrimage to Stonehenge and unreachable.

The seven founding families of Poppy Meadows had done what they could, and it wasn't enough.

And still, the scent of Jerusalem cherry tea trailed her around corners, and she woke with it curled up on the pillow next to her.

The house whispered its good morning around her as she made her way downstairs. It stretched its walls with creaks and its stairs with a groan. She opened the back door to let Abby and Bambi out, and there was a pile of peaches at the top of the stairs like an offering.

The day passed in a fugue. She barely remembered getting dressed and arriving at the café to open up. Her magic was too unpredictable to bake from scratch, so she pulled bread doughs out of the freezer and cookie doughs from the fridge.

She went through the motions until Jake showed up in the late afternoon. She saw him talking quietly with Gail, who nodded before he made his way to Sadie. She stood there as he untied her apron, took her by the hand, and led her outside. She didn't fight him.

"Where are we going?" she asked, and her voice sounded mechanical, even to her own ears.

"For a walk down Main Street."

Sadie glanced up at the sky, surprised to see how far the sun had trekked when it felt like she'd woken up only an hour ago.

The harvest-themed shop windows sparked orange and russet and cream. Mayor Elias must be proud. Though the town itself wasn't strictly magic, it had been founded by the seven magical families, and that meant there was always a trail of glittering enchantment if you looked close enough. The street lights chatted to each other through secretive winks of light, and the benches would move ever so slightly to track the patches of sunlight, so whoever sat there would always be warm.

The townsfolk had grown accustomed to it, never knowing that generations ago, the founding families had spelled the ground and blessed the buildings. Only some of them truly believed in magic, but even for those who didn't, it believed in them.

She took it all in, the gingersnap wind and the stained-glass window of the church where she'd first caught sight of Jake all those weeks ago. The prisms of light seemed to whisper to her.

"Sade," he said, now, catching her attention.

She looked up quietly and tried to smile.

"I closed on Rock Creek House," he said.

"So, we're officially neighbors."

"Speaking of, how's Chief?" he asked, though she didn't think that was the question he really wanted to know the answer to.

"I'm not quite ready to give him back yet. Soon, I promise."

"You can keep my damn dog. Please, just, tell me how you're doing. Tell me what's going on. This isn't just Gigi. There's something else, I can tell."

She thought about how easy it was to love this new version of him. The lingering love of their youth was still there, would always be there. The sarcastic, challenging, loyal traits were what had drawn her to him in the first place. His booming laugh that came so easy and the crinkle at his eyes when he smiled. But the way he saw through her, his new kindness and patience, the way she knew he'd drop everything to be there for her, that was her undoing. He held the love she'd always longed for but could never have. And still, she couldn't tell him the truth.

"I have ten days to fix something with Seth," she said instead.

"And you're not going to tell me what that is?"

"How's Bethany?"

"She's—" He ran a hand through his hair and stopped on the sidewalk. "You know, I never knew I wanted to be a dad. It was always this far-off thing. But when Bethany told me she was pregnant, it kind of woke something up inside me."

"You're going to be the best father," she said, and her smile was genuine this time. She tried not to linger on the images too long because jealousy was sitting just under the surface, clawing to get out.

"I'm excited. But it's like she's trying to block me out. She won't let me put my hand on her stomach. Won't tell me anything about doctor's appointments."

"Maybe she's just scared."

"I think *you're* scared. And I wish I could help."

"Jake, whatever happens, I believe in you. Whatever path you take, you'll make the right choices. And I'll be cheering you on." It was as close as she could get to saying, "I love you."

"And whatever this thing with Seth is, look, I know your family isn't—" He paused, searching for the right word. "Normal," he finished, and Sadie actually laughed. "But one of my favorite things about you is that you'll do whatever it is that needs to get done. You'll sacrifice anything, make the hard choices even if you don't want to. So, in ten days, I know you'll have it fixed."

When she hugged him goodbye, she held on a little longer than she should, memorizing his scent and the way his arms felt like home.

The house was utterly silent when Sadie arrived.

Her feet carried her to the tea cupboard, and her fingers clumsily moved jars until she found a small vial of what she was looking for. Jerusalem cherry tea.

In small doses it could be used as a sleep aid.

In a medium dose it would knock you out.

In a big enough dose, you would fall asleep and never wake up.

"Never-wake-up berries," she and Seth had called them when they were children.

The water was boiling before she realized she'd turned the kettle on.

She scooped in a big enough dose.

It would be so easy.

The sweet, bitter scent was like childhood and promises and fear.

She couldn't do much. But she could do this. It would fix everything. And that had always been her specialty. Jake had been right: she'd make the hard choice if she had to. It wasn't that the world would be better off without her, but that she would be better off without the world.

She'd shoved her grief aside as she tried to find a way to save Seth. But now, with the truth laid bare before her, that this was the only cure, it came roaring back. She didn't want Seth to die. And she didn't want him to live with this darkness. The emptiness. It was already killing her, even though she was still alive. And she could fix this for him.

The tea was too hot to drink so she went out to the back porch. A last look at her garden. Gigi's cigarettes and lighter still lay on the glass table, and wanting any piece of her grandmother she could get, she lit a Virginia Slim 120 and inhaled. The smoke curled around her like comfort.

Stubbing the cigarette out a few puffs later, she went back inside.

The tea was cool enough to drink.

She swallowed hard. *This is for Seth,* she reminded herself. Still, the physical act of bringing the teacup to her lips was one of the hardest things she'd ever done.

The first sip made her throat itch as tears began to fall.

She would fall asleep at the kitchen table, where she had so many times before. Only this time she wouldn't wake up.

She took another sip. The tears fell harder, each one bursting on the tabletop like a shattered dream.

And then another. She wished she could have kissed Jake just once.

Her eyes grew heavy, and somewhere, nagging in the back of her mind, a small voice asked if this was the right thing to do. But the darkness begged her to enter it. It curled around her like a promise of sweet release.

And Seth would be safe. That's all that mattered.

The thought of what her future might have been without magic and curses and life debts settled into her. It was a dangerous daydream that she rarely let in, but the present was all she had left, and a little indulgence seemed safe. She thought of Jake and a pair of toothbrushes and water splatters on the mirror from little hands brushing too vigorously. Of cold feet under covers that found warmth when they snuck over to his. Of family dinners and dancing under the moonlight and the magic of found things that had been lost.

Half the tea was gone now, and her limbs grew heavier in the space between moments.

I'll get to be with Gigi again, she thought.

And that's when she wondered if maybe that was the real reason she was doing this. If perhaps this was the easy way out. But as she brought the cup to her lips and said goodbye to the future she'd never have, she knew that this was the hardest way to go.

She was swimming through honey, or maybe it was jam. Each thought was murkier than the last, every movement growing sluggish.

When she heard a door slam, she thought it was a metaphor made tangible.

But then a pair of very real hands knocked the mug out of her hands.

"Damn it," a voice hissed. "Are you fucking kidding me?"

Seth.

"This is not the answer, you idiot," he half shouted, shaking her shoulders. And then he was gone, and Sadie thought she could finally fall asleep in peace. She wanted to tell her brother it was for him. Everything was always for him. But the words were too thick on her tongue.

There was a clatter of jars clanking and being tossed aside and onto the floor. It sounded like music.

And then he was back, one hand on her neck as he pushed her head back and none too gently forced her mouth open.

She tasted jewelweed. Ironically, or maybe not, also called touch-me-not.

An antidote to poison.

Realization turned like rusted cogs, and she tried to spit it out.

"You're an idiot," Seth hissed again. And the hiss slithered its way into her ears and Seth himself became a serpent with arms and slit pupils. She'd forgotten hallucinations were a side effect of never-wake-up berry tea. "I'll kill you for this," snake Seth spat.

She heard his phone ringing on speaker.

Was that Jake's voice?

Why was her brother calling her boyfriend?

Or wait. That wasn't right. Was it?

And then she was flying. At least that's what it felt like until the couch became solid beneath her and she realized that Seth had carried her there.

More jewelweed found its way into her mouth.

She knew somewhere that she wasn't supposed to want it. But her throat opened obediently, and this time the bitterness choked her, and the tangled mess of thoughts started to untangle in a way that made her head pound harder than her heart.

"How could you be so stupid?" Seth demanded.

"Was trying to help," she croaked, narrowing her eyes, trying to separate snake Seth from real Seth. And then she heard the labored breathing of someone who had been running. Even in a never-wake-up berry state she'd know his smell anywhere.

Warm, calloused hands took her pulse, checked her temperature, pried her eyes open to check pupils. His head rested on her chest and she wanted to smile. To sink into it. Run her hands through his hair and pull his lips up to hers. The future she could never have.

"Her breathing sounds stable," Jake said.

Ah. Right. Paramedic Jake. Not impossible future Jake. Checking her breathing. Not tenderly embracing her.

"Everything checks out. We should keep her awake, though. Why? Why did she do this?" Jake demanded, and there were broken shards in his voice.

"Because she's an idiot."

Sadie listened for the broken shards in his voice but heard only a swarm of angry bees. Or perhaps they were hornets. Wasps?

"I have to go call Raquel before she has an aneurism," her brother said. "I told her something was up. Stupid twin connection."

"Thank God for that," Jake said. "I'll stay with her."

The room swished with the air that Seth took with him as he left the room. And then the couch depressed as Jake sat next to her. She opened her eyes. How long had they been closed? She was hot but there were goose bumps on her skin. The ticking of the grandfather clock sounded like canons. She felt like Clara in *The Nutcracker*, everything around her growing impossibly large, stretching to dizzying heights and locked in a battle between gingerbread soldiers and the Mouse King. Only instead of sweets and rodents, it was life and death.

She reached out and touched Jake's arm to make sure he was real. His skin felt like cotton candy. She was there and not there, and she thought how sad it was that this was how she felt most of her life. One foot in, one foot out. *"Fold it in half, tuck it away."*

"Hey," he said softly.

She trailed her fingers up his arm, and he stilled. As though the movement cost him a great deal of effort, he took her hand and laid it on her chest, giving it a pat for good measure.

"Jake," she whispered. "I think Seth is mad."

"I'd say that's an understatement. I'm not too thrilled either. What the hell, Sadie?"

"I was trying to fix everything."

"This is not what I meant when I said you'd sacrifice anything," he practically growled.

She thought about answering, about telling him she'd been trying to save Seth's life, but the words were too thick and dull.

"Sadie," he said, concern in his voice. Like it wasn't the first time he'd said her name.

"I'm okay," she said, closing her eyes. "I'm fine." She sleepily wondered when that lie had gotten so easy to tell.

"My whole life, I've always felt like I was a step behind where I was supposed to be," he said, and even though it seemed to come from nowhere, she listened. "When everything happened with Bethany I thought . . . hell. Get married. Have a kid. And even though something was missing, I knew I couldn't put my own kid through a broken home. I wanted the happy ever after. I want to be a dad. But, when Seth called me"—he put his hand over his eyes and then pinched the bridge of his nose—"I almost lost it, Sade. You're the love of my life." His voice broke, and it sounded like waves crashing. Waves Sadie wanted to swim in. Let the undertow drag her down until she was suffocating with the beauty of it. But maybe that was the tea. "So, tell me," he said after a beat, "what am I supposed to do here?"

"I don't know," she whispered.

"You always know."

The front door opened.

"Raquel said she's going to kill you too," Seth said as he came back in, and as he did, Jake stood.

"I accept that," Sadie said wanly, her heart still beating fast from Jake's confession. "But can I go to sleep first?"

Seth looked to Jake.

"Wake her up every hour," Jake said. "And I should go. I need to figure some stuff out. Let me know if you need anything else."

"Thanks," Seth said.

"No problem."

After he left, Sadie couldn't look at Seth. She was so tired. And didn't want to be yelled at. But he surprised her by taking the place Jake had occupied next to her on the couch.

"I know you feel like you always need to do everything by yourself. And tomorrow I'm going to be so pissed at you. But for right now"—he cleared his throat—"I'm glad you're okay. And Jake is suspicious, by the way. I think he wanted to pass this off as your grief over Gigi, but he knows something is up. I'm in no position to give advice, but I think you should tell him what's going on. But don't worry about that now. Just rest, okay?"

"I'm sorry," she said, and it seemed a hollow sort of sentiment for what she really wanted to convey.

She closed her eyes, but the tears came anyway, silent and painful.

"I'm not going anywhere," he said, taking her hand.

And she slipped into sleep.

Awhile later, after Seth had woken her twice, she heard the front door open and the family filter in, noisy but trying to be quiet as they saw Sadie asleep on the couch. She kept her eyes closed and listened as Seth told them in hushed tones that she had drunk too much and was sleeping it off. A moment later she felt a cool hand brush the hair off her face.

It wasn't a familiar hand, which meant it was her mother's, and the tears began to sting again. Her mother had changed the course of her life to make her children proud, and Sadie finally wondered if she was the type of person her mother could be proud of. The hand vanished, and aunts and uncle and mother dispersed.

"I only told Raquel," Seth said quietly. "You can tell the others if you want." He shrugged in the near darkness. "But I didn't think it was my place."

"Thank you," Sadie croaked out. "For everything."

He returned to the chair by the fireplace and promptly fell back asleep.

Sadie felt something zinging along her veins. It felt like purpose. Or hope. Or maybe a little of both. The Jerusalem cherry tea had worked its way completely out of her system and she was wired.

She was tired of life happening to her. There was a hollow space in her soul that ached with Gigi's absence, but she couldn't use that as an excuse. What would it be like to trust herself? To trust the woman Gigi had raised her to be? She thought of Jake, how it would hurt him to follow his heart. If he could do the right thing, so could she. Because one thing she knew, now that her life was staring her in the face again and some of the feeling had returned to her, was that she wanted him in her life, even if only as a friend. She decided right then to invite Bethany over and get to know her.

The sharp fear of throwing away her life, losing her brother, her magic, made everything clearer. Her fingers itched by her sides. She tossed and turned on the couch until the sun filtered in through the curtains. A new day. A new promise. A new hope.

Athena's Tea

Wisdom of the head is useless without wisdom of the heart. Drink this tea to bring both in balance. This is a caffeine free tea meant to be sipped before bed to sweeten your dreams.

Ingredients

2 spoons of Rooibos tea
1–2 tsp dried apple
1 inch of cinnamon stick
½ inch vanilla pod
squeeze of honey (optional)

Directions

Steep in hot water 7 minutes, strain, and drink while it's still piping hot for full effects.

♦ 15 ♦

As the sun had risen, Sadie had finally fallen back asleep, and was woken by a bone-crushing hug and voices filtering in from the kitchen.

"I could cheerfully murder you!" Raquel whispered fearfully in her ear.

"I'm okay," Sadie promised.

"What were you thinking?"

"I wasn't, obviously," Sadie answered. "Or I don't know. Maybe I was. I thought I could be the solution. Gigi's letter said that if I sacrificed myself, Seth would be safe. It just—it made some kind of sense. At the time, anyway."

"Gigi would never say that." Raquel frowned.

Sadie pulled the letter out of her back pocket. She'd been carrying it around with her for days. The paper was worn soft and the creases smoothed.

Sadie watched as Raquel's eyes scanned the letter and then started at the top again, narrowing as they neared the end.

"This is like a riddle."

"Seems pretty clear to me."

"No, it's not. Because if you actually used the brain in that pretty little head of yours, you'd know Gigi would never, ever, and I mean *ever*, tell you to *off yourself*."

Sadie was silent, her brows pulled down. She had known that, surely. Realized it but not wanted to stare that truth in the face because it was easier to take it at face value. Her head still felt foggy and ached if she moved too fast.

"Gigi must have been pissed," Sadie said quietly.

"No shit," Raquel said, and Sadie laughed because it sounded so like something Seth would say.

"Starting to talk like each other now?"

"Shut up," Raquel smiled. "Are you really okay with us, by the way?"

"Hey, it's your funeral. And anyway, I feel like if you can forgive me for . . . you know, being stupid, then I can forgive you for loving my brother, aka also being stupid."

"So, now all we have to do is figure out what Gigi meant."

Sadie settled on that word: *we*. One syllable packed with so much promise.

"Also"—Raquel took both hands in hers—"I think you need grief counseling."

"I was only trying to save Seth," Raquel answered, her heart hammering.

"I know, I know. This has nothing to do with Seth, though. I've already been talking to him about seeing a therapist."

"I told him the same thing."

"Sometimes it needs to come from someone who knows what it feels like, though, you know? I didn't tell him he should or has to. I just told him how it's helped me."

"And you think it would help me too?" Sadie asked, even though she already knew the answer.

"I think therapy could help the entire planet," Raquel said seriously. "But yeah, this isn't something you want to walk through alone. Even though we're here with you, a professional can give insight we can't."

"Okay." Sadie nodded resolutely, vowing to find help after Seth was safe.

"Now, how's it going with Florence?"

"Weird," Sadie responded automatically. "Or maybe it's weird because it's starting to feel normal. I just wish Gigi could have been here. To see us all together. For everything."

"She's here." Raquel reached out and squeezed her hand.

Sadie's nerves felt calmer than they had in ages as she sipped honey chamomile tea. And when Sage padded in with sleepy eyes in her oversized T-shirt, clutching Cocoa to her chest, she poured her sister a bowl of cereal. Maybe her mother and sister would leave. But they were here now. And Sadie wanted to know this girl with secrets in her hazel eyes. She didn't know what to do about the life debt, but sitting paralyzed in fear wasn't getting her anywhere. It was time to switch gears. *Nothing like a brush with death to set things in perspective,* she mused. There were only nine days until the full moon, and with a jolt Sadie realized it was the same day as the fall festival.

"How would you feel about being my helper?" Sadie asked. "The Fall Festival is coming up. Gigi and I always have—I mean, *had*—a booth. What do you say?"

Sage's tired eyes brightened, and she beamed.

"We'll start with honey chrysanthemum scones." Sadie smiled. "I have a friend I need to make them for."

"Good morning," Florence said from the doorway, glancing between her two daughters. "Coffee?" she asked.

"Sure," Sadie said, and watched as her mother busied herself about the coffeepot. She thought of what she'd seen of her in the haze of the last week. She was always there to help, a Revelare trait, it seemed. She gave advice like candy but said it with such earnest honesty that the person it was directed at would nod, wide-eyed. Most of all, she hadn't pushed Sadie. Hadn't tried to force the bond. Sadie loved her just a little bit for that."

"Ew," said Sage. "Coffee is gross."

"You say that now," Sadie said, laughing as she stole a bite of her cereal.

Over the next hour, they planned and wrote down what they'd need for the festival, volleying ideas back and forth until everyone else woke up. There was coffee and toast and chatter and laughter, and it felt like Christmas vacation from childhood.

Uncle Brian cleared his throat.

"We won't be in your hair much longer," he said.

"You're leaving?" Sadie asked, and even though she'd expected it, been waiting for it, it still hurt.

"Before mom died, she spoke to each of us. It's time we're all together again. I've been feeling it for a while now. I want to open another location for my auto shop. And there's a garage for rent here in Poppy Meadows. So, Suzy and I, we put an offer on a house down the street. That's why we left—had to list our other place and get all our affairs in order."

"And I've spoken to my work about transferring," said Tava. "There's too many good thrift stores around here anyway. I needed more time in them," she smiled. "Kay and I are renting a little flat above Lavender and Lace's Ice Cream Parlor in town. Those girls are a hoot. And who knows, I might end up opening my own little vintage and refurbished furniture shop."

"And when Steven gets back, we're looking at a piece of property on the edge of town," said Aunt Anne. "We'll be able to have goats and chickens and dogs, and we'll only be about ten minutes from everyone. Close enough for Sunday family dinners. And for me to help you in the café, if you want it," she added to Sadie.

Seth looked at his sister and she stared back. When they were young, they had lived for the holidays when aunts and uncles and cousins would stream through the house, a rainbow of color and noise and activity everywhere.

"You're . . ." Sadie started but couldn't finish.

"You're staying?" Seth finished for her.

"This has been a long time coming, baby," Tava told her. "There were a lot of pieces in play that kept us from each other. But now we're all here. And we all plan to stay. Some of the kids are moving back too. Emily and Madison and the kids and husbands. The others that can't move because of jobs or school have already booked time off for Christmas so we can really do it up right."

"Every Revelare leaves, but they always come back," said Uncle Brian. "And now is our time, kiddo."

"Hey, you think you'll ever leave?" Seth asked, turning to Sadie.

"Haven't you realized yet that I'm the exception to every rule?"

"And so humble too," he answered. "But you know, it wouldn't be the worst thing in the world."

"Stop trying to get rid of me, Seth. I'm not going anywhere."

"Neither am I," Florence said. "At least, I plan on staying. If you'll have me, that is."

"Of course," Seth said, as though it were the most obvious thing in the world. Sadie seemed to have lost her voice. "Now all we need to do is figure out this conduit shit," Seth continued. "Sorry, I mean *stuff*," he added, glancing at Sage.

"We shouldn't talk about that in front of Sage," Sadie said, finally speaking up.

"She may be a child, but she's an old soul. And she'll know everything anyway," Florence said with a shrug as she slathered butter on a piece of toast. She offered no further explanation, and Sadie wondered about the particulars of Sage's magic. She looked at the child, with her wide, expressive eyes, but she was focused on her second bowl of cereal.

Sadie was so tired of not believing. Of expecting the worst. Of fearing the abandonment that always plagued her. So, she pulled out the vial of bright blue tansy she'd put in her pocket earlier and dabbed some behind her ears. Courage. To believe in the impossible. She smiled. And this time, it almost felt real.

A little later Sadie kicked everyone out of the kitchen so she and Sage could get started baking. With her magic somewhat settled and Sage there to help balance her out, an old, worn calm returned to her. The peace of treading the path from the counter to the fridge and back. Of the feel of flour rubbed between fingers and measuring cups perfectly fit to her hand. Florence asked if she could join, if only to watch and help where needed, and Sadie was comfortable with her place at the counter where she sat next to Raquel. The kitchen was warm, and the air was sweet and the *snick* of the oven door opening and closing was a Band-Aid over her bruised heart.

They spent the rest of the day in the kitchen and garden, where Simon pounced on Sage's feet and mewed at Sadie with indignance as she told him off. Abby trailed after Tava, ignoring everyone else. And Bambi sat at the fence line, barking every so often toward Rock Creek House.

Sadie was surprised at how effortlessly they all moved around each other. Laughter trailed them like sunflowers leaning toward the sun, and Sadie realized how much she'd missed being in the kitchen with someone.

They made jars of orange-infused honey that would bring joy back into the lives of those who ate it, sachets of snowdrop tea to give hope, and hard-candy wood sorrel drops to help new mothers. There was olive oil infused with rosemary and black pepper to encourage adventurous love, and yellow rose petal jam to make the eater forgive and forget.

Seth came in to help in the late afternoon, but he kept getting in the way and making Sage laugh so much they lost track of measurements, so Sadie banished him. He breezed in and out, sat at the high counter on his computer, and finally took Bambi for a walk.

She taught Sage how to cut in cold butter and they dipped their fingers in the orange-infused honey, watching as the fading sunlight caught the amber strands.

They ordered pizza for dinner, and everyone ate in the living room, with grease-stained paper plates on their laps and the coffee table, as an episode of *Bonanza* played quietly in the background. Bambi ambled from person to person, begging for scraps, with hearts in his eyes, until he finally took his usual place at Sage's side. The two of them were becoming inseparable, and Sadie idly wondered if she should give Jake his dog back but decided against it. It felt like having a piece of him there with her. Simon meanwhile had perched on top of the grandfather clock, looking down at Bambi and Abby with narrowed eyes, waiting to pounce.

It all felt so normal. And she wondered how different their Revelare blood really made them. Magic wasn't always spells and curses and charms. Sometimes it was the comfortable silence of a good meal, and smiling eyes that met across the room and spoke more than words.

She went to bed with tired arms, no closer to finding a solution but a little closer to rediscovering a small piece of herself. As she fell asleep, there was the tap, tap, tap of the oak tree against her window that sounded like fingernails against glass. She wasn't sure if the wicked growl of laughter was real or only echoing in her dream.

The next morning was quiet as the aunts were out doing mysterious errands about town. There were only eight days left, but she couldn't put it off any longer. The honey chrysanthemum scones were judging her silently every time she passed them. Finally, she plucked some heather from the windowsill and slipped it in her pocket, grabbed the container of scones, and set off toward Rock Creek House.

Her boots squelched through mud, and she wished she'd worn a hat as her ears pinked against the cold. But the walk was worth it as the rain had turned everything various shades of green. Vibrant moss and muted lichen, snowdrops bursting through clumps of brambles along the path. The crisp snap of fresh air against her face, chapping her lips and making her eyes sting. It was glorious. With only her thoughts and the sounds of her boot heels breaking twigs and a stream bubbling nearby, she let the sanctity of the forest press in on her, press her nerves away.

But all too soon, she was at Rock Creek House. There were swatches of paint colors on the front. A deep green to camouflage it among the forest, a tan that didn't belong, and there, on the right, the most perfect cream with yellow undertones. And she could see it all. The house in meringue with robin's egg blue trim. Flower boxes under the windows with bleeding hearts and gladiolas. All the details swam before her eyes before she blinked, and they vanished. She sighed. Wanting what she couldn't have was getting exhausting.

Friends, she reminded herself. *You're here to make a friend.* Her knock echoed and her heart beat fast.

The door opened, and Bethany appeared. She wore her thick hair piled in a bun on top of her head, patterned leggings, and a cream sweater.

"Oh, hello," she said. "Are you looking for Jake? He's not here."

"That's okay. I'm actually here to see you. I made honey chrysanthemum scones," she held up the Tupperware. "As a welcome to the neighborhood."

"Oh! Thank you so much. Wow. Why don't you come in? I can make us some coffee—or do you have time?"

"Absolutely," Sadie said, walking in as Bethany stepped back. The memories cascaded over her, and the attic whispered of the past, but Sadie shoved them down.

"I was sorry to hear about your grandmother." Bethany busied herself with a French press and the electric teakettle, getting down two plates and forks and setting them on the table.

"Thanks," Sadie said, trying to ignore the tightness in her throat.

"It does get easier, but for a while it feels like you can't breathe. Like you constantly want to pick up the phone and call her until you remember, and then it kind of sucks all over again."

Sadie nodded because she didn't trust herself to speak.

"These look delicious," Bethany added, opening the container and setting a scone on each plate.

"They're supposed to help you be open."

"Jake told me about that. How all your food means something." There was a hint of hardness to her words that she tried to cover with a smile.

"My grandmother taught me that everything has meaning," Sadie said. "I like to think it'll be a way to keep her memory around. How are you liking small-town life?"

"It's . . ." Bethany paused as the pushed the plunger of the French press down. "It's not quite what I was expecting," she continued. "Jake is trying to sell me on it, you know? But I only have a week of vacation left, and I'm kind of itching to get back to the city. How do you take your coffee?" she asked.

"Sugar, if you have it. And oh, I brought some orange-infused honey for the scones," she said, pulling it out of her bag.

Bethany got a spoon and the sugar bowl down from the cabinet and then sat down across from Sadie.

"I could live on sweets." Bethany sighed and closed her eyes as she took a bite of scone. "Mmm, God, this is seriously so good."

"Thanks," Sadie said. "How is pregnancy treating you? Any nausea or anything?"

"Um, no, actually. Not yet, anyway." She took a sip of coffee.

"How far along are you?"

"You know, I don't actually know." She took another bite and chewed slowly, her eyes turning thoughtful.

"Oh." Sadie was surprised but didn't say anything else. She plumbed around for another topic of conversation, but Bethany took over.

"So, you've known Jake a long time," she said, and for some reason it sounded like an accusation.

"About half my life." Sadie nodded and tried not to think about the pool of dread thickening in her stomach.

"These really are delicious," Bethany said again, finishing the scone. "Yeah, he used to talk about you a lot."

It was like they were having two different conversations.

"He did?" Sadie was surprised.

"Yeah, you and your grandmother, and your brother. Sam?"

"Seth."

"Right." Her eyes were growing dreamier.

Too much chrysanthemum, Sadie thought, her brows pinching together. A little made you open and trusting; too much would make you spill secrets. Secrets Sadie wasn't entirely sure she wanted to hear.

"Did you know Jake's sister introduced us? It was all kind of a whirlwind." She took a sip of her coffee. Black, Sadie noticed. A no-nonsense option, she'd always thought.

"He talked about you," she repeated. "And this place, this town. When he started having trouble sleeping—well, he talks in his sleep sometimes. I agreed with his therapist. Getting out of town would be good for him. But then he talked about *moving.* I could feel him slipping further away." Her finger drew circles on the table.

"Bethany, I don't think—" Sadie started, having no idea where the sentence would take her. But it didn't matter because Bethany looked up at her then, and there was so much guilt in her eyes, it shone like twin pools.

"When he talked about Poppy Meadows, I knew he was talking about you. And I didn't want to lose him. I—I do love him."

Definitely too much chrysanthemum, Sadie thought.

"I'm not sure what you're telling me," Sadie said softly. She should leave. Let the scones work their way out of Bethany's system—she'd forget everything. But Sadie was glued to her seat.

"When he said he was taking time off to come look for a house here"—her voice dipped to a whisper—"I told him I was pregnant. I didn't mean to. It just came out. I was afraid he'd come here and fall back in love with you. And he's—well, I knew he'd want to do the right thing. You know what I'm saying?" Her eyes were darting around now, wild and worried.

"But you should have seen his eyes light up when I told him about the baby. It was like a present he'd been waiting for his whole life but didn't know he even wanted." Her beautiful face was twisted in anguish. "He looked so hopeful, I thought we could fix what was broken. I couldn't tell him the truth. And then he proposed. And I said yes. And I've been miserable ever since. If he finds out . . ." She shuddered. "He's not the type of person to forgive that kind of lie."

"How—but oh my God," Sadie whispered, her brain whirring, trying to piece it all together. "Bethany, he's going to find out when you don't get any bigger. When you're not going to doctor's appointments."

"I told him I couldn't get an appointment until after he left to come here. I took a screenshot of a sonogram picture off the internet and sent it to him." She clapped a hand over her mouth, eyes wide, like she couldn't believe what she'd said.

"Bethany," Sadie groaned, her heart breaking for Jake.

"I've been trying ever since to actually get pregnant. Then I could tell him the dates were just a little off. But I—" She paused, "We haven't been having sex. Not since I got here. I'm a horrible person. I'm going to hell. I'm going to break his heart."

"You're not a horrible person," Sadie said automatically, hating that she always had to find the good. "You were just scared and made a bad choice. But you have to tell him. Bethany. You have to."

"I know," she wailed.

But even as she said it, Sadie remembered that Bethany *wouldn't* remember this conversation. It would feel more like a dream to her once the effect of the scones wore off. Which left Sadie as the secret keeper.

She looked at her own plate, the scone untouched, and wondered what kind of secrets would spill out of her. *Too many,* she thought.

"I got in too deep, and now the lies have just piled on top of each other," Bethany whispered miserably into her hands. "I just didn't want to lose his love. But I ruined everything."

"It's going to be fine," Sadie said, forcing a soothing tone to her voice. But Bethany's gaze was now staring off at a far point behind Sadie's right shoulder, her eyes reverted to their dreamlike state. Quietly, Sadie popped the lid back on the Tupperware and exited noiselessly through the front door. On her walk home, she dumped the scones in the river where the fish could keep counsel with their own secrets.

Florence was sitting on the back deck in Gigi's old chair, smoking a cigarette.

"You look like you've got the weight of the world on your shoulders," her mother said.

Sadie sank into the second chair and ran a hand up her forehead. Ever since Gigi had died, she'd felt like she was floating. And here was her mother, offering an anchor. It was too much to turn down.

"I fell in love when I was seventeen," she said. "And he broke my heart."

"Did you ever fall out of love with him?" Florence asked. It was a strange question. A knowing one.

Sadie's silence was her answer.

"Now he's back. And he's engaged. To a woman named Bethany. And she told him she's pregnant. But she's not."

"Well, shit," Florence said. "That does sound like a problem."

"You don't say." Sadie couldn't help but laugh at the tone in her mother's voice. "I don't know what to do. He has to know. Right?"

"You think if he knows that'll give you two a chance?" Florence guessed.

"More than that. Taking myself out of the equation, he deserves to know."

"But you can't be the one to tell him."

"I can't?" Sadie grimaced. "No, I can't. You're right."

"It would poison the well. Whether we like it or not, we're all human, and revealing that kind of secret could come back and bite you in the ass later on down the road. You don't think she'll tell him? Or that he'll figure it out on his own?"

"She said she's trying to get pregnant and she'd just fudge the due date."

"My God, she sounds like a piece of work."

"She's just afraid he'll leave her. We do crazy things for love."

"That's not love, honey," her mother argued. "That's loneliness. Trying to hold onto someone like that, it's control. Does he love her?"

"I think they both love the idea of each other," Sadie thought out loud.

"Half his heart is with you and half is with that girl's lies. The truth will always win out, one way or another. Trust me."

And for some reason, Sadie did.

"I wouldn't want him anyway if half his heart is with her." And she realized as she said it that it was the truth. If she was going to risk her last heartbreak, there could be no question about where his heart lay.

"When your heart is split in two, you can't be true to either piece. It's like you're two different people with one beating heart." And as she spoke the words, her eyes lit up. "Sadie. I have an idea that might satisfy the life debt."

Orange Honey Vanilla Scones

I like to use these when people refuse to talk to each other. Encourages openness and honesty with a little kick of joy. Made them for Dickie once, and they didn't work on him. Some people are just too stubborn, even for magic.

Ingredients

2 c. all-purpose flour
1 T. baking powder
¼ tsp. kosher salt
7 T. cold unsalted butter cut into 1 T. squares
¾ c. heavy cream
1 T. vanilla extract
2 T. dried chrysanthemum flowers
¼ c. orange-infused honey

Directions

1. Preheat the oven to 375°F.

2. Mix the flour, salt, and baking powder in a large mixing bowl.

3. Using a pastry blender or two knives, cut in the butter until it's well incorporated and you have pea-sized chunks.

4. Combine the heavy cream, orange honey, chrysanthemum flowers, and vanilla extract in a measuring cup, and pour into the mixing bowl.

5. Stir with a wooden spoon until the mixture starts to come together into a ball.

6. Transfer the shaggy dough and any unincorporated dry bits to a very lightly floured large cutting board or work surface. Knead briefly until it just comes together, and shape into approximately an 8 × 8-*inch* square.

7. Cut into *eight* 2 × 2-*inch* squares and, and then cut those into triangles. Transfer to your baking sheet.

8. Bake 8–12 minutes until cooked through with light golden edges.

9. Remove from the oven and allow to rest on the pan *for* 10 minutes before transferring to a wire rack to cool or serve warm.

♦ 16 ♦

"Go find your brother," Florence said breathlessly.

Her mom was actually excited. The most animated she'd seen her. And that was what made Sadie hop out of her chair and run into the house, heart beating triple time, her fingers trembling with hope.

Seth was on his computer.

"What's up, sister?" he said, and when he looked up, Sadie was startled by the hollowness in his eyes. It looked like the vestiges of fear had ravaged his face, and it took him a moment to focus on her, like he was crawling out of a darkness and searching for any kind of light.

"Florence thinks she has an idea for the sacrifice," Sadie said, trying to mask the worry in her voice.

"Thinks she does or actually does?"

"Shut up," she answered automatically. "I'm the pedantic one, remember? Let's go."

She turned on her heel and heard the laptop shut a moment later. He grabbed her shoulder before she reached the door.

"Sade," he said, his voice rough, "I'm scared. I can't sleep at night. And I fucking miss Gigi. The darkness is getting worse. I—I feel like I'm losing it."

"Me too," she said, taking his hand. "I'm literally terrified. And I know it's worse for you because it's your life in the balance. I'm so sorry."

"Not worse, just a different kind of bad. If it was your life hanging in the balance, I think I'd—no, I don't even know what I'd do." She'd never heard Seth talk like that before, and it made her want to be strong for him.

"Hey," she said, "we're in it together. I'm here. And this will work."

He nodded, schooled his features so that his brow was smoothed out and the tight lines around his mouth weren't so deep, and silently followed her outside.

Florence was pacing back and forth on the deck when they got there, her eyes wide and her short hair fanning about her in the wind.

"When your heart is split in two, it's like you're two people with one heart," she said. "But you two, you're like one person with two beating hearts. The life debt demands a sacrifice. But if each of you give half . . . well, we'll just have to see if it works."

"I don't get it," Seth said. "Is this like the story from the Bible where two women claim the same baby, and the king suggests they cut the baby in half and each keep a piece?"

"Really?" Sadie said.

"Sacrifices can work in different ways. Representational magic is just as powerful, if not more so sometimes, than traditional magic. If each of you can channel your essence into a totem, it'll create a whole self. At least, I hope it will."

"Smart." Sadie nodded in agreement. "I can't believe I didn't think of this before."

"Well, I'm a genius—what can I say?" Her mother smiled. "This might just work. You'd both end up with half your magic, which is a sacrifice in and of itself. But considering the alternative, I'd say it's worth it."

"Would there be other consequences?" Sadie asked.

"To be honest, honey, I don't know."

"Considering what you almost did, I'd say half your magic is nothing," Seth said.

"What did she do?" Florence frowned.

"Nothing," Sadie said quickly. "Tell us what to do."

"You each need a totem, something important to you that we can channel the magic into. Something that represents who you are or an important moment in your life."

Seth nodded and went back inside, all business. Sadie was lost in thought. Something that represented her. And then she knew.

When she was young, maybe twelve, right before the tea ceremony, Gigi had given her a crystal perfume bottle that had once belonged to her. She'd taught her how to mix oils to make a scent that would embody who she was. They'd spent hours going over an array of bottles, smelling and learning their uses and meanings, with breaks for whiffs of coffee beans to reset their senses. Finally, she settled on a drop of valor for courage, patchouli for her free spirit, white angelica for peace, and lavender for calm. Sadie had dabbed it on, and it was then she realized that this was what she was made for. Every morning when she sprayed it on, it reminded her that she wasn't alone, that her magic—and Gigi—were always with her. She hadn't used it since Gigi died, and when she grabbed the bottle from her bathroom, the crystal throwing light on the counter, she took the lid off and held it to her nose. It was the smell of memories and love, promise and hope.

Rushing back outside, she held it out to her mother, who nodded without asking questions.

Seth was already there, holding a silver ring that Sadie hadn't seen in a long time. It wasn't a complete circle, but ended in two wolf heads, jaws open, ready to consume each other with only a hint of space between their teeth. She opened her mouth to ask him what it represented, but he shook his head, only slightly, and Sadie knew he was saying now wasn't the time.

Simon snaked around her feet and followed them to the garden. Sadie and Florence walked through the gate first, but just as Seth neared it, it slammed shut. Simon meowed, and Sadie swore it sounded like a laugh. The cat slipped through the wood slats and then paused to look back at Seth with a "you incompetent human" look.

"Be nice," Sadie told the garden in her sternest voice.

Seth tried the handle but it wouldn't budge.

"I hear store-bought fertilizer does wonders," Sadie said, and the handle opened with ease, and the gate let him pass.

Seth opened his mouth with what Sadie knew would be a scathing retort, but before he could get anything out, she stopped him with a hand.

"I wouldn't," she advised him. "Unless you want a peach to the head."

"This is a delicate magic," Florence said when they were all in the garden with the ring and the bottle nestled on a small mound of dirt. There was a ring of salt around the items and four candles on the outside of the circle. "It requires concentration. A lot of it." She held out her hands. They each took one, and then Seth and Sadie clasped hands to complete the circle around the mound of dirt.

"Ashes, ashes, we all fall down," Sadie thought.

"Close your eyes," Florence instructed them.

They did.

"Focus on your breathing. Tune out all the noise. Climb into yourself. And go deep. Call on the ancient power that lives in us."

Sadie peeped one eye open to look at Seth. He'd usually scoff at that kind of talk, but his eyes were screwed tight.

"Close your eyes," Florence reprimanded her.

"Sorry," she mumbled, cheeks burning as she returned to focusing on the air passing in and out of her lungs. The rise and fall of her chest. Seth's hand in hers, anchoring her to the earth, to this moment. But she'd always been terrible at meditation. At stilling her mind. The moment she tried to clear her head, an avalanche of thoughts slammed in. For some reason, she thought of Gigi's chocolate pecan pie. She'd always said it was for healing strength, which Sadie could certainly use about now. And the chocolate was meant for calming. She could practically taste the sweet marriage of chocolate and karo, butter and vanilla.

"Sadie," her mother said. "You have to focus. Imagine a river. Every time a thought comes in, acknowledge it, then send it down the current."

She willed the taste of pecans away, and for several long minutes Sadie envisioned the river under Two Hands Bridge, sending every thought into the rapids until her breathing slowed.

"Good. Now, reach out with your mind and connect to your object."

Sadie's fingers grew warm, and her forehead broke out in a sweat. A moment later there was a hiss as all four candles lit at once. Sadie smelled the damp air, a hint of patchouli from her perfume bottle, the melting wax. She could almost hear the flames flickering and swaying.

"Yes," Florence whispered. "Keep going. Take that ember and stoke it, pour it down the connection. Let your magic free and into the object."

There was silence. And then a soft humming.

"Kanali Symbalo. Kanali Symbalo," Florence began chanting, low and intense.

A gentle breeze stirred around them, making Sadie shiver as her mother continued reciting those same words. She idly wondered what they meant but tried to keep focused on the task at hand.

The breeze turned to wind, the plants in the garden trembling.

And then the wind stopped abruptly. The leaves stilled. Silence echoed through her bones. There was only the connection, warm and honey filled, that connected her to that crystal bottle. And there, if she reached out, she could feel Seth's magic, pouring down to his ring.

Sadie felt stuck inside of a moment. She thought if she opened her eyes that the world would have stopped.

A crack of thunder roared from the sky, making her jump.

Her mother stopped chanting.

There was a sizzling sound coming from the mound of dirt and then what sounded like a small explosion. She jumped back as an ember popped and hit in her in the shin. She opened her eyes and watched as their totems burned, the candle flames rising two feet above the wick. And then, just as suddenly as it had started, the fire went out. Sadie smelled rain and the heavens opened. Big, fat drops that drenched them in moments, scattering the circle of salt and obscuring the smell of ash.

"Well, son of a bitch," Florence said.

"It didn't work," Sadie said quietly.

"Good one, Captain Obvious," Seth said angrily.

"Oh, what are you—twelve?" Sadie answered right back. But when she saw the fear back in Seth's eyes, the guilt came, fast and rich as Black Forest Cake, making her stomach hurt.

"That's enough. Both of you. It didn't work." Florence pinched the bridge of her nose and closed her eyes. Sadie knew that look. It was the face of someone trying not to freak out. "We'll figure something else out," Florence said.

"Yeah," Seth said, deflated. "Yeah, sure." He walked back into the house, and with a sad smile to Sadie, Florence followed.

Sadie stood there, the rain mingling with her tears, until they both stopped altogether. It hadn't worked. Her chest constricted. Her breath came in short bursts, and even though she was shivering, her body became a single flame. Her fingers tingled, and the feeling worked its way up her arms until they were numb. Until everything was numb. The rain-drenched world swayed. Or maybe it tilted. Did it matter?

The panic was suffocating in a familiar kind of way. Like an old friend.

If they couldn't figure out the sacrifice, Seth would die. The thought made her want to vomit.

I can't do this, she thought.

Maybe if she ran away, but no, her feet were too leaden. She looked down at them, bare and muddy. Her panicked thoughts chased after each other. The grass beneath her toes began to curl and crisp. It spread out from her feet, licking along the ground to the nearby zucchini plants, an invisible flame urging them along, and the more she panicked, the faster it spread.

The panic turned tangible, and she coughed from the smell as the garden died off in front of her eyes. It was tied to her. She could feel it. But how?

"Sadie," Florence called from the gate.

Sadie turned to look at her, her eyes wild. She tried to move but couldn't.

"It won't let me in," Florence rattled the gate. "You need to breathe. Find your calm."

"I can't," Sadie whispered raggedly. Her shirt was soaked with sweat and rain and sticking to her back, her breath coming in short pants. Her vision blurred.

"Let me try," Sage said quietly, coming up behind her mother.

Her hand had barely touched the handle when it sprang open. As soon as she was through, it swung shut again.

The girl walked to Sadie and gently laid a hand on her forearm.

Sadie inhaled sharply at the contact.

"It's okay," Sage said softly.

Sadie could feel Sage's calm trying to enter, but her body was fighting it.

"You have to let me in," Sage whispered.

Fear curled in Sadie's stomach. But there was no other alternative if she wanted to keep her garden and stop this madness. She'd spent her whole life pushing people away, and here she could feel the insistent knocking on her heart.

Let me in, let me in, it said.

And so, she did.

Before, she would have said there was no choice. But she knew now, there was always a choice. And the closer you get to desperation, the easier it is to accept what you've wanted all along, which makes the choice tangible, if not easier to make. After all, it was easy to let someone in when you were planning on pushing them right back out.

Her breathing slowed. She closed her eyes and focused on the calm. Let it soak into her marrow. Felt Sage's small presence beside her and her mother's at the gate. And without opening her eyes, she knew that Seth was there too. She grounded herself in that. And slowly, the numbness turned back to tingling, and then the tingling left altogether.

By the time she opened her eyes, the devastation had stopped. The tomatoes were decimated, all four varieties. The zucchinis were charred, and the rutabagas had just begun to wilt.

"It's me," Sadie whispered, the realization making her knees weak. "This is all my fault." She sank to the ground, mud squelching. Her magic was the thing doing this. Not some incorporeal spirit or malicious ghost. Her. Every burned bush was a testament to her fear and grief. It reflected what was inside her, she realized. The chaos and doubt. *She* was controlling it.

She thought back on every time a patch of garden had died off and remembered the panic that had taken over just before. Sage had helped her control it this time. But the girl wouldn't always be around.

"Let's go back in the house," Florence said, the gate having finally admitted her.

Sadie let herself be steered inside, and as her feet moved of their own accord, a startling thought occurred to her. If she was the one causing the garden to burn, what was the spirit doing? The one she'd seen a handful of times. Or more importantly, what did it want? She shivered and pushed the thoughts away.

The afternoon had turned so dark it looked like evening had come early. Sadie only wanted to bury her head under the covers and let the misery consume her.

But giving in to her grief, letting her fears consume her, was what was ruining her life. And she'd finally had enough.

The house was filled with creaks and groans as though it missed the noise and was trying to make some of its own. Sadie moved around those sounds, finding her place between one creak and the next, lost in the way time seemed to drip slowly and pool at her feet, begging to be stepped in. But she kept her feet dry and refused to listen to the ever more insistent chiming of the grandfather clock. It had stayed mostly silent since Gigi's death but now every day grew bolder. From rooster crows for vigilance and magpie chatter for luck to a crow's caw, which made Sadie shiver because it meant time was running out, and even the clock knew it.

She ignored the screen door as it creaked open, and ignored Florence as her mother took the chair next to her, pulling out a long, brown cigarette.

Like the one the ghost was holding, Sadie thought. *Or the spirit. Or whatever it was.*

"I didn't know you smoked," Sadie said, and her voice was scratchy from disuse.

"Bad habit left over from the old days. I started because it reminded me of Mom. I don't do it often, and only when Sage is asleep. But . . ." She shrugged and lit her cigarette. "How are you doing?" she asked on an exhale.

Sadie gave her own shrug and watched the plume of smoke curl and dissipate, leaving the smell of sweet clove and tobacco.

"Listen, is there anything I can do for you, honey? I hate to see you like this."

Her mother's voice grated. Sadie wanted silence. Ached for it. When she didn't answer, her mother continued.

"I know you're worried. But nothing is going to happen to your brother. We're going to figure this out."

"How?" Sadie demanded, finally speaking. "How exactly are we going to figure it out?" Panic was making her chest tight, her rage boil to the surface like a cauldron full of bubbling potion, thick and acrid and threatening to spill over.

"I don't know yet," Florence answered.

"You seem to have an answer for everything. And yet this is all your fault in the first place! If you hadn't gotten together with Julian, none of this would have happened. Gigi wouldn't have been forced to tie the darkness to herself, and she wouldn't have gotten cancer, and she wouldn't have died."

"If I hadn't 'gotten together with Julian,'" her mother quoted softly, "you and your brother would never have been conceived. And I will never, not for a second, regret that vile man coming into my life. Because beauty came from those ashes."

Sadie didn't have a response for that. She knew her mother was right. But fear makes sweet things bitter. There comes a savage kind of pleasure in making others hurt as much as you do. And Sadie felt like breaking bones.

"Beauty might come from ashes. But destruction does too. Maybe there was a reason you weren't supposed to have kids."

"Sadie," Florence said, and her name was a gentle reproach.

"You should never have come back here." The words rolled off smooth and landed hard and cold.

Florence left quietly after that, but not before pausing and briefly placing a hand on her daughter's shoulder. Sadie stayed and stared at the garden, at the charred ashes she'd created.

Chocolate Pecan Pie

They say pecans are good for healing strength and longevity, but really the family just loves this pie.

Ingredients

1 c. corn syrup (light or dark is fine)
3 eggs
1 c. granulated sugar
2 T. butter, melted
2 tsp. vanilla extract
1½ c. coarsely chopped pecans
1 c. chocolate chips
1 pie crust—I don't know the recipe; that's Sadie's domain. Buy it premade, or make her give you the recipe.

Directions

1. Preheat oven to 350°F, and place a baking tray in the oven to preheat.

2. Line the bottom of the pie crust with the chocolate chips.

3. Mix corn syrup, eggs, sugar, butter, and vanilla. Stir in pecans, and pour mixture over chocolate chips.

4. Bake for about an hour or until the pecans are toasty brown, or if you want to be precise about it, until the center is 200°F—that's what Sadie tells me. It's supposed to cool for 2 hours, but that girl can't wait more than 15 minutes before biting into it, and she burns her damn mouth every time, that stinker.

• 17 •

It was seven days before the full moon, and Gigi's letter was following her everywhere. And she kept steadfastly ignoring it. She'd memorized it, anyway.

When she got back from a walk to the garden, it was waiting for her on the back steps. When she got out of the shower, it was there on the counter, its edges curled from the steam like a finger beckoning her. When she opened a drawer to pull out her favorite socks, the letter was underneath. She finally had enough when she opened the sugar cannister for her tea and the letter was curled, like a scroll, inside.

"Fine!" she said aloud to the empty kitchen.

She mixed her tea and sat at the kitchen table and took a deep breath, her rib cage aching. Her shoulders were tense, the knots behind her shoulder blades sharp points of pain, physical manifestations of her stress. She rolled her neck and unrolled the letter, placing her mug on the top corner to keep it from curling back up.

"Hi Peapod," she started to read. And damn it all if her eyes didn't start to sting. It didn't make sense. The words were etched into her memory, but seeing them on the page, in Gigi's handwriting again—it was too much. Certain parts meant different things to her now than they had even days ago.

"I know how mad you can get sometimes."

Understatement.

"God knows Revelares are too good at holding grudges, and if there's one thing I regret, it's not letting go of them sooner."

She thought of her mother.

"It's always been so easy for you to forgive, except when it comes to the people you love the most."

Jake. Seth. Florence.

And then she got to the words that had been echoing in her head on repeat since she first read them.

"If you sacrifice yourself, Seth will be safe. When you give up who you are, you become someone new. And that means all the old debts are forgiven, the dark magic nullified. You're a new creation. It's a baptism of sorts, that kind of sacrifice. Just make sure you're prepared for it."

She reread those lines. The first time she'd opened that letter, when the paper was crisp and new, she'd gotten caught on *"If you sacrifice yourself, Seth will be safe."* But it was the words that followed that caught her attention now. *"Give up who you are,"* Gigi had written. But what did that mean? Who *was* she?

She climbed through the words again.

Become someone new.

She thought of who she'd become, the place she'd allowed herself to get to, the bitterness that curled its seductive fingers toward a living death where she made everyone as miserable as she was. And she longed to be someone new. To let go. To find joy even in the face of this utter heartbreak. But how? She wasn't strong enough.

"Give up who you are," she thought again, holding her head in her hands and exhaling through pursed lips. Gigi hadn't meant for Sadie to sacrifice herself by giving up her life, but by surrendering who she was. And she was many things. Bitter? Yes. Grudge holder? Gigi had been on the money about Revelares holding on to things for far too long. But more than that. She was rigid and wild, fearful and brave—and, most of all, afraid of being left behind. Alone. Because of her curse. The curse of heartbreaks. Which she'd taken on to keep her magic. And that, she realized, was who she was.

She was magic.

And *that* was what she had to sacrifice.

She swallowed hard, wondering why the thought of taking her own life had been easier than thinking about giving up her magic.

She remembered the look on her mother's face when she told her she wished she'd never come back. The way Seth kept trying to make up for leaving. Time and again they'd tried to prove that they weren't leaving. She needed to listen. Magic couldn't be her crutch anymore.

She would sacrifice her magic for her brother's life. But first, there were a few things she needed to do before it was gone forever.

She started to pull down the ingredients for another batch of honey vanilla chrysanthemum scones. Jake deserved to know. She couldn't tell him, but maybe she could get Bethany to.

She spotted a bag of pecans and remembered then that Jake had never had pecan pie. Not to mention the chrysanthemum had been a little risky, and if she ground up a little coltsfoot to mix with the pecans, neither of them would ever be the wiser. It had a different effect—*justice shall be done to you*—but the outcome, well, they could work that out for themselves.

As the pie was baking, she opened her text thread with Raquel and felt guilty about the ten unanswered messages her friend sent. Sadie swallowed around the tightness in her throat.

You were right, she texted her.

The typing bubbles popped up instantaneously.

Duh, she wrote back. What was I right about this time?

Gigi didn't want me to sacrifice my life. She was telling me I had to sacrifice my magic.

Holy shit, Raquel's answer zoomed back. Sadie could just see her fingers flying over the screen. You're going to do it?

No, I'm going to let Seth die. Yes, obviously I'm going to do it!

Rock on with your bad self.

Just wanted to say I love you and I'm sorry.

I love you too. Don't be sorry. We all have our dark days.

Sadie put her phone away with a smile and got out Gigi's recipe book.

Hyacinth beans were poisonous. But boiling them in two changes of water made them edible. The blast of steam pinked her cheeks as she lifted the lid on the simmering pot. Sorrow.

Forgiveness. Regret. After the second boiling started, she got to work chopping onions, letting her tears stream freely down her cheeks, where they left shimmering tracks that looked like stardust. While the onions were frying in the skillet, she cut potatoes, carrots, and tomatoes, and then added them to the onions with a dash of salt and thyme. When the beans were strained, she put everything in the slow cooker and turned it on low.

As it began to simmer, she looked through the window over the sink and watched Florence and Sage in the front yard. Sage was sitting quietly by the lemon tree, its blossoms barely open, playing with what looked like a folded-up piece of paper, and Florence was watching her the way Gigi used to watch Sadie and Seth.

She'd done so many things wrong. Pushed people away so many times. She wondered if it was too late. Even if it was for her, she refused to let it be for Jake. While the beans bubbled merrily in their pot, she took the chocolate pecan pie and walked over to Rock Creek House. The air smelled of moss and sunlight, and if Sadie felt the presence following her, she pretended not to. She thought of knocking but wasn't ready to face either Jake or Bethany. Maybe that made her a coward. But a trail of hope followed her all the way home. It tasted bright and pure like the first piece of stocking candy on Christmas morning or the sleepy thoughts you have right before you fall asleep. It was hope for Jake to find the truth; for Bethany to love herself enough not to have to lie to keep someone; for Seth's life; for a relationship with her mother. Hope was a dangerous thing. It was flighty and sharp and wicked in the way it made you dream. But it was also a wild force, a flicker in the dark that helped you face the endless night until the world turned right again. Even if it wasn't right in the same way. It was new. And though new could be terrifying, it could be beautiful too.

Back in the kitchen, surrounded by cookbooks and the comforting smell of hyacinth beans, Sadie started the rice, adding three tablespoons of butter and a dash of salt. She was making the salad when Seth came in.

"You're making dinner?" he asked in surprise.

"It's an apology dinner," she told him. "Think it'll work?"

"I don't know. You've kind of been a pain in the ass," he mused.

"Tell me about it," she said, laughing. "Help me set the table?"

"What brought all this about?" he asked, taking the silverware from her.

"I'll tell you at dinner. When Florence is here."

"You can call her 'Mom,' you know."

"When Mom is here, then," she said, and the word barely stuck on her tongue.

"Wow. Progress. What *is* the world coming to?"

"Armageddon," she answered seriously.

"Are you one of the four horsemen?"

"Famine, obviously."

"Obviously," he said, nodding and staring at the basket of naan bread she'd just put in the center of the table. "Guess that makes me death," he added as an afterthought.

"We'll see about that."

Just as the rice finished, Sadie opened the window.

"Dinner!" she called out, and Sage came running.

"Well, isn't this fancy," Florence said, her eyebrows saying more than her words.

"Yum," Sage said, sticking her nose in the air and inhaling.

Sadie ladled the soup into bowls, and Sage carried them to the table.

"This is hyacinth bean soup," Florence said in surprise.

"It's my way of saying 'I'm sorry,'" Sadie said.

"You really are Gigi's granddaughter." Florence laughed ruefully and took a bite. "Even better than Mom made it." She dipped a piece of naan in her soup and closed her eyes.

"Mom," Sadie said, and Florence stopped chewing and opened her eyes to stare at her daughter. Sadie could tell she was trying not to cry. "Remember your idea about the totems?"

"The one that didn't work?" Florence laughed harshly.

"It didn't work because the magic knew we were only giving half of ourselves." She told them about Gigi's letter and the sacrifice, and how she'd come to understand that she had to give up her magic. "If we take that same concept," she said, "but instead, I channel *all* of my magic into it, it'll work. I know it will. Her letter said that when you make a sacrifice like that, you become someone new. Your old self dies and you're reborn. It'll pay off the life debt."

"But . . ." Seth started and stopped, searching for words. "But, no. You can't."

"Shut up, Seth. I can do what I want."

"Honey," her mom said, reaching a hand across the table to her, which she took, "I know how much your magic means to you."

"It doesn't mean anywhere near as much as Seth. You're going to let me do this for you," she added sternly, turning to him.

"Are you sure about this?" he demanded.

"I have literally never been more sure about anything in my entire life," she said. "I mean, I only have one heartbreak left. I'm ready to stop living in fear. So, really, you're doing me a favor."

The chair legs scraped against the floor as Seth got up and surprised the hell out of Sadie by leaning down and wrapping his arms around her.

"Thank you," he said, his voice rough. "I've been nearly shitting myself every day trying to find a way out of this God-forsaken disaster."

"You know I'd do anything for you," she said around the tightness in her throat. "Literally. Anything."

"I know," he acknowledged.

"Magic is at its most powerful on the full moon. We have seven days. And I don't know how Gigi planned it this way, but it's also the anniversary of Julian's death. So, we'll do it at Old Bailer and kill two birds with one stone." She swallowed hard and ignored the flutters in her stomach. "It's also the day of the Fall Festival," Sadie continued. "And since Miss Janet will actually kill me if I don't show up, I figured we could do our booth and then be at Old Bailer by midnight, which is when the moon technically sets."

"My life," Seth said, holding up one hand. "The Fall Festival." He held up the other and moved them up and down like he was balancing a scale. "Good to know where I fall on that."

"Do you or don't you want me to save your life," Sadie demanded archly.

"Alright, alright," he grumbled. "But I'm not—" he started, and Sadie cut him off.

"Yes, you are working the booth with me."

"Oh God, a lifetime of servitude? Is this what I'm in for? Maybe it would be better to let the life debt take me."

"Sounds like you have it all worked out." Florence smiled, and Sadie thought she could see pride there.

"If you don't want to be there, I understand," Sadie told her. "Actually, I can do it by myself. It might be better that way. In case something backfires."

"Like that's going to happen," Seth scoffed.

"Not a chance," Florence echoed.

"Okay," Sadie breathed a sigh of relief, not ready to admit that sacrificing her magic alone was rather low on her wish list.

"Full moon magic," Sage said.

"Sacrifices and life debts." Sadie nodded.

"Just your average Friday night," Seth said.

Sadie laughed. Her hands were trembling, and her body was too jittery, like she'd had six too many cups of coffee. They were all quiet until finally Seth asked the question Sadie didn't want to.

"Do you think it'll work?"

"It'll work," she said.

"I can't even think about what it's going to be like. To be able to block out the voices. I'll be able to go out in public again."

She tried not to think about the fact that, after everything, Seth would be left with the magic he never wanted while hers would be gone.

She listened to the chatter and saw Seth's smile. The real one. Not the tight, close-lipped one he'd been wearing for the last few weeks as he tried to pretend he wasn't worried. The spoons clattered, and the bread was dipped, and the bowls were emptied, and it felt like she was looking in on someone else's life. But it was hers. And the knowledge wrapped around her like a hug that welcomed her home.

Hyacinth Bean Soup

If someone has a grievance against you or you're looking for forgiveness (for yourself or others), then this is the soup you want. Hearty and perfect for fall and winter. If you can't find hyacinth beans, substitute navy beans.

Ingredients

1 onion, diced
2 tomatoes, diced
3 medium potatoes, diced
3 medium carrots, diced
2 c. hyacinth beans (also called njahi beans)
3 c. water, vegetable stock, or chicken stock
salt to taste
1 tsp. garlic powder
dash of thyme

Directions

1. Boil the hyacinth beans twice, changing the water between batches (skip this step if using navy beans, and simply rinse and strain them)
2. Fry onions in oil until translucent, add tomatoes and carrots and let cook for 2–3 minutes.
3. Add beans, onion mixture, and potatoes to a slow cooker or stockpot. Add salt, garlic, and thyme. Let cook until the potatoes are done (but not mushy).
4. Serve with rice.

♦ 18 ♦

SADIE SPENT THE NEXT six days baking, in and out of the café, returning to her drop-offs at Wharton's, Lavender and Lace's, and Poppy Meadows Florist and Gift shop. Florence gave her lessons in focusing her energies, breathing techniques, and meditation practice to guide her magic into the totem . . . which she still hadn't chosen. She didn't hear from Jake. Had no idea if the pecan pie had worked. But one evening when she'd come back from the bakery, there was a small box on the garden gate. Inside was another spoon, this one from Wyoming. There was a bucking bronco perched on top of the handle, and the capital building was etched into the head. She tucked it in her pocket like an amulet.

The day of the full moon dawned bright and crisp as an Envy apple. The house, for once, was silent. No creaks or slamming doors or ominous threats from the grandfather clock. Like it was waiting in suspense with everyone else. A fire roared cheerily in the grate, and someone was making cinnamon toast under the broiler. Sadie found herself rubbing the amethyst on her ring every few minutes, sliding it on and off her finger. Her stomach was in knots, and she could barely stand to drink her coffee for fear it might come back up.

For something to do, she ran to the florist for sunflowers and baby's breath to arrange on the table for the festival.

She thought about Jake. About the pie she'd dropped off. Had it worked? She knew, even if she wasn't about to sacrifice her magic, she would've risked her last heartbreak for him. Love, real love, no matter how long it lasted, was worth it.

And that was exactly the kind of love she was going to save. Tonight.

She walked home feeling triumphant and stopped in her tracks to stare at the lemon tree in the front yard. Sage had been playing by the trunk only days ago, and the blossoms had been new, but now the branches were heavy with fully ripe lemons. She shook her head with a smile.

The house was practically humming now. Windowpanes rattled. The grandfather clock's pendulum swung in double time.

Bambi looked up when she entered her room and sat on the bed. Now, there was the question of her totem. It had to be something that was important to her. It had to mean something.

And, just like that, she knew what she wanted to use. But it seemed silly.

A minute later, with her mind made up, she was padding down the hallway to Gigi's old room. Her hand hesitated before knocking.

"Come in," Florence called. "Oh, hi, honey. I'm just tidying up." Her mother's hair was tucked behind her ears, and she looked impossibly beautiful.

"I decided on my totem," she told her mom. "What is that?" she added, her eye catching on a cheap gold picture frame as Florence was arranging things on the bedside table.

"It's the only photo I had of her," Florence said, following the line of Sadie's stare.

She hadn't seen Gigi's wedding photo for years. There was Gigi, wearing a skirt suit and pumps, her hair perfectly curled under a pillbox hat. And next to her, a man wearing a suit that, despite the sepia tone, was clearly white. With a white trilby. And a long brown cigarette in his hand, the smoke curling up like a question mark.

"He's the ghost," Sadie breathed, unable to believe it.

"What," Florence said, startled. "What ghost?"

"The one I thought was ruining the garden. I kept seeing him." She shook her head. It didn't make sense.

"Well, honey, Mom always said he was waiting for her," her mother mused. "Said he refused to move on without her."

Of course.

"I tried to call Gigi's spirit one day. In the forest. He tried to stop me."

"Sounds about right," Florence smiled. "Once he finally got her, there's no way he'd let you try to bring her back, even for a chat."

A weight lifted from Sadie's shoulders.

"But if they're together now, why'd he come back?"

"All his kids gathered in one place? I doubt he could stay away. He's been gone awhile, and from what I understand, the more time someone's been gone, the stronger their ability to project their spirit."

"Do you think I could see Gigi one day?" Sadie asked, her voice sticking in her throat at the thought.

"What did you decide for your totem?" Florence asked instead of answering.

Sadie held up a finger and then ducked into Gigi's bathroom. She rummaged through the cabinet until she found it.

"Mom's hairbrush?" her mother asked in confusion, staring at the old pale pink plastic brush.

"I know, but I knew I wanted to use something of Gigi's. I just couldn't figure out what. And every time I thought of her, I pictured her doing her hair. I'd always sit on her bed and talk to her while she pinned it into curls and tied it up with this brown scarf she had. And then she'd use this to tease out the curls when it was dry. I just—I love those memories."

"I understand," Florence said softly. "It's perfect. But . . ." She paused.

"I know. I'll have to destroy it. But I'll have the memories, and that's what matters."

Her mom didn't say anything to that. She just reached out and put a warm hand on Sadie's arm.

"You're going to do great. Come on, let's go get breakfast before Sage eats all the cereal."

They spent the rest of the morning baking and chatting about the festival. They made maple butterscotch walnut fudge and verbena loaf cakes with lavender and lemon icing. They made Sadie's rendition of the traditional Chinese moon cakes, round pastries filled with lotus seed paste and apricot jam in place of egg yolk. Sadie taught them, as Gigi had taught her, how to stew the dried lotus seeds until soft, and then they took turns mashing them by hand into a fine paste. After being watered down and passed through a sieve and into cheesecloth, they squeezed the mixture dry until it resembled a crumbly paste, then added sugar, honey, and sunflower oil to produce a smooth, sweet substance that paired perfectly with the pastry dough.

"Lotus seeds grow through muddy water," Sadie told Sage. "But even though its beginnings are dirty, they grow spectacularly beautiful flowers. That's why they symbolize spiritual growth and will help the eater to overcome obstacles. There's a small pond just beyond our property line where I keep these growing. I'll teach you how, if you want."

"I don't like mud." Sage frowned.

"Very well," Sadie said, suppressing a laugh. "Maybe I'll keep that task for myself, then. But sometimes it's fun to get your hands dirty." She winked at the girl.

Sadie made tomato and cheese sandwiches for lunch, with homemade dill pickles, which Sage turned her nose up at. And constantly Sadie had to fight the rising panic that scratched at the back of her throat and caused hives to break out on her arms, like she'd wrestled with stinging nettle.

It's going to work, she repeated to herself over and over. Because the alternative was impossible to consider. Even if a small part of her was still trying to figure out any possible way she could keep a sliver of her magic.

At two o'clock Raquel came over, and they started loading the cars with folding tables and lanterns. Sadie dressed in warm black leggings and a saffron-colored sweater that reached to mid-thigh. Her hair couldn't decide whether it wanted to be curly or straight, so she put it in a messy bun on top of her head, where its changes would be less noticeable.

By three thirty they were pulling out. Sadie, Raquel, and Seth drove in Sadie's old Subaru, and Sage followed with Florence in their car.

Main Street was blocked off to all but vendor traffic. All up and down the street, tents and E-Z Ups were being set up. Sadie drove slowly as Miss Janet led her to their reserved spot right on the corner where the best foot traffic would be. They got to work setting up the tables. Sage, who had an artful eye, helped organize the jams, olive oils, and honey around overturned old wooden crates. They placed small gourds and pumpkins on the table, and Sage found some colorful fall leaves to strew about. And everywhere, there was the hustle and bustle of other vendors doing the same. Neighbors chatting about the previous year's festival and exclaiming over new products. Soft music was pumping from someone's tent nearby.

When the chalkboard signs with pricing were propped just so and the lanterns ready to be lit, Sadie grabbed Sage's hand and, along with Florence and Raquel, strolled up and down the street, which was already filling with people.

The cross section of fall and winter in Poppy Meadows always smelled like apples and gingersnaps and possibility. This year, the festival seemed even bigger than usual. There were booths with caramel apple–dipping stations and an array of toppings. There were tents for children that offered face painting or stations where you could pour your own candles. Freshly spun apple cinnamon cotton candy wafted down the street, chasing you like desire until you gave in to the temptation. A towering rock wall that children could climb was set up at the end of the street, and an area had been roped off for live music. Firepits were dotted around so festivalgoers could stay warm as the night grew chillier. An antiques booth sold old furniture and rare books, set up like a cozy little living room, complete with a wingback chair and side table. Other vendors sold everything from hand-knit hats and scarves to fairy lights in mason jars. The air was warm and rich, the smells changing every few feet. Lavender and lemon from the handmade soap stall, exotic spices from the sweet and savory nut booth.

And then, the hairs on the back of Sadie's neck stood on end, and there was a tingle along her spine. She knew, before her eyes found his in the crowd, that Jake was looking for her.

"Hello," Sage said, looking at Jake as he approached.

He looked at Sadie, whose heart was beating rapid-fire. She couldn't read his beautiful face. He held a small paper bag in his hand, and there were dark circles under his eyes. Even after all this time, they were eyes she wanted to fall into and never find her way back out of. Her stomach dipped as his eyes hungrily searched hers.

"Sage, why don't we get back to the booth; I think these two need a moment," Florence said.

Raquel gave Sadie a look that said, *"You okay?"* When Sadie nodded subtly, she dipped her head in acknowledgment and said, "Well! Look at that! Kitten calendars!" and walked away, leaving Sadie and Jake swimming in a bubble of silence as the Festival moved around them.

"Come over here," he said, taking her hand and pulling her behind a tent stall. The light was darker there. Pressing in on them. An invitation for secrets and twined fingers.

"Thanks for the pie," he finally said.

She didn't move. She didn't breathe.

"I wanted to tell you . . . Bethany faked the pregnancy," he said quietly.

"I know," she answered, barely breathing.

"Why am I not surprised?" His low laugh rumbled in his chest, and Sadie felt it in her fingertips. "I would have come to see you sooner, but I needed time to process. I broke it off with her. She's staying at the Elmwood and leaving tomorrow. I'm having her things packed up and sent to her."

"Oh." Sadie could barely talk through the small space that separated them now.

"Look, I was mad at her at first. I was pissed. But I mourn the loss of"—he paused, the words seeming to stick in his throat—"the idea that I could have been a father, not the relationship. You have to know that. I *need* you to know that. But I can honestly say I wish her the best. Just not with me. It's always been you."

They were the words she'd always wanted to hear, so why didn't she feel better? Because there was still more truth to tell.

"Listen, I need to tell you something." And she told him everything: she knew he'd had an inkling about the magic, though he didn't know the full extent of it. Now he did. She told him about the pie and her curse of four heartbreaks.

"Sadie—" he started, then stopped, searching for words.

"It's a lot to take in, I know. But . . . I thought I should tell you. You deserved to know the truth."

His eyes snapped to hers. "The truth," he said. "You want to know the truth?"

She nodded, her heart in her throat.

"I fell in love with you ten years ago. And I could never love anybody else the way I love you. I've been stupid and angry and broken. And I want, more than anything, for you to forgive me." He handed her the bag he'd been carrying.

Confused, Sadie looked inside. There, like little jewels of hope stacked on top of one another, was box after box of collector spoons.

"The first time I bought one, it made me feel closer to you. And then, I think I started traveling more just to get more spoons for you. I'd go to every little shop until I found the perfect one. It's pathetic, I know, but it's always been you."

She looked up at him, barely able to breathe. She didn't answer at first. Instead, she approached him gently and ran a hand through his hair. Down his neck. Tension crackled at her fingertips.

"I forgive you," she said, and before the words were out of her mouth, he'd pulled her hard against him, his fingers digging into her hips, anchoring her to him. His forehead leaned against hers, his chest rising rapidly.

"Jake," she whispered.

"Sadie," he said, and her name was a prayer as he kissed the spot below her ear. "Sadie." This time it was an offering as he kissed her neck. "Sade." A plea. And then his lips found hers.

Sadie shivered, her fingers threading through his hair, every delicious inch of him pressed against her. The kiss was soft, like coming home. But it wasn't enough. Not after a decade of waiting. She pressed into him and gasped as he angled his head to deepen the kiss, his tongue brushing against hers with a new urgency. All she could think was *more.*

Her hands clawed under his shirt, needing to feel him. He let out a rough breath as her fingernails trailed his stomach just above the waistband of his jeans. Everywhere they touched her body warmed like molten sugar. And then without warning he scooped her up by the waist and walked forward, balancing her back against the brick wall. Her legs wrapped around him, ankles crossed to bring him even closer. The brick biting delectably into her back.

They were breathing each other in. Inhaling each other's scents. Committing them to memory. His teeth catching her bottom lip in a bite that had her groaning into him. It was a slow, maddening slide, growing more frenzied by the second. Her blood thrummed. Her skin crackled. Each stroke of his tongue against hers was a word. A war. An invitation. *Come closer,* it said. *I dare you. Let me show you what we've been missing.* And he did, his hands sliding up the back of her thighs. A delicious heat pooling in her core, Sadie inhaled sharply as his hands, calloused and rough, the hands she'd dreamed of too many times, made their way under her shirt and up her waist. She arched into him and he groaned, breaking away to pay tribute to her neck with a kiss. Lick. Bite. Repeat.

There was a sudden yelp from a child nearby. It was enough to pull them both out of the kiss, though they didn't pull away.

"I think we may be brought up on charges of public indecency," he murmured against her skin.

"I don't care," she breathed. "I never want to stop. I should have forgiven you ages ago if it meant this."

"Wait until we have a bed. I'll show you just how grateful I am for your forgiveness," he said against her lips. "I don't want to put you down."

"Then let's walk around like this forever," she answered, her voice laced with desire and a hunger for more. Always more.

"I can't pretend to understand . . . magic, or any of it. But I did the wrong thing once. And I'm not going to give up this second chance. I'll be here for you. With all of it."

"Are you asking me to go steady?" she teased.

"I'm asking for a lot more than that, but sure, let's start there." He tucked a strand of hair behind her ear and kissed her gently.

They made it back to their booth fifteen minutes before opening time, Sadie's cheeks flushed, her hand in Jake's. Raquel gave a slight smirk and bumped her shoulder, her eyes smiling.

Already there were a few customers browsing the table. Sadie finished wrapping up their purchases just as she noticed Seth's fidgeting. It would only get worse as the night wore on and more people came.

"Go," she told him. "Raquel, you go with him. We've got this covered."

"Thanks, sister," he breathed quietly. "It's just, it's hard to deal with it all. All the secrets and voices and—all of it."

"You won't have to deal with it much longer," she whispered, her heart beating fast at the thought of what was coming. "We'll meet you at Old Bailer."

When Seth was gone, she let herself enter into the enchantment of the festival, all thoughts of Old Bailer and conduit magic forced away. Until Sage gasped.

"Look!" She pointed to the sky, where the pale shadow of a full moon was rising.

Sadie's heart beat double time, her muscles tensing. She suddenly wanted to throw up.

The rest of the festival passed in a blur. Finally, Jake and Sage went to get the car to load up while Florence and Sadie broke down the tables. They'd been wiped out, every single jar and pastry bag gone except for a single lone Black and White cookie that had been hidden behind a crate. Sadie suspected Sage.

"I'm proud of you," Florence said as she folded the tablecloths.

"For what?" Sadie laughed.

"Everything. For making the hard decisions. Facing your greatest fear to sacrifice for your brother. The life you've built here. I know I had nothing to do with it. But I've got some damn fine kids. I know I don't deserve it. Deserve all of this. But everything is going to work out. Just you wait and see."

And Sadie knew, in that moment, that being afraid didn't make someone weak or a coward. Doing something in spite of heartbreak and fear, that's where courage came in.

Do it afraid, she told herself. *Your brother's life depends on it.*

Orange-Infused Honey

This is sure to bring joy back into the lives of those who eat it. Don't have too much, though, because when your life is full of blessings, you tend to forget gratitude. And that right there is the key to keeping a happy life.

Ingredients

honey (preferably raw)
oranges, sliced thinly
mason jar

Directions

1. Stack the orange slices and place them in the mason jar. Pour the honey over until nearly full. Put the lid on tight, and slowly tilt to make sure the honey coats everything.

2. Let sit in the pantry for 5 days (the longer you let it sit, the stronger the flavor).

3. Strain—be patient, this may take a while.

♦ 19 ♦

This was it. The moment her brother would finally be free. The balance would be paid.

No more magic, a small voice whispered in her head. *Are you sure you want this to work?*

Shut up, she told the voice, and it snickered, but the echo faded.

As her foot pushed harder on the pedal, her thoughts were wild things, chasing futilely after each other until her head spun. She could still feel Jake's kiss on her lips. The way his fingers curled into her hair, her skin. The maddening way his body suspended hers against the wall. And before she knew it, they skidded into the Old Bailer parking lot, and their mother's beat-up old red Corolla that Seth had driven was already there. A faint red glow surrounded the old building, reflecting off the chain link fence that still circled it.

The air had turned wickedly cold, biting into their bones as though it knew what they were trying to do and wanted to thwart them. After all, magic was about balance, and the earth was owed its dues.

Sadie took a container of salt from the trunk and started scouring the grounds, looking for the right spot. The silence compared to the noise of the festival was jarring. Only the whistle of wind through trees and the stars, clear and bright looking down on them. The scent of pine and brick and damp earth smelled like lost secrets and dark promises.

"Here!" Sadie called to the rest. She was forty paces from the main building, in a field of grass. Around her she'd poured a ten-foot circle of salt. The wind picked up, and Sadie pulled her jacket tighter against her, trying not to be sick, ignoring the clamminess that had broken out on her forehead and the back of her neck.

"You sure there's not some blood sacrifice we can do instead?" Seth asked his sister, stepping into the circle with her.

"I'm sure," she answered. "Hand me that bowl," she said, gesturing to the items next to her bag on the ground.

"From a few twigs of sacred oak," she explained, dipping her finger in the ash of the wood she'd burned earlier and drawing a Y shape on her and Seth's forearms. "The Elhaz rune, for the divine might of the universe. We'll need all the strength we can get. This is where Julian is buried," she added.

"And I'm the one who helped bury him," said a voice behind them. And there was Aunt Anne with Kay, followed by Tava holding Sage's hand, and then Florence and Uncle Brian coming close behind.

"You came," Sadie breathed, as they each took a position outside the salt circle.

"Of course we came. And I brought this." Anne pulled a rope out of her purse and had everyone grab onto it, directing them around the salt until they formed their own circle. "We're in this together," she said. "All the extra power you can get."

This is it, this is it, Sadie kept saying to herself over and over. Her skin was jumpy, but there was a sureness in her bones. This was right. The whole family together. Putting a stop to something that should never have happened in the first place.

She took Seth's hands in hers.

"Are you ready?" she whispered.

"Are you?"

"Over a cliff," she said.

"Over a cliff." He squeezed her hands.

She closed her eyes.

The earth below my feet, she thought, bringing her mind to focus. *The molecules of air I'm breathing.* She drew in a deep, steadying breath. *Focus on the purpose.* The wind picked up, whistling a sad tune as the full moon shone its cold light.

"I'm going to use you as the conduit," she breathed out. "My magic will flow through you and into the totem. It's going to get worse before it gets better."

He nodded mutely.

"At the exact moment my magic goes through you and into the totem, I'm going to use the last vestiges to destroy the brush. And the totem will be channeled into the earth where Julian is buried."

"Won't it drain you?" Seth demanded. For the first time in as long as she could remember, he sounded scared.

"We'll be linked. You'll have double the magic, but we'll be united as one. All of our magic—together. And when my magic separates and leaves you, the curse won't know the difference between magic and life. The debt will be fulfilled."

"That didn't really answer my question," Seth said in a shaky voice.

"I'll be fine."

The shadows looming from Old Bailer seemed to turn corporeal and loom over them. The towering birches that surrounded the property shimmered silver in the moonlight and rattled their leaves in the ever-growing wind. She closed her eyes again. Smelled the fresh paint from Old Bailer; the grass beneath her feet; and there, Seth. She breathed him in. The comfort of him. Her brother. Her twin. Around them, Florence, Kay, Tava, Anne, and Brian all nodded to each other. A dozen feet back, Sage stood encircled in Raquel's arms.

The well deep inside of Sadie had been building for what seemed like her whole life. And she tapped into it. Drawing it out. Directing it down the bond between her and Seth. And then she heard the voices.

They were coming from Seth. It was a cacophony. A symphony. She opened her eyes and his face was a mask of pain. The magic was pushing him through his own personal hell. His face was twisted in agony, eyes shut tight, and even in the dark, she could see his skin had turned a ghoulish white.

The breeze picked up and corralled into a wind so strong it whipped Sadie's hair against her face, stinging her cheeks. And then she felt the darkness seeping from Seth into her. She pushed back. *He* was the conduit. *He* had to hold all the magic, or it wouldn't work.

But the voices kept coming and they were hers now. The horrors, her own. The living, waking hell sitting on her chest, suffocating. The void called to her. The blackness. The demons of despair and depression.

"Sadie," she heard her mother shout her name, but it was an echo in the mist, eaten up by the endless abyss.

Kay was praying, tears streaming silently down her cheeks.

The air grew savage, and shadowy talons sliced at their ankles, trying to break through the circle they formed. The siblings closed rank, drawing closer to the twins, and then they heard the voices too. Felt the wretched weight of misery that Seth had been plagued by.

Was this what he had been dealing with? No wonder he'd left.

She couldn't fight it. She had never been strong like he was. The pit beckoned, and she longed to crawl into it.

"Sadie," Seth screamed her name, and her eyes, half glazed, turned to her twin. Her brother. Her best friend. This wasn't for her. It was for him. Family was strength.

"We're here," Anne shouted.

"We're with you," Brian echoed. His features were hard, but they did nothing to hide the panic burning in his eyes.

And she felt them. She could taste their fear, feel their pain, and sense their secrets. They beckoned her to look, whispered what power it would give her. The pull was too much. But with Seth's magic flowing through her, she also knew what they needed. And that was for Sadie to be strong. To use them. Lean on them.

She focused on their combined energy and used every ounce of willpower to fight through the darkness with her own light. She poured that light into Seth. Every last speck of her magic. Her skin grew clammy, her hands shook, her knees trembled.

The ground between them ignited with green flames, and Sadie, in her haze, felt the same malicious presence she had at the edge of the woods. Not her grandfather, but the other spirit. And the fire licked closer, and sweat dripped down Sadie's face.

It was almost gone. She could feel it evaporating, and it left her cold and shivering uncontrollably. The chasm yawned before her, and she pushed harder, drawing strength from the circle outside the salt. Her family.

She could feel the curse. Dark and rough and violent, it was trying to keep her out. And there, just as the last of her magic tore from her, she directed it through Seth, into the totem on the ground and the decades-old grave beneath.

Seth yelled out in pain as Sadie fell to her knees.

The flames died down, leaving the earth scorched. She knew it would never regrow.

"Seth," Sadie whispered. His name had barely left her lips when he was blown back outside the circle of salt and collapsed to the ground.

Despite the echoing ring pounding through her ears and the lightning-like pain searing through her body, Sadie fell forward, grabbing Seth's shoulders, cradling his head, calling his name. The ground was still smoking, its acrid stench making Sadie gag. And then Sage and Florence were there on either side of Seth.

They each took a hand in theirs, and they closed their eyes. The harsh wind still blew, but the connection points of their skin emanated a heat so strong and sweet it smelled like hope and remembrance. They were siphoning their energy into him to bring him back.

Sadie could barely breathe, the iron cage around her chest constricting until her skin prickled in pain. The aunts and Uncle Brian were still linked, their eyes closed, heads tilted heavenward, mouths moving in silent prayers and spells.

And there was nothing she could do. Her magic gone. No spark remaining. Florence held her tight as she sobbed, silent and watchful as she held Seth's hand.

And finally, Seth opened his eyes. They were clear.

He looked around. At the charred spot in the center.

"I think we destroyed the Death Star," he choked out, and Sadie laughed through her sob as she threw her arms around him.

"Did it work?" Sadie asked, looking to Florence, who she suddenly realized was ghostly white and looked on the edge of collapse. Anne rushed to her before Sadie could, sliding a strong arm around her sister and holding her up.

"I'm okay," Florence said with a wan smile, reaching a hand out to Sage, who looked shaken but healthy and relieved.

"It worked," Seth answered for her with wonder in his eyes and awe in his voice. "The darkness—it's faded away. I can feel the control now. I can even feel . . . the earth?" he said questioningly. "It's humming. I can feel the energy, the living things." He put his palm to the ground and then slowly pulled it up. Out of the earth came a single yellow daisy. "That's why the garden always kicked me out as a kid," he whispered. "Because of the curse."

"Great." Sadie sighed. "Now you'll have another thing to be better at than me."

Seth laughed shakily.

"It's over," Seth said in wonderment.

"It's over," Sadie echoed. And she cried. From relief and exhaustion and guilt that she'd lost her magic but saved her brother. There was an emptiness she'd never felt before. The hum of the earth that Seth had mentioned, that she'd always been able to feel, had vanished. She reached for the light she'd always held inside her, that spark of magic, and came up empty.

"Hey now, Ugly Duckling," Seth teased, pulling her into a hug, "it's going to be alright."

"I can't feel it," she sobbed. "It's really gone."

"I'm sorry." His whisper sounded pained.

"I'm happy. I really am. I would do it again—it's just . . . I feel lost."

"I promise I'll be here to help you find yourself again. You've always been so much more than your magic, Sadie. But I'm sorry. I'm so sorry."

She leaned against his shoulder, and he kept his arm around her as they walked back to the car.

"Thank you," Sadie said to Aunt Anne. "For bringing everyone."

"Wouldn't miss it, baby," said Kay.

"Who needs a margarita?" Uncle Brian asked, and Sadie laughed through her tears.

"Hot chocolate for you, little miss," said Tava, giving Sage a squeeze.

"You go ahead," Florence said to the group at large. "I need some time here alone. To say my piece and complete the ritual for Julian's grave. I want to do it by myself. I need to," she added when Seth opened his mouth to argue. She pulled Sage into a hug and kissed her on the head before turning to Sadie. "Well, honey, you did it. I couldn't be prouder."

Sadie swallowed so hard it hurt, but couldn't stop the tears from coming again. She hugged her mother. Really hugged her for the first time in her life. And doing so made her feel closer to Gigi somehow. "And my golden boy," Florence continued, pulling Seth into a hug. "You've been fighting your demons for so long. You deserve this. Don't waste it," she added. "Now, go."

When they pulled into the driveway, Uncle Brian was carrying a sleeping Sage inside, and Jake was waiting for her.

"Hey." Jake grabbed her hand and held her back as the others went in.

"Hey," she said, leaning into him, relishing the touch of his palms as they rubbed warmth into her arms. "I always wished you'd come back, you know. For a while I even prayed you would. But then the years went on, and I started to think of all the things I'd say to you. I'd play out these whole conversations in my head. But then you did come back. And now I can't for the life of me remember what I said to you in all those imaginary talks." She laughed, and even that sounded tired.

"I'm not going anywhere. This? You and me? It's going to be good."

"That sounds like a promise."

"Oh, it's a guarantee."

"Shut up and kiss me, please," she murmured as he pressed her against the car.

By the time they went inside, her cheeks were flushed, and she wasn't quite as tired as she'd been before.

"I guess you can keep my dog," he murmured against her hair.

"*Our* dog," she corrected him.

Raquel had made tea, and the back door to the garden was open. The faint smell of a freshly lit cigarette trickled in. Seth met Sadie's eyes across the kitchen table and nodded. Gigi was there.

Raquel's head rested on Seth's shoulder. Uncle Brian and Kay were arguing about the proper way to make a margarita while Anne rolled her eyes and Tava spoke in a baby voice to Abby (curled on her lap) and Bambi (curled at her feet).

She'd spent more than half her life in fear of heartbreak, reveling instead in being strange, different, latching onto the Revelare name like she had no other identity. And for the longest time, perhaps she hadn't. Her days had been structured around order and tradition, control and fear. Now, the unknown settled into her bones like adventure instead of panic.

She'd only ever trusted her magic. Now it was time to trust herself.

She kissed Jake goodbye and hugged Raquel as she left. Anne put Sage to bed while Brian fell asleep on the couch, snoring within seconds. Tava and Kay left to stay in their flat above Lavender and Lace's Ice Cream Parlor.

She and Seth were the only ones left in the kitchen. And still they waited. In a silence that had grown heavy with expectation, until Anne came in with a look of determination on her face. And Sadie knew in a way that didn't need words or magic that her mother wasn't coming back tonight.

"Why?" Seth asked, sensing the same fact.

"Here," Anne said, sliding an envelope across the table.

Sadie opened it, and Seth leaned over her shoulder as they read it together, their mother's elegant script spilling across the page like a spell.

Seth and Sadie,

First of all, I'll be back. I promise. But I've made a lot of mistakes in my life, and its time I made up for one of them. Sadie, I know how much your magic means to you, and I'll be damned if I don't do everything in my power to help you get it back. Because I believe you can get it back. Seth, now that you're safe and your magic is under control—explore it. I know, like me, you wanted to be normal. But if there's one thing I've learned, it's that being normal is an oxymoron. There is no "normal." Even without magic, every single person is so uniquely significant that there's no plumb line for being ordinary. That's what makes us all extraordinary. Embrace it instead of hiding from it. And let your sister help you.

Sage will be staying with Kay and Tava. Check in on her for me, will you? I'll be back, hopefully with answers, and we'll be a family.

Your loving mother

"There's no way," Sadie said breathlessly. "Is there? For me to get my magic back?"

"If anyone could find out, it would be Florence," Anne said.

"Yeah, you're the one who's always talking about hope and believing," Seth said with a grin as he slid the letter back into the envelope and into his back pocket, like a talisman.

"Hope," Sadie said, and the word sounded like a blessing.

"Yeah. And no more curses either," he said.

"The thing about curses is that sometimes they're actually blessings in disguise."

Seth merely gave her a pointed look.

"But yeah." She laughed, feeling light. "No more curses."

"And I'm going to go to therapy," he added. "Now that the curse is gone, it's like I can feel which parts of the darkness were because of the life debt and which parts are just me. I know the sacrifice wasn't a cure, but it feels like the start of understanding how to manage it, you know?"

"I suppose we have Raquel to thank for that decision?" Sadie smiled.

"She made some valid points," he admitted. "And I see how different she is, how much it's helped her. And I want to be the best version of myself for her."

"My brother and my best friend," Sadie said, shaking her head, still in disbelief. "Well, then you'll also be happy to know I'm going to go to grief counseling," Sadie said.

"Raquel strikes again. And hey," he said, patting her on the head like a dog or a child, "when you're ready, I've spent the last few weeks researching the best literary agents to query for a cookbook. I have a whole spreadsheet. And a bunch of links for legal and business stuff you need to fill out to teach cooking classes."

"Seth," Sadie started, but her throat was too constricted with the effort of holding in her tears.

"Stop," he said, holding up a hand. "I needed something to do. And you needed a kick in the ass to do something for yourself."

She threw her arms around him and squeezed until he groaned in irritation.

"Thank you," she breathed. "Thank you for being the best brother in the whole world."

"Thanks for almost dying for me," he answered with a soft smile.

Sadie walked to the back porch in a daze, staring at the rustling leaves of the peach tree and the patch of dirt where her magic had once grown. The fairy lights were glowing, and the night-blooming jasmine perfumed the air with a flourish. Security, she realized, wasn't an impossible dream. It was a garden like the one before her. Vulnerable and in need of constant tending, but beautiful and bright.

And now, it was time to navigate her new world with the man she loved, family by her side, her town, Gigi's memory in her heart, and the Revelare heritage to carry on.

The nightingale's song fluttered through the trees, and the deck hummed in approval while the grandfather clock chimed gently from inside. And as the wind whispered, her fingertips tingled. That old familiar feeling. The one she thought she'd never feel again.

She didn't breathe, but watched as Gigi's rosebuds, pale in the dawn light, unfurled before her eyes, their scent staining the cold air like a promise. She thought of Gigi's lessons and rules that still clung to her. *"Always bury found pennies in the garden at midnight to make a wish come true. Never whistle indoors or you'll invite bad luck. Always wear green in some form or another."* And *"A little bacon, butter, or sugar can improve just about any recipe."* But most importantly, *"Hold on to hope no matter the cost, because as long as there's hope, everything else is just the unfortunate side effects of heartbreak and magic."*

ACKNOWLEDGMENTS

FIRST, THANK YOU, GOD, for putting this dream in my heart and bringing it to fruition.

Second, none of this would be possible if my agent extraordinaire had not plucked me from the mire and made it possible. Natalie, you exceed my wildest dreams at every turn. You go to bat for me and answer my hundreds of questions, and you gave me hope when there was none. Thank you for not giving up on me!

Third, to Holly—you took my sad tea and breakfast and turned it *right around*. This book is at least six thousand percent better because of you and that's a solid math statistic.

To the whole team at Alcove Press: what you do is true magic, and I am so grateful this book found a home with you.

Mom and Dad, words can never express how much you mean to me. Thank you for watching the girls and giving me space to chase my dream. I could write a whole book about my gratitude to and love for you. Everything I am, I owe to you.

To my love, your unfailing support and the way you celebrate every little win makes me fall more in love with you every day.

To my darling daughters, Evelyn and Rosalie, thank you for your grace and patience (usually) while Momma worked.

Grandma and Grandpa, thank you for your unflagging enthusiasm and for being so proud of me. And Uncle Matt, thank you for always checking the weather with me. I sure love you.

Alyssa, your love sustains me. Mac, you are my Bookish Wonder Twin forever. Uncle Teddy, it all started with you. Jinnae, you'll always be my Tweedle Dee. Or is it Dum? Kienda, my kindred spirit, your gifs and voxers are life.

To my TikTok family—you brought the excitement and turned this into something far bigger than I could have imagined! Thank you forever.

And to anyone who reads this book—you have my eternal awe and gratitude. I wrote it to process through the grief of my grandmother's death, and if it connects with you in any way, it's an honor to her memory, and for that, I am forever humbled.